Rise of a Kingdom

A.L Maruga

Rise of a Kingdom

ISBN: 978-1-7782508-8-0 Paperback

ISBN:978-1-7782508-7-3 Ebook

Cover design provided by: Cady Verdiramo of Cruel Ink Editing + Design

Formatting & graphic design provided by: Mark Suan of WeLoveWriters Design Studio

Editing by: B&R Edits

Spotify Play List

Burn it all down: League of Legends, PVRIS

Running out of Roses: Alan Walker, Jamie Miller

Fighter: The Score

Enemy: Imagine Dragons, JID, Arcane, League of Legends

Super Villain: Stileto, Silent Child, Kendyle Paige

Bizzkill: Mothica

Phoenix: League of Legends, Cailin Russo, Chrissy Costanza

Devil: Lowborn

Chain My Heart: Topic, Bebe Rexha

Dummy: Cheat codes, Oil Sykes

Are You Ok?: Yves V, Dubdogz, ILIRA

Kingdom of One: Maren Morris, Game of Thrones

How Not to Drown: CHVRCHES, Robert Smith

The Wolf in Your Darkest Room: Matthew Mayfield

Heartless: The Weeknd

You and I: Pvris

Devil Side: Foxes

Who Are You: SVRCINA

Man or Monster: Sam Tinnesz, Zayde Wolf

Heaven: Julia Michaels

Sinner: Dezi

God is a Woman: Ariana Grande

You Don't Own Me: SAYGRACE, G-Eazy

The Other Side: Ruelle

Take the Crown: CRMNL

F U Anthem: Leah Kate

Million Dollar Baby: Ava Max

Y OU CAN FIND THE complete playlist on Spotify.

A Note from A.L Maruga

HELLO, MY LOVELIES,

This book is a complete standalone outside of the **Casbury Prep** world, although a few of the characters of that series will make an appearance in it. It can be read independently or before the ***Reign of the Queen.***

This book follows two characters filled with possessive and destructive tendencies, the need for control and power, supercharged emotions, and a controlling alpha hole that can't seem to help himself.

All characters are over the age of eighteen, and none are blood-related. Please note that this book does **NOT** end on a cliffhanger but has a bonus epilogue that leads you into the world of ***Casbury Prep***.

If you have read any of my other books before this one, you know my little dark soul leaves traces of itself everywhere it goes. If you're hoping for a sunnier book from me, run for the hills! We are about to plunge headfirst down a dark, spiraling path of destruction and chaos that will take us to the beginning of our journey. If you are seeking answers, you may just find them. I hope you return with your sanity!

This is an adult, dark romance and is strictly a work of fiction. I do **not** condone or approve of any behavior, actions, or scenarios that take place between these characters. This book is <u>intended for 18+ only</u>.

Many potential triggers are waiting to rush forward and bring you to your knees in this book, along with its resident *alphahole*. Please, for your sanity and mental health, heed my warning. I have placed international resources at the end of the book for those who may need them.

Content in this work may contain graphic scenes of physical, sexual, and/or emotional abuse, consensual, non-consent, and dubious consent, murder, slight cheating (before the relationship starts), gun use/violence, knife use/violence. If these may be triggers, don't walk, **run** away from this book.

It may also contain scenes of violence, pain, primal behavior, light BDSM, sexual manipulation, an over-the-top possessive alpha, corruption, depravity, breath play (Asphyxiophilia), knife play, semen play, and blood play. Also featured in this book are degradation, Agoraphilia /Exhibitionism,/Voyeurism; if any of these may be triggers for you... **go no further**. This is not the book for you.

There will be explicit profanity throughout the pages of this book. The characters are unreasonable, morally questionable, and lack self-preservation at times. If that will cause you distress, this is not the book for you. *I am not the author for you.*

Don't say I didn't warn you.

For those who want to take the return journey, welcome to the beginning of the empire. This book has caused my sanity to run and hide. I hope you return with yours.

A.L Maruga xoxo

Dedication

To my mother and mother-in-law,
the two strongest women I know,
who take no shit,
&
To all the other women who will never settle,
refuse to cower and be forgotten.
This one's for you!

A.L Maruga

xoxo

Author's Quote

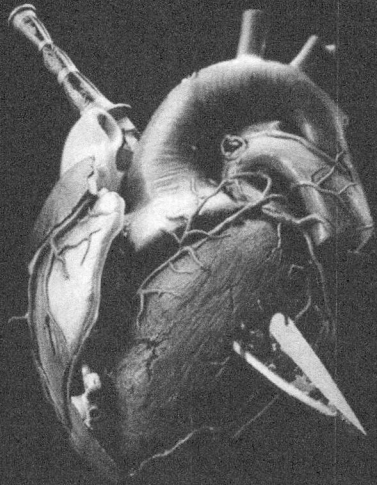

The blade didn't enter her flesh,
it entered her soul.

A.L Maruga

Introduction

I am a commodity. One to be traded between the selfish and dirty hands of wealthy men. I am a prize to be won. One that is pursued relentlessly against my wishes.

I am a bargaining chip between two players with no intentions of seeing me as a human being. I am a pretty object to admire, crave and amuse oneself with.

I am vengeance, with the yearning for the blood of my enemies pounding mercilessly through my veins.

I am determination, I will win at all costs. I am the harsh blade in the night, they don't see coming.

I am a woman. They thought I was the weaker sex. That I would go quietly, and meekly into my existence, powerless to define my own destiny.

They were wrong...

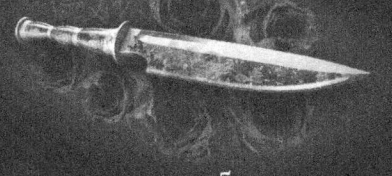

Stella

"Anger takes your freedom, anger imprison you in jail of regrets."
Josephs Quartzy, Sweetest song I know

"**I**S THAT REALLY NECESSARY?" A cultured, deep voice asks from behind me, causing the hair on my arms and nape to stand on end. Bright sunshine streams through the windows, professing this to be a beautiful day, except I know the truth. It is a day filled with dismal despair and categoric doom. It's the day a part of me dies.

"Is what really necessary?" I turn around and try to contain the evil grin that wants to burst across my face, instead providing the intruder a sheepish smile. My eyes trail over the classic black tuxedo, black polished shoes, and crisp white shirt and continue upwards to a strong chiseled jaw, clean-shaven face, strong Roman nose, and dark haunting pools of malice for eyes. The devil himself, in all his damned glory, stands before me, raking his eyes over me like I'm already his.

He is beautiful to look at, and if I were a weaker woman, I would be counting my blessings, but I'm not a weaker woman, and he's about to learn that firsthand when I plunge a blade into his callous fucking heart.

"You're not going to your own funeral, Stella. Is the black wedding gown really necessary?" His brows furrow, and his jaw clenches. He's displeased with my outfit choice, *fucking good*. I'm infuriated that he's breathing. One of us can remedy their displeasure, and I have no intention of changing out of this gown.

"Of course not; I'm going to yours." I dismiss him with an arched brow and give him my back. My gaze locks solely out the window at the freedom that is escaping me. Minute by minute, this day continues to move along, drawing me closer to my impending destiny. My desire to run from this room, from this church, and this whole mess, vibrates through my system and becomes throbbing in my veins. *Escape!* My mind and heart yell, but my feet remain firmly planted.

"Is this how it's going to be for the rest of our lives?" A deep, irritated sigh leaves those traitor's evil lips. His soft footsteps echo off the stone floor and approach me. Unease skates down my back. I don't want the monster behind me to come any closer, but I also refuse to show him any weakness. An impasse, I must weather to prove a point not only to him, but also to myself.

"I wouldn't worry too much, Jaxon; I don't plan for you to live long enough to find out." Ice drips from my voice as I answer him and I bite down hard on my lip to keep from verbally lashing him like my heart demands. *Control. We need to keep control.*

"I don't understand why you are so fucking angry, Stella, you get everything you want and you didn't even have to lift a finger to get it." I feel him move even closer to me, his body giving off heat in the frigid room.

My body turns angrily towards him, hot fury racing through my limbs. My features are filled with sheer contempt at how callous his words are. How fucking dare he utter them to me? I'm going to ensure that he regrets his choice of words and the breaths he continues to take. He's lucky I don't have anything within reach to bludgeon him with. My asshole of a father, made sure everything I could use as a weapon was removed from this room beforehand. The first intelligent action the man has ever taken, and it was against his own daughter.

"I get everything that I have ever wanted? What exactly is it that you think I wanted, Jaxon? Please enlighten me, why should I be happy today?"

"Stella, be reasonable. There was no choice here for either of us. You're not making out too badly from this situation. You get to be the new reigning queen of the Manhattan elite, and everyone will worship at your perfect ice queen feet. You're about to become one of the richest women in the world. What more could you need?" He throws his hands up in exasperation, his face perplexed.

A shrill laugh leaves my lips. "What more could I need? What a despicable man you are, Jaxon Stratford. For your information, I was already one of the richest women in the world, your money is just an extra zero in my bank account. As for being the new reigning queen of Manhattan, I never asked for that title, nor do I desire it."

I shove both my hands against his chest, forcing him to take a step backward and then another. His molten steel gray eyes widen dramatically at my actions. "As for having no choice, I beg to differ. I had no fucking choice in marrying you... but *you* could have refused. You could have found a willing victim to be shackled to you. You chose me because *YOU* need my family's name, connections, and money. Do not flatter yourself that you are the better catch in this scenario."

He grabs onto my wrist in his tight grip, pulling me forward towards his hard body. His gaze predatory, his nose flaring in anger and teeth grinding together. "You're right, Stella, I had a choice, and despite you being the coldest, most haughty bitch in Manhattan, I still accepted the terms your father put before me." His tongue peeks out, and he licks his bottom lip, the movement capturing my interest. "Either way, Stella, it's done. You are about to become my wife and a Stratford. With that comes responsibilities and respect, respect you will show me, *little wife*, or I will make all your waking and resting hours hell on earth."

He releases me with a disgusted grimace as if the mere touch of my skin repulses him, and steps further back away from my body. His gaze sweeps over me from the top of my crown and black veil-adorned head to the tips of my black satin *Yves Saint Laurent* heels and everywhere in between, leaving fire in its wake. I almost think I see a spark of interest or desire in his gaze, but he shuts it down quickly. After all, he doesn't need to desire me to force me down the aisle. He just needs the determination of a wealthy, privileged man.

A knock at the door has both of us startling and moving further away from each other. The person doesn't bother to wait for our acknowledgment to enter before the door swings open, and my father and mother glide into the room. My father's shocked gaze lands on me and then quickly turns to anger as he tries to control his impending explosive temper. His face immediately resembles an ugly tomato the more he stares at me in disbelief. My mother sweeps her disapproving gaze over my wedding attire but keeps her mouth glued shut, just the way my father likes it.

"Stella, what is the meaning of this? Where is your wedding dress?" Thomas Jefferson Penticton is a menace and a tyrant in a well-dressed custom tuxedo. He stalks towards me, rage vibrating with each heavy step. My meek mother trails behind him in her light pink chiffon dress, head bowed, and hands grasped together. *Ever the dutiful and submissive wife.*

"Whatever do you mean, father?" I smirk my most mischievous smile, the one I know causes his blood pressure to rise. I want him to explode, I want him to acknowledge this fucking tragedy that he is putting into motion. "I'm in my wedding dress." The reminder that this dress just cost him over fifty thousand dollars, only to bring him nothing but rage, brings me immense satisfaction.

"It's black Stella, a wedding dress is white." He states with irritation, like I'm some incompetent imbecile that didn't know she was supposed to wear white to her own wedding. *Fuck that shit!* He wants a sacrificial virgin lamb in white, but I have no intention of playing the part of the lamb or the virgin for him.

"Yes, well, since I didn't ask to be married and am being forced into a union with this horrendous, malignant creature before me. I thought it was best to dress as if I were going to a funeral. After all, father, this will be the death of me. You have sold me off to the highest bidder and killed any possible happiness I could have ever had. I think the color is very appropriate."

A harsh grunt leaves his lips, and he moves to grab my arm, no doubt to drag me across the room. His usual brutish tactic of making the women around him cower in fear. Before he can get more than two feet from me, Jaxon slips in front of him and blocks his access to me with his large wide shoulders. The move has my father stopping in his tracks. "It doesn't matter what she wears, Thomas, as long as she makes it down that aisle. She could be naked or wearing a brown paper bag, for all I care. She will be a Stratford by lunch, and no one touches a Stratford, *not even you.*"

The large, ugly vein on the side of my father's head is currently doing jumping jacks, a sure sign that the volcano of his temper is about to detonate to the absolute misery and misfortune of everyone around him. "Are you threatening me, Jaxon? I can still pull out of this arrangement." A trickle of sweat drips down my father's ruddy face, he is so overflowing with rage that he physically trembles before Jaxon.

A whimper escapes my mother; it sounds pitiful and timid in the air, just like the slave she is. My mother only seems to fear for herself. I can't say I blame her. My father is Hades personified, and she is an imprisoned Persephone, except without the love story to match. She, too, was sold off by her father. One can say the sins of the father always tend to be repeated in our bloodline, and I will be no exception, it seems. It's so fucking unfair, this wouldn't be happening if I had a dick between my legs.

"Let's not bluster, Thomas; we both know there is no way you're pulling out of this deal; the humiliation alone would be social suicide. You need this deal, you need a legitimate heir to the mighty Penticton throne, and you want that heir to be a Stratford. Your desire to see your precious little dark-haired princess as the reigning queen of our elite society, motivates your actions. Don't try to play with me, Thomas; you're not the biggest predator in the room."

Jaxon turns back in my direction, his dark slate irises meeting mine. A devious smirk quirks at the side of his lips, and the fucker winks at me. I think he might actually be enjoying this whole situation. After all, it's not every day that someone gets the upper hand on Thomas Penticton. I have been trying for years, and look where I have ended up and what it has cost me.

"My little ice queen, if you're not down that aisle in the next ten minutes, I will find you, throw you over my shoulder, and drag you down with your ass red and on display for all our friends and family to see. Do not make an enemy of me, Stella; you will regret it." He turns, shoulder checks my father hard, causing him to stumble into my mother, and I watch with horror as the both of them get tangled in her dress and fall on their wealthy, privileged asses.

Holy shit! I don't know whether to be livid at his threat or slightly aroused. The door slamming is loud in the space and causes my heart to clench tightly. *SHIT!* What should I do? Do I try to run? Where would I be able to run to, that Jaxon Stratford won't be able to find me? *Nowhere*, my mind immediately provides.

"Stella, please, darling. Maybe we can have someone run out and grab a white gown." My mother cries, as she tries to help my overweight father back to his feet. It's almost comical, really. She's barely five feet and a hundred pounds wet, and he's a hulking giant, at five foot eleven and three hundred pounds. I would laugh, except right now, all I feel like doing is sobbing at my unfortunate demise.

"No, mother. I will not change, and there is no time. You two made this bargain without my consent and have sent me to be a lamb at the slaughter. You can now watch me walk to my death."

I don't bother to assist either of them, walking towards the full-length mirror in the room. When I reach it, I take one last good look at Stella Penticton; an hour from now, she will no longer exist. I lower my expensive French lace veil in front of my face, square my shoulders back, raising my head held high.

If they want a powerful reigning queen, I'll give them one. I will set fire to their world and grab as much power as I can. No man will ever be able to control me or my fate again after this. I will be the rocky cliff that rich men break themselves upon.

6

Jaxon

"An angry woman is vindictive beyond measure, and hesitates at nothing in her bitterness." Jean Antoine Petit-Senn

I WALK DOWN THE aisle, greeting the elite of the world's wealthiest sycophants with a fake smile across my face. The room may be full of the most beautiful and wealthiest people in this world, but underneath all that glitter and shine, they are nothing but toxic, decaying reptiles willing to destroy each other at a moment's notice, and I'm their new king. I hold my head high, my gaze glittering and ice cold. I will bask in their worship and glory, ensuring that each one of them becomes another tool to help me achieve my plans. I'm no different from them; evil and ruthlessness speak to each other.

My blood is still pounding in my ears from my encounter with Stella and her fucker of a father. I should have knocked him on his ass when his fat mouth offered that threat. No one threatens a Stratford and lives. *Didn't Stella just threaten us too?* My mind exclaims with glee. She's different; she's about to become a Stratford and my property. I will take distinct pleasure in teaching her some newfound respect, preferably with a collar around her neck and a leash chained to my fucking wall.

Once again, the nagging in the back of my mind starts to try to wear me down. *We shouldn't be forcing her to do this. She's a young woman with her own dreams and aspirations. We're taking everything away from her with the placement of a ring on her finger and the slash of a pen on paper.*

A snort leaves my lips at the thought. Even though I know all of these things are true and my consciousness tries to move me, it will find no purchase here. She is fucking mine now; her life and dreams belong to me. I keep moving toward where the priest and my best friend, Ajax, stand before the ornate golden altar. The thought that God could smite me for being the devil in his house of worship makes a chuckle leave my lips. *Go ahead and try fucker.*

I'm a ruthless cunt, and there is nothing that will stop me from achieving my goals, not some deity from above and certainly not Stella Penticton and her misery. She's about to learn that firsthand, living in my depraved and power-hungry world. A sick part of me hopes to see tears trailing down her pretty face as she walks towards me and her demise; just the thought makes my cock harden. Stella is proud, but I will make her bend and bow at my feet, preferably with my cock shoved down her miserable throat while those arctic eyes stare up at me with tears streaming down her face. *Do you hear that, God? She will be praying at my altar going forward.*

When I finally reach Ajax, his intense hazel gaze meets mine, and I see fierce anger in their depths. His hands are shoved into the pockets of his pants, I'm sure, to prevent him from wrapping them around my neck. From the looks of it, he's going to need dental work with how hard he's clenching that fucking jaw of his. I know he disapproves of this whole situation. He doesn't want me to force Stella to marry me for my own personal gain. He has made his opinion of the subject known to nauseating lengths, and frankly, I'm tired of hearing it. He's lucky we haven't come to physical blows over the subject in the last couple of days. Not that the fucker could take me down if we did.

Ajax forgets that we have been friends since the fifth grade, and I know his mercurial heart. He has had a childish infatuation with that viper I'm about to marry since we were in our sophomore year of high school, and she was a freshman. His adamant objections are not about me forcing Stella to marry; they are about me forcing her to marry me. He would have taken her for himself, had her father not approached me first. *You snooze, you lose, motherfucker.*

"Stella?" He questions with a raised eyebrow and a whisper as he removes his hands from his pockets, looking for all before us like the proud and supportive best friend that he isn't. *Cunt.*

"About to be a blushing bride." I taunt, wanting to get a rise out of him. I know it's a dick move, but what can I say? I'm a fucking dick, and I'm not apologizing for it.

I don't miss the tightening of his hands into fists and the scowl that crosses his face before he schools his features. The piano and violins start to play at the end of the room. The music starts out slowly and then builds in volume and strength. *What the ever-loving fuck?* These fuckers are playing *'Chopin's Funeral March,'* if I'm not mistaken, and not the wedding march my new father-in-law insisted on.

It doesn't take long before I hear the gasps and whispers all around the room, and they bring a smirk to my lips. I survey the crowd, and their faces are shocked and horrified. I have to give her credit; she is a devious and dramatic little hellion. At least I know things with Stella will never be boring. These maggots better get used to her doing as she pleases; she's about to become their queen. The thought of my conquest of Stella Penticton brings a smile filled with satisfaction to my face.

Stella has always been untouchable. She is the cold ice queen that men crave, if only to tarnish her appearance and convince themselves that she is but a mere mortal and not some beautiful fae, brought here to tempt man into destruction. I've never been immune to her; I've just hid it better than others. Now, all that beauty and strength is about to be all mine. My wife is a Stratford queen, one that I plan to tarnish over and over with all my darkness and depravity.

Stella stands at the end of the aisle next to her robust father. The man's face is still bright red and getting redder by the moment with the song the orchestra is playing. He holds his arm out stiffly for Stella to grasp, and they move steadily forward together. Stupid fucker has no idea what treasure he just bargained away, but I do, and I have no intentions of letting it slip between my hands. His quest for unending glory and legacy will be his undoing but will cause mine to soar to undeniable heights.

The black lace veil partially obscures Stella's features, so I can't see those threatening, blue arctic eyes. The ones that cut right through me every time she glares at me. She looks stunning in the dress, regardless of it being black, a full strapless ball gown with lace cutouts and embroidery. The front meets in a sweetheart neckline that shows off the swell of her round, full, creamy breasts and that gorgeous, elongated neck that I dream of wrapping my hands around nightly. Her head is held high, and her shoulders are back. My reigning, elegant little queen is filled with malice and defiance. My cock jerks in my pants at just the thought of breaking her and making her beg for my mercy. *Soon. Soon, I will have her down on her knees.*

I was hoping that she would have given me a reason to chase her and spank that perky uptight ass of hers and then drag her down the aisle kicking and screaming. My cock pulses again at just the thought of having my hands on her creamy skin and marring it with my touch. If I'm not careful, I'm going to have a raging hard-on here in front of all these well-wishers.

There is no conceivable world where Stella wouldn't be mine once I set my mind on her. A Stratford always gets what they want, and we always win. I hope my ice queen wife learns that lesson early. Actually, scratch that; I might enjoy teaching her that lesson over my knee a few times. *Stop fucking around before we bust the zipper of our pants, motherfucker!* My mind screeches at me.

As the two of them reach the end of the aisle, her father places her hand dutifully on mine after the priest asks who gives this woman away. I hold my breath for her objection or snide comment, but she seems to hold her tongue as her hand settles in mine more firmly. From the side of my eye, I watch as Ajax attempts to catch her eye. I know what he's trying to do, but there will be no stopping this wedding. I give him a harsh glare, my fingers tightening into a fist at my side, and turn my attention to the priest, who starts droning on about love.

Love. What does love have to do with two of the wealthiest families in the United States marrying? This is not a love match, there aren't too many of those made in our world. No, in our world, you marry for power, wealth, or sometimes both. Stella always knew this, she was brought up in this world just like I was. We have a duty to strengthen our families. *Love plays no part in that.*

I catch her peeking at me from the corner of her eye through the lace veil. Her stunning blue eyes are large, and her hand is slightly clammy in my grip. My ice queen, it seems, is a bit nervous. You would never know it by looking at her. Stella Penticton has always exuded class, sophistication, and coldness. I wasn't the one to nickname her *"ice queen,"* even though it's an apt description of my soon-to-be wife. That name has followed her since we entered high school, and she never did anything to discourage it, quite the opposite, actually. Right now, if I weren't holding her hand, I would never know she was feeling anything at all.

This is the woman I need by my side to grow the Stratford name into a dynasty that will never be forgotten. With her name, money, and countenance, the woman before me will help me build a kingdom that will outlast us all. Whether she wants it to be or not, her fate and mine are tied together, and anyone who tries to impede that will be met with swift destruction.

"Do you, Jaxon Philip Stratford, take this woman, Stella Rachel Penticton, to be your lawful, and cherished wife?" The priest questions. *Cherished? Will I cherish Stella?* I'll cherish the power she brings me. As for the viper herself, I don't plan to ever hurt her. Well, that's not exactly true either; I plan to enjoy myself vigorously between those toned thighs of hers. If, in the process, my hands end up wrapped around her slim neck and stop her from breathing a time or two, well, I own her now; I can do whatever the fuck I want with her.

Once she provides me with an heir or two, I will leave her to her coldness and the solitude she seems to prefer. I have no intention of spending the rest of my life having to deal with her sharp, wicked tongue. Even if she makes my cock hard just by opening that pretty mouth of hers. I can pop in every once and awhile and fuck her throat raw as a reminder of who she belongs to. After all, we don't have to live together forever in order to make this work. Marriages in our world are all about appearances, but behind closed doors, spouses rarely have anything to do with each other.

It's one of the reasons I haven't given up my man-whoring ways, despite telling Thomas that I would. I don't see Stella warming up to me anytime soon, and honestly, other than filling her frigid belly with a child and forcing her to submit at my feet, I'm not interested in spending any more time with her than I have to. Sex should be pleasurable and passionate. Stella gives off a cold, in-the-dark missionary vibe. Breaking her might be enjoyable for the short term, but I will tire of her quickly. *No fucking thanks, my tastes run a lot more kinkier and darker, and I don't plan on giving them up for Stella.*

The priest clears his throat just as I feel the sharp heel of Stella's shoe dig into my toes and I have to bite the inside of my cheek to muffle the pained sound that wants to escape my lips. *Damn it.* My mind ran away with my thoughts about Stella's frigid cunt.

"I do," I raise my voice and meet the priest's gaze.

"Do you, Stella Rachel Penticton, take this man, Jaxon Philip Stratford, to be your lawful and cherished husband?" I almost feel sorry for the priest. He's holding his breath, waiting for whatever Stella will do. It's been no secret amongst those intimately involved with this wedding that the bride wanted no part in it. It's a good thing no one took her objections and desires into consideration. *I'll probably be paying for that fact for the rest of my damn life.*

Stella never turns her eyes towards me; she stares straight ahead and past the priest. I can almost see the scales in her mind as she undoubtedly weighs the consequences of refusing me. *It's no use.* She, like I, knows there is no changing our fates. I'm power-hungry, and she is a prize I'm determined to take—the crowning jewel in my new empire. I will have her by any means necessary.

Silence fills the air, and we all stand like statues, afraid to move, waiting with bated breath for the ice queen's words. I can feel a trickle of sweat down my back. The desire to wrap my fingers around her impertinent throat seizes me. I grind my back molars to prevent me from doing anything further to embarrass myself. Just as I turn my face towards her with a raised brow and the look of retribution on my face if she denies me, her words ring out, loud and reserved.

"I do." Her cultured voice is strong in the silence of the church. The congregation releases a breath they all seem to have been holding. I watch out of the corner of my eye as Ajax stiffens, his eyes riveted on Stella before lowering to the ground with a grimace. That motherfucker better wipe that grimace off his face before someone in the crowd catches on that the best man was cheering for the groom to be left at the altar. *Fucking traitor!*

The need to slam my fist into his pretty boy face is almost overwhelming. Heat is rising along my body, prickling my skin, as my temper tries to get control of me. My foot takes a step in his direction, before I pull myself back to the here and now. A smug grin crosses my face with the realization, it doesn't matter what Ajax wants or feels. I already fucking won; *she's mine.*

The priest continues on for a few more minutes about the sanctity of marriage, but I tune him entirely out. My thoughts race ahead to all the power plays I mean to make in the next couple of months. I tune back in just as Stella tightens her grip on my hand, squeezing my fingers in a bruising embrace. My glance returns to her, and even through the veil, I can see her displeasure. Her lips are in a tight line, and her nose is flaring with obvious rage. *Well, shit.*

Ajax moves forward and places two platinum and diamond-encrusted bands in my hand before returning to his spot. I hold up the smaller of the rings and slip it on Stella's finger, pushing the square Stratford diamond I sent her by courier weeks ago further back as I slip the band in next to it. I know it was a dick move and not one that won me any brownie points with her, but I just couldn't be bothered to play up the charade of two bestowed lovers. Stella takes the band from my hand and slips it with bruising force on my finger, sinking her nails into the skin of my knuckle before releasing my hand. *Fucking bitch.*

The words I have been waiting weeks to hear are finally uttered. "You may now kiss your bride." Hell, I'll willingly kiss the ice queen; after all, she just became my most valuable possession. I reach forward and lift her delicate black veil over her glittering crown, revealing her beautiful features to me. The breath in my lungs momentarily stalls. She is a stunningly beautiful woman. If it weren't for her viper tongue and arctic personality, I would be beside myself with glee at having such a stunning wife. Instead, I'm constantly weary and waiting for her to plunge a blade into my chest.

Before I can lean forward and take her lips in the obligatory kiss, she shoves her bouquet of blood-red roses at me, makes an unladylike snort, and turns away from me to walk back up the aisle alone, head held high and back rigid.

Gasps, murmurs, and giggles are breaking out around the room, and the poor priest looks mortified. My beautiful, uncontrollable bride just left me standing at the altar like an irredeemable asshole holding her flowers rather than allowing me to kiss her.

She's going to pay for that.

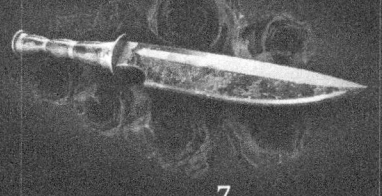

7

Stella

"Anger is a violent emotion, vindictive, and as dangerous to he who is driven by it as to anyone on whom it is turned." Dean Koontz

I LEAVE HIM STANDING at the altar holding my damn flowers and walk out on him. He doesn't bother to give chase; he now has what he wanted. I'm a Stratford and his possession. *Fuck, him. I'm no one's possession.* I make it to the black chauffeured vehicle outside of the church that is meant to take us to our reception lunch with hurried steps.

The back of my mind is shouting miserably that I'm weak, running away from my monsters, but I try to ignore those tempestuous thoughts. The driver rushes around to open the door and to help me quickly get inside with this overbearing dress. Once I'm safely in the confines of the vehicle, I instruct him to take me directly to the Stratford estate rather than the country club where our reception is to be held. I'm finally able to release the strangled breath that has had my chest tightening for the last hour. *It's done, there is no turning back now.*

All my personal belongings were transferred to his home this morning. There is no point in returning to the Penticton estate; I'm no longer a Penticton. At least at the Stratford estate, my father will not be able to get his furious hands on me. His rage was palpable, and I know if the world wasn't watching, he would have wrung my neck for my show of defiance. I close my eyes and try to calm my racing heart from the ordeal of the ceremony. *It will all be alright; we can survive this, too, my mind reassures me.*

Jaxon, *the fucker*, couldn't even pay me the minuscule amount of respect of paying attention to our wedding vows. Not that any vows he makes to me, I would put any weight in. I could tell he was lost in his thoughts, probably already scheming, now that he has his desired prize. He has another thing coming if he thinks I will just sit back and let him use me.

The look on his face was priceless when I refused his kiss, shoved my flowers at him, and turned and walked away. I could hear all the gasps and murmurs all around the room. The disappointed sheep, bleating that their new queen will not fall in line with what is expected. They hunger for the type of power that we now have together. The one my new name provides me. I will not put on a show for any of them if it does not benefit me. I'm the untouchable ice queen; why should marrying Jaxon formally change that? If anything, it fills me with more disdain and fury that they all watched as I was forced to the altar—a sacrificial lamb, sent to the slaughter at the hands of powerful men.

I know that most of the women in that room have slept with my new husband. Whether they themselves are married or not. Nothing in our world is truly a secret. That man is despicable and can't seem to keep his dick in his pants. I have heard rumors of his various kinks, ones that cause a shudder to race down my spine. Will he try to force those on me now? He pursues women relentlessly, and even in my self-imposed glass castle, I hear the stories of his exploits. I will not be one more notch on his belt. He can force me to take his name, but he cannot force me to desire him and willingly let him touch me in intimacy. *What if he tries to take it by force?* My mind questions. *Then it will be the last thing he does alive on this earth before I slit his delectable, evil throat.*

I almost feel sorry for my pathetic father, who so desperately craved a male heir that he sold his only daughter to a monster in order to get one. He did it for nothing. I will rip out my ovaries and set fire to them before I provide him with what he and Jaxon want. No, as far as I'm concerned, the Penticton's and Stratford's lines will end with us so that we don't force the next generation into the same predicament.

The gates open upon the vehicle's approach, and I watch as the large gray stone house appears, a short drive from sixty-second Street. It's ridiculous the opulence in the middle of the city, not that the Penticton estate isn't as grandiose. We are all living in a rich man's world, regardless of what is happening just outside of our gates.

The limo rolls through the gates, and they immediately close behind us. One can never be too careful when one comes from a powerful, wealthy family. I know there are those who mean to do my father and my new husband harm. I will be fighting enemies at every turn going forward. That thought should scare me. Instead, it fills me with anticipation. I was made for war; just like the goddess *Athena*, I welcome the blood of my enemies.

I've never stepped foot in Jaxon's family home, having preferred to live in complete denial that there wouldn't have been a way for me to extract myself from this mess. Now that I've failed, I need to accept that this will be my new prison for the foreseeable future, or at least until I make myself a willing widow.

The limo stops before the large Grecian-styled columns on either side of the resplendent wood and glass front door. It opens, and a butler and housekeeper, both in navy uniforms, make their way outside to the driveway. As I extract myself from the car, tearing the train on my fifty-thousand-dollar dress as I get out of the vehicle and almost end up in an undignified heap on the cobbled driveway. *Fucking hell!* I'm so glad I wasn't in love with this dress, otherwise I would be in tears right now. As it is, it is one more shackle confining me to this miserable life. I will be so relieved when I never see the despicable thing again, and I would love to be a fly on the wall when my father gets the bill.

"Mrs. Stratford, it is a pleasure to have you home, ma'am. We were... not expecting you... before the completion of the... bridal lunch. I am Fergus, the Stratford family butler, and this is Mrs. Pox, the housekeeper." His lined face seems kind, and I can see that I have caused both of them agitation with my untimely and unexpected arrival and my black dress. I feel horrible for causing them stress, but I just couldn't take another moment of pretending to be content with the wedding and since this is my new home, there was nowhere else to go. I would have boarded a plane anywhere had Jaxon not taken my passport days ago to prevent that very thing. *Fucker.*

"I'm truly sorry for causing you any distress. I was exhausted from the ceremony and decided to come to my new home for a reprieve." I watch as they both take in my black attire and the use of my word reprieve. Yes, that's right, this wedding was an execution of myself at the hands of my father and Jaxon Stratford. There is no point in mincing words anymore. The deed is now done.

"Ma'am? Uh... Mr. Stratford is not with you?" Fergus seems perplexed by the fact that no one else has vacated the vehicle other than me. I nod my head no and start moving towards the front door.

"He stayed with his guests. I'm sure there are lots of people who want to offer their congratulations or..." I bite my lip hard to keep from laughing. "Condolences to the groom."

"Yes... ma'am." They are too well-trained and polite to call me out on my crazy behavior and instead lead the way into my new home with blank expressions. *Great.* Not even ten minutes in my new home, and the staff already think I'm insane. *Great going, Stella. You will need allies here. Try playing nice for once in your miserable, entitled life.*

I step forward into the grand foyer only to be accosted with oil paintings of past generations of Stratfords and a silver knight uniform on display. The foyer floors are all black and white marble with inlaid details that meet a dark, sprawling wood staircase that leads to the second-floor landing and a large embankment of windows. The multiple crystal chandeliers give off prisms of light across the champagne-colored wallpaper and all the deeply rich-toned brocade and velvet upholstery.

Great, we are living in the Middle Ages instead of the end of the 20th century. I roll my eyes at all the pretentiousness of wealth on display and turn my attention back to Fergus and Mrs. Pox. I guess redecorating will be one of my very first tasks as lady of the shitty manor.

"Mrs. Pox, if it wouldn't be a great inconvenience, may I have a pot of tea and some assistance removing this dress?"

"Yes, ma'am. Of course. I will put the kettle on right away. Your belongings have arrived, and I have taken the liberty of hanging most of your clothing in the master suite. Fergus will show you and I will be up shortly with the tea to assist you." She turns as if her backside is on fire and rushes down the hallway in the direction of what I'm guessing is the kitchen.

A deep sigh leaves me, and I turn my attention back to a waiting Fergus. I indicate with my arm that he should precede me on the stairs. The man must be in his mid to late sixties; there is no way I'm risking taking him down that flight of stairs if I fall with this dress on. He gives me a look of displeasure but turns and walks up the stairs. "The master suite is in the east wing, ma'am. The west wing holds all of the guest suites." I admire all of the beautiful, priceless art on display and the exquisite artifacts that should adorn a museum but are instead here in the private home of a tyrant. *I wonder how angry I could make him if I donated them all to charity?*

All of this is now as much mine as it is Jaxon's. My cunning father insisted there be no prenup, amalgamating both of our vast wealth into one entity, therefore ensuring the survival of the Pentictons and the Stratfords. Too bad I mean to end it all and ensure that the only one who survives is me.

We reach the large double doors of the main suite, and I get my first glimpse of the space. A large dark wood canopy bed meets my gaze, decorated lavishly with creamy white linens and rich navy accents. I wonder how many of my female acquaintances have been draped across that thing? Disgust curls my lip as I look away. That mattress will need to be burned and replaced. Large windows allow natural light into the space, and there's a beautifully furnished sitting area with a chaise for reading or lounging. I walk further into the space and push open two double doors, which lead to a massive walk-in closet.

The space is divided into his and hers, and I can see that Mrs. Pox indeed put away my belongings across from Jaxon's fine Italian wool suits. The space smells like him, a heady mix of citrus, musk, and spices. I breathe in the scent and rather than agitating me, it helps to calm me and bolster my confidence. *Well, at least the heathen smells good.*

I leave the room and walk directly across the hall into a large ensuite bathroom with a massive glass and marble-enclosed shower, a huge sunken tub, and his and her pedestal sinks. Everything in the space is white and gray marble with touches of navy accents. It's beautiful, and I can picture myself spending some luxurious time in that tub—that is, *after I dispose of my wretched husband.*

I re-enter the bedroom area just as Mrs. Pox walks into the space with a tray filled with tea and pretty little cookies. I give her a small smile and reach for one of the cookies. Taking a quick bite, a moan leaves my lips. *Oh my god, the cookie melts in my mouth.* Maybe living here won't be so bad if Mrs. Pox keeps supplying me with cookies! Can one have an orgasm from a baked good? I watch as she sets everything down on the coffee table in the sitting area and moves back in my direction. She nods her head at Fergus to leave and motions with her finger for me to turn around.

Before I can do that, a wicked thought on how to further mess with Jaxon enters my mind. I bet the fucker thinks he's going to have his wedding night and pillage the blushing bride. *I would rather slit my own throat than allow that man inside of me.*

"Fergus, wait. You mentioned that there are other suites in the west wing?" I raise an eyebrow, and a smirk reaches my lips as he eyes me questioningly.

"Yes, ma'am. There are six suites on the other side." He stands there, completely confused by my question. I catch Mrs. Pox's eye and notice she's trying to suppress a smile. It looks like she and I may end up understanding ourselves perfectly. Maybe we can be allies. It would be lovely not to have to watch my back while I'm here.

"Fergus, as quickly as you can, please have Mr. Stratford's clothing and personal belongings moved to the largest of the suites in the west wing." His bushy gray eyebrows meet his hairline at my words, and his mouth goes slack. "If no one else can assist you in completing the task quickly, I will change, and Mrs. Pox and I will help. I would like it completed before Jaxon returns home."

I watch as his Adam's apple bobs up and down, and his mouth opens and closes, then he seems to shake himself. "Yes, Mrs. Stratford, right away. I will get the two maids to help me while you are changing." He quickly leaves the room, and a snort escapes Mrs. Pox. "Oh, deary, I hope you know what you are doing. Jaxon tends to have a hellish temper." She motions to the ensuite bath, and I follow her in after grabbing clothing from the closet to change into.

"I'm not worried, Mrs. Pox; he needs me too much to really do me any harm. He can rant all he wants; he asked for this reckoning." We quickly make work of removing my dress, veil, and crown, and I slip into a pair of blue jeans and an off-the-shoulder cashmere sweater.

We re-enter the room to the bustle of Fergus and two maids, quickly removing Jaxon's items from my new space. I hope he enjoys being the master of nothing. He's about to learn that the queen is the most important piece of the board, and kings just don't hold the same power.

8

Jaxon

"On wrongs swift vengeance waits." Alexander Pope

I'M LIVID, AND MY face hurts from all the fake smiling I've had to do all day. Once Stella dramatically snubbed me at the church and disappeared with my damn limo, I had to commence damage control. I can't allow these wealthy families around me to believe that my... *wife*, god, I hate that word. My wife can walk all over me.

Stella has no idea the rage she has awoken in me, but she's about to find out when I get home. The only thing that gives me a measure of calm is the knowledge that my little ice queen will pay me back every slight and insult on her knees.

I had to hitch a ride with my new in-laws to my wedding reception lunch, as if the humiliation of being left standing at the damn altar holding my wife's flowers wasn't enough. Stella's mother, Rachel, tried unsuccessfully to start a conversation in their limo, but I barely uttered two words. My thoughts are solely on my ice queen and what I'm going to do with her spiteful ass when I next see her. The picture of me spanking her with my full palm over and over until her ass is red and her cunt is dripping while a ball gag is wrapped around her face races through my mind and gives me a semi-right at the most unfortunate of times.

Thomas Penticton was unusually quiet in the vehicle. The man likes to boast about his business conquests at length, but other than to agree that the priest did a splendid job, he hadn't uttered another word. *Thank fuck for that.* He did, however, stare at me with rancor and displeasure the whole way to the country club. Maybe he was regretting his choice of groom after all. Regardless, there is no way back for any of us now. *We are one miserable wealthy family now.*

The country club was just another horrendous and humiliating affair to endure. *How does one have a wedding lunch without a damn bride?* Her parents made a toast to the beautiful missing bride, much to mine and everyone's amusement. I will be on every gossip newspaper across the country by morning, and all because my little hellion of a wife was displeased with the hand fate played her.

She went through with the ceremony, and for that, I'm grateful, even though I will never admit it to her. There were a few moments there when I thought that for sure she would deny me or, better yet, slap me. But she didn't, and if I'm honest with myself, that worries me. Stella doesn't seem the type to roll over for anyone. Case in point, leaving me at the altar after completing our vows. She's a planner, just like I am. A planner with access to an unlimited fortune and massive amounts of power now that she carries the Stratford name.

I do not doubt that we are about to go on a rollercoaster ride of trying to punish and tame each other. The thought alone of how I will bring her to heel has my cock hardening in my tuxedo pants, which is unfortunate as the company around me won't appreciate the desire for my new wife. Maybe I can warm up that frigid temperature inside of her, and melt some of that ice so my cock doesn't end up with frostbite.

I tuned back into what Ajax, Thomas Penticton, Fisher St. John, Jeffrey Cain, and River Stanton were discussing. The discussion centered around buying up low-income housing in the South and revitalizing it into condos for the wealthy—*fools, the lot of them.* Don't they realize the housing market is about to crash? How about the fact that they will have to deal with the local gangs?

I should let them invest in whatever scheme will cost them vast amounts of their wealth and then sweep in and buy up all their assets. I can use my underworld connections with those very same gangs to make their lives miserable. That's what my father would have done before me. He would have gone so far as to have their buildings burnt to the ground and then benefited from his soiled hands. The apple doesn't fall very far from the tree; I have no issues with getting my hands muddy.

Patrick Stratford was a ruthless, conniving business shark before his untimely death from a heart attack two years ago, leaving me the sole heir and inheritor of the Stratford line. I wonder if he's up there somewhere smiling today at my calculated move to expand our empire. All I have ever wanted to do was make that man proud of me. Make him see the value in me, after years of ceaseless disappointment. I was unable to do that before he abruptly passed away, but I'm determined to make it my life's mission, and Stella Penticton Stratford will help me achieve it. *Who's the idiot now, dad?*

"Are you even listening, Jaxon?" Ajax inquires with annoyance in his voice. I know he's still mad I married Stella and he seems to really be enjoying my humiliation at her hands at the moment. The urge to break his perfect nose fills me, and I have to restrain myself from reaching out with my fist. *Some best friend, this fucker is.*

"He's too busy dreaming of his little ice queen of a wife, isn't that right, Jax?" River asks with amusement and wags his eyebrows.

"That and all the empires I'm about to destroy, maybe even yours, River," I smirk and excuse myself from the conversation. Having had my fill of their obnoxious bullshit and sly jokes at my expense.

I'm just about to return to the bar to grab another much-needed drink when Stella's mother stops before me. Her large blue eyes are reminiscent of her daughter's, but where Stella's are arctic, Rachel's are pools of sunny skies. "Jaxon, may I have a word, in private please?"

My eyebrow arches at her request. I watch as she steels her shoulders, and determination fills her delicate features. I nod in the direction of the balcony, and we make our way out to the fragrant, chilly area. "What is this about, Rachel?" I inquire as I lean my body against the railing, my mind filled with curiosity.

"Jaxon... Stella..." She takes a deep, fortifying breath. "Jaxon, please don't hurt my daughter." I go to interrupt her, but she raises her hand between us, indicating I should remain silent. It irks me to comply, but I do. "My daughter is fearless, strong, and frighteningly intelligent. Had she been born a man in this world, she would have had all of you on your knees as your king. Unfortunately, that was not her fate, and her father could not see her worth as anything other than a pretty chess piece to maneuver on the board."

I watch as her features darken at the thought, and her small hands clench at her side. *Interesting*, Rachel Penticton is not the meek little thing she portrays herself to be. "She will not bend willingly, and if you try to force her to her knees, she will set fire to your world, Jaxon. You don't realize it yet, but my idiot husband has given you more than a prize; he has given you an asset. If you're the intelligent man I believe you to be, you will work with her to build the empire that you crave. Make her a willing part of the conquest, or you will never achieve what you desire without her."

She moves closer to me and grabs my chin tightly in her delicate pink-tipped fingers. I stare at her in surprise at her bold move. "If you hurt my daughter Jaxon, I will have you murdered and decapitated in the middle of the night, leaving my daughter as the sole heir to all of our fortunes. I am only weak because I have to be, but I refuse to allow you or anyone else to turn my daughter into me. Do we understand each other?"

She tightens her hold, her fingernails slightly digging into the skin just below my jawline. *Holy fuck, Rachel is a little spitfire.* I'm not sure why I'm even surprised; after all, Stella had to get her spirit from somewhere. I meet her eyes and see the sincerity blazing there. She will have me murdered; I have no doubt about it. A wealthy woman like her, I'm sure, can arrange a murder without much of an effort.

"Understood. I have no intention of hurting her, Rachel."

"Good," she says, releasing my chin, stepping back, and turning towards the open doorway. "Oh, and Jaxon, leave her wild and free. Do not try to control or contain my daughter; you will scorch yourself in the process." She moves forward and away from me, leaving me stupefied and with revolving thoughts in my head.

God damn it! Are there no meek women left in this godforsaken privileged world? Are they all secretly demented banshees just waiting to cut off the heads of the men that cause them displeasure? I wonder if Thomas Penticton even truly knows the strength his wife hides? *Probably not*; he would have beaten it out of her by now if he did.

I crack my neck and shrug my shoulders to try to relieve the fucking stress that threatens to drown me. I won't be making his mistake. I know I'm a dick forcing her down the aisle and trapping her for my own ambitions. Hell, the thought of forcing her to submit to me, the ice queen of Manhattan, makes my cock throb, but I'm not her father. I don't want to beat that spirit out of her. I plan to know my wife in every way, to ensure she never hides her true self from me and that I don't one day end up with a blade in my back. I may not love Stella or even like her at the moment, but I can respect her fierceness and determined spirit. Her mother is right; Thomas never saw Stella as anything more than a prize to hand off to the highest bidder, but I see the fire within her.

She will be my queen and rule alongside me. Together, we will master this world and ensure my name lives on for hundreds of years. I just have to convince her that I don't mean to break her spirit and that I see her as an equal first. *Good luck with that!* My mind roars.

Stella Stratford, I'm coming for you, and you will be mine in every way.

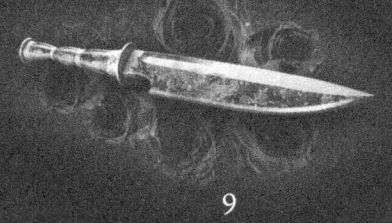

9

Stella

"Rage became a layer of my skin." Soraya Chemaly, Rage Becomes Her: The Power of Women's Anger

I T'S ALMOST MIDNIGHT, AND a storm is brewing both outside and in my veins. There has been no word from Jaxon since I left him at the church hours ago. There has been nothing from my parents either, which I don't know whether to be relieved or concerned about. Deep seeds of resentment are building inside of me. Now that both my father and Jaxon have what they desire, I'm once again an afterthought, easily discarded like a pair of dirty shoes.

A part of me that I don't understand hoped Jaxon would chase me back to the house and argue with me. The need to push all of his buttons until he veritably detonates is a humming deep in my blood. Is it just the need for spite and vengeance, or is it something more?

The desire to hurt him first before he can inflict pain on me wars with my common sense. Other than agreeing to my father's terms and forcing me down the aisle, he hasn't really hurt me. If anything, he just gave me unlimited power to play with. He just doesn't realize it yet. *What an idiot.*

The thought alone of all the wealth and power that I now have lights a fire inside of me. I always wanted to take over Penticton Industries from my father. Our family dynasty started in the late seventeen hundreds when we came over from England to colonize the American east coast. My family consisted of wealthy merchants back in England, and we set up trading posts across the eastern United States, buying and leasing goods and land to all the new hopeful European immigrants. The beginning of the Penticton dynasty, take something that doesn't necessarily belong to you and make it profitable selling it to someone else. We have never looked back since. Now, most of our wealth is in real estate holdings and industrial acquisitions.

I've heard rumblings about how my father doesn't have the drive or business mind of his forebears and how the company hasn't grown at the rate expected under his tenure. I imagine that was why he was so determined to tie us to another tyrant of industry to ensure our survival, and Jaxon was all too willing to be a part of it. If only my father had given the slightest thought to my worth as anything other than a piece he could bargain with, he would have seen that I have a shrewd business mind and understand how the game is played, even more than he does.

I would have led Penticton Industries into the future, growing our already vast fortune to unprecedented wealth and power. He could have been proud of having a daughter, rather than lamenting the lack of a son.

He did educate me in the finest schools, and although I have a business degree from Browns, he saw no future where I wouldn't be just some rich man's wife—a pretty trophy on a man's arm, much like my mother. For that, I will never forgive him. His lack of faith in my abilities has long been a wound on my soul, one that he continuously inflicts without mercy.

I watch out the window as a dark green Porsche races down the lit driveway of my new home before coming to a sudden screeching halt in front of the columns. Both doors open, and my new husband slides out of the passenger side of the sports vehicle, still in his wedding attire but looking disheveled and, if I'm not mistaken, inebriated. That, however, is not what catches my interest; it's the blonde female with the low-cut, short red dress that pops out of the driver's side and laughs at whatever he is saying. Kalista Cain, one of the most beautiful women of the Manhattan elite and my new husband's ex-girlfriend. That term may not be entirely accurate by the looks of their current touchy interactions. My teeth grind together as I watch them through the glass without a care about who their audience might be.

Kalista is beautiful in a way that puts supermodels to shame. Her features are delicate and refined with high cheekbones, deep emerald green eyes, a perfect nose, and pouty lips, finished off with a body made for sin and every man's wet dream. By the way, Jaxon is looking at her, he is no exception to that sentiment. I watch with a flash of irritation as he rounds the car, still laughing at whatever they are saying to each other. He grabs her elbows and pulls her into his embrace, wrapping his arms tightly around her as she tilts her head back to stare up at him. Their eyes meet, and

I can sense the scorching desire from my perch at the bedroom window. I watch as Jaxon licks his lips before lowering his head to the side of her neck, kissing, and dragging his tongue along its length as his hand squeezes her breast in his large palm. She digs her hands into his hair's dark, thick tresses before arching her back and giving him further access to her sun-kissed skin.

My sight is mesmerized as his lips trail a path down her neck to the low-cut neckline of her dress and kiss a path over the swell of her breasts before returning to her neck. Her jaw, and finally, his mouth seals over her red-painted lips in a fierce kiss that, even from a distance, is giving off heat. I watch, stunned, with my pulse pounding in my veins as both his hands reach around Kalista's waist and grab handfuls of her ass cheeks, lifting her off the ground until she wraps her toned bare legs around his waist and rubs herself against his cock.

A gasp leaves my lips; my mouth goes dry at the scene before me. I have never been kissed the way he is kissing her, never experienced that unrestrained passion. It looks like he is consuming her, and she is in paradise. I should be furious; I should be running down there and stabbing both of them. How dare they disrespect me in my new home, on my fucking wedding day!

However, my feet remain planted, watching the vision play out before me as if they have grown deep roots. They are so lost in each other and the lust between them that they are oblivious to me watching them. If I ever held the slightest hope for something more in my wretched life, the image before me just decimated all of it. This will truly be a faux marriage in name only. Jaxon thinks to humiliate me by bringing women to the home that we share, unabashed and unworried about the consequences.

He might as well have just declared war on me. The sting of betrayal makes its way across my skin, and my heart hardens further towards him. For every small sliver of rage that he makes me feel, for every hurt that he inflicts going forward, I will pay him back a hundredfold. I vow it to my soul. I will not allow any man to destroy me.

An emotion that I have rarely felt before rises as I continue to watch my husband kiss his gorgeous girlfriend with lustfulness. *Jealousy.* For a moment, it rises within me, and I wish it were me he was kissing with such passion. That it was me draped in his arms and feeling the scorching heat of his kiss. Then reality settles back in, and

I know that it will never be me. He doesn't want me, just my name, wealth, and an heir. I'm an ice queen, and he prefers his women hot-blooded, witless, and putty in his hands. I swallow down a fresh surge of rage, and it burns and swells in my belly and courses through my body, reminding me that I'm alive and still in one piece. This will not break me. I will not shatter at the sight of his disdain and obviously intended disloyalty.

A large bang emerges from somewhere in the house and must vibrate outside as Jaxon breaks the kiss and steps back from Kalista. His gaze rises over the house and meets mine through the large window, the bright light behind me doing nothing to disguise my presence. A look of shock crosses his features before he masks them. He steps back further from Kalista and opens the door to her vehicle, waiting until she returns to the driver's seat again. Once the door is closed, she braces one of her arms with her head out the window. She says something to him with a smile that he doesn't return before reversing, turning the car around, and driving back down the driveway.

My new husband once again meets my gaze through the window before turning towards the front door of our home and moving out of sight. I brace myself for the interaction about to happen. I push down the feelings of jealousy and any other emotion other than rage and humiliation, allowing them to fuel me. He wants a war, I will fucking give him one.

It doesn't take him long before his rapid, hard footsteps make their way down the hallway toward the main suite, and he pushes the door wide open. He stands there in the glow of the hallway lighting, a well-dressed menace that just willingly inflicted pain on me without the slightest concern for the consequences. *Fucking monster.*

"Wife." He raises a dark eyebrow in question, and wipes at his mouth with his fingers, trying to remove Miss. Cain's red lipstick. *It's too late for that fucker.* Irritation pricks at me at the action. Does he think I'm stupid? How about easily manipulated? I move away from the window as if to confront him. He braces his body as if in fear of flying projectiles.

Oh no, I have no intention of being one of those women who throws things and cries. Jaxon Stratford has no idea what I'm capable of, but he's about to learn that I can be patient and ruthless. He will pay me back in blood for that little scene on the driveway, and so will his little whore. *Vengeance will be mine.*

I feign an unbothered calmness I don't feel and move further away from the window, taking a seat on the chaise and pouring myself a glass of wine from the decanter at my side. I'm projecting the image of being unperturbed by what I just saw outside and his unkempt appearance. "Did you enjoy your wedding reception, husband?" I question with a haughty glare, raising the glass and sipping the rich red wine. How I wish I were spilling his and Kalista's red blood right now. *Patience Stella, good things come to those who know how to plan.*

"Our wedding reception, Stella. Despite your lack of appearance, it was quite enjoyable." He strolls into the room, removing his tuxedo jacket, draping it on the back of a chair, and taking a seat. His body slumped down, and his legs wide open and bent. My eyes are drawn to the spot that Kalista was rubbing herself against on his pants, and mercifully, there is no mark present. I'm not sure I could contain the anger thrumming inside of me had I seen a wet spot on the fabric.

"I'll just bet it was. Did Miss Cain feel the need to continue the festivities?" I arch a dark brow, malice dripping from my tone.

For a fleeting moment, I think I witness regret across his features before he schools them into his unreadable mask. "Kalista just gave me a ride home; someone took our limo."

"How generous and kind of her." I grit through my teeth. "Please remind me to reward Auggie, our driver, with the same reward when he brings me home."

A scowl crosses his features at my threat. "Stella... it was nothing. Just two old friends parting ways."

"Yes, well, don't part ways on my account, Jaxon. I have no intentions of stopping you from being the manwhore you really are. After all, you will need to get your needs filled somewhere. It certainly won't be here."

He jumps to his feet and stalks angrily towards me. "What are you talking about, Stella? You're my wife. You will fulfill my needs."

A snort leaves my lips, and his words send both fury and heat down my body. *His wife. His needs.* "Yes, well, you seemed to have forgotten you have one, mere moments ago, Jaxon." I let an evil grin cross my lips. "Don't worry, husband, whatever you do,

I will follow your lead. If it's good enough for you to do without thinking of the consequences, it is good enough for me to do too." A smile graces my lips, and the malice I feel towards him drips into my eyes.

He reaches down, grabs my arm, and pulls me to my feet, causing me to drop the glass of wine all over the cream area rug. Before I get the chance to react, he crashes into my body. The impact has a grunt, leaving both our lips. "You think you're so clever, my little ice queen. I wouldn't make idle threats, Stella." His deft fingers slide into my dark waves and yank hard, bowing my neck as a gasp of pain leaves my lips.

His soft lips skate down my neck, and goosebumps erupt across all of my skin. A shiver racks my suddenly heated body as his lips suck hard on my pebbled skin, no doubt leaving a mark behind in his wake. For the briefest of moments, I want to give into the sensation and pleasure that he is creating across my body. Wisps of heat and shudders skate up my limbs, my core clenches in response to his lips sucking and licking my skin. I've never felt spontaneously turned on by anyone, and I've never wanted to give in immediately to wanton behavior. Then my mind comes to a devastating halt and reminds me that not mere moments ago, his lips were on another woman's lips, and it's as if a bucket of ice-cold water is poured over me, welcoming me home.

I raise my knee hard between his spread legs and slam it into his cock, while digging the fingers of my right hand into his hair and yanking forcefully on the strands. My other hand wraps around his throat and squeezes, my nails digging into the soft, warm flesh until I feel them puncture the skin. He releases a pained cry and starts to fall to his knees despite the hold I have on his hair, which has dark strands ripping out in chunks between my fingers. "My threats are never idle, Jaxon; you had better learn that now. Do not ever touch me, I'm not one of your willing whores."

I squeeze his neck once more as his fingers reach up to crush mine while he still tries to get himself under control from the knee to the groin. He's breathing heavily, and sweat is dotted across his forehead. His eyes are two twin pools of the darkest flint, and the fury in them brings a thrill to my heart. "You're a fucking cold bitch, Stella." He grits, pushing himself back to his feet while still cupping his crotch.

"I have never denied being one Jaxon." I move further away from him towards the crystal candle holders on the console by the far wall. I need to get myself under control. His touch momentarily made me lose my wits, and I cannot allow that to happen.

"I would like you to leave my room, Jaxon," I state with rancor, meeting his eyes with defiance.

"Our room, Stella, this is our room now." He stands up straight to his imposing six foot one height, yanking his loosened bow tie off, and starts unbuttoning his shirt, heading in the direction of the walk-in closet. A sinister smirk crosses my lips as he opens the door and enters the space. I hear him loudly shout, "What the fuck!" before he reappears in the room. "What have you done with my things, Stella?"

"My room, Jaxon. This is no longer your space. You have been moved to the west wing, as far away from me as possible. I will not share a room or a bed with you."

He strolls towards me, his shirt wholly undone and his large, muscled, golden-skinned chest on display. I see the hint of black ink just off to the side, but I can't distinguish what it is behind the parted sides of the shirt. His abs clench as he moves, and I have my eyes transfixed on the area that leads to a dark, happy trail and a defined 'V.' Fuck, he is a gorgeous specimen of a man; too bad he is the devil himself. "We'll just see about that, Stella."

I reach over and grab the heavy crystal candle holder, brandishing it in front of me like a weapon. "Get out, Jaxon. I don't want to even have to look at you."

"I could force you, Stella, you know that, right? This little game you are playing, there are no winners." He stops before me, his dark gaze meeting mine. He bites down on his full bottom lip as he reaches out and trails a finger slowly down the side of my cheek. "How could something so beautiful be so disturbingly vicious?" His words are soft, and a flash of heat enters his eyes. I feel traces of fire everywhere that his fingertip has been.

I pull my face away from his touch, the effort harder than I would have liked, raising the candle holder between us; I make my intent to hit him with it present. "If you try to force me into anything further, Jaxon, I will cut off your cock and make you swallow it before slitting your miserable throat. Get the hell out of my room."

For a moment or two, neither of us move. The air around us is ripe with scorn. He doesn't look like he will back down from my threat, and I start to worry that I may actually have to bludgeon him with the weapon in my tight grasp. My mind is a whirling mess of sensations and thoughts. Will he force me? Do I want him to? What will I do if he refuses to leave?

It's not like anyone in this house will come to my rescue if he decides to be violent with me. He is a stranger to me; I don't even know if he has violent tendencies, and Mrs. Pox mentioned he has a temper. *If he raises a finger to hurt us, we kill him.* My mind screeches like an unhinged banshee. My hands are starting to get clammy holding the candle holder, and soon enough, I won't be able to continue to hold its heavy weight at this angle.

Just when I think he is going to reach for me, he steps back, giving me a final perusal from my bare feet, over my body, and to the top of my dark head; then his eyes meet mine once again before he turns and walks out the door. *Thank fuck!*

The air that was trapped in my lungs finally leaves in a ragged breath, and I lean my body against the wall behind me. I slide down the wall until I'm on my ass and release my tenuous hold on the candle holder, which makes a dull thud as it meets the floor. I trail both my hands down my face, I wonder what I have just gotten myself into.

Is this to be my life now?

10

Jaxon

"Youth is a blunder; Manhood a struggle, Old Age a regret."
Benjamin Disraeli

*F*UUUCK! MY COCK *IS still throbbing from Stella's hit. Fucking bitch!* Who does she think she is moving me out of my own room? THIS IS MY GODDAMN HOUSE! The threats leaving her villainous lips only stir up my fury and my ardor more. The intensity of resentment scoring through my veins is close to exploding if this beauty of a bitch keeps this shit up. How can something so pretty be so fucking destructive and violent? She's like a tsunami in her destruction, so horrifyingly beautiful you can't take your eyes away from it, and you wait too long to realize that she means to drown you in her depths.

The devious viper fucking attacked me, and I just know she would have hit me with that candle holder if I pushed any further. My body is strumming with fiery rage, the desire to go back in there and wrap my tight fist around her swan-like throat and force her to her knees before me is burning in my veins. I want her to submit; I want her to acknowledge that I own her, every fucking inch of that delectable body and that ice-cold heart. *I will have her, she's mine now.*

You started it by bringing Kalista here. So what if I brought my ex-girlfriend home on my wedding day? This is my fucking house, *mine*, not Stella's. Just like this house, she belongs to me now. She's one of my fucking assets. I can do whatever the fuck I want. It's not like Stella doesn't understand the score, she's fully aware of how our world works. *I don't owe her shit.* Fuck her and her miserable coldness, even a chainsaw couldn't cut through it. Thoughts run rampant through my mind, causing me to yank on my hair. Bringing with them fury, but also the sprinkling of unease. That's not exactly true; I do owe her at least some respect; she is the new Stratford queen. *Fuck!*

Did you need to hurt her like that? Be a fucking callous dick right out of the gate? As if forcing her to marry you wasn't enough. I drag my hands down my face as I lean against the wall outside of *my* bedroom—the one my new wife has seen fit to steal and bar me from.

DAMN IT! How could I have been so fucking reckless? Messing around with Kalista on my wedding day right after Stella's mom threatened to murder me if I hurt her daughter. *Fuucckk! Stella's mom is going to shank my ass.*

How would you have reacted if she pulled that shit on you? Irateness and a ferocious fury fill my body at the thought of watching Stella cuckold me from a window with another man in my fucking house. I would strangle her. I would make sure she watched as I tore her lover to pieces in front of her and set him on fire. She's fucking *mine,* and I don't share.

Yeah, asshole, exactly! Is it a wonder, her reaction, and the knee she slammed painfully into my groin? Fucking hell, she had every right to be enraged with me. I'm a stupid cunt, that does reckless shit with no thoughts of the fallout. A good man does not hurt his wife the way I have. I disrespected her in her own home by bringing Kalista here. A home she has been forced to. *I am a fucking walking moron.* I can't even claim I wasn't aware of what I was doing when Kalista cornered me outside of the country club and kissed me brazenly. I should have walked away then and stopped it from going any further. Did I, however, do any of those things? *Nope,* the fuck up that I am, I went recklessly forward into the abyss without a care.

My displeasure with Stella at humiliating me at the altar and leaving me to have to face all our friends and family alone, made its way to the forefront of my mind, and I wanted to repay her in kind. My slightly inebriated state didn't help matters either. It's why I agreed to allow Kalista to drive me home, knowing we wouldn't be able to keep our hands off of each other. Somewhere on the drive home, I actually forgot about my little ice queen waiting for me back at the Stratford mansion, and the whole burden of the stress of the last couple of weeks began to melt under Kalista's flirtations and wicked hands. Especially when those hands stroked and gripped my hard cock through my pants, making it weep and stand at attention for her. *Shit, I almost had her pull over on the side of the road so I could fuck her pretty face.* Thank fuck now, that I didn't.

Shit, when that bang startled me out of my passionate infused drunkenness, and I looked up into my wife's arctic blue eyes, promising me a world of fucking pain, my stomach dropped, and my body went ice cold. Even my breath stuttered in my lungs at the disappointed and hurt look on her face. The one I put there with my callous actions. How could I have allowed things to get so far, outside of my front door, in the house my new wife now inhabits? On her first night in this house, no less.

I never thought about Stella actually seeing us, but I also did not discount the possibility. The truth is I didn't care. I let it play out like the entitled piece of shit I am, and now I will have to deal with the fallout. *Why do we care now?*

The thought has me stopping in my tracks. Stella is not the forgiving type, and I was already on her shit list for forcing her down the aisle. This one reckless action of mine will cause irreparable damage to our non-existent relationship. She's going to make life even more difficult now. She will make sure I pay her for the hurt inflicted. Stella is a dark, vengeful force, just waiting to be unleashed on the world, and the fucker that I am, I just gave her a target to aim at. *Jesus, fuck, I'm screwed.*

Her threats to repay me in kind for my actions skate across my mind. Would my little ice queen even dare? Would she allow another man to seduce her where anyone could see? Let passion ride her sexy little body as another man touched and kissed her? Just the thought has anger racing through me, making me see nothing but red.

Fucking hypocrite! My mind blares. A red haze slides across my eyes as my fists clench at my side. *She is mine!* No one will take my fucking prize, and I will destroy anyone foolish enough to try.

I continue walking down the hall towards the guest wing, cracking my neck, anger, and jealousy riding me. Mrs. Pox climbs the stairs and as I meet her at the top, I immediately notice the disapproval on her features before she schools them away. "Mrs. Pox." I nod towards her, but she won't look me in the eye and instead looks over my shoulder. *Fucking great!* Is every woman in this house mad at me right now? *When it rains, it fucking pours.*

"Sir. Congratulations to you on your... nuptials. I hope everything was... to your enjoyment." Her lips grimace into a straight line. I know she's not thrilled with me forcing Stella to marry me. She refused to play an active role in my wedding because of it. The woman has been with me since I was ten years old, and my mother died.

She is the only real mother figure I have ever known; I can always tell when I have done something to disappoint her. Right now, she doesn't only look disappointed; she seems hurt and disgusted with me. The feeling of remorse crawls across my chest as I stare at her. "You saw."

She sighs deeply, her shoulders slumping and her dark brown eyes meeting mine. I see a whack of emotions there, ones that cause my chest to tighten painfully. "Yes, Jaxon, all of us witnessed through the windows how you just humiliated that girl up there on her wedding day, after forcing her to marry you with that... that woman you brought home." She moves to go around me, and I reach for her arm. "Where are you going?"

She recoils back before my touch reaches her, displeasure evident in her eyes. "To ensure she is alright in her new home, Jaxon. Something that you should have done instead of causing her pain. I raised you better, Jaxon Stratford." She turns away from me and stalks down the hallway towards the master ensuite. "You are in the largest of the west wing guest rooms. I suggest you make yourself comfortable. I don't foresee you moving back to your bedroom anytime soon." With that imparted over her shoulder, she moves out of my sightline.

FUCK! Does everyone in this house hate me now? Mrs. Pox being ashamed of me is devastating. She's right; she didn't raise me to be this selfish; my father, however, did. I grip the handrail tight, wanting to rip it off and fling it at the wall. I grab a painting off the light beige wall and throw it down the stairs, watching as it crashes and splinters, a priceless artifact destroyed much like my first day as a married man. I literally couldn't give a shit what anyone but Mrs. Pox thinks of me. She has always been a constant in my life and strength at my back. *What about Stella? Do you care what she thinks of you?* The thought whispers through my mind.

No... fuck, yes. I should care what Stella thinks of me if we are going to build an empire together. How could I have lost myself like that in Kalista? I was reckless, led by my hard cock instead of my brain. I told Kalista yesterday that we were over and that once I married Stella, she would have to be my priority, at least until we had conceived an heir or two. I urged her to move on to someone else, someone who wasn't trying to actively build an empire with another woman. I clarified that I could never give her what she wanted because I was marrying Stella. Yet not even a mere twenty-four hours later, I allowed her to give me a hand job over my pants in a moving vehicle and kissed her passionately in front of my new fucking wife and all of my household staff, it seems.

I drag my hands through my hair as I make my way down the stairs to the den. I need a fucking drink or maybe ten to get through what remains of this day. I'm an idiot, a disappointment, just like my father always claimed. I can never think clearly about the weight of the consequences of my actions. An attribute leftover from my spoiled, rich boy, motherless childhood.

The mere thought of how my father would be chastising me over my actions makes the hairs on the back of my neck stand on end. He would be berating me endlessly with his loud voice about how my reckless actions may have just jeopardized all my plans and ambitions for the future of the Stratford empire. The empire he left begrudgingly in my hands, the heir he hoped to shape into an image of himself. Sometimes, I feel like his ghost is trapped inside this house, determined to haunt all my waking moments and oversee all of my resounding failures as a man. At twenty-eight, I should be wiser, more decisive in my thinking, and more aware of my actions. I'm no longer a schoolboy out there playing the field and making mistakes that someone else will clean up for me. My actions now are my own, and they will have dire results if I'mainm not careful.

As I pour myself two fingers of amber scotch, my thoughts return to the beauty currently holding court in my bedroom. Her rage was palpable, as was her intent to maim me with that crystal candle holder. I hurt her mentally and emotionally, and she, in turn, inflicted physical pain on me. *Fuck, that's hot.* That knowledge makes my already throbbing dick rise, causing a harsh groan to leave my lips in the empty room. My neck is still smarting from her tight grip. I rub my fingers over the punctures left from her nails, and my fingers come away streaked with my blood. *Fucking sexy, vicious cunt.*

The vision of an enraged Stella causes my temperature to rise, and my heart quickens in my chest. The way her eyes seared into my very soul and the pretty pink flush across her chest, neck, and cheeks after I kissed her soft skin, hell, I need more of that right now. The smell of her, something tantalizing and delicate that called to my senses, still surrounds me. *Fuck, Stella Stratford is a dream and a nightmare all rolled up into one.* One that now carries my name and is irrevocably mine. The knowledge brings me heated pleasure and satisfaction.

As I down the scotch and pour myself another, I wonder if there is any way that I can remedy the havoc that I have already created. It will take a substantial gesture to make it up to her. For a moment, I stop and question, why do I even care? It's not like I have feelings for her, well at least ones that don't revolve around her choking on my thick cock when I force it down her throat. I wonder if it's even worth it to try. *I own her. She's already mine.* I will never release her from this marriage while she's still breathing.

Even then, Stella can try to run off to hell. I'll drag her back by her fucking hair. Do I really need to do anything here? Sure, Mrs. Pox is mad, but she'll get over it. Do I really care if Stella is up there in my fucking suite, upset at my actions? She should realize who she married, after all.

She's our wife, dickhead. My mind seethes. I hurt and disrespected her, and despite everything that happened today, she didn't deserve that. This will make it so much harder to get her to cooperate with my plans. I need to put a baby in that frigid fucking womb of hers right away, without her ripping my cock off.

I plop myself in the oversized brown leather wing chair to think through what I can do as a grand gesture for my wife that is short of walking through glass naked on my hands and knees or making her a widow. The only two gestures she probably craves at the moment. As I close my eyes and allow the smooth scotch to warm my core, arctic blue eyes flash in my mind.

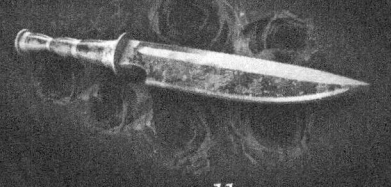

11

Stella

"Women have discovered that they cannot rely on men's chivalry to give them justice." Helen Keller

I CAN FEEL THE morning sunlight penetrating through the open window curtains on my face, the orange glow behind my shuttered eyelids bringing me a sense of much-needed peace. I burrow further under the deliciously warm and luxuriously soft covers. A moan of appreciation escapes my lips as I keep my eyes tightly shut, needing a few more minutes before I have to face the unrepentant world.

"You keep making those sounds, Stella, and I will crawl right under there with you." The deep voice filled with humor has me jolting up in bed and pulling the covers all the way up to my neck. *Jesus fucking Christ!* Jaxon is sitting in a chair next to the bed, watching me intently with a coffee mug in his hand. The devious smirk across his face has the hackles at the back of my neck standing on end.

"What the hell are you doing in here, Jaxon?" My voice comes out sharper than I intended, and I can feel the heat of his eyes on my skin, causing a blush to rise up my neck. Those slate gray-blue eyes track every exposed inch of skin that I haven't covered with the sheet. The knowledge that I'm only wearing a scrap of lace and silk underneath has my stomach cramping in mortification.

Last night, when I went looking for my night clothes, I was horrified to discover that my mother had all of my comfortable sleeping shirts removed from my things and only silk and lace nightgowns and frilly undergarments placed in my trousseau. *What the hell was she thinking?* That I would need to seduce the man that is already my husband? How outrageous! I don't need to seduce Jaxon; he already bought the damn cow so he could have the milk!

"I'm here to bid my *wife* good morning, Stella." I watch as he places the mug on the side table, those elegant long fingers trailing over the table's edge before languishing comfortably in the chair. He looks like a sleek, sexy panther, all long-limbed, sinewy, and seductive in his dark gray dress pants and royal blue dress shirt. His dark hair shines in the sunlight, and his eyes sparkle with mischief. The corner of his mouth rises as he notices my perusal of his body. My blood is rushing so loudly in my veins that I can hear it in my ears, and my core tightens with the way he is staring at me. Like he wants to take a bite of my flesh and sate himself on my taste. *Shit, shit, shit.*

"Get out, Jaxon; you are not welcome in my room." I break eye contact, needing a moment of respite from the onslaught of his gaze which is trying to read my every thought. I don't understand the effect that Jaxon has on me. Why does this man cause heat to rise throughout my body? Yes, he's handsome, but he's not the only attractive man I have ever been around. I'm not some wilting virgin, like my parents like to believe. *That ship sailed long ago.*

The way he glares at me, like he wants to take a huge bite of my flesh, and the way his gaze lingers on my skin, mixed with the tone of his voice, has me fighting my own mind. My mind and heart war with each other in his proximity, one wanting to decimate him, the other wanting to jump on him and ride him like a damn beast. The train of my thoughts, coupled with his presence, has goosebumps racing across my skin and my nipples hardening painfully against the lace of the negligee. The sensation of the raspy material against my hardened, sensitive tips forces me to have to bite on the inside of my cheek to swallow the moan that is attempting to escape.

"Our room, Stella. This is our room, one which we will share, together. That bed you are so seductively lying in with all that gorgeous skin on display is our bed. One I plan to partake in with you, wife."

A snort escapes me at his audacity. How dare he slither in here without my knowledge, watch me sleep like some devious pervert, and then announce that he will be sleeping with me. Jaxon Stratford has a lot to learn about women. Maybe the bimbos he sleeps with fall at his mercurial feet, but I won't be so easily persuaded.

"You find that thought amusing, Stella?" He shifts forward in the chair, his body leaning closer to mine, and causing his tantalizing scent to reach my nose. *Why does this man always smell so delicious?* I try not to inhale a deep breath of his citrusy, musky, and spicy scent. His eyes focus on my mouth, and I can't help biting my lower lip at the attention. "You are a beautiful tease, Stella." His words come out soft and with a deep growl that has me almost dropping my hold on the precarious sheets.

"Nothing about you being in my room like some sort of deviant watching me is funny." My body tenses, waiting for whatever he's about to do. I tighten my grip on the sheet until my knuckles are white. The way his long limbs are positioned like a cat about to pounce, I can tell that Jaxon Stratford is about to invade my personal space.

A sharp laugh escapes his full lips, and a blush rises on his high cheekbones, making the few light freckles that he has across them darken and become more pronounced. In the next moment, he grabs all of the bed linens between two tight-fisted hands and stands, pulling them off of me. The power behind his move forces me to relinquish my hold on the sheets or come tumbling down to the edge of the bed.

I wrap my arms quickly around myself after pulling down the nightgown that had ridden up while I slept, the one that barely covers my crotch. *Fuck my mother and her meddling ways right now.* I'm intimately aware that I have a ton of skin on display. As his eyes skate over my bare legs, my body does the unthinkable and shivers as if he were physically caressing me.

"I enjoyed watching you sleep. You look so peaceful, soft, and warm, so unlike the ice queen you are when you're awake." He moves one knee onto the end of the bed, and my breath stutters in my throat. "I especially enjoyed looking at your creamy round breasts and those sexy pink nipples against all that lace. Did you buy that nightgown for me, Stella?" Another knee approaches the mattress, and I get ready to bolt off the bed.

"What do... you want?" My voice sounds breathless and whispery in the air between us, and I immediately regret my display of weakness. My heart is pounding in my chest, and I know he can see it. His eyes travel down my face and lock onto my heaving chest before making their way back to my gaze. My skin feels like a trail of fire has been left in the aftermath of his study.

"I came with noble intentions to beg your forgiveness, Stella." A smirk crosses his features. Did I bruise your ice-cold heart with my actions or just your pride?" He shifts his body forward a little more, his pant-covered thigh now touching my bare toes. I send him a cold, scathing look, watching as his chest rises and falls, just waiting to try to trap me, like the weak captive that he believes me to be.

"It's funny that you think you are the only wronged party here, my little viper. After all, you left me standing at the altar like a goddamn fool, stole my fucking limo, and forced me to attend our wedding reception without my fucking bride and do damage control." He licks his lips, and the image makes me think of a hungry wolf about to devour its prey. Except he hasn't realized that I'm not his fucking prey, I'm just as much a hunter as he is.

"One would say I deserved a little something in the way of re-compensation, Stella. To help soothe my rage and prevent me from coming back here and strangling you." A look of doubt crosses his features, his shoulders slump forward, and his posture relaxes. I push at his thigh with my toes, trying to force more distance between us. I clench and unclench my clammy hands, the need to rake my long nails down his face and gouge his eyes calling to me. Whispering that I should hurt him, before he hurts me.

"Maybe I shouldn't have brought my prize home on our wedding night. It wasn't my classiest moment, but I didn't think it would have affected you as it did. You are an ice queen, after all. Is that frigid heart capable of feeling real emotions? Why are you so angry, Stella? Is it the thought of me with another woman that has you so upset?"

A snort leaves my lips, he thinks I am weak and purely ruled by emotions. That jealousy is the catalyst for my actions last night rather than the disrespect he paid me by bringing that whore here. My will is forged in steel, I am resilient as he will learn to his own detriment. I try to calm my racing heart, to project the image of aloofness. I will never let Jaxon see how much that hurt me last night. "I thought you came here for forgiveness, Jaxon? It doesn't seem like that is your true intention. I don't hear any remorse in your words."

"You want me to beg for your forgiveness, Stella? Will you beg for mine?"

Beg him for his? Is he deranged? I have nothing to beg forgiveness for. "Forgiveness, Jaxon, you think you deserve some after trapping me in this marriage against my will. Forcing me to be your unwilling wife and trying to parade me around as the prize you think you won? Then bringing your bimbo girlfriend to the home we are to share and rubbing your insolence and disrespect in my face."

I watch as his eyebrows furrow, and his jaw clenches at my words. Remorse briefly flashes across his face as his teeth trap his bottom lip, biting into it. Dark pools of ash meet mine, and I can see the lust in their depths.

"There's remorse there, baby, and my intention is to make peace between us."

"How do you expect peace between us, when you started this with deceit and betrayal, Jaxon?"

He sighs and drags his fist through his thick, dark hair, disrupting the strands and making them look disheveled. I can see the bulge clearly defined in his pants, he's not even trying to hide that he's aroused. "You're right, Stella, I'm a cunt. Last night was wicked and reckless of me. As for forcing you down the aisle, at this moment, looking at your sexy, creamy breasts, I don't regret shit about that." His thigh pushes against my toes once again, and I feel the thick, hard muscle clench. "What can I do at this moment in time to allow us to move forward? There is no going back."

"Beg my forgiveness, Jaxon." My mouth is dry, my nipples hardening against the lace, and my core clenches at his words. They shouldn't cause that reaction in me, but the look in his eyes that promises nothing but a raging inferno of lust has my blood ringing in my ears. I'm playing a dangerous game here, egging him on to get a rise out of him. My mind is muddled on why I even want a rise out of him, *we should be pushing him to leave the room, not tempting him to lose control.*

A chuckle leaves his lips, followed by a growl that has him baring his teeth at me like a feral animal about to attack. "Before I beg on my knees, Stella, to soothe your viper heart, I think I will have a taste of my wife."

He lunges at me before I can even move to the other side of the bed, his large muscular body landing across my chest and lower half, trapping me underneath him with his weight. I try to buck him off of me with my hips and push at him with my legs, but he bears down hard on me with his hips and crotch. I can now definitely feel that he's enjoying this whole interaction. His hard dick presses up against my panty-clad pussy and nudges my needy clit with every movement. His hands reach out and grab onto my wrists, pushing them flush against the mattress as I try to force him off of me.

Jaxon leans forward and brushes his warm lips along my jaw, stopping my thrashing movements and causing a whoosh of air to leave my lips and prickles of heat to rise on my skin. His teeth leave little nibbles as he makes his way to the space where my ear and neck meet, his tongue slowly licking down the side of my neck before he blows warm air on it. *FUUCCKK!*

Goosebumps break out across my body, causing my arm hair to stand on end. "Just a little taste, Stella." He whispers in my ear before sucking hard on my neck and causing my core to tighten and my pussy to clench on nothing but air. The traitorous bitch is weeping for him as his lips continue to cause havoc with my senses. I should fight to remove him, but heat is invading all of my limbs, and the press of his body feels delicious against me. *Just a moment, I'll enjoy it just for a moment, then I'll throat punch him.*

He moves his way down my neck to my collarbone, leaving nibbles and kisses along the way and no doubt leaving marks as claimed territory. The knowledge that he is marking me should infuriate me, but instead, it has my core heating and my pussy clenching with desire and the need to be filled. Once his lips reach my heaving chest, he laves the swell of my breast with his warm tongue, a deep moan escaping his sinful lips. His gaze returns to mine as his tongue strokes the hardened tip of my nipple through the confining lace. A whimper escapes me, causing me to arch up into his body, and I stop fighting against his hold. The sensation of his warm, wet tongue and the rough lace are aphrodisiacs to my senses.

His warm lips seal over the lace-encased tip, and he sucks deeply; a moan rumbles up his throat, and my body arches further into the embrace. He pushes his fabric-covered hard cock against my swollen pussy. The thick crown nudges my clit over and over and causing moisture to seep from inside of me and soaking the thin fabric of my panties, and leaving a mark on the front of his pants coated in my wetness. *Fuck, yes,* my mind crows. His tight hold on my wrists releases as one of his hands moves to stroke and squeeze my other breast, kneading it roughly and causing the most delicious lust-induced pain. His other hand reaches the base of my neck, his fingers spanning the delicate space and teasing the skin.

For a moment, my breath is trapped in my throat. My body and mind warring with the hope that he tightens his grip and stops my breathing. The possibility turning me on and causing me to rub harder against the erection pressing against my opening but being denied by the confines of his pants and my silk panties. "You taste like heaven, Stella."

A mumbled breath fills the air as he groans deep in his throat into my breast, and I shut my eyes, allowing myself to fall into the sensation of his mouth on me. I should be pushing him away. I should be kicking and screaming at him, not allowing all my bones to turn to pliant mush under his touch. *So good, he smells and feels so good.*

His hand grips and pulls on the nightgown, and I feel the thin spaghetti straps give way across my breasts; then his lips are sealing over my hard nipple without a barrier. My hands slip into the dark hair at the back of his neck, and I pull on the strands, causing a low moan to leave his lips. *Fuck, that sound has my toes curling.*

"More." The word leaves my lips without my permission as my body arches again into his, seeking friction on my clit and his mouth on my other breast. His sultry wet mouth releases my nipple with a pop and moves over my skin, licking and sucking a path across to my other breast as his hand trails down my ribs and to my hip. He slides his warm fingers into the band of my panties just as his teeth nip my nipple. A sharp cry leaves my lips, and I grind hard into his thick cock. "Fuck Stella, you keep doing that, and I'm going to fuck your needy cunt."

His fingers tighten around my neck at the same time as he pulls his bottom half away slightly from my body and makes room for his fingers to trail over my soaked pussy lips, moving the drenched silk of my panties to the side to give him full access to my swollen lips. "God damn, Stella, bare. Look at those pretty plump lips."

A deep guttural moan leaves his throat, and it has my blood singing for him. His deft fingers strum over my clit, playing me like a delicate guitar. The sensation causes a fire to burn across my body and an electric current to sizzle down my spine. My breathing is coming in huge, harsh pants, my head moves restlessly against the wood headboard and pillows behind me. One of his thick, long digits makes its way to my slick opening, and his mouth pulls back from my breast as he sinks it inside of me in one pleasurable go. A cry leaves my lips at the sudden invasion. "Jaxon." His name leaves my lips in a gasp, and my fingers pull hard on his strands. A pleased and animalistic noise vibrates from his chest as his head pulls back into my tight grip.

"You're soaked, Stella; your cunt is craving my touch, *little wife*. Your soft, bare pussy wants to be filled up by my fingers and my cock. My thick cock is going to stretch this tight hole, baby. I'm going to make you scream."

His dirty words have me biting down hard on my lip as his finger strokes inside of me, thrusting slowly in and out as my traitor of a pussy clenches around it. I need and want more; my body is not satisfied with the thickness he's providing. He senses my need, and a second finger slides inside of me as a groan leaves his and my lips simultaneously. The digits slide across the front wall of my heat, reaching a spot that has my toes curling and my legs opening wider for his touch as surge after amazing surge of pleasure races through me. "So fucking tight, Stella... I'm going to enjoy destroying this pussy with my cock."

The sounds of wetness fill the air around us, I'm so drenched that it's embarrassing. His fingers move with harsh thrusts that cause my impending orgasm to race through my body and barrel down my heated channel like a runaway freight train. My grip on his hair releases, and my fingernails scratch down his neck and shoulders, causing a pained moan to echo in the room. He tightens his grip around my neck until not a whisper of oxygen is making its way past his thick fingers, and light-headedness starts to make my vision swim. At the same time, his thumb creates slow circles on my throbbing clit, and my body detonates with a sharp cry. A gush of warm liquid coats his fingers, still deep inside of my pussy, as a deep growl leaves him. He releases his tight hold on my throat, and oxygen soars back into my lungs with a jarring breath.

"Look at what a *good girl* you are, cumming all over my hand. My pretty *little slut*."

His dirty words have a wave of heat flowing through me. No one has ever spoken to me that way, disrespected or degraded me. I want to be angry, horrified even, but the truth is they turn me on, and I want more of them.

Jaxon continues to stroke me through the shattering waves of my orgasm and the aftershocks that are singeing all of my hypersensitive nerve endings. I open my eyes to half-mast and watch as his hooded eyes are riveted to where his fingers are still providing shallow thrusts, and my body is still clenching around them. He licks his lips like a man desperate to eat his favorite meal, and it makes my pussy clench down tightly on his digits.

A low moan leaves my lips, and his hungry, predatory gaze rises and meets mine. His eyes are bright with lust and need. There's a pink-tinged color across his cheeks, his lips are swollen, and he's biting down on his lush, full bottom lip. I've never craved sucking on anything before, but right now, I want to suck on that lip. No man has ever looked sexier than he does at this moment, with passion and vulnerability riding him. Now that my orgasm is subsiding, I immediately feel self-conscious and acutely aware that his fingers are still deep inside of my pussy, and there is a wet spot underneath me.

"Jaxon," His name leaves my lips in a moaned whisper that has me sealing them tight in both embarrassment and desire.

"Oh no, Stella. Don't hide from me now." His thumb strums once more over my clit as his fingers slide from inside of me, and I watch as he raises them to his lips, his tongue sliding out to lick at the digits coated in my release. A deep moan leaves his mouth as he slides both digits in between his lips and sucks them clean. The image in front of me is both obscene and molten-lava hot. I watch as he sucks every drop of me off, his eyes never leaving mine. "You taste like the richest nectar I have ever tasted, Stella, and I mean to satisfy my hunger for you daily."

Mortification and awareness finally have me spurring out of my orgasmed bliss and shoving him off of me. *What the hell is the matter with me?* I just let Jaxon Stratford finger fuck me the day after he forced me to marry him and brought his girlfriend home on our wedding night. My hand rises of its own volition and slams across his jaw. The sound of skin smacking skin is loud in the space. For a moment, we both stare at each other in shock at my actions. I roll away from him and off the bed, getting to my feet and putting space between us. *Fuck, fuck, fuck.*

"How fucking dare, you!" I shout with indignation, my legs trembling and threatening to give out on me.

"How dare I, what? Give you a leg-trembling orgasm that had you cumming all over our bed?"

"Get out, JAXON!" I'm quickly losing all control, my blood rushing in my veins and pounding in my ears. I move to round the bed, but he quickly stands in my way. I can't keep my eyes from staring at the large erection that is now tenting his gray dress pants. The size alone causing my mouth to go dry. *Jesus, does he have an anaconda in those pants?*

"Stella, fucking stop trying to beat on me! Stop running from me and what we just had, baby. Let me make you feel so good. I promise, baby, I'll have you seeing stars in just a moment." He tries to step towards me, but I tighten up both of my hands, prepared to punch him if he attempts to touch me again.

"Get the fuck out, Jaxon! You came here to play games, not to show the remorse you lack."

He holds up his hands with a gesture of platitude and submission and takes a step back, giving me more room. I watch him wearily, not trusting that he won't reach for me again. He drags one of his hands through his dark hair, his shoulders slumping and his body deflating before me. "I really did come here to apologize, Stella. I'm not, however, going to apologize for giving you that orgasm. Consider it a wedding gift." He smirks.

A wedding gift? For a fucking wedding I didn't want? Some gift, that is. I roll my eyes at him and move across the room while trying to convince myself that I am not, in fact, running from him. That I am stronger than that, and lust cannot weaken me. He doesn't move from his spot, and for that, I am grateful. I can't trust my body right now; it has betrayed me by enjoying that interaction a little too much.

"We need to talk, Stella. To figure out how we move forward... together." His expression is still heated, but I see determination there, too. Fuck, I need him gone, my body is still trembling with the remainder of my post-coital. I need to be able to breathe air that is not saturated in his scent and not see the heated lust on his face.

"Please leave, Jaxon, so that I can get dressed in peace. Then, if you would like to speak to me, I will attempt to listen." I wait to see if he will comply with my request. I can feel heat traveling over my skin as his gaze lingers on my body, and the ardor never leaves his eyes.

"I'll meet you in the breakfast room, Stella. Ten minutes, or I am coming back up here to grab you." He walks past me towards the door, stopping with his back to me. "You are a beautiful woman, wife." Then he opens the door, walks out, and closes it behind him, leaving me with a pounding heart and the after-effects of one of the best orgasms I have ever had.

12

Jaxon

"A society that does not respect women's anger is one that does not respect women; not as human beings, thinkers, knowers, active participants, or citizens." Soraya Chemaly, Rage Becomes Her: The Power of Women's Anger

I CAN STILL TASTE Stella's cum on my tongue, and I relish the flavor as I make my way down the hall towards the guest wing. I need to bottle that shit up, it's about to become my drink of choice. Who knew my little ice queen of a wife was passionate and hot-blooded underneath that frigid exterior? My tented pants definitely tell a different story. *Fuck, I cannot go downstairs and risk running into any of the household staff like this*. I'm already on most of their shit lists with the crap I pulled yesterday.

I make my way into the first guest room in the hallway, lock the door, and move quickly into the bathroom while already unzipping and pulling out my stiff cock. I'm so painfully hard from rubbing against Stella's perfect bare, pink cunt that tears of precum are leaking down my shaft, and my balls feel full and achy. The memory of how tight and swollen her pussy was as I slipped my fingers inside of her and the little moans that escaped her lips has me stroking myself hard and fast.

The image of Stella with her back arched, her lithe body moving in time with my thrusts, and her little gasps when I tightened my hold around her slender throat as she gushed all over me has my heart galloping in my chest and my legs feeling weak. She was so deliciously wet, and when she came, I knew I had struck fucking gold. That tight little pussy is going to need to stretch to take all of me, and she *will* take all of me. The only thing that could have made it better would have been if I had shoved my hard cock into all her tight holes. *Fuck, that pretty pink pussy and the tight puckered hole were a temptation I almost couldn't resist.*

I brace myself against the vanity and increase the tempo of my fist, while pulling on my balls with my other hand. *FUCK ME!* The orgasm races down my body like a tsunami, and cum spurts out of the end of my cock, all over my hand and down on the floor in thick creamy streaks. My breathing is coming in harsh pants, and my vision is a kaleidoscope of colors. I just came like a fifteen-year-old boy to a daydream of his crush, and I'm already semi-hard again at just the thought of getting to touch her once more.

Images of all the depraved things I want to do to her flash through my mind, and I have to brace myself against the counter. How fucking sexy would she look with her arms tied above her head, forcing her body to stretch while I pump my cock into her ass or down on all fours with a belt wrapped around her neck, while I fuck her hard and deep from behind? She would look amazing covered in my bites and marks, the impression of my fingers across all that creamy skin. *Fuck, yes!*

Fuck, I'm painfully hard again. Once again, I tighten my hold on my cock, stroking it quick and hard until I cum all over the counter and sink. My breath is coming in ragged pants out of my chest, and sweat is beading along my hairline. I have never cummed so hard from just an image in my mind.

I turn to the vanity and wash my hands, trying to settle my breathing and the erection that, even now, just doesn't seem to want to quit. As I stare at myself in the mirror, a pang of regret fills me when the thought of yesterday's actions crosses my mind.

If I hadn't brought Kalista here and behaved like a callous cunt, would I have been enjoying my wife's bed last night? Would I have found the same scorching passion between her creamy thighs? How could I have been so wrong about her? There is nothing frigid about Stella; if anything, she is like the sun, hot, destructive, and devastating.

Fuck, I am such a miserable mess. How am I going to fix this with her? There is no way, now having had a preview of the type of heated, sexually responsive creature that Stella is, that I'm not going to desire that permanently. What am I willing to give her, to make peace? What penance can I pay that will appease her righteous anger?

As I leave the guest room after cleaning my own cum from the floor and vanity, I make my way to the breakfast room. I realize that my cunning little wife is testing me. I told her ten minutes, and I would come and get her. I know I was in the bathroom cumming like a schoolboy for more than ten minutes. A grin crosses my face at the realization that maybe, just maybe, she wants me to chase her and punish her. The thought, of course, does nothing to help the current predicament of my rapidly hardening dick. *Damn it.*

As I enter the breakfast room, the sun shines through the windows, and the table is immaculately set for two. The thought that this is now my married life, having breakfast daily with the spitfire that is my wife after having woken her up with an intense orgasm. I've gone to fucking heaven! Why did I wait to get married? I should have fucking rushed her to the altar the same day her father proposed the marriage.

"Good morning, sir." Fergus nods as he enters the room carrying a coffee pot, which has my naughty thoughts abating. I notice he won't look me in the eye; in fact, he is doing everything he can not to meet my gaze. *Damn it, another one that is obviously upset with me about last night.* The old man has been with my family my whole life and has never been ashamed of my actions before, and trust me, I have given him plenty to be ashamed of. He's watched me stumble my way into adulthood and never given me the look he's wearing now. Hell, if I wasn't regretting my actions last night, thinking that I don't owe anyone shit. I'm regretting them now in the light of day.

Just as I am about to open my mouth to apologize for my behavior to Fergus, Stella walks into the room, her dark brown hair cascading down her shoulders in thick waves. She's dressed in a fitted white pencil skirt, a navy and white off-the-shoulder puff sleeve blouse, and a thick belt accentuating her tiny waist. *Fuck, was she always this hot, and I just never noticed?* She consistently looked beautiful at every event she attended with her parents, her classical beauty always giving off a pristine and out of reach air. She was never this fucking arousing before. Is it the knowledge of what she hides behind that cold exterior that is causing this reaction inside of me?

As she moves tentatively into the room, she graces Fergus with a smile that lights up her face and reaches her stunning eyes. "Good morning, Fergus." The poor man blushes beet red and gives her a shy smile back as he pulls out her chair. "Good morning, ma'am."

The swinging door between the kitchen and the breakfast room opens, and Mrs. Pox enters carrying a platter of eggs and pancakes, followed by Molly, one of the maids, with hashbrowns, bacon, and fruit. *Jeez, they went all out this morning.* Each of them exchange good mornings with Stella and pointedly ignore me. I watch helplessly and with envy as all three of my staff fuss over her until she gives each of them a bright smile. No one bothers to serve me any breakfast. After a moment or two of waiting and having each of them look away, I understand that this is part of my punishment for yesterday. *Well fuck you too, I'll serve my fucking self.*

I should be outraged that my staff is deliberately giving me the cold shoulder and treating my new wife like she's the best thing since sliced bread. But honestly, I am relieved that they like her, that they are on her side, and that they have gravitated to protecting her—even if it's against me, *as it seems.*

They all vacate the room after ensuring that Stella has everything she needs. Mrs. Pox is the last one to leave, and she provides me with a warning look that, had I been a weaker man, I would have had my balls shriveling up and tucking my tail inside of my body. I am going to be seriously outnumbered in my own home if they continuously take her side in everything. *Maybe we could stop doing stupid, harmful shit?* My mind questions.

I stare at my new wife as she takes a dainty sip of coffee and avoids my direct gaze. As she pushes her hair back from her face, I notice the marks blooming on her neck from this morning. Each of my fingertips is clearly on display on her soft skin, and a sense of pleasure and achievement races through my blood. She didn't even make an attempt to hide them. That pleases me even more, to know that everyone that looks at her neck and collarbone today will see them. My brand of ownership, clearly evident on her skin. Then they will know that she belongs to me. SHE IS *MINE!* The beast that lives inside of me roars.

Clearing my throat, I realize that I'm a bit nervous. *What the ever-loving fuck is wrong with me? Man up, motherfucker!* I've taken a bat to a man's head and never been nervous before. Shit, I have decimated whole companies and not broken a sweat. One little wisp of a woman, just over five feet, has me over here doubting myself. Doubting actions, I'm not even a hundred percent convinced I regret. I'm sorry that I disrespected her, especially since the staff saw it too. I shouldn't have brought my ex here, there are classier ways of doing shit like this. I wanted to hurt her, but I went too far with shoving her face into the lust I feel for Kalista.

Especially since my cock is still semi-hard at just the thought of Stella's pink pussy. I bite down on the inside of my cheek, the realization of how much I want to drive my hard cock into the tight hole my fingers got to experience, making me force the groan in my throat down. *God, her pussy was so tight and plump. Fuck, I need more of that.*

I know I have to apologize to her in a way that she senses my sincerity and forgives me for my trespass against her last night, or I'm doomed to live in purgatory, knowing heaven is just out of reach. Now that I have seen and experienced her taste and the feel of her cunt, *I want more. I need more.*

"Stella..." Her beautiful arctic blue eyes lift and meet mine, and I watch as she schools her features, hiding her thoughts from me. "Stella... about yesterday... our wedding, and then what happened... afterward."

A perfectly sculpted dark eyebrow rises as my words tumble awkwardly from my lips. She's not going to give me an inch here, making me work for this apology. *Would you have so quickly forgiven her, if the tables had been turned?* The question slithers across my mind, bringing with it an unfounded rage at the mere thought of Stella bringing a man back to our home and kissing him. *God damn it, I am a fucking hypocrite.* Here goes fucking nothing. I'll be lucky if she doesn't knee me in the balls again. *Fuck, I should have asked Mrs. Pox to remove all the knives from the room.*

"Look, Stella, I am a giant fucking ass. What I did yesterday was uncalled for and unconscionable. I know I have no right to ask for your forgiveness, but I am here asking for it nonetheless." I don't know what to make of her expression. Is she pensive, conflicted, or enraged? She hides her thoughts so well from me. Her perfect mask on display before me. The picture of a beautiful ice queen, a part she plays so well.

"You're right, Jaxon; you do not have the right to ask for my forgiveness, and not only for your activities last night, but for all of it." She breaks our connected gaze and takes another sip of her coffee, her fingers clenched tightly around the cup. "Regardless, I will not grant it without *penance*."

"Penance?" I question with a raised brow of my own, the word feeling like acid as it leaves my lips. My hellion of a wife, it seems, is out for blood. "What type of penance, Stella?"

She places the cup down carefully and crosses her hands over her plate, her expression stern and her lips in a tight grimace. I have a feeling whatever my little ice queen is about to say is going to have me losing my shit and probably flipping this fucking table over. How can one small woman have such volatile emotions traveling through me without the slightest hesitation? Does she not fear for her safety, constantly provoking me? *Remember the knee to the groin and the smack you still feel the heat of on your face? Yeah, she doesn't fear you fuckhead.* My mind laughs sarcastically at me.

"The way I see it, Jaxon, you have two options, two ways that you can make it up to me." She leans forward towards me on the table. "And you will repay me, Jaxon, *one way or the other*."

My eyes are riveted to the smirk starting on her pouty red lips. Stella Stratford is sitting here prim and proper, dressed immaculately with not a stitch of makeup on her stunning face, but she's a shark underneath all that beautiful exterior. All of it is a facade, one she uses to disarm others into thinking she's emotionless, an ice queen without a heart. My wife is out for red, hot blood, and I am the idiot who put myself in her shark-infested waters to begin with.

"Firstly, you can pay in blood and sacrifice, Jaxon, or you can pay in sacrifice and wealth. The choice is yours, but choose wisely, there will be no refund on your pound of flesh."

I lean forward towards her, intrigued and tempted to wrap my hands once again around her slender neck and choke the fucking life out of her for sitting there and threatening me. Her exterior is calm and unfazed but I'm watching the pulse in her neck jump. She's aware that she's pushing my buttons and the restraints on my limited patience. She should fear me; my control is precarious at best, and violence is always my go-to answer when pushed to the depth Stella is closely reaching. "Explain, Stella. What are the terms for your pound of flesh?"

"Let's begin with blood and sacrifice, shall we?" She doesn't wait for my response before licking those delectable lips and proceeding without caution. How fucking amazing would they look wrapped tightly around my cock while I choked the life out of her? I shift my throbbing cock at the image my mind provides me with and try to focus on her words.

"The blood will be yours, husband, and any women that you come into contact with. I will actively destroy any female that you try to cuckold me with by any means necessary. You will remain faithful to me, regardless of whether I allow you in my bed or not. If you don't, you will suffer my wrath each and every time, and I will repay you in kind with your closest friends and business acquaintances." She watches as my hand tightens on the breakfast knife before me at her threat. "The sacrifice part will be easier to bear. You will relinquish all the shares of Penticton Industry and the seat on my father's board to me, that you just received as a dowry for marrying the Penticton heir."

Rage fills my blood and heats it with her threats. How dare she try to strong-arm me into giving away my prize. Those shares and the seat on the board, were spoils won for marrying her. Her little threat about fucking my friends in retribution is another matter altogether. I will murder any man that touches her and make sure their bodies are never found. *She is mine.* "And the other option, wife?" The word *'wife'* leaves my lips with venom. I drop my hold on the knife, and it clatters on the fine china before me, loud in the tense and silent room. Her eyes never leave mine, she doesn't even acknowledge my little threat to stab her. *The balls of fucking steel on this woman amaze me.*

"The other option is no less daunting, husband, but perhaps my favorite pound of flesh. The sacrifice, perhaps at this very moment, is not as harsh to bear but will have lasting consequences for your empire. The one you are so desperate to build and expand, that you would trap me into marriage against my will. You will forfeit the right of an heir. I will give birth to none of your children, Jaxon. *None.* Your name will die with you and me. I will guarantee that I have my ovaries medically removed to ensure you can't get me pregnant *ever.* I will never willingly lay with you, but you can keep your little whores. The wealth part is perhaps harsher to stomach. All of the assets and fortune that I entered into this falsehood of a marriage with will be signed over to me alone, or I will divorce you. You will not benefit from this marriage financially, Jaxon."

I'm out of my seat in a flash, the chair tumbling behind me with a large thud. My hand wrapping around the column of her swan-like neck and squeezing the delicate organ as she stares at me with no fear in her conniving, spiteful eyes. "You think to play with me, Stella, to threaten me? You belong to me now; you are a possession." I tighten my grip until her color starts to rise on her creamy skin, and her nails dig into my flesh. She doesn't fight me, though; she doesn't try to force me to release her. *My brave little viper of a wife.*

I release her and stand back, watching as she takes a gasp of air, her eyes never leaving me. "You hurt me first, Jaxon. You put all of this in motion, forcing me to marry you and then daring to humiliate me. What did you think would happen? That I would be some weak, little wife, bending over for you and looking the other way while you had your cake and ate it too?" She stands from the chair abruptly and it falls backwards as she stands unafraid before me. She is the image of pure power and strength. It's startling in the sunshine streaming through the window, how much I misjudged her and this situation. Here, I thought a few words of platitude, some declarations of faithfulness, and maybe some new jewelry would have her giving her forgiveness willingly. *How fucking wrong I am.*

This little ice queen of mine will never bow or bend to me. I will be fighting the daggers in my back every day of my goddamn miserable life. That's if she doesn't slit my fucking throat in my sleep. How could only an hour ago, she have been so warm and inviting with her perfect little body and now be coiled and ruthless? Which one is the real her? *Are they both, each one, a different side of the same coin?*

Her threats echo in my mind, each threat harsh and punishing in its own way. *How could this have happened?* Are you seriously questioning that fuckhead? My mind seethes. *Fucking hell!* I could just disregard her threats, believe them idle, and wait to see if she will make good on them. If she will destroy my whole world. I close my eyes tightly, trying to get my harsh breathing under control and to stop the desire to murder my wife not twenty-four hours after we have just been married.

Stella isn't threatening me lightly, every cold and punishing word out of her mouth was well thought out. She didn't just randomly come to these consequences.

The little viper probably stewed on them all night, coming up with the harshest way of repaying me for my offenses. She won't sit back and not retaliate; I can feel it in my bones. *Fuck!* Can I have her locked up somewhere so she can't cause harm to herself or my empire? *Are we going to chain our new wife to a cell?* My mind questions with rancor. Stella wouldn't even hesitate to hurt herself, knowing it would hurt me in turn. Her threat of having her ovaries removed carries terrifying implications. Would a woman really do that to herself just for vengeance? *Stella would, she won't back down.* She means to take away the one thing of true value to me, my empire and legacy. Without an heir, the Stratford line will end with me. I will be the downfall of the Stratford's legacy, just like my father predicted and feared. *Fuck, what do I do?* She really has left me no choice here, backing me into a corner, like the cunning cold snake that she is. Instead of being my beginning, she will be my end, and she will do it with that malicious cold smile on her face.

Molten anger rolls through me, and the desire to throw the table into the wall fills me once again. With a sweeping arm gesture, I send all the china flying off the table and crashing onto the floor. I bare my teeth at her like a fucking wolf that would love nothing more than to rip her apart. She's standing there unafraid and sewing seeds of resentment between us, as if her very life and our future doesn't hang in the balance.

I don't believe for one miserable second that her threats can be taken idly. I will have to swallow my pride and choose the lesser of the evils she has proposed, if I want to keep her and have some semblance of a future and a marriage. One that I very much doubt right now can ever truly formulate when both parties have nothing but disdain for each other. Fuck this vindictive cunt for making my life harder than what it needs to be.

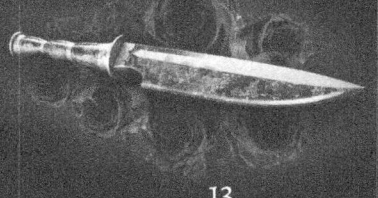

13

Stella

"Revenge is an act of passion; vengeance of justice. Injuries are revenged; crimes are avenged." Samuel Johnson

I WATCH, CAPTIVATED, AS various emotions trail across his handsome features. The most prominent being rage. I can still feel the ghost of his hands squeezing tightly around my neck. I swallow and the tightness in my throat tells me I will have the imprint of his hand as a bruised necklace within hours. He could have done further damage to me at my threats, but instead, he relinquished his hold as if my skin seared him. *Does he hate me now? Does he regret his moment of passion in the bedroom?*

His flash of rage decimated our breakfast but the look he just gave me indicates he's holding himself back from doing me further physical harm. He looks like a predator, his lip curled back in a snarl, his jaw clenched and teeth bared. His neck is corded and his body tense, on the verge of springing towards me. Does he want to hurt me? Perhaps slam me into the table or the wall and take me by force, to show me that he is in charge here? That he is a man and I am just a weak and fragile woman. My eyes glance down at the sharp knife near my foot. If he tries to force me into anything I will stab him in the fucking eye. He has no idea of the fury that lives within me, the abuse I have already suffered at the hands of a man who thought he owned me. One that was supposed to protect and cherish me, yet sold me to another monster.

I wonder what is going through his mind at rapid speed. Does he think my threats are idle? *They won't be.* I have every intention of hurting him the way he has hurt me. I spent a large part of the night going over my options and the weapons at my disposal. Part of me hopes he doesn't choose at all, so that I can make good on all my threats, taking the choice away from him. *Jaxon Stratford needs a reckoning and I mean to be the weapon.*

I'm enthralled as I watch him begin to pace back and forth in front of me, periodically raising those stunning eyes and stabbing me with the malice I don't doubt he's feeling towards me. The memory of his touch this morning on my skin brings heat to my flesh. Have I just forsaken that forever with my threats? Will he always look at me from this moment onwards with hate? Will I be able to live in the falsity of a marriage without ever feeling the warmth and pleasure of his touch?

A part of me wants a repeat immediately, knowing that sex with Jaxon will be mind-blowing. The other part of me is screeching that I keep my wits about me, not letting this man corrupt my intentions for my future. Too many men have now laid claim to owning and controlling me. I will stop at nothing to be the master of my own fate. Jaxon Stratford is an obstacle I mean to steamroll right over if he gets in my way. *Fuck him and thinking he owns me, no one owns me.*

He stops before me, raising a finger to my face and trailing it softly down to my cheek and over my lips. The sensation causes the hairs to rise on my body as my eyes meet his intense ones. "You are a viper, Stella, cunning and cold. You mean to try to control me, but you're mistaken if you think I will allow it." His finger continues down my chin to my jaw and down my neck where his fingers lightly trail and caress across my warm flesh. A morsel of fear rises within me, but I push it down.

"You will have your pound of flesh. I will transfer the shares and the board seat to you. I will, however, require an amendment to your vicious and calculating demands. One that you will not negotiate if you're as smart as I believe you to be." His fingers press into my skin, causing my breath to stop in my throat. "You will sleep in the same bed with me every night starting tonight. I will fuck you raw in any way I want, use you for my pleasure, and lose myself between your creamy thighs. You will wake up every morning to my cock lodged in your fucking throat or you can take your chances at going to war with me, Stella."

His hand tightens, not stopping my airflow but in a subtle warning that he could if he so desired it. My throat aches from his mistreatment but I don't dare ask him to relinquish it. His other hand snakes behind my back, pulling me forward until my body meets the hardness of his, and his warm coffee-scented breath skates across my lips. "I will fuck you over and over, Stella. My cock bottoming out ruthlessly inside of you nightly. My cum filling you until you're drenched in my scent." His fingers tighten, this time ensuring that my breath struggles to leave my lips.

"You will wake to my hard cock every morning in that vicious mouth of yours or that sweet dripping pussy. I will fuck that tight puckered hole and stretch it with my thick cock until you can barely fucking sit down. I mean to get my money's worth out of you, Stella. You are about to be my constant cum whore." He leans forward letting his lips briefly rest against mine, allowing me the option to pull back from him.

My body is a riot of nerves and sensations. Heat is coursing through my skin everywhere that our bodies meet and my pulse is racing, which I am sure he can feel in my neck. His dirty words having the instant effect of soaking my panties and turning me on at his demands. I'm not afraid at all of Jaxon or his threats. If anything, my body is soaring at the thought of him using me for his pleasure and providing me orgasms in return. He means to make me a slave to passion, but I have no intentions of falling down that rabbit hole alone. I'll be taking his ass right along with me.

Is it really a penance to sleep nightly with him? To let him invade my body with the hard cock that I felt through his pants earlier? To allow him to use me for his own pleasure while providing me with mind-blowing orgasms? I could do much worse in a negotiation, and he knows it. He could have refuted any and all of my threats. Instead, he agreed to give me the shares and the board seat in my family's company. Although he hasn't expressly indicated that he will be faithful to me, his amendment makes me believe that as long as he is getting laid here at home, and finding pleasure between my legs, he will not wander. I might be foolish to believe that, but I trust that Jaxon understands the consequences if I find out he has defaulted on our agreement.

Regardless, I will have my pound of flesh from the whore that he brought home last night. My wrath will not be so easily assuaged with her. She will pay me in spades for the humiliation she caused me. I know that all of the household staff witnessed Jaxon's interaction with her on the driveway. I also plan to make an example and a warning of her to other women who would think to try to seduce my husband. Stella Stratford will be the queen of their nightmares, and I mean to haunt them all.

I press my lips against his, my tongue lightly tracing his bottom lip, before demanding entry into his mouth. I mean to make a point to my new husband. I will never back down, and I will never cower from him. He had better learn that lesson now.

He deepens the kiss with a groan, his tongue meeting mine in a fierce dance that has a moan leaving my lips as he pulls me closer. His soft lips consume mine, and his grip on my neck tightens before suddenly releasing. He breaks the sizzling kiss and takes a step back from me. His eyes alight with passion, and his breathing heavy. The color has once again risen in his cheeks making him look younger than his age. *He really is an extremely sexy man, and he's all mine now.*

I clear my throat, never breaking eye contact with him. "I agree to your amendment, Jaxon. Do not think to manipulate me with your dick. Better men than you have tried and failed. I will have your monogamy, or you will suffer the repercussions."

A devious smirk crosses his lips. "Oh, little ice queen, when I am done with you, you will have a permanent imprint of my cock inside of you. Every waking moment you will feel me and the memories I intend to leave you with. Any man that has been there before me will be a forgotten memory; of that, I promise you."

He leans forward, his warm breath skating across the skin of my neck and my exposed collarbone. "A warning, Stella, one that I suggest you heed. I am a possessive and jealous man, and you are *mine*. If I discover that another man has laid a hand on you, in any way." His tongue trails out and licks a line up my neck to the soft flesh of my ear lobe. "I will have all of his fingers sawed off from that hand." He bites down on my lobe, the sting making my core tighten deliciously in response, and a little whimper leaves my lips. "Do I make myself clear?"

When I nod in confirmation to his bloodthirsty warning, he places one more hot kiss just below my ear lobe, the spot causing my toes to curl up inside of my shoes. *Holy crap, that feels amazing.* He pulls back, his steely gray eyes hooded and meeting mine. He takes a step back, his chest rising and falling in rapid movements and his cock tenting the fabric of his pants. *Jesus, fuck.*

He slides past me towards the breakfast room door, and I turn to watch him go with a raised eyebrow. *Is he running from me already?* Perhaps he cannot stand to be in the same room with me any longer, knowing that he does not, in fact, hold the upper hand in this situation. He stops at the threshold of the room, his shoulders stiff and his head held high. "I never intended to hurt you, Stella. I didn't think it would have mattered to you. I am truly sorry for my actions yesterday."

He leaves the room and disappears from sight, leaving me feeling empty, horny, and confused. His apology was sincere, I can feel it in the caliber of his words and in his tone. Regardless, the fact is that he did hurt me and will continue to do so if I allow it. I need to draw the line in the sand now of our future relationship or I will have failed to free myself from the hands of yet another man that believes himself my superior and captor.

14

Stella

"Deep vengeance is the daughter of deep silence." Vittorio Alfieri

"**G**OOD AFTERNOON, MRS. STRATFORD; what a pleasure it is to have you with us." The man before me is almost salivating at having me in his presence. I wouldn't put it past him to get down on his pathetic knees and grovel at my expensive Louboutin-heeled feet. His round face, red and coupled with sweat dotting his cheeks shows me his unease. *Good, let him worry about displeasing me.* My father and Jaxon wanted a new reigning queen of the Manhattan elite. I mean to ensure that all here fear their new monarch.

"My table, Jepson." I indicate with a nod of my head for him to lead the way. I'm impatient to get this show on the road so I can move on to more important things. *More important than ensuring your husband doesn't cheat?* My mind laughs at me.

When I called earlier to inform the country club that Jaxon and I would be requiring a new permanent table as well as some much-needed assurances to ensure our continued patronage, they were immediately accommodating. Of course, they would be; I am now one of the richest women in the United States, some would say top ten in all of the world, with my union to Jaxon. Power and money call to places like this, wanting to attract and keep membership exclusive and for the uber-rich. Maggots and corruption are what surround my privileged world. *Perhaps it needs a cleansing by fire?*

I watch as other patrons nod and smile at me as I pass them on my way to my highly visible and coveted table by the window. My head held high, and shoulders back with an air of aloofness surrounding me. *Sheep, the lot of them, paying me civilities now that I have married their most eligible bachelor and one of the most powerful men on the East Coast.*

None of them were outright rude to me before yesterday. My father and mother have always been part of the top of the food chain, but none of them ever made any effort to befriend me, either. They nicknamed me Ice Queen and then left me to my fortress of ice. I foresee a change in that as I take my seat and allow my eyes to trail over those in attendance here for lunch. A redhead gets up and starts to approach my table, but at the harsh, cold look I direct her way, she turns around and sits back down. My resting bitch face is on point and very useful for situations like these. Although I need to be here to put my plans into place, I don't relish the idea of being around fake people. I am not naive enough to believe any of them will ever truly be my friends. There is no such thing in this world of privilege, where you keep your enemies close.

The country club is a giant fish bowl surrounded by glass windows and views of Central Park with its lush green grass and blooming trees. Springtime in Manhattan is one of my favorite times of the year. The rich Japanese cherry blossoms are in bloom outside of the confines of this room. How I wish I was out there inhaling their rich scent instead of in this awful space. The country club's decor is artfully modern, with too much glass, chrome, and bright flashy red booths. I detest coming here and always have. Even when my mother and father demanded it of me so that they could be seen by the elite. Now I have come here willingly to sit and be admired by these assholes that take pleasure in the misery of others.

It grates on my nerves to be forced by Jaxon's actions to be as malignant as everyone else in the room or the reality that I will actually have to be much worse than them in order to be feared. My only solace is that I will enjoy tearing this miserable world apart piece by piece. No doubt, my social butterfly of a mother will be hearing of my attendance before I even leave the building. *Will she be proud, I wonder, or will she burst into pitiful tears for having raised such a willful and cold-hearted daughter?*

A pretty waitress fills my glass with water and then takes my order, scurrying off to ensure that I do not wait long for my food. *It wouldn't do to displease the new queen, now would it?* An un-lady-like snort leaves my lips at the very thought, and I watch as the woman seated closest to me, her eyes growing large at the sound. I let my gaze roam over the tables closest to me, meeting the glance of various women who no doubt would change places with me in a second as Jaxon's wife. I purposely left my neck and collarbone exposed with the marks Jaxon left on my skin. Let them note that my husband has laid claim to me. *They need to be forewarned that he is mine, and I do not fucking share.*

After a few minutes of meeting various pairs of eyes with a look of utter distaste on my part, my annoyance at having to even be here starts to rise. Men don't have to play these games with each other. They provide warning with their fists and words. Women, however, require more subterfuge to obtain their goals. Just as I am rethinking whether or not I am, in fact, interested in having lunch here, I hear a loud commotion at the entryway of the restaurant. A devious smirk crosses my lips before I wipe it off my features and school my face so those around me cannot read my thoughts. *My ice queen mask.*

A blonde woman is pushing harshly and loudly against the manager's round body and one of the uniformed waiters, trying in vain to force her way into the restaurant and towards me. I sit back, crossing my hands in my lap and giving off a relaxed vibe, one that I don't realistically feel, but no one in this godforsaken room needs to know that.

"You cold, conniving bitch. How dare you!" She screams in a high-pitched voice and pushes past the waiter who tries to block her, moving towards where I am sitting at my new, highly coveted table.

I raise an eyebrow in her direction, my jaw locking tight and displeasure evident on my features, nodding to the manager to let her continue to move past and closer to me. She is creating a spectacle of herself, and all eyes in the country club are now on us. What is happening here will be on the front page of every gossip paper by morning and spread on the lips of every member of the elite within hours. I counted on it; after all, it's why I am sitting here, subjecting myself to this fishbowl. "How dare I what, Kalista?"

"How fucking dare you blacklist me from my entire life! Who do you think you are? You had me barred from all of the spas. The elite nail salons and the hair salons have all notified me that I am no longer a client. All my accounts have been closed at every fashion house in the city. I have been fielding calls all morning, Stella. You ensured that all my sponsors and client labels have now parted ways with me, you *vicious bitch*! You even had my assistant resign with no notice, terrified for her own life." Her beautiful face is filled with ugly rage, red blotches making their way across her skin, and if I am not mistaken, she's been crying. "You have destroyed my life and livelihood! Why have you done this!" The feeling of satisfaction fills my blood. If she thinks it's bad now, just wait, it's about to get much worse.

"Ma'am, I must insist that you leave immediately. As I explained at the door, you are no longer a member here and cannot enter the country club." The obtuse manager speaks through gritted teeth, looking at me from the corner of his eye as beads of sweat trickle down the side of his face.

"You frigid whore! He will never be yours! He bought you like a prized horse, and when he's done playing with you, he will return to me." Gasps fill the space around us, but I don't bother to take my eyes off the woman falling apart before me. Her comment about being a frigid whore bounces right off of me. I guarantee that my new husband would not agree with her assessment after this morning.

"Your words have no impact on me, Kalista. Go ahead and make more of a spectacle of yourself." I allow the tiniest of smiles to grace my lips. My gaze is cold and filled with malevolent energy. I don't bother to look around at those surrounding us, knowing from the hush my words are bringing that everyone is watching and listening to what is transpiring in front of me.

"I will give you no further warnings, Kalista. The world you built up around you." I motion with my finger, pointing dramatically at the tabletop and then snapping my fingers. "Is gone, poof! Up in smoke, it went this morning. All of your modeling and endorsement deals are gone. Even Walmart won't touch you now. Your life is done." A full, devious smile crosses my lips as I sit back comfortably in the booth. "Your parents, I'm sure, are also trying to reach you. They too will have found that their access to certain amenities will have been denied."

"Why? Why would you do this to me? He married you." Tears trickle down the side of her gorgeous face. The sight should move me, perhaps even make guilt rise inside of me. After all, she is a woman trapped in the same world as I am. But all I see is the vision of her kissing my husband in my new driveway on my wedding day, her hands trailing over his body and the smear of her lipstick across his lips.

"You are an unfortunate warning to those around us. You are learning firsthand the consequences of crossing me, Kalista. You thought that I would allow what happened between you and Jaxon to continue, unfettered?" I lean forward, my words leaving my lips in a harsher, lower tone. "You thought what happened last night would have no consequences, that I was weak? How weak am I now, Kalista?"

"He doesn't love you." She wipes at the tears trailing down her cheek with the palm of her hand, smearing more of her makeup across her face. She really does look a tad disheveled, no doubt from running from one place to another all morning trying to stop the destruction I caused with mere phone calls once Jaxon left the house.

"He doesn't need to, I am his wife. A fact that you seemed to have forgotten in your haste to bring my husband home last night from our wedding reception. I am Mrs. Jaxon Stratford, and with that comes responsibilities. Like the removal of trash from my husband's presence and acquaintance. " I let my eyes trail over the faces of those watching the destruction and chaos I am engineering before them. Let them feel my anger, hate, and determination to destroy each and every one of them if they cross me. I am fucking dark vengeance reincarnated into Stella Penticton Stratford.

I nod to the manager and he pulls on Kalista's arm, attempting to pull her from my presence as she tries to pull out of his tight grasp, spittle flying from her perfect lips. "I hate you, Stella. Jaxon will never leave me for you, he loves me. You think he will stand for the way you are treating me?" She continues to screech all the way to the door before being ushered out of the building.

I don't bother to hide my thoughts or feelings from those still watching me with stunned looks on their faces. I place my elbows on the table and steeple my hands in front of me. A thrill of energy makes its way through my system at the look of fear on their faces and the feeling of power that surrounds me. I don't raise my voice; there isn't a sound being made in the room right now, and I know they are completely enraptured with my every word.

"Those of you who thought you would continue having certain... relationships with my husband, fair warning: Miss Cain is an example of what will befall you should you raise my ire. If she attends any of your events or crosses your thresholds, consider yourself barred from mine and Jaxon's presence. I suggest you not present yourselves in my path; I am completely without mercy."

I dismiss them all with a nod, indicating to the nervous waitress holding a tray laden with my lunch to serve me. I have no appetite right now; in fact, my stomach is tight as a knot, but I need all of these cockroaches to believe that I am, the ice queen that they named me. They should begin to fear me, it will keep them away from my husband and ensure they don't meet with my wrath.

I raise a sip of the glass of white wine the waitress poured me to my lips in a toast to the first day of being Mrs. Stratford.

What is that term they use to salute a queen? *Long may she reign?* I fucking intend to.

15

Jaxon

"Don't mess with her, she isn't delicate like daffodil, she is delicate like dynamite." Amit Kalantri, Wealth of Words

I'M FURIOUS AS I drive home in my scratched-up gray Aston Martin Vantage Volante to the Stratford estate. My blood pressure is skyrocketing, and the desire to wrap my fingers around my wife's slender neck is so strong that my grip on the steering wheel has my knuckles white. *Fucking willful bitch!*

Someone took a sharp tool to the sides of my two hundred-thousand-dollar vehicle and carved the words *"cunt & man whore"* into the front doors. If that wasn't bad enough, the giant phallus painted on my hood is the cherry on fucking top. Of course, no one saw a damn thing in broad daylight, in a private company parking lot. As if I wasn't already on the verge of exploding, the images of the day play out before me and distract me from my drive. The one I am currently doing at a speed guaranteed to get me a meeting with my maker.

Kalista entering Stratford Industries and my office in a blind panic, with make-up smeared across her beautiful face and begging me on her knees to stop my wife's destruction of her life and livelihood. I couldn't make sense, at first, of what she was even rambling about. She was so hysterical that every other word was an anguished sob.

Then, the phone calls from acquaintances started to pour in rapidly. It wasn't lost on me that it was mostly women calling me to beg me to keep my wife from destroying their lives. Shit, even certain husbands that had enjoyed me cuckolding them in the past were calling, desperation and fear laced in their voices.

Apparently, my little ice queen of a wife, decided to flex her power muscles as the new reigning queen of the elite. Her first target, not really a surprise, *Kalista*

Cain. She decided to teach both Kalista and me a lesson it seems. One that everyone watching the utter destruction she has caused won't soon forget. The vindictive little cunt, even after I agreed to her pound of flesh. I should have realized that she would retaliate. I underestimated my wife, something I don't plan on doing again.

Stella is not taking chances with my faithlessness, and instead has stacked the deck in her favor. Ensuring that any woman I would have dabbled with is now utterly petrified of her wrath, and the majority of husbands who would have previously looked on indifferently to their wives' dalliances are now paying strict attention, not wanting my wife to come after their empires. I almost want to applaud her for her deviousness, that is, if it wasn't my life, she was playing with.

To add insult to injury, my assistant refused to come within a ten-foot radius of me all day, and her face paled every time I spoke to her. All the other women in my office scampered off and hid as if I were the devil coming for their souls anytime I stepped out of my office. Word has apparently reached everywhere of my wife's ruthlessness.

As angry as I am, I have to acknowledge that it was a well-played offensive move. My wife is cunning, cold, and calculating. She also doesn't seem quick to forgive, a warning that I am taking very seriously.

I had the shares and board seat transferred to her name this afternoon, per her new assistant's request, which she didn't even bother to acknowledge. I am sure she was too busy ruining others' lives. Thomas Penticton will have a coronary when he realizes how many shares his daughter now holds. My shares, combined with hers, almost give her the majority shareholder position with forty-nine percent. He should fear my wife; it seems he has underestimated her brilliant mind, and she will no doubt make him pay for using her as a bargaining chip. *She's out for blood, and all of us should be wary of her.*

I pull past the opening gates of my home and try to calm my enraged breathing down. I can't go in there with my temper ready to explode and try to deal with Stella. She will no doubt be expecting my wrath and will have a way to push my buttons further so that I don't proceed with plans to fuck her little cunt raw. The only thing keeping me sane at the moment is the knowledge that I will be punishing her with my cock later. Ensuring that she submits to me in every way. The thought has me rock hard in my pants as I pull into the vast six-car garage.

I immediately notice a little blue *Lamborghini Countach* parked in one of the slots in the garage. A vehicle that was definitely not there when I left this morning. It seems my wife is full of surprises; I know for a fact that she didn't own that car before our marriage. All of her assets were listed in the marriage documents. She's been shopping and it doesn't seem like she showed restraint.

I trail my fingers over the hood of the car, it's sleek and sexy like my new wife and made for thrill-seeking, smooth riding, and speed. I wonder if my Stella will give me half the same experience tonight between her creamy thighs. Her tight pussy this morning and the way she rode her passion to completion make me believe she will.

As I enter my home, no one greets me. *What the fuck is going on here? Where is Fergus or Mrs. Pox?* I move quickly from one room to the other on the main floor and find not a hair of my usually well behaved and attentive staff. As I make my way to the dining room, I notice that the table is set for dinner, but the room is empty. My agitation is rising further as I play hide and seek with the members of my household. *What. The. Fuck!*

"Stella!" I bellow, the vibrations of my shout echoing off the walls of my vast home. I take the stairs to the second floor two at a time, unable to stop myself from losing the precious control I just admonished myself to keep on the way into the estate. As I slam open the door to the master suite, I hear the low murmurs of jazz music playing. The room is shrouded in shadows except for some well-placed candles, giving it a muted and warm glow. My eyes trail across the expanse, and I locate my wife, sitting comfortably and utterly at ease in the upholstered chaise with a glass of red wine in her manicured hand.

She watches me stalk toward her, her face a careful and blank mask, so I can't determine her feelings or thoughts. She's changed from earlier and is sitting there in nothing but a flimsy red sheer nightgown, even though it's early evening. One that leaves very little to the imagination and sets against all that beautiful and velvety skin, making it appear luminous and warm. Her dark hair trails down her shoulders, and thick, wavy strands curl around her round breasts, just tempting me to run my fingers through them. *Shit, she is a fantasy come to life, a life-size doll for me to play with.*

I trail my eyes up from her red-painted toes, over her toned calves, up past parted and bent knees to her thick, toned thighs. Ones that I want wrapped around my head, and to the prize of her core, still partially covered by the flimsy material. My heated gaze continues over her tiny waist and to the round, full globes of her breasts with their erect, dark, pink nipples. My mouth waters instantly with the desire to suck them deep into my mouth and trail my teeth along their hardened tips.

I pull my eyes away with difficulty up her chest, along the long, graceful column of her neck that still bears my earlier marks, causing perverse pleasure to rise inside of me and my hands to itch with the need to wrap themselves around and squeeze the delicate skin once again. My gaze continues upwards to trail over her beautiful face. One that has my breath momentarily stalling in my chest. *She is gorgeous. No, that doesn't even seem like a strong enough word to describe the creature before me.*

A small smile graces her red-tinted lips, and her arctic blue eyes are unreadable and steady on me. She raises the wine glass to her full lips, taking a small sip, but her gaze never leaves mine. I can feel my pants tenting in front of me, my erection so painfully hard at the vision before me that I worry that my zipper is leaving an imprint. My wife is a goddess before me, who comes to destroy and tempt me with carnal thoughts and pleasures of the flesh. *Peitho has nothing on Stella.* Does she mean for me to worship at her feet? *I just fucking might.*

I almost give in to the desire to rush her, part those toned legs, and bury my cock into her sweet heat in one forceful go. Laying claim to her and ensuring she knows and feels my brand on her skin and in her core. That, however, is what she wants. She wants me to lose complete control, be enthralled by her, losing myself in her so that she can continue to manipulate and control me.

Stella seeks to make me a puppet king, while she makes the moves behind our empire. A lesser man would allow her, maybe even thank her as he reaped the benefit of the pleasure she no doubt can provide. Unfortunately for Stella, she married a Stratford, we are made a little differently. If my gorgeous wife wants power, she will have to earn it on her knees with my cock down her throat.

Stella Stratford does not play fair and uses any advantage that she has available. Right now, the most powerful tool she has in her arsenal against me is herself. *I want her, and she knows it.*

I have to try to reel in my desire for her. I refuse to be a puppet on her strings. I want her, but I am not alone in this sentiment. She wants me too, and I mean to make her beg for my brand of passion, to *make her needy for me just as much as I am for her.*

16

Jaxon

"The flame of anger, bright and brief, sharpens the barb of love."
Walter Savage Landor

I FORCE MYSELF TO move closer to her in measured steps, taking the seat opposite of her and watching as her chest rises and falls with deep breaths. Her blue eyes watch every move I make with rapt attention. Her gaze causing my skin to heat and longing to fill me. *Jesus, she's so beautiful.*

Stella may appear calm on the surface, but it's nothing but a mirage. Her pulse beating rapidly in her neck confirms my thoughts. The pretty bruises left from my fingers along the surface call to the animal inside me, daring me to add more to her flesh. I watch as she moistens her lips with her pink tongue. The desire to take it into my own mouth filling me. The remembrance of her taste from this morning makes my cock throb in the confine of my pants.

Stella plays a great pretense, but I'm almost positive my little wife has limited experience with seduction. In fact, I am not even sure if she's not a virgin, despite her passionate behavior this morning. The thought of being the first to breach her channel and lay claim to her warm and wet cunt, makes precum leak from the tip of my cock and coat the inside of my tight boxers. Fuck, I hope that tight pussy bleeds all over my cock when I slam myself home. The desire to see her red blood streaked across my dick is all-encompassing.

"Where are the staff, Stella?" I question with a raised eyebrow as I watch her part her legs slightly giving me a more enhanced view of her bare cunt. *Fuck, look at those pretty pink lips, just ripe for me to run my tongue and fingers through.* I shift my cock in my pants and almost groan at the painful sensation of how hard he is. *Down boy, you will get your turn shortly!*

"I gave all of them the night off." Stella's voice breaks through the unadulterated mesmerizing effect her pretty, pink pussy is having on me, and I force myself to meet her gaze. A slight pink blush streaks up her neck and across her high cheekbones. She's not as unaffected as she's trying to play. Stella is turned on, and it's a beautiful thing to witness. I bet if I ran my finger through her plump pussy lips right now, it would come away drenched.

"I see, and who will be serving us dinner?"

A small, crooked smile graces her lips, and her eyes alight with mischief, causing my chest to tighten at the way it transforms her face from being beautiful to earth-shatteringly stunning. Again, the thought crosses my mind of how I never noticed that this woman, whom I agreed to marry for wealth and power, was so devastatingly gorgeous. "I'm sure we can find something to eat, Jaxon," her breathy response has my balls tightening painfully and my cock begging to be let loose.

Her sultry voice and words are a seductive force trying to lure me closer and to my knees. No doubt where my little wife would like to see me and keep me. As I stare at her, the thought of getting on my knees and giving up some of my power doesn't repulse me; in fact, it starts as a deep yearning. I would love nothing better than to suck and lick that sweet cunt right now. My pride, however, understands that this is a game that Stella is playing. A move on the chessboard of which she is now the most valuable piece.

A queen, one that will lay waste to rooks, knights, and kings to get what she wants. What is it that my little, devious viper truly wants? *Freedom? Power? The heads of the men that bargained and negotiated for her without her approval or assent?*

I knew this morning when I agreed to her terms that she would make me pay for my trespasses against her. I just didn't realize I would be paying so soon and that the tools she would use would cause me to want to be willingly on my knees. I bite down hard on my bottom lip, trying to use the momentary sharp pain to break this hold that she is having on me. *Jesus fucking Christ, she is a seductress, just tempting me to fuck her against that chaise.*

"You have been busy today, Stella. Care to tell me about your day, wife?" I spew the word *'wife'* out with as much spite as I can produce. I want her to hear the displeasure in my words and tone. She caused chaos and humiliation on day one of being my wife, starting by leaving me standing at the altar like some useless cunt.

Day two has seen utter fucking destruction at her hands and our world trembling with fear at her feet. As much as I am starting to admire her cunning behavior, I also need to be cognizant that she is trying to use those same skills against me. I won't have it. She is mine, and she needs to understand that I am her master and that I will demand her obedience and respect. *Like the respect you showed her last night?* My mind questions with snark.

"I went shopping and bought myself a little car." She grins deviously.

"I see, anything else other than the new hundred-and-fifty-thousand-dollar car parked in our garage?" I thread my fingers together to prevent myself from reaching for her. The desire to run my fingertips along her soft as-silk skin is a thudding craving in my bloodstream. How pretty will she look with fingerprints marked red across that perky ass of hers when I spank her for being deceitful and prideful?

I watch as she places the wine glass down on the small marble table to her side, her breasts moving underneath the sheer material and causing me to have to bite down on the inside of my cheeks. She smooths her hand down the front of her negligee, causing the material to press into her skin and the appearance of her perky nipples to become more pronounced. Temptation beacons to me, the wisp of lust calling my name and daring me to fight its thrall. I watch as she once again parts her knees, her red-painted toes digging into the material of the chaise and her elegant feet arching. *Fuck, even her feet are pretty.*

"I might have done a little housekeeping and removed some trash to get our house in order, Jaxon."

Her insolent words have my temper erupting and I'm out of my seat and straddling her in the chaise in a brief second. I bear down part of my weight on her thighs and grab onto her wrists, pinning them against the back of the chaise as her breathing stutters.

"You little viper. Do you know the destruction and chaos you caused today?" I tighten my grip until a pained flinch crosses her features. Her eyes meet mine without even the slightest hint of fear or remorse.

Her features, this close up are pure perfection, not a blemish or mark. Her stunning eyes heat at my restraining manner, and a pink tinge stains her high cheekbones. Her tongue skates out, wetting her lips before her front teeth bite down on her pouty bottom lip, urging me to take it from her and use my own teeth on it. *Is that fire that I see in her eyes? Is she enjoying my tight hold?* Maybe my little ice queen likes to be restrained? That definitely has possibilities. Once again, the image of tying her up and collaring her pops into my mind, and I have to swallow the moan that tries to escape me.

My teeth grind together as I tighten my punishing grip on her flesh. She will have the imprint of my fingers when I am done, a circle of bruises on her flesh to remind her that I am her master and she is my possession.

"Did you have to be so petty going after Kalista, Stella? I had already agreed to your pound of flesh." I bear all my weight down on her thighs and waist, trapping her beneath me. The sensation of her breasts pressed against my chest is not helping my raging hard-on, and I am sure she can feel my cock pressed firmly against her soft skin. It throbs painfully, wanting to rub against that velvety skin and stain her with my precum. Yet, I refuse to relent and give in to my baser needs.

She doesn't bother to respond to me, she just raises her eyebrow at me in a taunting manner and shrugs off a response. "I am sorry that I hurt you, Stella. I already apologized this morning. Was it really necessary to destroy her and provide the spectacle that you did to all of those around us?"

She leans forward as much as my weight will allow her. Her lips barely a hair's breadth away from mine, and the sweet scent of rich wine and her own vanilla and floral scent making its way to my nose. "Oh Jaxon, did your little whore go crying to you on her hands and knees, like the trash she is?" She pulls on her wrists, trying to release them from my hold. "Did you really think that your brief words would be enough to satisfy the harm you caused me? That somehow I would forget your humiliation just because you apologized? Maybe you truly believed that she would walk away unscathed, Jaxon?"

Her warm lips meet mine in a crushing embrace that has me immediately parting my lips so that I can get a taste of her. All my good intentions to resist her go out the window at the brush of her tongue against mine. *Fuck, her personal taste, along with the rich wine, is a heady combination and makes me crave more of her.* I release my hold on her wrists, allowing my hands to dive deeply into her dark, thick tresses and begin pulling on the silk strands of her hair. My other hand wraps around her soft, full breast, and my fingers pull on her hardened tip until a gasp leaves her lips. My chest rises and falls in an erratic rhythm as the noises escaping her cause my cock to throb in its confinement. *Fuck, I need her right now.*

I know I should be holding back and trying to show restraint against my crushing hunger for her, but right now, all I want to do is have a taste of her. Scorching heat surges through my chest and groin, and my heart slams against my ribs. I need her. I need to dominate her, to control her. To make her fucking mine. *Fuck it.* I will teach her a lesson with my cock, one I hope that she doesn't learn so that I can repeat it daily. I have a feeling once will never be enough with Stella.

I pull away from her lips, trailing my own down the side of her face and to her jaw, my tongue slipping out to lick at all her creamy flesh and then continuing its path down the column of her neck and to her chest. Where I leave open-mouth kisses, sucking the flesh tightly as she trembles below me. I move back further on her legs until I'm sitting on the chaise between her toned thighs. My fingers kneading her soft breast and eliciting whimpers from her mouth that I'm not even sure she knows she is releasing. She arches into my embrace, her breath hitching as I apply pressure to the soft globe and pull her nipple between two fingers. The sounds are music to my ears. She is so receptive to my touch. Who knew that below all that frigid exterior, hot, scalding lava resided?

"I mean to discipline you, Stella, for your reckless behavior today," I mumble into the soft swell of her breast. My teeth nip the skin, and her flesh pebbles underneath my touch. Her skin smells delicious, with hints of vanilla and notes of rose mixed with fresh citrus. She is an aphrodisiac that I mean to consume regardless of the consequences. "I have a feeling, though, that you will enjoy it, my little wife. Are you going to be a *good girl* for me now, Stella?"

My voice is husky and filled with the desire to make her mine as I tighten my grip on her hair, a whimper leaving her lips. I pull on the scrap of fabric that is keeping her other breast from me, and it tears easily, exposing the beautiful swell of both her breasts to my waiting mouth. I take her hardened tip in between my lips and suck deeply on the delicate flesh until a moan leaves her mouth, and she moves restlessly before me. Her hands make their way into my thick hair, and her fingers yank harshly on the strands, causing me to groan in pleasure. "Don't threaten me, husband; I'm not afraid of you." She moans seductively, her voice low and filled with pleasure.

My cock is trying desperately to poke its way out of my pants and to find the warm oblivion of Stella's cunt. I move back, removing my lips from her soft flesh, and stare at her. Her eyes are heated, large, and such a dark blue that they remind me of troubled ocean waters. They call to me to give in and continue to give her pleasure, to awaken every nerve ending in her body, and make every part of her mine. Her red lips are parted and there are marks already starting to bloom on her fair skin from where my mouth traveled. *More*, my mind demands, every inch of her needs to know she's mine. Her pink nipples stand at attention before my gaze, just daring me to suck them deep into my mouth.

I will my control back into place. I want to have her, but I need to ensure that she understands that she will not top me. I am her master, not the other way around. She will submit to me and stop this foolish game of trying to win over me. "Are you wet, Stella?" My voice comes out thick and filled with heat as I move my fingers down the front of her abdomen towards her pussy.

When I reach my prize, I shift the flimsy material out of my way, and her bare pussy lips sit glistening before me. The skin is all pink and swollen and so very tempting. Stella has the prettiest, most delicate-looking cunt I have ever seen, and a part of me wants to mark it up and leave my personal brand on it. The only thing that would make it prettier still, would be my cum dripping down and coating it. I part her folds with my fingers, revealing her clit to my eyes, and my mouth waters, needing a taste of her.

"Up, Stella," I demand, grabbing her underneath her arm and pushing her to a standing position before me. She looks a little shocked and confused at my intentions, and she stumbles for a moment before righting herself. *Good, I want her off balance. I want her to wonder what I will do to her next. How I will control and devour her.*

"You're going to stand there with that pretty cunt above me, spreading your legs wide and riding my face, Stella, while I eat that delectable pussy of yours." My words cause a gasp to leave her lips and her body to sway. I can tell she enjoys my dirty words as much as the promise behind them. I wrap both my hands around her calves to steady her on the chaise, while moving into position just below her juicy pussy. I slide one of my hands up her legs, over her soft folds, and around her waist, holding tight to her hip and pulling her down toward my salivating mouth. She smells fucking delicious, her arousal musky and sweet, and has my eyes rolling to the back of my head in anticipation of her taste. *MINE.*

The first lick of my tongue across her pussy lips has a moan leaving both of our lips and her swaying slightly. I lick through her folds up to her clit and suck hard on the little nub, then lash it back and forth with my tongue, breathing against her molten center. Her hands make their way back into my hair, pulling fiercely on the strands as she lowers herself more fully on my face, pushing my face harder into her needy cunt. I move my tongue down her flesh and spear her tight hole to a harsh gasp from her lips. "Jaxon!" The way she moans my name has my tongue thrusting harder into her core, wanting to elicit more cries from her lips.

She tastes amazing, a rich nectar and a flavor that is all Stella. I rub my nose, lips, and chin across her pussy, coating myself in her wetness while whimpers leave her parted lips. My gaze rises up to meet hers. Her heated eyes are at half mast, her pupils blown, and pink tints both her cheeks. I watch with satisfaction as her plump lip is once again firmly between her teeth, trying to restrain the moans from leaving them. *Naw fuck that baby; I want to hear those screams; they're mine.*

I fuck her over and over with my tongue, in and out of her tight hole, while her body rides my face from above. I slide my hands slowly up the inside of her thighs, caressing the skin on the way to my ultimate destination. Once I reach the soft folds of her pussy lips, I pull my tongue out and lash her clit over and over while slipping two of my thick fingers deep inside of her, scissoring my fingers.

"Oh my God!" Her whimper is the sound of music to my ears. Her ragged panting is the most beautiful sound I have ever heard. Move over Mozart, my wife's cries are the best concerto. I pull back with a smirk, "Your God is right here, Stella, eating this soaked pussy."

I feel her body tightening above me as her breathing increases in speed. I pull my face back to watch her expression but continue to fuck her with my fingers, and dare to slip another one inside of her until her pussy grasp is so tight, and her moans are so loud that I know she's about to come. I hook my fingers upwards, finding that delicate spot inside of her and caressing it with my digits. *"Fuck."* The word leaves her lips over and over as her head tips back, and her dark hair cascades down her back and over her shoulders. A breathy chant as her orgasm races through her.

Jesus, she is the sexiest woman I have ever seen. She comes undone over my face, with my fingers deep inside of her. Soaking my digits and her cum dripping down my hand. I reach forward with my tongue lapping up all her wetness, not wanting a single drop to be wasted. She slumps over me, her body deflating and boneless. I slowly remove my fingers from her pussy and help her to lie back down on the chaise before me. The desire to fuck those pretty lips of hers almost overwhelming me. I would love to watch my hard cock choke her and move in that tight throat.

I drape my body over hers, grabbing her chin. Her eyes are dilated, as she's still in that amazing euphoric state. "Open." I pull on her lips, forcing her mouth to part for me. Then I spit some of my saliva with the taste of her cum into her mouth.

"Swallow, Stella. You taste delicious." My eyes narrow on her mouth as she closes her lips and then swallows my spit. *Fuck, that is so sexy*. I want her to taste herself so she knows how intoxicating she is.

I pull back, unbuttoning and unzipping my pants. My cock is desperate to be freed from its confines. The tip peeks out over the band of my boxers, all swollen, flushed red, and dripping with beads of precum.

"Do you see what you do to me, Stella, with that pretty cunt of yours and those vicious lips?" I stand up and pull my pants and boxers down, stepping out of them and standing next to her face. Watching as her eyes widen at my size and proximity to her face. *Oh, baby, you're about to choke on my snake.* I'm not a small man and she will be feeling every inch of me come tomorrow. *That is if I leave her breathing.*

"Have you ever deep-throated a cock before, Stella?" I thread my fingers through her hair, yanking on the strands harshly, and tilt her face upwards towards my cock. When she opens her pretty mouth to reply, I don't hesitate, pushing my cock through her lips and to the back of her throat. I hold tight to her hair and the side of her face, forcing her to take me into her tight throat, even though she gags on my cock and uses her hands to frantically push at my legs. Her struggle is just another level of seduction for me. I want her to panic with my hard cock down her throat. I want her to feel the air draining from her as I control her breathing and close off her airway. She should realize that I am her everything. Her master, husband, and the asshole that decides how much air she will get into that sexy treacherous mouth of hers. *She is fucking mine, a fact she will learn.*

"You're going to be a *good little slut* for me and swallow my cock deep down into your pretty little throat. I'm going to fill it with my cum until you're choking on it."

I pull back, only leaving the tip inside her lips, spittle coating my cock and dribbling out the side of her lips. Her eyes are wide, and a tear trickles down the side of her face from my harsh treatment. *Fuck, I want to see more tears running down her face.* She looks beautiful like this, ready to be used for my cock's pleasure. I push back inside her warm, wet mouth, not being any gentler than I was the first time, and hitting the back of her throat. Forcing myself once again down it and keeping her face and head held in my tight grasp. Her gagging noises are music to my ears. I start a punishing rhythm of fucking her mouth hard, each time I plunge in, hitting the back of her throat and making her gag loudly and choke on my hard length. "Relax your throat, Stella; you need to swallow all of me."

Her hands grip me in desperation, trying to slow my onslaught of her mouth and throat, but I will not be denied. The sounds of her slurping, gagging, and her harsh breath are a symphony of sounds to my ears. Beethoven, Chopin, and Bach have nothing on the music my Stella is making. The only thing that could make this even better would be her cries of pain. I grasp a fist full of her hair and yank, ripping out strands as she screams around my cock. *There it is, what a beautiful sound.*

The orgasm starts to race down my back, a live current soaring through my skin and causing heat and sweat to break out across my body. Her fingernails dig into the back of my thighs, and that little pinch of pain causes me to go right over the edge and roughly cum down her throat. I push her head forward until her nose is flush against my pelvis and spurt over and over down her tight throat as she tries to swallow as much as she can. She struggles in my hold, scratching up the back of my legs with her sharp nails. I don't release her until the final rope of cum has left me, and even then, I hold her face tightly in my grasp. Her struggles continue to excite me as aftershocks race back up my spine, and she continues to gag on me.

Pulling back, I watch as my cock vacates her mouth, inch by inch, covered in her spit and my thick cum. "Swallow every last drop, Stella. Lick those pouty lips of yours to make sure you get all of me inside of you." I yank hard on her hair, and tears slide down the side of her cheekbones as I watch her do exactly what I have instructed her. *She is so exquisite when she obeys me.*

I let my hard cock slap her lips and then her cheek, coating both in my cum and her spit until she looks a mess. I release my hold on her and back up a step to stare at her. She's an alluring wreck, her hair in complete disarray from me fucking her face and pulling on it. Her lips are red, swollen, and spittle, and cum is coating her chin and splattered across the top of her chest. Her arctic blue eyes are reminiscent of a tempestuous storm about to make landfall. She's breathing heavily, her chest moving harshly like she can't catch her breath. *That's it, my whore; you only breathe because I allow it.*

I reach down and run my fingers through the mess on her chin and chest, bringing two fingers up to coat her lips. "What a messy, *good girl* you are, Stella. You take cock in your throat like an expensive whore." A whimper leaves her lips, and her tongue comes out to lash at my fingers, cleaning them of her spit and my cum. I watch as her thighs tighten, her pussy needy for another orgasm.

One I wish to give her, but instead, I pull back and away from her. Needing to get myself under control and my bearings around me. I can't allow Stella to seduce me into being her willing puppet. The point of fucking her mouth ruthlessly was twofold. One just because I wanted to see my cock shoved hard down that pretty throat of hers and two, to make sure she understands that I own her. She is mine to do with as I please. Her little manipulations and maneuvers won't alter the fact that her father essentially sold her to me.

"You are mine, Stella, to do with as I please. You will be my whore for the rest of your life. You had better get used to me using you." I lean forward, my lips touching hers and tasting myself on them. I lick and nibble her bottom lip. The combination of her taste and mine, fucking delicious.

"Don't try to control me, Stella, and manipulate the rules of the game. You will find that you are outplayed and inexperienced every time you come up against me."

I move back another step, watching as her eyes narrow, no longer in pleasure but in anger. "I will allow your move today, *wife*. Take care you do not overplay your hand." I turn and walk out of the room, the bottom half of my body bare and my cock standing erect and hard. *Fuck, I'm ready to go again, just like I guessed, once with Stella would never be enough.* My cock is already craving the tightness of her throat once more. I force myself to walk away from my little viper of a wife before she becomes an addiction for me. The desire to keep fucking her over and over until she can't stand or breathe, running through my limbs and causing me to want to backtrack into the room.

I keep forcing myself forward, though, heading to the guest room I slept in last night. I need to teach my little ice queen a lesson. I will use her like she was meant to be used, as *my wife, my queen, and my whore.*

17

Stella

"Women are just as motivated by the desire for power as men; it's just that our cultural ideas about power don't associate it with femininity." Soraya Chemaly, Rage Becomes Her: The Power of Women's Anger

SHOCK IS RUNNING THROUGH my system as I watch Jaxon's tight, muscular ass walk out the door after fucking my throat raw and giving me one of the most intense orgasms of my life. I should be appalled at his harsh treatment, but the reality is my pussy is drenched, and I almost begged him to fuck me. Begged him to use me and degrade me further.

You're a weak, dirty whore. My mind whispers, reminding me that the desires I hide are weaknesses in a man like Jaxon's hands. He will have me on my knees as a willing slave if I allow it. Despite how much his filthy words and his domineering and controlling treatment turn me on. I need to remember that he is a tool to get my vengeance and independence over the men in my life that would subject me to being some rich man's possession. *His possession.*

Didn't he himself just utter those words? Ones that should have rage flowing through my veins. Yet instead, I'm lying here sprawled on the chaise, like a sex doll that he used and abandoned, covered in cum and spit. Contemplating slipping my fingers back inside of myself, so that I can ride them to another orgasm.

Jaxon Stratford is dangerous! My mind and self-preservation seethe. I have to be careful with the hands I play against him. I lost control of myself in a moment of pure lust. I thought I had my move down pact for seducing him and bringing him to his knees. Instead, he turned it quickly around on me, gave me another body-shattering orgasm, and used me savagely for his own pleasure. Then he left me here, like the slut he named me, without a look back.

I rise from the chaise on trembling legs, heading in the direction of the bathroom to clean myself up. I can still taste his warm, salty cum in my mouth and the slight musky taste of myself. I want more of that taste and the feel of his hands on my skin. I just need to figure out a way to play him and get him under my control before he does further damage to me.

I will never allow him to treat me like a possession, bought and paid for. *But you will allow him to treat you like a whore, correct? Is that not the same goddamn thing?* My mind questions. I falter in my steps at the thought of Jaxon forcing me to my knees before him. *Fuck!* My core clenches painfully at the thought of how brutish he was and how I wanted him to be even more vulgar with me.

Get your shit together, Stella, or you will end up in a worse situation than you left. Do you want to just be some rich man's plaything? A whore for his amusement? How will he ever respect you if you fall to your knees or spread your legs willingly for him?

As I step into the large glass shower, turning the water to scalding hot and washing the feel of Jaxon's hands and cum off of me, thoughts start to roll through my mind on how I'm going to turn the tables around on him. *Fuck you, Jaxon Stratford, I will never belong to you, not as your prize, possession, or whore.*

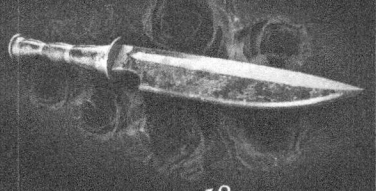

18

Stella

"If you don't challenge things, all you have done is passed it onto the next woman to deal with." Julia Hardy

THE SUN IS SHINING through the large windows out here in the wide, cream-paneled hallway. It's warmth across my skin, a soothing sensation for the nerves that are playing havoc on my body. I take a deep breath as I prepare myself to do battle with one of my strongest adversaries. For just a moment, a deep pang of regret fills me. I wish I didn't have to do this. I wish my father had seen me not just as a pretty, delicate prize to bargain with but as a proud extension of himself.

One that he could have helped shape to rule his empire. Instead, I have to face the hand that I have been dealt. I am a woman, only valued for what men seek as a trophy. My value is in my looks, name, womb, and the zeros in my bank account. *Well fuck that shit, I am more than that!*

Determination fills me once again to set this world on fire. This world which would have me believe that because I am a woman, I am worthless and incapable of ruling. That men are the stronger of the species and destined to control women forever. They will watch as I burn their world down to ashes only to reshape it in my image. I am a queen with a king for a consort, not the other way around. Once I'm done proving my point to these other men that would have seen me kneeling, and simpering at their entitled feet, I will go after Jaxon Stratford with all my strength for thinking he could buy me and treat me like some wanton whore. *My new husband will learn what it means to be conquered at my hands.*

I nod to my new assistant, Tyson. He's a young, good-looking man with dark brown hair and a slim build. His dark brown eyes exhibit an eagerness to learn and rise in this world of privilege and wealth. He had no objections to working for a woman and seemed to salivate at the concept of tearing this male-dominated and chauvinistic world down. At first, I was hesitant, thinking that perhaps I would be better suited with a woman as an assistant, but I quickly realized that I was playing the same double standard game as my father. Here, Tyson stands by my side, strumming with nervous energy, ready to assist me in tearing my father's whole world down. I look forward to taking him with me into the many battles to come.

He opens the dark wood double doors to the boardroom wide and stands aside as I enter the space with my head held high and my shoulders back. All conversation ceases as I move within the space. Cream walls greet me with photographs of all the board members' faces framed and hung on the walls. Large windows allow the New York sunshine to filter inside, giving me strength for what is about to happen. I meet my father's stunned eyes across the large dark wood board table without flinching. *Here goes everything.*

"What is the meaning of this, Stella?" His loud voice bellows through the room. I watch as a few of the men seated at the table flinch in response, but I hold firm, not giving him the satisfaction. *Weaklings, the lot of them.*

"Father." I nod my head to him, never taking my eyes off him as Tyson moves into the room, depositing dark navy folders on the boardroom table in front of each of the four board members present. "This is a board meeting for Penticton Industries, is it not?" I feign indifference that I don't feel and shift further into the room, assessing the situation for any further threats or weaknesses.

"You do not need to attend these meetings, Stella, as I have reminded you in the past. You have meager shares. Your husband will attend on your behalf if he sees fit and deal with his own shares." *Meager shares, this fucker really thinks he's fooling anyone.* Even before my marriage to Jaxon, I held twenty percent of the shares of this company. No one would call that meager, but him. There are board members sitting here with fewer shares than I own, and he treats them with respect. The only difference is the cock I wasn't born with, but make no mistake, my balls are bigger, as he's about to find out.

A smirk crosses my face, and I watch as the large vein in his forehead starts to throb. He's angry at me for the interruption, perhaps even a bit embarrassed that his only child decided to attend a meeting of her family's empire. A woman, no less, one that he has deemed inferior to him and those present. *This will make this whole situation even sweeter for me, I will enjoy inflicting pain on him as he has on me in the past.*

I tear my eyes away from my father's outraged and disappointed ones and look over each of the preceding board members. All men in their mid to late forties, fifties and sixties. Not a single woman is present on the board of my family's company, even though both my mother and I are shareowners. That will need to change. I have no intention of allowing this toxic male superiority to remain at Penticton Industries or at Stratford Industries. The world is changing, and these men are about to experience a rude wake-up call. *Hey, assholes, the world is half female, and it's our turn to shine. Forget the glass ceiling we are going even higher.*

"Is that so?" I move closer to the end of the oval board table, directly opposite my father, and stare at the man sitting in the plush chair. "It seems, father, that you may be unexpectedly and unmercifully misguided. My husband will not, in fact, be present for any board meeting for Penticton Industries as he owns no shares."

The gray-haired idiot before me opens the folder that Tyson dropped in front of him, which contains only one document. The one that clearly shows how many shares I currently own. He stares at the document in disbelief and then raises his brown eyes to meet my unrelenting ones. "I suggest you move; you are in my seat." My words leave my lips in cold, calculated malice.

"What are you babbling about, girl! Of course, your husband has shares in the company; I myself provided him with them for your matrimony." A dowry, of course; he provided my husband with a dowry to marry me like we are living in some medieval world. Thomas Penticton's face swells up with anger and agitation, he reaches over and rips the folder from the board member next to his hands. The room is silent as he contemplates what he is seeing before him. *Gotcha, dad.*

I quirk my lips as I take the newly vacated seat, crossing my hands before me on the desk, demurely. The perfect picture of a dutiful queen, one that he ensured I knew how to play the part of. He should congratulate himself once the fury has settled down a bit. He is partially responsible for making me the woman I am today. Without his mistreatment, lack of support, empathy, and general sexism, who knows what I may have become?

"As you can see from the document before you, father." I sneer the word out, making sure that all present hear my disdain for it. "Jaxon generously signed over his shares and his board seat to his wife yesterday. That would make me, *his wife*, the majority shareholder in Penticton Industries, not you." The biggest surprise was that my timid mother also signed over her shares to me when I requested them, without any hesitation or questions.

My father slams the folder down on the desk before him, rising to his feet and leaning over the table, his large belly protruding over the belt of his black dress pants. His face filled with rage, blotchy and red, sweat dotting his receding hairline. I'm almost sorry that I'm hurting him, he is my father, but the mistreatment and disdain over the years at his hands stays any sentiment that rises within me. He will be the first of many that I will have cowering at my feet when I'm done. I don't think he will enjoy the trip down to the bottom. To be subjected to my rule, and my control, but oh well, life is never fair. *After all, I should fucking know first hand, I'm a woman.*

"This is ludicrous. You cannot have the majority shareholder's position, Stella!" He slams his fist down hard on the tabletop, ensuring that the water in the glasses before each of the shareholders sloshes out and wets the tabletop before us. His breathing is harsh and his chest is rising and falling with angry pants. He is working himself into one of his rages. The ones he subjects my mother and me to. The ones that portray a less civilized version of Thomas Philip Penticton than the world gets to see. The tyrant is actually an abusive monster behind closed doors.

"Why is that father?" I raise my eyebrow and meet his affronted glare. "Could it be because I am a woman?" I sit back in my chair, demonstrating to all those before me a rational, collected, and serious countenance. I will not allow any of them to judge or misalign me with the stereotypes attributed to women. I am not prone to hysteria, fear, or tears, and I will not cower before a group of men.

"What have you done, Stella? You think this little stunt will change anything? You are a woman. Your place is at home, running your husband's house and ensuring that he is taken care of, giving birth to the next generation. Not in a corporate office and certainly not heading Penticton Industries."

Indignation fills me, and I have to stop the outraged retort that wants to leave my mouth. How dare he insinuate that all I'm good for is being my husband's property, breeding, and running his home. I tighten my fingers on the edge of the table until they are bloodless before me and take a few short breaths through my nose, glowering at my father. The man I once worshiped with a little girl's admiration for her poppa. He never deserved it, even when I was a child. Always lamenting the lack of a son and making me feel small and unwanted.

"Regardless of your opinion, father, the fact is right there in black and white before you and indisputable. I am the majority shareholder, with even more shares than you. I have my shares, Jaxon's shares, and my mother's, which gives me fifty-one percent. Which means that I will be heading this company going forward from today onwards." I raise my hand to silence whatever wrathful words are about to leave his lips. "Be wary, father, I have no qualms about taking my shares public and selling our family legacy to the highest bidder if you try in any way to stop my takeover."

"You would destroy over two hundred years of Penticton legacy in spite, Stella?" Spittle flies from his mouth as he moves around the table towards me. A huge lumbering presence seething with wrath. I feel Tyson move forward at my back and spy the other board members moving further away from the table at my father's approach. *They are smarter than they look, bastards.* He is a volcano about to explode, and they don't want to be in his immediate vicinity when he does.

"I would burn it all to the ground and sleep well at night. Your legacy, your name, and the empire that our family built."

He reaches out with his large hand and grabs my chin in his tight grasp, tilting it so that I have no choice but to meet his ferocious gaze. The sweat that at first dotted his forehead is now trickling in drips down the side of his face, and his nostrils are flaring. He looks like an enraged bull, ready to attack. His large body is locked tight, perhaps with the restraint of not raising that meaty paw in punishment. If he were to slap me here, like he so often does, these men would know what type of man Thomas Penticton really is. The type that uses his hand and fists on his wife and daughter to ensure obedience and fear.

Someone clearing their throat behind me catches everyone in the room's attention and has my father releasing his tight hold on my chin. I move my jaw back and forth to loosen up the feeling of his fingers. I have no doubt that his meaty fingerprints will be present there tomorrow. *Motherfucker!*

"Thomas, I thought that I had already warned you about touching a Stratford, in particular the one your fingers were just on." Jaxon's voice rings out behind me, filled with cold malice and a vibrant threat.

I watch, enthralled, as my father swallows painfully, his face rising with further color as he moves away from me. His body is almost trembling with the resentment he is trying to suppress. His hands are now clenched at his side, and he's grinding his large, meaty jaw. I don't bother to turn in my seat, I can picture the look of malicious intent on Jaxon's face. He did warn him and even though I don't need him to fight my battles, a warm satisfaction fills me at the look of abject fear on my father's face.

"She is my daughter."

"She is my wife, Thomas. That trumps being your daughter. She is also the majority shareholder at this company, and you will show her the respect that both those titles require or... *I. Will. Destroy. You.*" Jaxon's voice never raises with the threat but the deadly intent behind his words has a shiver racing down my spine. He moves further into the room, his scent reaching my nose and helping to release some of the tightness in my chest. I should question why his mere presence is having that effect on me. Something to ponder at a later opportunity when I am not surrounded by enemies.

"How could you have done this, Jaxon? Have you lost your mind?" Thomas seethes.

"Done what exactly, Thomas? Given my wife, the shares that rightly belong to her as Penticton Industries, is her family's legacy? Provided a highly educated and business-savvy woman the right to lead her own empire? Which part vexes you the most? That she will be your superior and run the company, or that she is a woman and outsmarted you?"

19

Jaxon

"There's something special about a woman who dominates in a man's world. It takes a certain grace, strength, intelligence, fearlessness, and the nerve to never take no for an answer."
Rihanna

A s I AWAIT MY new father-in-law's reply to my question, my eyes fall over the young man positioned as a sentinel at my wife's back. This is the new personal assistant she hired. It seems my wife, and I will be having words about hiring good-looking young men as her right hand.

Hypocrite, my mind whispers. I know that it's a double standard. I have no qualms about attractive women working for me at Stratford Industries, but I don't want my wife surrounded daily by handsome men. The little kernel of emotion rising within me has a vibrant green tinge to it and I don't for one second enjoy it.

"She will never be my superior; you are misaligned and insane for even suggesting it. You need to get firm control over my daughter, Jaxon." I snort at his comment and his attempt at reminding me of ownership. Stella is no longer his, she's all mine now. The fucker is insane. He obviously doesn't know the first fucking thing about Stella, if he honestly believes anyone can get control over her. I have no doubt that she will fight me tooth and nail for the rest of our lives over control, and I may never come out the victor. Yet the thought of all the battles I am going to face and all the ways I'm going to try to force her to submit to me, make me feel alive.

"Of that, you are correct, father. I will not be your superior. In fact, as of this afternoon, you will be entering retirement. You will no longer be an active member of this board or have any say in the daily actions of this company." A smirk crosses my lips at the way she spews the word *'father'.* She has no pity for the man, just disgust. Gasps fill the room around us and the side of my mouth quirks up at their reactions to my destructive viper of a wife. God, she's a sexy little thing when she's being ruthless. I've got a semi just watching her. If these fuckers weren't in the room, I might even have slipped under that skirt she's wearing and eaten her pussy, while she tried to boss me around. *Still might, fuck now my semi is a full hardon.*

I observe as Stella meets her father's furious gaze without hesitation or flinching. She's a queen sitting court and utterly unafraid. Desire races through me at the show she is putting on, at the power she is demonstrating to all these men. I want to kneel at her feet and be the man at her back. Too bad I can't do both at once. I move closer to my wife, giving her assistant a harsh glare, and the promise of violence.

For a moment, I don't believe he will back down, but at the last minute, he tips his head and steps back, allowing me to position myself at my wife's back. I will have to watch the sly fucker. If he thinks he will be spending any time reaping the rewards between my wife's thighs, he is fucking mistaken, and I will have him murdered and dismembered. *She is fucking mine, and I don't plan to share her.* I lay my warm, tense hand on her shoulder, a show of support but also of possession, one I have no doubt she will make me suffer for later. Other than tensing minutely, she doesn't even acknowledge its presence. *What a good girl she is.*

"I will be doing no such thing! How dare you even suggest that!" Thomas' voice echoes through the room. He is losing control of his emotions, and my wife is purposely pushing his buttons. She wants the world to see what type of man he really is behind the expensive exterior. After all, is that not why I'm here? I knew there was a board meeting today; the invite was hand-delivered and crossed my desk yesterday, mere hours after I transferred my shares to my wife.

The memory of the way he behaved with her the morning of our wedding played as a nagging thought all morning in my mind. Would he have struck her if I hadn't been present? Has he hit her in the past? The mere thought has rage bubbling in my veins, and the desire to knock him on his ass fills me.

I had a feeling that Stella was going to pull something today at this board meeting. Her assistant was very insistent that the documentation of the transfer be completed and sent immediately to her. My wife is out for blood, and as much as I don't appreciate the tactics that she uses when used on me, I can't but admire her determination to slay her demons. Even if I happen to be one of them.

Do I believe my show of support will diminish her ire towards me and the forced marriage? *No fucking way.* I will still be paying with blood and flesh; of that, I have no doubt. Will I allow anyone else to hurt her, though? *The fuck I will.* If anyone is going to bring Stella Stratford to her beautiful knees it will be me, and me alone.

An adorable snort of amusement leaves her, and for a brief moment, a smirk crosses mine at the sound. She is such a cyclone of contradictions. Beautiful, elegant, and sophisticated meshed with viciousness, cold, and calculating. *So many layers to my little ice queen.*

"The fact that you still don't understand that you have no power here, that your time as ruler of this kingdom is over, shows that you are not fit to lead. Let me put this in layman's terms, father. You have been dethroned and conquered; the empire is now mine. You will leave with your tail tucked between your legs and head into retirement, or I will use the full force of my inheritance, plus the Stratford name, you forced on me to ruin you and your *legacy.*"

Once again, there are gasps of shock across the room. The men in attendance feel the full power of her words and intentions. She will not back down, and her threats are not idle, as witnessed by poor, unfortunate Kalista yesterday. *Fucking beautiful!*

I could intercede. I could, in fact, refuse her the power behind the Stratford name, but why would I? She is helping to ensure that all of these minions go forth and spread the word of the might of the Stratfords. My father is in his grave, clapping for her right now. She is probably more the son he always wanted than I am. She will bring the world to heel at the strength of the Stratfords and help me to build the empire that I crave. *That is, if she doesn't destroy me, too, in her quest for power.*

Her father's mouth opens and closes, like some demented blowfish. His eyes meet mine, and whatever he sees there makes him realize that I will not stop her. I will, in fact, ensure that her threats are carried out. He gave her to me without realizing the power that he once held in his hands. *I won't be so ignorant.*

He shifts to move past me towards the door, his breathing heavy and his body filled with frustrations at being bested by my viper of a wife. Just before he makes it to the door, Stella pushes back from her chair, dislodging my hand in the process, and turns towards her father's back.

"If I find out that you took any of this out on my mother, if even a minuscule scratch is found on her body, I will not only be displeased; I will ensure I retaliate in kind. Do not touch her." Her words are strong and uttered without a hint of any other emotion than the promise of retribution. Her words cement my previous thoughts that her father has laid hands on her and her mother before in anger. The strength her mother presented me at our wedding reception makes a shiver race down my spine. Thomas Penticton is lucky that his wife and daughter haven't had him murdered yet.

Thomas storms out of the room and the rest of the board scampers up immediately and leaves the room behind him, none of them meeting her gaze or even uttering a word. *Cowards!* Little wealthy mice running away from my lioness of a wife. I'm so fucking proud of her right now, I could roar like a satisfied lion.

"Tyson, ensure he vacates his office immediately and does not take anything of value with him. Have security posted on each floor of the building. The board members are also to leave the building today without any files. Have their access to top-tier documents restricted and their passwords cloned. I want to see everything they're doing."

"Yes, Mrs. Stratford."

I move forward and take the vacated seat next to her. Appraising her appearance and expression as I do. She looks lovely dressed in a hunter's green business suit. The cream silk shirt underneath her suit jacket shows the barest amount of cleavage. My mouth salivates with the memory of how delicious she tastes and how full her breasts were in my hands yesterday.

I can almost see all the thoughts and plans circulating through her mind. "That was quite a takeover, Stella. Well done, little ice queen." I let the pride and desire I am feeling show on my face. There is no point in trying to hide it. I want her, and I will have her, over and over. That pretty pink pussy that torments my waking and sleeping moments will be laid before me and used for my pleasure.

"Why are you here, Jaxon?" She turns her arctic gaze on me. Her expression is reserved, and I am unable to read her thoughts. Is she truly displeased that I came?

For some reason that I can't fathom, that thought upsets me. She didn't want me here to witness her victory and support her. She is my wife. Does she not understand that I will always have her back, even if I don't agree with her methods?

"I came to bear witness to your destruction and rise in power, little ice queen. Does it displease you that I wished to watch you humble your father while you seized the company that is rightfully yours?"

Her arctic eyes meet mine, flashing with emotion. *Is that satisfaction or need in their depth?* Does she finally understand that she is mine and I am hers, and together, we will build an empire? "You are an extremely sexy woman when you play with power Stella." I lean forward, my lips a hair's breadth away from hers. Her lips open, and her warm, minty breath trails across my mouth. My eyes meet hers, gray, fighting a losing battle against the blue arctic night. "Does it turn you on?"

I run my finger up the smooth, creamy skin of her bare calf. "Are you soaked right now, Stella? Does conquering men and striving for power make you wet, baby?"

20

Stella

"When a woman is talking to you, listen to what she says with her eyes." Victor Hugo

H IS TOUCH AND WORDS cause goosebumps to rise across my skin. Those slate-gray eyes meet mine with heated seduction and promises of debauchery. His charcoal suit is perfectly tailored to his large, powerful body. Those wide shoulders stretch the material, and that broad, powerful chest pushes against the fabric of his crisp white dress shirt, causing saliva to pool in my mouth. I watch as he first licks and then bites his full bottom lip, tempting me to lean forward and take it into my own mouth. Did he come here to tempt me as the snake did to Eve in the Garden of Paradise?

He is temptation, and the promise of sin all rolled into one, and he knows it. The sexiest, most intriguing man I have known, waiting to destroy me and bring me to my knees. Everything about him is designed to entice the female race. He was crafted by divine hands to be our downfall, and it seems I'm no more immune than any other woman.

He leans further into my space, his scent tickling my senses and causing my body to soften for him. His fingers slide further up the inside of my leg and below the hem of my dark green conservative pencil skirt. They don't stop until they reach the trim of my panties, and I can't seem to force myself to end his actions. I tell myself that I just want to see how daring he will be. That this is a game, we are both playing, but the truth is I want him to touch me. I want him to ravish me over and over, and then I want to drag him to his knees before me so that I, too, can have a taste of power. Power over Jaxon is a drug, and I'm about to be a willing addict.

"Open wider, beautiful wife. I want to feel how drenched that pretty pussy of yours is right now." There's a rose flush starting on his jaw, his gaze is locked on mine with tantalizing intent and suggestive of all the enjoyment he can provide me. The look of longing and desire across his features has me doing his bidding and opening my legs as wide as the skirt allows.

His fingers slip under the leg band of my panties and caress my warm flesh as my core clenches tightly and weeps with the anticipation of his touch. "Jaxon, someone could walk in," I exclaim in a low tone and try to reason with him as well as with myself. I shouldn't be allowing this to happen, and certainly not here, where I need to command the respect of the men around me and not be seen as just a woman with a pussy to be used. *Shut the fuck up, we need this!* Even though the rational part of my brain knows all this, I still don't stop his wandering fingers from gliding across my wet skin.

"Soaked Stella. Your cunt is weeping. Is she drenched for me or for power, little wife?" He lets out a groan that makes his chest vibrate. "Who cares if anyone sees? Let them bear witness to your power. I'm not here to take from you but to serve you, Stella. Tell me what you want, and I will provide it, my little ice queen."

His finger grazes my hard, swollen clit, and a moan escapes my lips. I close my eyes, leaning my head back against the leather chair and contemplating his seductive words. The pull of his command reaches into the darkest, deepest part of me. The part that hides the need for anything but power.

He starts rubbing methodical circles over and over on my sensitive nub, quickly causing electric currents to rush through my body. The thought that anyone could walk back into the room and find us causes more wetness to seep from inside of me. A thrill shoots through me at the possibility of being caught, exposed, and being watched. *Fuck, why is that so hot?*

I want him to continue, to bring me to completion, but I also want to ensure he knows his place.

Today is about me, Stella Stratford, not him. It's about my rise to power and my empire. I want him to subjugate himself at my feet and prove to me he understands that. I want to use him like he did me last night. I crave control and power over him. I reach out and grab a fist full of his dark, thick hair, pulling him forward as I take his lips in a rough, impassioned kiss that is all teeth, tongue, and heated ardor.

He groans as he comes willingly into my mouth, his fingers never ceasing their exploration of my pussy and playing with my clit. I need more than that, however. I want to cum with a desperation that I can't control. I break the kiss and use my hold on Jaxon's hair to pull him from his seat, and down to his knees before me.

"Pull my skirt up, Jaxon, and my panties to the side." My voice sounds wanton and filled with passion to my ears, and I watch as his mercurial eyes dilate. Need, and hunger cross his features as he licks his lips like a man starved before a banquet. *Jesus, fuck.*

He slides his fingers away from my pussy, and a whimper leaves my lips at the loss of his touch. He grabs the crotch of my drenched silk panties and yanks hard on the material, a tearing sound retching the air around us. Then his warm, large hands skate down the inside of my thighs until they reach the hem of my skirt, and he pulls it up, his eyes never leaving mine.

I lift my ass to allow him to pull the tight material over and up to my waist, leaving me naked and exposed from the waist down to him and anyone else that may enter the room. The thought of someone catching us, of seeing my heated and drenched flesh on display, causes my pussy to clench and a tempoed throbbing to start inside my core. My wanton need for exhibitionism on display. I would have imagined I would be feeling shame at the prospect of being so thoroughly on display. But instead, all I feel is searing heat rising, excitement, and power flowing through my veins. Power at having this man on his knees before me. He waits for further instructions, his fingers lightly stroking my heated flesh.

My grip on his hair tightens further until a grimace crosses his handsome features as I pull him closer to my sex. His warm breath skates across my scorching skin, and a shiver trickles down my limbs, leaving goosebumps in its wake. "Do you want me to eat this drenched cunt, Stella? Right here where anyone could see?" His words have a moan leaving my lips before I can trap it.

"Shut up, stay on your knees, and worship the queen you helped create, Jaxon." A harsh breath leaves his chest at my words. He grasps both my legs just below my knees, pulling me slightly forward on the seat and raising my legs to drape over each of the chair's arms.

I am wide open and exposed for him. My pussy, slick and on display like some shameless creature for his heated inspection and the warm breath leaving his lips. The way he is staring at my center has butterflies filling my stomach and heat rising through my body. He looks like a lion that wants to devour me, and I am his willing victim and his next kill. *Fuck, what a sexy predator he is.*

The first warm lick of his tongue through my pussy lips has me clenching tightly on nothing but air and a whimper, leaving me at the empty feeling. His tongue strokes through my wetness up my swollen and throbbing clit, and he lashes it with his tongue until I'm starting to see nothing but bright colors before me. I pull on his hair, wanting him to get closer and be rougher with me. Needing more of him, the longing to explode on his mouth and all over his face, creating wave after wave of pure lust and energy inside of me.

"Patience, little queen, I mean to savor this delicious cunt." He moans into my flesh, the rumble of his words causing shocks of electricity to rise within my core. His tongue makes its way into my needy hole, and his eyes meet mine as it slips inside, causing a moan to leave both our lips. His thumb takes up the relentless stroking of my clit, and I have to close my eyes to try to catch my breath. I'm moving restlessly in the seat, my legs trembling over the chair's arms. His other hand comes to lay flat across my pelvis, forcing my movements to still so that he can fuck my tight hole with his ruthless tongue. His palm raises and slaps my clit hard, causing a gasp to leave my lips and my eyes to shoot open in shock.

"Jaxon," I moan as he repeats the action, slapping my poor swollen clit with the meaty part of his palm. The sound of flesh meeting flesh, coupled with my whimpers, are obscene in the large, empty room.

His eyes are heated pools of gray metal and form to slits as he studies my reaction to his tongue penetrating me over and over. He removes his warm tongue only to replace it with two thick fingers that have my ass rising off the seat, a deep groan leaving my lips.

"You're so sweet and wet, baby, this pussy wants to be ruined by me, doesn't she?" He licks my clit with his tongue flattened at the same moment he slips a third finger inside of me. The stretch and bite of pain feel so good as I tighten my hold on his thick digits. His unoccupied hand slips up my body and squeezes my breast, causing another gasp to leave my lips.

"Jaxon, harder." The words leave my lips in harsh pants. The orgasm is so close that my whole body is tingling. His grip on my breast loosens as his hand makes its way to my throat, and his fingers tighten around it, causing the airflow to stop and a ragged gasp to escape me. His fingers move with harsh, deep strokes inside of my clenching core and rub against the spot deep inside of me that has me crying out my release and gushing all over his mouth and chin. He pulls back from my clit. "You crave darkness like the one that inhabits my soul, Stella. Let me push you into the dark, let me corrupt you."

His fingers tighten around my throat until the edges of darkness start to crush my vision as he returns to feast on my pussy like a madman, causing aftershocks to roll through me on an unending loop. My body stiffens completely, and he grazes his teeth against my sensitive clit and rolls me into another shockwave of an orgasm. My hands pull on his hair, and I gasp for air, mewling sounds escaping me. My body is completely rolled under his unmerciful treatment and begging for more as darkness calls to me.

Finally, his grip releases on my throat, and air rushes back into the abused organ, causing me to suck deep gasps through my mouth and cough. He licks me once more through my swollen pussy lips and then pulls back on the fierce hold I have on his hair and removes his fingers from inside of me. I watch as he brings all three digits to his mouth and sucks them deep, his passionate eyes never leaving mine. Jesus, he is so erotic and fucking hot.

He groans as he sucks my taste off of his digits and then removes them from his mouth, reaching forward and laying a gentle kiss on the soft skin of my pelvis. "I will gladly bow at your feet, Stella, if I get to eat this juicy cunt."

He pushes back up from his knees and stands before me. A king dressed in expensive finery staring down at his prize. He may have subjected himself to his knees and my whim, but the expression on his face indicates he thinks he has won. His large cock is tenting the fine fabric of his dress pants, and there is no way to hide his substantial size or affliction.

For a moment, I want to reach forward and pull down his zipper. Let my mouth trail across his hard length and suck him back into my abused throat. I want to watch him come undone like last night, knowing I have complete power over him when I do.

"Congratulations, Stella, you seemed to have brought every man within the vicinity to their knees." He wipes the palm of his hand across his glistening lips and chin, wiping my moisture off of its surface. He leans down and picks up the scrap of silk that I am sure are my panties, slipping them into his dress pants pocket. "I look forward to seeing what you will do next, little ice queen."

With those parting words, he moves away from me and leaves the room with his raging erection on display, a smug grin across his lips, leaving me fully exposed and spread open in the boardroom chair, like the brazen slut I am becoming for him. *Fuck.*

My body is completely liquefied as I try to force myself to sit up and pull down my skirt. Little aftershocks are still racing through my system, and my core is sore and throbbing. He fingerbanged me so exquisitely, two orgasms later, and my demanding core is still begging for more. She wants his huge cock deep inside, and frustration is once again setting in at being denied the feel of him within me.

His words repeat inside my head. "I will gladly bow at your feet, Stella, if I get to eat this juicy cunt." Fuck, his dirty words, and that expression on his face will have me cumming again just from the memory. Jaxon Stratford is a distraction and threat that I should be worrying about how to handle. He will not go meekly before me, regardless of his claim to want to bow at my feet. I need to get control of myself and not fall into a puddle of orgasms at his touch.

I will bring you to your knees, Jaxon, and then keep you there.

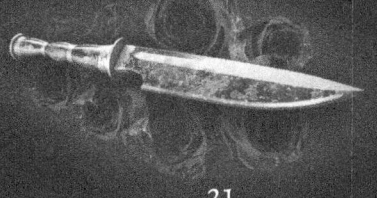

21

Stella

"Jealousy is a dog's bark which attracts thieves." Karl Kraus

"**Y**OU LOOK STUNNING, STELLA." Jaxon's slow steps greet me, and his words cause a flush of pleasure to rise within me at the compliment. I've never been swayed by pretty words, especially ones from men, but I can tell that his words are sincere by the look on his face. His gaze moves down to stare intently at my feet, the red five-inch heels giving me much-needed height against Jaxon's six-foot-one frame but also making my legs look impossibly long. "Later, I'm going to fuck you with those heels up by my ears, Stella. I might even cum on your face."

Every filthy word out of his delectable and sinful mouth causes shivers of anticipation and need to cascade through me. His gaze shifts over me with heat and admiration from my feet to my short black dress and over my waist, until his gaze centers on the deep "V" neckline that is showing off a large amount of the swell of my breasts. The dress is daring for me and completely out of my comfort range.

The reason behind wearing it causes me even more discomfort than the amount of skin I'm currently exposing to the eyes of strangers and my new husband. When he suggested that we dine out together at one of the top restaurants in the city. One that is frequented by most of the elite and top models. Models that have had previous sexual relations with my husband. I decided that I wanted to prove to them and to myself that I was not just a woman he got saddled with in this arranged marriage. That I could hold my own against them and keep Jaxon's attention on me all night long. I know I'll never be Kalista Cain beautiful, but I know I'm not an ugly hag either. Men do look at me occasionally with heat in their eyes.

The only man's attention I'm interested in capturing tonight is Jaxon's. I want him to desire me, to look at me with longing and sexual attraction. The reasoning behind why I want those things is confusing and causes me to doubt my sanity. Regardless of my crumbling willpower and mental instability, I might have gone a bit overboard and let the woman at the exclusive Fifth Avenue boutique talk me into this dress. One that I would never have even considered under normal circumstances. The one she guaranteed would have my husband drooling over me all night long. So far, she was right on the money.

Jaxon takes a step closer, leaning his upper body towards mine, his scent wafting over me as his warm breath slithers over my bare shoulder and neck. "I'm going to fuck those perky tits too, Stella." My core throbs painfully empty at his words, and my nipples pucker tightly with anticipation. His warm palm slides up the side of my waist, over my ribs, and cups my breast, the thin material of the dress offering no resistance against his hand. "I can't wait to cover these beauties with my cum."

His words are shocking, erotic, and filthy and turn me on instantly. The scrap of lace I'm wearing as panties is now drenched, and any minute, my arousal will be dripping down the inside my thighs. He must sense how ramped up I already am, a devious chuckle leaves his lips, and his hand slides back down to my waist, pulling me closer to him. His lips skate across my cheek, before meeting my lips in a quick peck. The heat from his body doing delicious things to my already over-stretched nerves.

"Let's go eat, I'm fucking starving, and the faster I feed you, the sooner I can go home to my own feast." He pulls me forward and we walk into the fine dining Italian restaurant together. All eyes are on us. I can feel their gazes like little ants crawling across my skin. Jaxon seems completely unperturbed with the attention and other than nodding to a few acquaintances here and there, he gives no one any serious attention. As I trail my gaze across the room, I notice the longing on various women's faces as they stare at Jaxon, before quickly averting their eyes when my warning glare lands on them.

The maître d seats us in a small round upholstered booth, fresh white linens adorn the table, and various candles are lit and surround us. The whole atmosphere gives off a very romantic vibe, one that I should be wary of, but instead, for tonight, I'm throwing caution to the wind and enjoying myself in the company of the sexiest man I know. When Jaxon phoned me at the office to ask me to meet him here tonight after our interaction in the boardroom of Penticton Industries, I wanted to refuse him. The words were on the tip of my tongue, but instead, I found myself agreeing.

Has all the orgasms this man has been pulling from my needy body, finally fried my brain? I found myself thinking about him throughout the day. Remembering how it feels to have his skin against mine. His fingers deep inside of me, and the taste of his cock in my mouth. All the sensations have me in a constant lust-filled fog. I'm struggling to concentrate on my own plans to conquer the world around me and bring it to its knees. The only man I seem interested in bringing to his knees before me, at the moment, is the one sitting across from me, eyeing me like I'm a slice of heavenly cheesecake or a prime steak.

"How did the rest of your power domination go today?" He inquires with a smirk and a raised eyebrow. I roll my eyes at him, knowing he's baiting me to get into an argument with him. Just as I'm about to reply, the waiter appears before our table. His dark eyes meet mine, taking his time to peruse my face, frame, and dress before even acknowledging Jaxon's presence. The guy is hot, like magazine cover hot, and come to think of it, I may have seen him inside of one or in a commercial or something. An embarrassed blush rises on my skin at the overwhelming and intense way he's staring at me. He looks like he would like nothing more than to have his way with me, regardless of our current company.

Jaxon clears his throat, and the blond-haired handsome waiter finally turns his attention towards him. "Good evening, welcome to Santa Lucia. Can I start you off with some wine? Perhaps a special drink for the lady?" Jaxon's jaw locks tight, and I try to hide a chuckle at his irritation with the waiter. His hand is clenched on the fine white tablecloth, and he is grinding his molars. Is my new husband perhaps a little jealous of the attention I'm receiving from another male?

"The lady and I will have a bottle of your Domaine de la Romanee." Jaxon raises an eyebrow, almost daring the waiter to utter another word. The man nods and quickly slithers away but not before trailing his eyes once again over me. I'm starting to feel self-conscious; do I look like a slut? I don't want that type of attention from anyone but Jaxon. *It doesn't matter what you wear, you could be sitting here naked, people can only make you feel uncomfortable with yourself if you allow it to happen, my brain admonishes me.* My eyes shift to Jaxon, and I notice his gaze is still on the brave waiter. I try to defuse the situation and bring his attention back to me by answering his original question.

"We had to forcefully escort one of the board members out with security. The idiot really thought he would be able to leave with classified documents in his briefcase. He caused quite a scene, kicking and screaming and threatening me with a lawsuit."

Jaxon's fingers slide across the table, his long fingers tapping the table top and meeting mine. His middle finger skates over my ring finger and the massive square cut Stratford diamond that now resides there. "Fuck 'em, Stella. You see this shiny rock here. This means you can destroy and ruin whoever the fuck you want to, anyone but me."

My breath leaves my lips in a staggered exhale, and I try to hold in the chuckle that wants to escape. A sheepish smile crosses my face. "Anyone but you? Why not you, too, Jaxon?"

"Oh, little viper, you know that diamond means you're mine, in every way. That's my name and ownership, plain for everyone to see across your delicate finger. Although I'm open to much more creative ways of demonstrating that you are my possession," his eyes linger on the length of my neck and collarbone, the one still demonstrating the marks from his lips and fingers.

Irritation fills me once again at his crude words indicating I'm nothing more than an object to him, a possession he coveted and then won. "I don't want to be your possession Jaxon. I'm your fucking wife and your equal." I get ready to stand and move out of the booth, annoyed that, once again, I have been diminished to nothing but an object. His fingers tighten on mine, holding me firmly in place before I can rise.

"If you move out of that seat and try to leave me here like some fuckboy, I swear to you, Stella, I will have you down on your knees with my cock shoved painfully down that pretty throat in front of all these fellow diners. Do not tempt me to take you here. I'm barely holding onto my precarious restraint with that dress you're wearing."

His threat is shocking and makes me pause. Would he really attempt to do that to me here? If he tried, I would stab him with the cutlery currently on the table. *Would you, though? Let's be real here: you enjoy it when he makes you come where others can get a peek.* The cynical bitch in my head replies. Our gazes clash in a standoff, the heady threat of punishment if I try to leave a live wire between us. A part of me wants to push his buttons just to see if he really will comply with his threat. The other part of me, the logical side that has a shred of self-preservation left, argues for me to sit my ass down and avoid this confrontation. This will not end well; I could end up being front-page news tomorrow with Jaxon's cock in my mouth.

The waiter returns with our wine and some complimentary appetizers, placing them down and filling my glass just as a man approaches our table and gets Jaxon's attention, totally disregarding me, like I'm not even present. Jaxon turns his attention towards him with a scowl across his face. The waiter takes the opportunity to lean a little forward and whispers near my ear. "You're the hottest woman in here tonight. What are you doing with the overbearing tyrant?" His fingertip skates down the length of my arm, causing goosebumps to form and the hairs to stand on end. "I'm off in a few hours, I could show you a better time, beautiful."

My mouth opens and then closes in complete disbelief. This guy is either really daring or really stupid, trying to pick me up while my husband sits a mere two feet away talking to someone else. Something drops in my lap lightly, and my fist closes around it. It's a piece of folded paper, no doubt, with this idiot's number. *Outrageous.* Should I say something to Jaxon? Should I even acknowledge this fucker's attempt? Maybe I should punch him in the dick. The thought of how that will completely ruin the rest of our night stops me from doing anything. I drop the folded paper next to me on the seat and disregard it.

The menacing and cold look I give the waiter has him taking a step back and realizing his mistake. I'm not one of these rich bored wives here to make arrangements to fool around behind her husband's back. "Step back and take our order, or I will dick-punch you," I whisper so that I don't interrupt Jaxon's ongoing conversation with the rude guy who didn't even greet me.

Jaxon's conversation finishes up and we proceed to order our food, the earlier conversation seemingly forgotten. For the remainder of the meal, the waiter finally behaves professionally, and luckily, I don't think Jaxon even noticed the man's blatant attempt to pick me up. Jaxon's quieter, the flirtation gone from our night and leaving me on edge. We speak about trivial things, two strangers enjoying a meal.

As we are leaving the restaurant and approaching our waiting limo, Jaxon suddenly stops and glares at me. "What did I tell you about what's mine, Stella?" The question throws me off a bit. I can see he's angry. His fists are clenched, his jaw is locked, the muscles in his neck are strained, and his eyes flash with molten silver. *Holy fuck, he looks unhinged.*

"I have no idea what you are talking about, Jaxon. Can we just get home? I'm tired, and this night has become tedious." I shiver from the cold air around us, regretting wearing this napkin-like dress and even coming tonight.

"Get in the fucking car, Stella., I'll be right back with a little reminder." He stalks off back into the restaurant, and I'm utterly confused about what is going on here. Has he lost his mind? What the hell is he even going on about now? The night I envisioned for us has gone down the toilet, and once again, I am left feeling less than. Why did I even try to make this night work? It's not like I need to seduce him for my plans to work.

Just as I'm getting into the limo and seriously contemplating demanding the driver leave without Jaxon, a pained shout sounds from the restaurant's entrance. I pop my head back out of the open doorway and watch as Jaxon roughly drags the waiter who served us by the hair and neck, kicking and screaming, towards the vehicle. Oh. My. Fucking. God.

"Jaxon, what the hell are you doing? Have you completely lost your mind?" I screech as I emerge from the vehicle.

A sinister grin crosses his face as his hand leaves the guy's throat, clenching into a fist and landing on the waiter's cheek in a hard crack. He pulls back once again and swings, this time landing on the guy's nose with a crunch, and I watch horrified as blood gushes down his face. The guy is trying to pull away with frightened eyes, but Jaxon's hold on his hair has him falling to his knees on the sidewalk. Jaxon starts kicking his abdomen and back. He's lost complete control, he looks insane and unhinged right now, hitting the waiter over and over.

"Jaxon! STOP!" I beg and try to pull his grip away from the guy's hair, but he shoves me, and I'm forced to step back or fall in the stupid shoes I'm wearing.

"You thought you were so slick touching my wife and dropping your phone number in her lap." *Crack.* "You thought I didn't notice." *Crack.* "I saw when you touched her arm, motherfucker." *Crack.* "NO ONE TOUCHES WHAT'S MINE!" *Crack.*

"Jesus! Jaxon, stop, you're going to kill him! Please stop!" I beg, my voice raised and filled with terror.

The guy can barely open either of his eyes, he's groaning in pain, and I'm pretty sure a couple of his teeth have popped out. Yet Jaxon refuses to release his hold on the man's hair. The waiter weakly tries to use his arm and hand to push Jaxon back and away from him. In a moment so quick I'm not even sure I'm seeing it correctly, Jaxon releases his hold on the man's hair, grabs his hand, and snaps it back until the horrific and sickening sound of bones breaking fills the air. A high-pitched screech sounds loudly, and I think I'm going to be sick, my dinner lurching up towards my throat.

"She is mine, fucker. *MINE!* I don't share and you touched her. You tried to take her from me!"

I wrap my arms tightly around my waist to hold myself up from falling to my knees and purging everything I ate tonight, just as Jaxon yanks back on the waiter's arm, and I hear the bone snap, breaking his arm and most likely dislocating his shoulder. I can't hold the bile back any longer, turning to the side and vomiting everything I had for dinner on the sidewalk.

Sirens can be heard coming towards us, and our poor driver, Auggie, tries to usher me back into the limo without ever touching me. "Mrs. Stratford, we have to go. Please get inside." Then I watch as he shouts something at Jaxon and finally breaks through to him. I can't hear the words; it feels like a million bees are currently residing in my head. How could this have happened? Is he insane?

Jaxon drops the waiter to the ground and gives him one final kick, spitting on him before moving into the open door of the limo. We're in motion before the door is even closed firmly. I move as far away from him as I can inside the confines of the limo, fear skating down my spine and my heart racing in my chest. Jaxon's breathing hard, his outfit splattered in the guy's blood. His knuckles are split open and covered in blood, and his chest rises and falls in dramatic exhales while he grinds his jaw over and over.

The only thought running nonstop through my mind is that I've married a deranged, violent psychopath. His eyes meet mine, and I witness no shame or regret in their depths. He stares at me with fury across his handsome features, and dread fills my body. My mind is screaming for us to get away from him, to run as far as we can. *He is fucking dangerous!*

"Let that be a reminder to you, Stella. You are fucking mine, and anyone who tries to take you will meet with the same fate, if not worse."

We don't utter another word to each other all the way home. I slip the heels from my feet and abandon them inside the limo. The minute we pull up to the front porch, I'm dashing up the two steps, and pushing through the front door. I pass a shocked Mrs. Pox, but I don't stop to acknowledge her. I take the stairs two at a time and run for my room as if the hounds of hell are chasing me. Once I'm behind the locked door of the master bedroom, I let my body slide down the wall until I'm sitting on the plush area rug, and tears are pouring down my face.

He's insane. He could have killed that man, and for what? Flirting with me, trying to give me his number. The horror of the situation fills me. Jaxon Stratford is violent and unhinged. I've left one violent man only to be placed with another.

How am I going to get out of this mess? How am I going to protect myself from him and build a world for myself that will never have me cowering like I am right now?

Jaxon

"Jealousy, that dragon which slays love under the pretense of keeping it alive." Havelock Ellis

MY POWER-HUNGRY WIFE HAS been avoiding me for over a week since the restaurant incident. She rises and leaves before I do in the mornings. My naughty staff have been running interference between us, so I never know when she is home. I'm sure, at her request, *the traitors.*

She has taken to locking the master suite's door firmly at night, and unless I want to cause a spectacle of myself and break it down, there is no breaching it. Last weekend, the little viper disappeared to Portland to check on one of Penticton Industries' holdings and didn't even bother to tell me. I only found out that she had left the goddamn state from her assistant. *The smug bastard enjoyed my ire and surprise just a bit too much, if you ask me.* I think I might need to break a few of his bones to make him understand that Stella is not the only one he should fear.

My behavior was a bit unhinged at the restaurant; I will admit that to no one but myself. I lost complete control of myself in that situation after watching that stupid fuck try to seduce her while I sat a mere foot or two away, talking to that asshole that didn't even bother to greet her. I'm not usually such a jealous man, after all, I'm guilty of sleeping with other men's wives.

Something about the way that fucker was even looking at her had rage boiling inside of me. When I noticed out of the corner of my eye his finger trailing over her soft skin, skin that fucking belongs to me, I almost lunged at him. Then, when he dropped the paper into her lap, thinking he was being discreet and sly, I watched her shocked expression. I wanted to plunge the steak knife on the table into his throat and watch the blood pour out of him. I don't know what she said to him, but whatever it was had him stepping back and acting right for the rest of the dinner. The damage was done, though. I couldn't get the red haze to leave my vision. I needed him to pay for touching and daring to try to take what was mine.

Her response in the limo and then at the house to run from me like I was the devil incarnate hurt my pride a bit. I wanted her to see me as an avenging knight—a husband defending her honor and his territory. My words were harsh and unrestrained, and I know that I frightened her. *Shit*, I frightened myself, if I'm being honest.

Auggie, our driver, did some follow-up and let me know what happened to the fucker. I put that guy in the hospital with a broken nose, dislocated jaw, broken wrist, and arm. The fucker, for sure, isn't going to be so handsome going forward or chasing after any more pretty wives. I would be worried about a lawsuit coming my way, but my contacts on the dark and shady side of the business have it handled for me.

Now Stella is running fucking scared both from my unhinged behavior and from this mutual attraction we share. She's playing a perilous game with me and my patience. *One that I'm determined to win at all costs.* Stella Stratford had better finally recognize that I own every part of her. I want her to bend for me while I drive my hard cock into her cunt until she begs me for mercy. *Even then, I have no intention of granting it. She is fucking mine.*

I drive up my driveway, having left the office early due to my lack of concentration and rising frustration, all stemming from this situation with Stella. *Why does she have to be so fucking stubborn?* Right now, we could be enjoying our honeymoon somewhere tropical, and I could be face-deep in her pussy. Instead, I'm here filled with anger, longing, and sexual frustration, which my own palm doesn't seem to alleviate.

As I reach the end of my driveway, I notice a familiar car parked in front of my front door. What the hell is Ajax doing at my house in the middle of the day? I quickly park the car and enter the house through the garage. For some reason, I cannot explain, my mind urges me to be silent in my steps. A feeling of unease skates down my back as I enter the mostly silent home. I can hear very muted voices coming from the direction of the den. Looking around, I don't see any of the household staff as I move down the corridor. *Where the fuck are they?*

I make my way to the door of the den, which is partially ajar. I can see through the crack that Ajax is standing before my wife, his hands placed on her upper arms, and she doesn't seem to be trying to move away from him. A red mist of indignation fills my body, my heart pounds in my chest, and I have to clench my hands tightly. The desire to punch Ajax first and ask questions later enters my mind. *Fuck it, I will rip both his fucking arms off and beat him with them, then ask questions.*

"Stella, be reasonable. You have gotten what you needed out of this arrangement. You now have the controlling shares in Penticton Industries, and you will walk away with half of Jaxon's fortune when you leave." Ajax's voice is filled with the telltale sounds of frustration. I can only see his back from the angle I'm standing in. His back is taut in his navy-blue dress shirt, his shoulders rigid and filled with irritation as he holds on to *my* fucking wife. I'm going to take pleasure in breaking every one of his fingers before I dislocate his fucking jaw. He shouldn't be touching what is mine, and she shouldn't be allowing it. I warned her beforehand about men touching her. *Did she learn nothing from the restaurant?*

"Ajax, please." My wife's voice sounds small and restrained in the room filled with emotion. *What the fuck is she begging him for?* I force myself to remain where I am rather than storming the room and breaking my best friend's face, and wrapping my fingers around my little ice queen's throat. The desire to hurt her, too, fills my veins. *Is she being deceitful with me? Trying to play me for a fucking fool?*

Was this all a game to get the shares back? How could that be, though? I was the one who forced her into this marriage, didn't I? Thoughts are a rapid tornado in my mind, throwing out possible scenarios and clashing against what I think I know as reality. *One thing is for sure, these two fuckers will suffer if they think they can fuck with me.*

"Please, what Stella! He doesn't love you! He will never love you like I do. You are a game piece to him. A fucking prize to be won. He will never desire and love you as I have for all these years." Ajax leans his forehead against my wife's, and I watch as she closes her eyes. *She closes her eyes, fuck!* My stomach clenches tightly at the image before me. The image of two despondent lovers. *How can this be? How did I fucking miss this? What the ever-loving fuck is happening here behind my back?* Has my best friend been cuckolding me behind my back this whole time?

"I am his wife." Her voice sounds small as she grasps onto Ajax's arms, preventing him from pulling her further into his embrace. The anguish on her face has my breath trapping in my throat. *Does she have feelings for him?*

My stomach feels like a boulder is sitting inside it. I can hear my blood rushing in my ears, the sound loud and causing nausea to rise. I've walked into a fucking nightmare, one where my wife, the woman I crave above all else right now, might be in love with my best friend. The fucker that has been my very best friend since my childhood, playing me for a fucking moron. Both of them, lying to me, probably laughing at my obliviousness at what is happening right under my nose, in my own damn house.

"You were mine before you were his. I was your first Stella. It's me that has claimed you. It's me that has always wanted you." Her face tips up to his, and I see the emotion in her eyes, no longer filled with arctic fire but with tears. Ones that trickle down the side of her delicate face like shimmering diamonds. *Fuck, no!*

"Have you fucked him, Stella, or is it still only my dick that has been inside of that pretty pussy of yours?" The emotion and dread in Ajax's voice have my hands clenching and unclenching at my side. *How fucking dare he ask her that! Her cunt is fucking MINE!* Every part of Stella Stratford is mine, and my fist is going to make sure that Ajax is made very aware of that.

She pulls out of his embrace and takes a step away from him, wiping the glistening tears from her face with the palm of her delicate hand. Tears that are for another man other than her husband. Tears for a man who has already had the treasure that I seek. My traitorous best friend, the one who I've always trusted, had her first and never mentioned a word of it. A man I'm going to enjoy breaking every bone in his miserable body before I end his life and leave him in an unmarked grave. *Fucking cunt.*

He loved her first, my mind whispers. *I don't fucking care! She is fucking mine!* His cock has been inside something that is mine and defiled it. *When?* When were they together? Before the wedding? Have they been fucking each other since the day we exchanged vows? Is this why she won't let me near her? So many questions are stampeding through my mind at once. Rage, violent rage, is flowing through my veins.

His pleas to walk away from her before our wedding, then his fury at my proceeding with it, now makes sense. It wasn't just that he had some high school infatuation for her. It wasn't that he had fancied himself in love with her all these years, and she was resistant to him or any other male's attention. He had her first. She had already given him her virginity. Who knows how long they were together behind everyone's back? I feel like an imbecile. How did I not see what was going on here? Bile races up the back of my throat, and I have to force myself to swallow it down.

She was forced to marry me at her father's demand. She didn't want to proceed with the wedding, even daring to wear a black gown to her wedding in protest. Did Thomas know that she was in love with Ajax? Would he have forced her into a marriage with me even if he did know? *Yes*, my mind replies. I was the better catch, the Stratford name more powerful than that of Ajax Pickering.

Sweat breaks out along the back of my neck as I watch Ajax reach for her again, and she takes another step away from him, putting distance between their bodies. I release a harsh breath of relief at watching her putting much-needed space between them. *I may not have to kill both of them after all.*

"It is irrelevant whether he has or hasn't. Jaxon is my husband now; I am his wife. Don't touch me again, Ajax. This has to stop." She takes another step backward. "You can't keep trying to see me and convince me that I should leave him. We ended months ago; you need to move past this. You can't keep trying to pull me into your arms, I don't belong there, and it's wrong. I won't cheat on Jaxon with you or anyone else. You are his closest friend; he would be crushed to know you are trying to take his wife." Her hands clench at her side, her shoulders straightening to her formal posture. The one she uses to put distance between herself and everyone else. She is closing herself off from him, just like she does with me and anyone else she interacts with.

"You are wrong, Stella! The fact that you haven't allowed him into your body speaks volumes about how you feel. You know he doesn't love you, and never will." Ajax paces back and forth as Stella watches with a blank expression. Desperation is etched across his features, and his eyes keep returning to my wife, pleading with her. "He will always belong to Kalista or some other woman. He'll never be faithful to only you. He is incapable of monogamy, and once you bear his children, he will discard you."

Ajax's words are daggers penetrating my skin and hitting their intended targets. *Is he right?* Is that why Stella has kept me at arm's length despite the heated passion towards each other that we both feel? *Does she wish I was Ajax?* Just the thought makes wrath and desperation fill my body. Desperation to hear her deny that she doesn't want me. I want her to tell that fuck face she is mine in all ways, not just as my named wife. *Every part of her is mine.*

As for his comment about Kalista, is he right? I did bring the woman here on my fucking wedding day. *Will I never be faithful to Stella? Will I grow tired of her and her games?* I want to deny his accusation. I want to run in there and punch him in the throat for putting those thoughts into her head. However, I can't, he may be right. I don't love Stella. I'm not sure I have ever loved a woman, but I know the closest I ever got was with Kalista.

Would I discard Stella after she had my children? Didn't I have the very same thought on my wedding day? Didn't I plan to go on with my life separate from hers once she provided me with an heir? *That was when you thought she was frigid and harsh.* My mind reminds me, and nothing could be further from the truth where Stella is concerned.

She is neither frigid nor cold in the bedroom. In fact, she is the polar opposite and the hottest, most sexually satisfying woman I have ever been with. She makes me crazy with thoughts of her day and night. I can feel the ghost of her soft skin against mine. Her smell and taste are my constant companions, driving me insane to have another hit of her. I'm now a willing addict of Stella Stratford's, and there is no way I want to be cured of the addiction.

Can I let her go? If she wanted to be with Ajax, could I release her from this marriage? *NO! She is mine!* She is a Stratford now, my wife, and regardless of her feelings towards Ajax, I will never release her from this arrangement. My body will lie cold in the ground before I free Stella from my grasp.

Just as I'm about to crash into the room to knock my best friend out and fuck my wife into the rug in front of him, I see a dark shape in the window directly behind her. The glint of metal reflects off the sunlight, and my heart races into my throat as

I run into the room without thinking. I manage to get in front of her and pull her body behind mine just as the shot shatters the glass and hits me in the chest instead of her back. The air whooshes out of my chest, and a harsh grunt leaves my lips.

There's a fire burning in my chest and loud sounds all around me, but they somehow seem muted, like I'm underwater. I stare down at the red blossoming across my white dress shirt, making a macabre abstract print. Hands grab at me, pulling me forward. Somehow I end up in one of the chairs, and I can finally focus my eyes on my wife and the noise in the room.

She's shouting at someone around us, and tears are sliding down her beautiful face. She has blood splattered on her chin, and her fingers are pressing a pillow hard into my chest. "Jaxon, oh my god! Please speak to me!" She demands in a high-pitched voice. Her beautiful arctic blue eyes, ones that I have grown to desire and look forward to seeing, are so wide on her face. Is the expression on her face only fear, or is there a tinge of regret? Even in her panicked state, she is the most beautiful woman I have ever seen, and knowing that she is mine, fills me with lingering satisfaction.

"The ambulance is on its way, and so are the police. The shooter is gone!" I can hear Ajax's panicked voice around me, but he's out of my sightline. *Thank fuck! I still owe the bastard a punch to the throat for touching my wife.* However, the pain in my chest and my ragged breathing suggest that it will have to wait.

"She... is... mine!" I pant the words through the searing pain ripping through my chest. I watch as Stella's eyes meet mine, a look of shock across her features. She pulls back from me like I have hit her. *Good, now she realizes that I heard them, that I know.* There shall be no more secrets between her and me. I raise my trembling hand, reaching for her beautiful face and cradling her chin.

A sharp pain rumbles through my chest, and I drop my hold on her. A ragged breath leaves my lips, and it feels like spittle is dripping down my lips and chin. Stella's panicked eyes zero in on it, and whatever she sees there must be bad, a tear trickles out of her eye, followed by another one, and they cascade down her beautiful face.

"Jaxon, we need to stop the bleeding. You need to stay conscious. Stay with me!" She begs, her voice shaking and her hand trembling as she reaches for my face, cradling my cheek in her palm. The feeling of her skin on mine brings me a sense of peace I have never felt before. She calms the racing thoughts inside my head. *I need her.* The thought races in my mind.

"Don't... worry... Stella, I... refuse... to free you... and make you... a widow. You... are mine... for all... eternity." The words leave my lips in a slur as I try to focus on her beautiful features. Ones filled with worry for me and not Ajax. The look of pure anguish on her face is the last thing I see before darkness takes me.

23

Stella

"Regret doesn't remind us that we did badly. It reminds us that we know we can do better." Kathryn Schulz

"**D**ON'T WORRY, STELLA, I refuse to free you and make you a widow. You are mine for all eternity." His words run on a vicious cycle in my mind as I pace back and forth in the corridor of the hospital outside of the surgical wing, awaiting information on Jaxon's condition. *Jesus fucking Christ, why has there been no news yet!*

He was rushed by an emergency helicopter to the private hospital favored by the wealthiest patrons of Manhattan and straight into surgery. The fear that the bullet may have hit an artery and he is bleeding out internally is of the utmost urgent concern.

I have never been so frightened as I was holding that pillow to his chest and trying to stop his blood from seeping out of him. Then he uttered those words, "She is mine!" like some commanding force, and my heart clenched in my chest. In that moment, I wanted to reassure him that I was, but the words would not leave my lips. I couldn't utter falsities as my last spoken words to him in case they were the last thing I ever got to say to him.

He had heard Ajax's and my conversation. Shame filled me at that moment, and I felt like the worst traitor for even allowing Ajax to enter our home. How long was he there before he ran into the room and put himself in front of me, taking a bullet for the woman who was listening to another man trying to convince her to leave him? *Why did he even risk himself after hearing Ajax's words?*

"She is mine!" Once again, his voice echoes in my mind, and I can't stop the tears from cascading down my face or the trembling in my hands. My limbs feel weak, and my stomach is filled with wretched acid and the knowledge that Jaxon now knows I slept with his best friend. Regardless if it was a year ago, it was still something that I should have told him, not let him find out in that horrific way. Then he took a bullet for me, after everything he must have been feeling.

He took a fucking bullet for me, the lunatic! I drag my hands down my face, unable to understand why he did it. My hands, which are still tinged in his red blood, despite wiping them. The knowledge that someone was trying to kill me is not even of the slightest importance when balanced against the actions of my possessive husband. My husband, the one I have been avoiding and running from. The one that terrified me a week ago and had me contemplating leaving him.

I watch as Ajax once again tries to approach me. His hands held before him in a placating and soothing manner that indicates that he means no harm, his shoulders hunched in and fear across his features. Pure rage like I have never felt before fills me just by looking at him, just by his mere presence here in this corridor. Outside of where my husband is fighting for his life. How dare he try once again to confront me after Jaxon just took a bullet intended for me! How dare he even be here right now after betraying Jaxon and attempting to convince me to leave him!

My hand slams out before I can think clearly, connecting with his chiseled face. The sound is loud in the empty hallway as he stumbles back a step from my attack. *It's not enough. I need to hurt him like we hurt Jaxon!* I move forward and slap him again and then again. I'm unable to stop hitting him as my body and mind loses control to my rancor. "Stella, fucking STOP!" He shouts, using his arms to cover his face to prevent the blows I'm raining down on him from landing.

"You traitor, you despicable man!" *Smack.* "How dare you come here!" *Smack.* "How dare you come here after you tried to convince me to leave him!" *Smack.* Ajax grabs onto my arm and pulls me hard into his body, the air momentarily rushing out of my chest. I try to fight his tight embrace, pushing and shoving against his body. I raise my knee to try to hit him in the crotch, but he sidesteps me at the last moment, preventing the blow from landing.

"He took a bullet for me!" I scream. "He... took... a... bullet." I can't even get the words out. They devastate me, breaking my heart into fragile pieces, my lips tremble, and I press them together.

"I know Stella, I know." He tightens his grip and cradles me into his body. The smell of his cologne and the feel of his hard chest against mine causes the bile I was trying to suppress to race up the back of my throat.

"No! Fuck, no!" I push against him, and he loosens his hold, releasing me so that I can take steps away from him. My head is spinning, my chest is tight, and I feel like I'm having a panic attack. I can't stop the trembling that is taking over my whole body. My body sways back and forth as my legs turn to Jell-O. I try to take deep breaths but end up with my body doubled over and my hands on my knees, panting harshly as vomit races from my throat.

"Jesus, Stella." Ajax tries to approach me, but I lift my hand warding him off. I don't want him to touch me. I don't want to feel his skin on mine. Both of us are traitors for what we were doing. I am a *Judas* for allowing Ajax to even speak those words to me.

Once I have nothing left to spew up, I lean my head and shoulder against the cool white tiled wall, taking deep breaths to clear my head. "You need to leave, Ajax," the words come out raspy and on panting breaths. My stomach clenches painfully once again, threatening to bring me to the ground.

I turn my glare toward the offending figure before me. He's all light in direct contrast to Jaxon's darkness. The sunlight through the windows glints in his golden hair. His dark brown eyes are filled with emotion and pain. His lean, tall body is encased in the fine fabric of his dress shirt and pants with my bloody fingerprints as macabre splatters across it. Fingerprints that are coated in my husband's sacrificial blood.

Ajax has always been handsome, and his spirit was always peaceful to me. Never causing me distress or volatile emotions, unlike his best friend. It's why I gave him my virginity all those years ago and then kept seeing him quietly without my parents knowing, but that ended months before my father gave me away as a prized pig to Jaxon.

I couldn't find any joy with Ajax. Yes, he brought me peace, but I craved passion. Something was always lacking, and because of it, I forced myself to end it. Ajax never stopped pursuing me, never accepted it as our ending. Even now, he refuses to accept it while wearing Jaxon's blood.

Looking at him now, he no longer brings me peace, just torment that I was even in that room with him. I allowed him over the last week to appear at Penticton Industries and the estate, trying to convince me to leave Jaxon. Like there was ever going to be a possibility of that. Jaxon would have never let me out of our marriage. *"She is mine!"* His voice once again bellows in my mind causing sobs to leave my lips.

"Get out of here, Ajax. It's over! Whatever our past was, it's over. I am his wife. I will never fucking leave him!" The words spew from my mouth in a scream so high-pitched that it sounds ripped from a deranged animal. He takes a step back, his eyes wide and shock across his face. "I never want to see you again. Do you hear me! NEVER AGAIN!"

A noise from the end of the corridor catches my attention, and I raise my eyes to see Mrs. Pox and Fergus rushing toward me. Fergus reaches Ajax and pulls him away toward the elevators, and Mrs. Pox envelopes me in her arms. "It's going to be alright now, dear." Her voice is soothing and commanding, and I burrow into her warm embrace, hoping that her words are correct and that I haven't just caused my husband to go to his grave, thinking I betrayed him.

It's been eight hours since Jaxon was taken into surgery, and still no word from the doctors in the operating room. I lean my head against the back of the chair of the private waiting room I sit in. Mrs. Pox left thirty minutes ago to find us food, despite me indicating that I had no appetite and there was no way I could stomach anything. Nausea is still plaguing me, and my stomach is tied up in knots of apprehension.

My mother is somewhere in the hospital trying to procure tea for us. She came immediately once she heard of the shooting, my father absent from her side. No doubt he is sitting somewhere with a drink in his hand, hoping that Jaxon succumbs to his injury for siding with me against him. *The fucking selfish, bastard.*

Once again, the thought of who could have shot at me or sent someone to shoot me runs through my mind. The officers that questioned me earlier had no leads as of yet. Just that it appeared to be one shooter and that he wasn't an amateur as he left very little evidence and somehow knew how to get past the cameras on the estate.

Someone hired a man to shoot me. Could it have been my father? Perhaps one of the disgruntled board members that I had terminated in the last week? Was it Kalista Cain? I did ruin her fucking life and take Jaxon from her. So many new enemies at my door. *Great job, Stella, your first eleven days as Mrs. Jaxon Stratford, and you have ruined lives, been shot at, and almost become a widow. Great fucking start!*

"Darling, I couldn't find a proper tea latte, but this pitiful excuse for a tea was available. I will have Stanley deliver us proper tea shortly." My mother walks back into the room, holding two Styrofoam cups of steaming liquid. She looks so distressed and disheveled that it's almost comical. I don't think I have ever seen Rachel Penticton with a hair out of place, yet here she is, wrinkled, hair falling out of her chignon and makeup smeared. If the situation wasn't so dire and I didn't feel like my heart was being ripped apart with guilt, I would wrap my arms tightly around her.

"I am sure it is fine, mother." She hands me the cup, sits beside me, and reaches for my hand. My mother has never been overly affectionate, knowing that my father disapproved of that. Today it seems, far from Thomas Penticton's eyes, she has decided that she will be motherly. Emotions clog my throat at her act of soothing compassion. Right now, I need her unwavering strength to help keep me together. I know I have to be strong, I'm a Penticton, but I'm also a Stratford, and Jaxon would be disappointed to see me falling to pieces here. I have caused him enough pain. I refuse to add to that by being weak.

I clear my throat, holding the cup in my hand and meeting her distressed gaze. "Do you think it could have been father that sent someone to shoot me?" I hold my breath, awaiting her reply. Part of me honestly believes he would be more than capable of issuing an order like that to assuage his bruised pride over being ousted at Penticton Industries. The other part of me hopes with all my might that despite us never seeing eye to eye on anything, he wouldn't attempt to murder his only child.

"No, Stella, I don't. He is too desperate to continue the Penticton legacy, which would end if you died. He has no one else to pass on this curse of an empire to." She sighs and takes a sip of her tea, grimacing at the subpar taste.

I let out a relieved, deep breath at her words. If it wasn't my father, then who was it? Who would dare send a shooter to my home, to Jaxon's home, to attack me? Who would have even had the knowledge that I would be there?

"Stella, what was Ajax doing at the estate? Was he there with Jaxon? I saw him down in the entryway. He is beside himself with worry and covered in bloody fingerprints." My mother raises her beautiful eyes, ones that are identical to mine, and waits for my answer. *Well, shit.*

I shut my eyes and bite down hard on my lower lip. I don't want to ruin this mother-daughter moment we are having, but I also don't wish to mislead her into thinking that Ajax was there with Jaxon. "He was there to see me." My voice sounds small and guilty even to my own ears. I watch my mother's expression carefully. She raises a concerned eyebrow and takes another sip of the hot tea. "I see. It seems he has not managed to move past his infatuation for you, regardless of your marriage to his best friend."

The shock of her words must be evident on my face as hers fills with a devious smirk. Her features lighten, smoothing out the fine lines and appearing younger than her years with the expression. "You knew?"

A very unladylike snort leaves her full lips. "Of course, I knew. I have my little spies everywhere, and I am not oblivious to the comings and goings of my only child." A chuckle sounds in the air between us. "That man has been sniffing you out since you were fourteen years old. Even after he left high school, he would find a way to be in your company." She raises both of her eyebrows and narrows her eyes at me with a disapproving expression. "Honestly, dear, give your mother some credit. If I believed for one second that you were not interested in his attention, he would have been floating in the Hudson River."

I open my mouth, but no words leave my lips. Who is this woman before me? She is so different from the meek and frail woman I see when my father is around. One that I can't stand as she cowers in his presence and caters to his unreasonable demands.

"All this time, you knew I was sneaking around with Ajax behind dad's and your back?" I don't even know what to think. Perhaps we weren't as discrete as we thought we were. "Does father know?"

"That you two were sleeping together, and his precious princess was compromised? Of course not! Ajax petitioned your father for your hand when this whole mess with looking for a family to tie ourselves to started, but your father immediately denied him. His family is not wealthy or strong enough to further the Penticton lineage."

Lord, how many things are going to be revealed to me today? I sit dumbfounded at her words. I never knew that Ajax had attempted to get my father's agreement to marry me. Would I have said yes, had he asked me? The answer immediately arises within me and not just because of my current outrage with him. *I would have never married him, not willingly.* He never saw me as anything but an object to cherish. There is no way Ajax Pickering would have enabled me or supported me to run Penticton Industries as Jaxon has.

He also wouldn't have brought another woman home on your wedding night, my mind reminds me, regardless of what Jaxon did to me that first night. I know that Ajax, despite believing that he loves me, wants a wife like his own mother—one who is dutiful and remains at home raising babies. Just the thought of that life forced on me raises my hackles and makes me want to run screaming.

"Jesus, mother. I feel like a complete fool. You knew all this time." I release my hold of her hand and stand, pacing before her as she watches me with rapt attention.

"You are not a fool, Stella. You do not understand the inner workings of this life. Especially for wealthy, privileged women like us, but you will have to learn quickly, daughter." She releases a deep, tired breath, one that I feel in my own soul. "Someone meant you harm. You have power now, Stella. You are one of the wealthiest and most powerful women in the world. You married a man other women covet. That comes with various threats."

She stands up, places the tea next to her on the side table, and reaches for mine, placing it next to hers. Then she pulls me into her embrace and squeezes me tight. "I could have lost you today, Stella—my only child. I beg of you, daughter, show some restraint moving through this powerful world. You are making waves when you should be making ripples."

24

Jaxon

"Our deepest fear is that we are powerful beyond measure. It is our light, not our darkness, that most frightens us." Marianne Williamson, A Return to Love

I'M SWIMMING IN WHAT feels like deep molasses. I can barely move my limbs; they feel so heavy and weighed down. I struggle to open my eyes, but they feel glued shut and, like a ten-ton truck is holding them closed. There's a searing pain in my chest at each forced breath entering my lungs. I'm not even sure if I am actually breathing on my own anymore. Muted noises surround me, but I can't make any of them out clearly. *Where am I?*

Rapid images flash before my eyes in technicolor, causing my body to lock up tight at their dizzying speed and ferocity. The first image to assault me is of me arguing with Stella through our closed door last night, where I raged against it to no avail, and she refused to open it to me. I felt fury and defeat as I walked away.

The image changes quickly to me driving angrily back to my estate because I couldn't keep my wandering mind or unfortunate hard dick from thinking about my little ice queen. The desire to strangle her while my cock choked off her airway was all I could think about.

The image flips once again, causing my stomach to lurch, this time to Stella in the den with Ajax. Her tears and the devastated emotions across her beautiful face as he declared his love for her and urged her to leave me. *My fucking best friend is a traitor.* I should have strangled him at that very moment. Instead, I stood there like an idiot, allowing his words to reach Stella's ears. Words urging her to leave me, to be with him, to take my most valuable possession from me. I have allowed myself to become weak over that woman when I should have been strong.

At that thought, I can hear loud beeping happening around me through the deep fog I'm currently anchored in. "His blood pressure is rising! He's going into cardiac distress!" *Who the fuck are they talking about? Who's going into cardiac distress?* The pain in my chest feels like it is exploding into the rest of my limbs. My head is swimming, and the darkness is once again calling me. I want to scream for Stella. To demand her presence before me, but my body refuses to obey and traps me once again in the utter void of nothingness.

"Will he eventually wake up?" The voice sounds small and hesitant, making my body want to wrap around it and bring it comfort. To protect it with all of my strength and being. The sound calls to me from the darkness I'm residing in. I try to wade through the thick void that is keeping me trapped, but I'm losing the war against it. The urge to fight rises but is immediately drowned out, as if my body has no energy and I am completely spent. *What is happening to me?*

Once again, images accost me at rapid speed, blinding lights making me shudder from the racing streams in my mind. This time, the image that greets me is of my father when he was still alive—the look of disappointment across his stern features at my constant rebellious antics.

"You need to grow up, Jaxon, and behave like a Stratford and a titan of industry, not some spoiled playboy plowing through all of the spread legs available to you. You need to prove to me that you are worthy of the Stratford legacy!" He downs the scotch in his hand, dismissing me like he always does. He can't bear to be in the same room with me for long. I'm such a miserable failure of a son. Such a disappointment to the Stratford name, a fact that he never hesitates to point out. The weight of that sentiment and knowledge crushes me until I'm struggling to breathe. Alone, I am always alone.

The image switches, and now it's of a small dark-haired boy dressed in a black suit, holding fiercely to an older woman's hand before an ebony casket, laid with red roses cascading down its sides. The smell of the roses permeates through the air around them until it's an almost suffocating smell.

"Don't coddle him, Mrs. Pox. He needs to learn that death is a part of life. Pain and suffering will make him stronger." My father's harsh voice causes the boy to flinch and cower, hiding his face in the woman's abdomen.

"Sir, he just lost his beloved mother." Mrs. Pox's grip tightens on the boy's hand, and she shifts more of her body in front of him to block my father.

"Yes, well, I lost my wife. You don't see me here sobbing, do you?"

"Doctor! Doctor! FUCK! Someone help!" I can hear the shrill sound of a female shouting through the darkness, stopping the images of my father from running through my mind and bringing me nothing but pain. My chest feels so tight, like a balloon someone keeps blowing into that is ready to pop. Once again, my limbs feel weighed down, and the pain that I was feeling in my chest increases until I can't think or feel anything else.

"Dammit, he's having another heart attack! Mrs. Stratford, you need to get out of the way!" A male voice is yelling.

Who the fuck is he yelling at like that? Is he yelling at my Stella like that? I will get up from this darkness and beat his fucking ass. No one talks to my Stella like that. She's a goddamn Stratford. In just a moment when I can catch my breath and open my eyes, I am going to break the jaw of whoever this fucker is, talking to my wife like that.

"Stella, you can't remain here like this. It's been a week, and he hasn't woken up. The doctor is not even sure that he will, in fact, wake up." The soft feminine voice sounds distressed at the words she is uttering. She is speaking to my wife, and I can hear her through the nothingness that I am residing in—the void that keeps me trapped with constant memories and harsh truths.

I have heard Stella at my side begging me to wake. Then, losing her temper and demanding that I come back to her. My awareness of time is nonexistent. *Has it really already been a week that I've been trapped in this hell? That can't be correct, can it?* Even though I would like nothing more than to open my eyes and pull her defiant, stubborn ass into my arms. Something is keeping me a trapped prisoner here. Perhaps it's my fear that she will readily leave me when I wake. Will she leave me for Ajax? Does she love him? A sharp burning pain accosts my chest at just the thought.

"He will wake and come back to me. He will not leave me here alone, I know it." I can hear her precious defiance in the tone of her voice. Stella Stratford will walk into hell and fight the devil to get what she wants. My wife has strength and a will that will not be defied, even by me. Her angry tone calls to my soul, insisting I return to her. The urge to go to her is so strong that I feel myself pulling against the barrier, keeping me a prisoner here and away from her.

"Stella, perhaps it's best if he doesn't. We have no way of knowing in what condition his mind will be in once he awakens. He's had three heart attacks and been in a coma for a week, daughter. You may end up with an invalid on your hands." The voice reasoning with my wife sounds miserable but resolute at the prospect.

Have I really had three heart attacks? Holy fuck! Am I in a coma? Is that why I can't seem to rise from this miserable darkness but can hear every word spoken? The one that has me trapped with my past and my demons? The one trying its hardest to break me.

Will I be a burden to Stella instead of the formidable man at her side? The one determined to rule an empire and create a lasting legacy that causes fear in the hearts of our enemies. Will I never get a true taste of my stunningly, wicked wife? Never have the chance to bury my cock deep inside of her and produce a spawn that is half her and half me. A new line of Stratford's to rule this world? Who will protect Stella from the threats coming at her from every direction?

"Jaxon Stratford is not weak nor a coward. He will not leave me here alone to face the Stratford & Penticton empires without him. He will return to me, or I will go into fucking hell and pull him back from the devil's hands. He is mine, and I refuse to lose him now."

Her words cause heat and fire to lick up my body. The desire to see those arctic eyes filled with fury fills me up. She wants me by her side to rule our empire. She is demanding my return to her and the living world. *Who am I to deny my ice queen?*

I fight harder against the nothingness, knowing that I must return to her, and when I do, she will submit to me in all ways. *Mine for all eternity.* I will never let her go, and if she tries to leave me, we will both end up in hell together.

25

Stella

"Hope... is the companion of power, and the mother of success; for who so hopes has within him the gift of miracles." Samuel Smiles

I'M FILLED WITH A restless energy and an anguished heart that I do not understand. It's been over a week since Jaxon was shot in the chest, missing his heart by mere millimeters. A shot that he received in order to save my life. I had to watch helplessly, an emotion I don't particularly fucking enjoy, as my husband of almost two weeks suffered three heart attacks in my presence. Ones that, by all accounts, should have ended his life. Yet he persisted and fought to stay alive. He is a warrior, and no one can keep him down, not even death with its clawing hands. *Come back to me, Jaxon.*

My eyes once again return to his pale face, his normally golden skin has an ashen tinge to it now. My eyes linger on the long white tube that is affixed to his mouth. He looks broken and weak before me. The total opposite of his cocky, frustrating, and determined self. I watch with trepidation as his chest rises and falls with the machine's forced breaths.

Is my mother right? Will he never wake up, or if he does, will he be an invalid? How will I cope with that on top of everything else? Do I want to be trapped with a man who can't take care of himself? *In sickness and in health... remember you made that promise when you married him*, my mind whispers. I let out a harsh breath that feels like it's strangling me, and my hand shakes in my lap. I can't fall apart, not now. He needs me to be strong for him.

No, fuck that! I refuse to believe that Jaxon Stratford, the man who forced me down an aisle to grow his empire, would be reduced to such a pitiful existence. Not even the devil can keep Jaxon Stratford against his will. He will cheat death each and every time. *"You are mine,"* His words once again vibrate through my mind. He will come for me, his prize, his possession. I have to remain strong; I have to fight for him, just like he fought for me.

What if he ends up with a broken mind, unable to think and function clearly? What if he is incapacitated of body, then what? Are you prepared to take on a man who will depend on you for everything? What about your plans? My mind questions. The thoughts race through my mind, but I keep returning to the same thought. I will do what I must to ensure that both our empires grow and survive. I will not allow anyone to take that away from us, not even Jaxon Stratford himself. He will still be my husband, no matter what. I will ensure he lives out his days with me at his side. He risked his life for me, and that is a debt that I will pay until my very last breath leaves my body.

I stare at my mother, sitting in the chair against the wall in rumpled elegance. The woman has refused to leave other than to bathe and change daily. She has been by my side here, holding vigil for Jaxon ever since he was shot. Even going as far as to disobey my father and incurring his malignant wrath when he demanded her presence back at the Penticton estate. Her beautiful hair shines in the natural light from the window, her complexion pale and drawn, and her beautiful eyes filled with pain, no doubt at the situation I find myself in.

I never realized the strength and determination that my mother hid behind her frailty. She is someone to admire and learn from. How to be both fragile and strong at the same time, without having to sacrifice one for the other. I wish I had more of her inside of me, that I wasn't filled with this urgency to be successful, to prove others wrong about me. To show them that I am so much more than just a spoiled, rich woman. Who knows, I might have already found peace and happiness if I had been more like her.

A flutter of motion catches the corner of my eye. For a moment, I'm convinced that my tired eyes are seeing things. I drag my hands over my exhausted face, my back and shoulder aching with the stress of dealing with this situation and not knowing what will happen next. I have barely slept in the cot the hospital provided next to Jaxon's hospital bed. Unable to rest easy while my husband fights for his life in the same room.

It's not only the stress of Jaxon being in a goddamn coma that has anxiety rising inside of me and threatening to have me screaming like a lunatic. The amount of paperwork Tyson has been bringing me daily from Penticton Industries and Stratford Industries is overwhelming. *How am I going to run both of those companies alone?* The thought once again presses harshly down on me. *You wanted this; you wanted to be the head of an empire.* The thought slithers through my mind with malcontent. I know, but fuck I didn't think it would be this difficult, this all-consuming. The desire for power seems lackluster in light of Jaxon lying in a coma next to me.

My eyes focus back on Jaxon, his body covered by the stark white sheet and blanket on the bed. The golden skin of his arms are a high contrast against the crisp material. His tattoo is just peeking over the sheet; the Stratford crest imprinted on his skin. As I watch him with a pang of regret in my chest, his right arm twitches, lifts a bit off the bed, his hand clenching into a fist, and then lands on his thigh. *What the fuck?* I watch as once again the limb lifts, this time higher, his hand unclenching and fingers reaching out as if grasping for something or someone. I rush to his side and grab onto his fingers with my own, clutching his hand tight and squeezing it. Hope soars through my body like a blazing light, banishing the shadows that have been oppressive weights on my shoulders. *He is fighting to come back to me.*

"Come back to me, Jaxon." I lean forward and whisper to the side of his face, laying my lips on his clammy skin. His fingers clench mine tightly at my words and have me pulling back. I watch with excitement as his eyes flutter rapidly before opening a crack. "*Holy Shit!* Mother, go get the doctor; he's waking up!" My voice leaves my lips in a high-pitched noise. My heart is pounding like a drum in my chest. *Is he finally waking up?*

"Jaxon, can you hear me?" I move my body across his. His grip tightens once again on my fingers as he starts to struggle, trying to release my hold on his fingers. His other hand reaches toward the tube in his mouth that is helping him to breathe. He moves to try to dislodge the tube, and panic seizes me as I press my hand down on his, preventing him from tearing the tube from his lips.

"Don't, Jaxon, it's helping you breathe! Come back to me, Jaxon!" I beg as tears race down my face. A surge of relief floods me, almost causing my trembling limbs to give out before me. *Get your shit together, Stella. You are a fucking Stratford now.*

You cannot behave like some weak-minded female. My mind chastises me rudely for my overly emotional response to Jaxon's awakening.

"Step aside, Mrs. Stratford." The rude fucking doctor that is about to get my fist in his face demands, pushing me aside roughly and dislodging Jaxon's hold on my fingers. This motherfucker is going to get a rude awakening, treating me as he has for the last couple of days. I have bitten my tongue over and over because he is one of the best heart surgeons in the country, but I'm at the end of my patience. He's about to discover why they call me an ice queen and a viper.

"Mr. Stratford, I need you to remain calm. You have a breathing tube installed in your mouth. We need to remove it and check your vitals. Please stop trying to dislodge it." I watch as he roughly swats Jaxon's hand away from his face, and my blood pressure rises. I move without thought and grab the back of his neck, digging my nails into the skin and causing a high-pitched cry to leave Dr. Bernard's mouth.

"You will treat my husband with respect and humility motherfucker, or I will ensure the only place you are practicing medicine is at a fucking third-world zoo." I tighten my grip as he stiffens at my threat. "Do we understand each other?"

"Yes."

"Yes, what?" I demand, my fury getting the best of me and my emotions riding me.

"Yes, Mrs. Stratford... ma'am." The words leave his lips on a trembling breath. I watch as he bites down on his lower lip, trying to stop it from quivering. His eyes are prominent in his ruddy, blotchy face, fear is clearly present on his features. The way he is cowering before me fills me with instant satisfaction and glee. *Maybe I am a psychopath, after all.*

"I am so glad we understand each other." I release my hold and step back, moving to Jaxon's other side as he stares up at me with frightened slate eyes. "You are alright now, Jaxon. I'm here with you." I grasp onto his fingers and squeeze, trying to calm my own erratic heartbeat and breathing.

The doctor clears his throat and brings his attention back to Jaxon. "Mr. Stratford... sir...we... I am going to remove the tube now." He gently pulls the tube from Jaxon's mouth as gagging noises fill the room.

Jaxon takes a few harsh breaths, the sound loud and raspy. I tighten my hold on his fingers, knowing I'm almost crushing them in my tight grasp. His eyes never leave mine, despite glassing over and a tear trickling down the side of his face. I watch as he opens and closes his mouth, but no words escape his dried lips. I reach forward, wiping the tear with my thumb, my skin connecting with the thick dark stubble on his face—the one I long to press my lips against in relief.

"Mr. Stratford... sir, please do not try to speak yet. Your throat will be ragged and parched. We are going to commence some vital checks. Please, can I have your focus on me for the moment?" The doctor peeks at me from the corner of his eye. I guess my threat worked, and now the fucker is afraid. *Good, he should be, my threat is not idle. I will destroy him.*

Jaxon tears his gaze away from mine and peers up at the doctor, following his instructions to nod to the questions asked. I watch with a sense of relief as he understands the commands and questions that the doctor is uttering. His gaze returns to mine every few seconds as if he can't stop reassuring himself that I am here. His mind is working, at least on a fundamental level. The tightness in my chest lightens a bit, and I feel my mother place her hand in comfort at my back.

Once the doctor has completed his questioning and checks, he leaves the room, and I bring a straw with refreshing cold water to Jaxon's parched lips. "Drink slowly, Jaxon."

His eyes meet mine steadily as he sucks on the straw. *Fuck, I have never been envious of a damn straw before, but I am now.* The color is returning to his cheeks, and he's not looking so ashen as he was. He must have an inkling of my inappropriate thoughts because the fucker winks at me as he sucks harder on the straw. Mischief temporarily appearing in those gorgeous gray eyes of his. *There he is...* the thought brings a streak of joy to me.

"Stella..." His voice sounds strained and raspy, as if he had been screaming and lost it. He pushes the cup away with one hand while his other reaches up tentatively to my face. His cold fingers make contact with my cheek, and a rattled breath leaves his chest.

"Safe?" He questions, his eyebrow rising and his lips forming a stern line.

"They haven't found him. There is security outside of the room and around the hospital. I added additional security measures to the house to keep Mrs. Pox and the staff safe, just in case." I watch as he nods, his eyes flickering over my features. What does he see when he looks at me? Does he see a woman filled with ambition and regrets? Does he see a betrayer who repeatedly allowed Ajax to try to convince her to leave him? Who am I in Jaxon's eyes?

It's almost like he can sense the direction of my thoughts. His fingers reach up and touch my face, one cold finger tracing across my lips. His intense gaze meets mine, turbulent slate gray meeting arctic blue. My eyes are riveted to his sinful lips as he licks them. "Mine, Stella." The words leave his lips not in question but in a demand. A demand for submission, acknowledgment, and obedience. For a moment, my rebellious and independent spirit balks at the demand. I belong to myself; no one fucking owns me. *Are you sure about that?* My mind questions quietly.

Various sensations fill my body and creep into the shadowed areas of my heart and mind, *acceptance, need, and desire.* The need to be wanted and accepted the way Jaxon is demanding. The desire that his two softly spoken words accelerates inside of me, causing havoc with my very thoughts. He wants me despite hearing the traitorous words that left mine and Ajax's mouths.

My emotions give rise to new fears. I don't want to lose who I am to this need for Jaxon. I don't want to just be his wife, some woman behind the powerful man. Jaxon is strong, capable, and demanding. His mere presence is able to overshadow anyone. *Do I want that to happen to me?* The desire that is running through my veins for him, is it enough to give up my dreams to lead my own empire? Does he mean that much to me, or is it the guilt of him being shot that is causing these emotions to rise inside of me?

All these questions run rampant through my mind while Jaxon stares up at me with an emotion I can't read. Is it fear or hope that is crossing his expression? His fingers move towards the side of my face, cradling it in his cold embrace, and I welcome the chill they bring. His grip tightens slightly, and his eyebrows furrow. "Mine." He declares with more strength behind the word than I would think capable of a man who just awoke from a coma.

A part of me wants to deny him. Laugh off his demand as delusional, but as his word skates across my mind, a fierce look crosses his features. My core tightens painfully at the force and ownership of the word. *Yes, I am his, just as much as he is mine.* Will that cause both of us to destroy each other? Time will tell, I guess.

26

Jaxon

"Control your anger, before your anger starts controlling you"
Atef Ashab Uddin Sahil

*F*UCKING HELL, NOT AGAIN! I try to quietly shift about in the room before Mrs. Pox and the antichrist of a personal nurse my wife hired find me once again. I'm a goddamn powerful man, yet all the females in this house, *my fucking house*, treat me like a wayward naughty child.

Coddling me and forcing me to take medicine and eat foods that taste like a donkey's ass. They tell me when to rise, when to exercise, when to fucking nap. And even disturbingly, when it's bedtime, *shit*, I'm surprised none of them tuck me in and read me a bedtime story. Like I am not the master of this home. *Ha-ha; that's funny, you think you are still the master here!* My mind laughs like a deranged hyena at me. *I am, aren't I?*

It's been three weeks since I left the hospital. A whole month since I came out of a coma that, by the doctor's account, I should have never woken from. My demand to be released from the hospital fell on silent ears for the first couple of days. Then it was only granted by Stella and that fuck-face of a doctor, based on getting a personal nurse for round-the-clock care to help at home, like I'm some sort of invalid, too weak to even wipe my own ass. *Let's be fucking clear; I still wipe my own ass.*

I hope that damn doctor doesn't think I have forgotten the way he spoke to Stella while I was in my coma. I mean to go back there and beat his miserable ass for his harsh tone and disrespect. A Stratford never forgets an insult and always pays his due. Dr. Bernard better pray for the meager time he has left before I come after him.

A shadow crosses over the window, blocking the meager sunlight we are getting today. I watch as the new security guards, dressed in all-black tactical gear, patrol the perimeter of the Stratford estate. Also, something my lovely wife established without a word to me. We now have a small private army of armed guards protecting us at all hours. This place feels like a fucking prison and not a residence.

Stella neglected to inform me that the very painful and devastating bullet to my chest had not been the only incident of threatening behavior to her life. According to Fergus, who was persuaded to tell me with a few glasses of my most expensive scotch, someone left a dead headless chicken on my wife's desk at Penticton Industries three weeks ago. Then, most recently, someone tried to attack her in the massage room of the local spa. Luckily for her, the new security detail she hired was just outside the door. The assailant managed to escape, but the poor massage therapist ended up with a knife wound to her side instead of my wife.

Once again, the fear of who is after my wife fills me with anger, worry, and helplessness. How can I protect her from whoever is daring to come after her from the inside of my estate? Stella has made it almost impossible for me to leave, using my recovery as an excuse to keep me under lock and key.

The knowledge that my ice queen of a wife is very much my keeper right now grates on my damn nerves. How dare she treat me like I'm weak! She leaves the estate daily to head to either Penticton Industries or to Stratford Industries, running our empires, while I remain here, trapped eating fucking homemade applesauce like a chump. *I fucking hate applesauce, but does anyone listen?*

When she does decide to grace me with her presence at the end of the night, she treats me more like a child rather than her husband, who desires to take her over his knee and spank the shit out of her. *Fuck, just the thought of my palm warm against her soft flesh has my cock hardening in my pants.* It seems that lately, just the mere thought of my wife's creamy perfection is all that is needed to have my cock weeping pearls of cum in my pants. A very unfortunate effect which I have to continuously hide from the staff so they don't think I'm some degenerate.

The fact that she is still sleeping in the master suite while I have been once again relegated to the guest suite in the opposite wing grates on my nerves and causes me endless sessions with my own fist. She won't go anywhere near me, and she refuses to be in a room alone with me. We always seem to be chaperoned by either Mrs. Pox, the nurse from hell, or Fergus. If I didn't know any better, I would say my little ice queen is afraid of me and uncomfortable around me. *I mean to change that immediately; Stella is about to be reacquainted with my hands, mouth, and cock.*

After I awoke that first day from the coma, she never again spoke to me with such affection and need as she had while I was asleep. Does she regret calling for me? Demanding I return to her and not leave her here alone? Perhaps they were moments of weakness that made her demand I return to her and not blatant affection for me? *No. I refuse to believe that. She is mine, and I mean to have her at all costs.*

"Mr. Stratford, you must return to your room for a nap, sir." The shrill voice of Sebastiana, the nurse from the fucking underworld, meets my ears, causing my shoulders and hackles to rise. I turn slowly from my position at the window of the library and stare back at the behemoth of a woman entering the room. I try to give her my most haughty and frightening stare, but it seems to just bounce off her six-foot-one frame. She is one hundred percent a demon from the beyond; there is no other explanation for her lack of fear when I stare her down. I have flayed powerful men with the look I'm giving her, yet she looks at me like I am a loathsome child under her care. *Fucking hell, not again.*

I would bet any money that my wife hired this particular nurse just to vex me. She is impervious to my charms; I know because I have already tried to use them on her. She ushers me around like a naughty two-year-old and not a grown man who is a billionaire and owns half the goddamn country. It seems like she always seems to know where I am at all times, despite me trying my best to avoid her. I have had enough! My pride and manhood can only take so much! *One of us has to cave, and it won't be fucking me, of that, I am sure.*

"No, I will not, in fact, be doing that. I will be heading into the office to see to my affairs." I raise my hand harshly to stop the words that are about to leave her thick lips, the hairy mole above her eye rising with her eyebrows in disdain. "You may think you are in charge here, nurse, but you are wrong."

"Actually, sir, your wife is in charge here." Sebastiana throws back at me with no doubt glee. I watch with rancor as she moves further into the room, unperturbed by my obvious dislike of her. *Is every woman I meet lately certain to make my male ego shrink in upon itself?* I can feel my balls wanting to shrivel up, tuck tail, and hide inside of my body at her miserable disposition and approach. *Man up, bitch, we may have to fight the she-bear!*

I roll my eyes at her words and move toward the doorway to pass her. "Sir, I really must insist! Shall I contact Mrs. Stratford?" Her threat breaks what precious little hold on my civilities I have left. I stop before her, my breath coming in angry pants. I can feel my neck and face getting hot, and I know my nostrils are flaring like an enraged bull about to knock her on her ass. I have never struck a woman, never desired to even raise my hand in anger at one, but this bitch is trying my fucking sanity. I clench both my hands at my side to avoid grabbing this insolent woman and shaking her until her fucking teeth rattle out of her head or I end up putting a million holes in the walls of my house.

"If you ever want to work again, never mind take another breath; you will do no such thing. No one is my master, not my wife, and certainly not you." I move closer until my body is mere inches from hers. "If you alert my wife that I have left the estate, I will ensure that you meet with a regrettable accident on your way home, nurse Sebastiana. Oh, and your precious cat, Snuffles, will disappear off the face of the goddamn planet. Don't for one second doubt that I can make that happen with a quick call."

A gasp leaves her lips, and I watch with satisfaction as she swallows whatever words were bound to leave her miserable mouth. I turn away from her, trying hard to keep the smirk off my face. *Fuck, that look of fear in her eyes made me feel good; I want more of that.* Two arctic blue eyes appear in my mind, ones I would love to see cowering before me or, better yet, filled with molten passion. One I know she is more than capable of. Stella gagged, bound, and on her knees before me is the shit fantasies are made of, and I'm about to make mine a reality. *Hell, yes!*

Yes, I think it's time I paid my little viper a visit at the office and determined how our empires fare. Perhaps the little ice queen will be made to drop to her knees in front of her king and apologize with her villainous lips for her actions. Just the image of all the ways I want to shove my cock inside all of Stella's holes has me hardening painfully. I might need to stroke one out before I head off to see her. I wouldn't want to terrify the office staff, walking around with my cock tenting my pants.

After that, my first stop is to teach a doctor some bedside manners. I hope he doesn't learn quickly. I have a huge amount of pent-up anger to work off before I wrap my fingers around my wife's pretty throat.

27

Stella

"It was pride that changed angels into devils; it is humility that makes men as angels." Saint Augustine

MY OFFICE DOOR SLAMS open with a hard bang, hitting the side wall and embedding the handle into the plaster. The framed art rattles on the walls loudly before one of them crashes to the ground, shattering upon impact. Panic fills my body as I push back my chair and grab onto the blade I never have far from my grasp anymore. When my eyes lift and meet cold, slate-gray ones, I almost drop the damn knife and end up cutting myself on its sharp edge. A red blood drop wells up on my skin before sliding down and landing on the fabric of my navy-flared skirt.

Fear and annoyance fill me and threaten to take my very breath away. Fear because, for a moment there, I thought another assailant had arrived to finish what the last two hadn't been able to manage. Annoyance, because my unwanted husband is standing there looking smug and delicious with his hands in his pockets instead of at home, where I left him under lock and key.

I watch as my assistant Tyson rushes in with an alarmed look on his face and the armed security guard right behind him. They both look ready to attack my husband at the slightest provocation. Jaxon gives both of them such a menacing stare that they each take a step back, and then their gazes meet mine in question.

I roll my eyes at the spectacle Jaxon is creating and nod my head no when Tyson's face questions whether I need Jaxon removed from my presence. As I shift my eyes from the two men sworn to protect me, back to the menace before me that has already sacrificed himself for me, I hear his threat to Tyson. "I'll deal with you later, fucker." Tyson smirks back at Jaxon without the slightest hint of fear and shuts my office door behind him. He is a brave fellow; it looks like my decision to keep him on was a smart one.

"Hello, little viper. Not happy to see me?" I watch as he strolls nonchalantly into my office, the picture of power and entitlement. His head is held high, his nose crinkled in amusement, and a devious smile across his gorgeous face, disrupting my already taxing day. He's a Greek god of the underworld, here to tempt me and make me lose my precious sanity. *Fuck, he really needs to stop looking so delicious; my lady parts do not need the temptation.*

"Jaxon, do I need to fire the nurse or send a search party for her?"

I sit myself back down in my office chair and try to avoid meeting his glare while pressing my trembling hand against my thigh out of his sightline. Ever since he woke up from his coma, it's getting harder and harder to be in his presence and resist my need to touch him and reassure myself that he is, in fact, alive. Guilt eats at me every time I look at him, knowing that he was shot and almost died, saving me—a sacrifice I don't deserve.

Fuck deserving it; we should take him up on the promise of tremendous sexual gratification. It's there in every line of his body and in the heated looks he keeps sending me nightly. He almost just died; we can't just jump on him... can we? *Bitch, if he dies while we ride him, he dies!* My inner voice cackles which has a small smirk crossing my lips at the naughty thought.

He looks amazing standing there in his dark gray dress pants and crisp white shirt. *Wait... what the hell is that splattered up his arms and on the waist of his shirt? Is that blood?* What has he done now? Did he actually fight the bear of a nurse I left in charge of him? I wouldn't put it past him. The thought makes a smile want to break across my face, but I fight the urge to let him see any of my emotions. *We are both psychos; is there a wonder we ended up tied to each other? Fate and karma are two destructive bitches.*

"She's alive and well. You should have known better, though, Stella. I won't be managed or controlled."

A sneer crosses his handsome, chiseled face, and it has me biting the inside of my cheek. Jaxon Stratford is one of the most stunning men I have ever had the misfortune to meet, never mind marry, even when he is practically growling at me. He is temptation and sin, all wrapped into a glorious and exquisite package—*one that I want to unwrap with my teeth.*

Yet I force myself to keep my distance from him every night when I return to our estate. The task becoming more challenging to force myself to endure. As for controlling or managing him, it seems an impossible feat. Even almost dying has done nothing for his possessive, demanding personality. I don't think there is a being on this earth that could force Jaxon Stratford to do anything he doesn't acquiesce to, not even me.

"I see; so fired then." I shrug, my eyebrows furrowing and my jaw tensing as I return my gaze to the document before me on my desk. I'm trying hard to look dismissive of the man who has corrupted my every waking thought and caused havoc with sinful dreams in my sleeping ones.

Every time I close my eyes, he is there. Calling to me, tempting me with his naughty words, demands, and the promise of sweet ecstasy. The memory of the feel of those lips and fingers on me haunts me and causes a flame to be lit from within. Slowly burning all my willpower and good sense. One that I can't seem to extinguish on my own, it seems, despite my frustrating attempts. My body craves his touch like an addict, willing to do anything for another hit. *Just one more taste...* my heated blood begs.

I close my eyes and force myself to take calming breaths. I cannot let Jaxon see the overwhelming need I have for him. One that is frightening me down to my very core. A man like him will use it to control me. He is still weak from his ordeal with the chest wound, but he won't be for long, and it would be a horrendous mistake to give him power over me. *Would it, though... to let him control us, to bend to his will? I bet he would make it feel so good.* My mind teases me.

He strolls to the side of my desk, his intoxicating scent of spicy citrus and musk filling my senses and almost causing me to moan out loud. Damn it! I am becoming a wanton whore, just like the ones that always chased him around. *We want to be his dirty whore...* my mind tries to tempt me with the thought. I almost choke on my own saliva at the thought of being just that, Jaxon's whore.

He perches that outrageously firm ass of his on the corner of my desk, and his finger reaches out, caressing my cheek before titling my chin up to meet his dark, anthracite gaze. What might be amusement along with desire is featured in his sultry depths, and it has my breath hitching in my throat: just *one taste, one lick*. My mind begs of me as a shiver races up my spine.

"That's better, little ice queen. I prefer it when you are looking up at me, Stella." His tongue peeks out as he licks his bottom lip, making my core clench painfully and the rest of me wishing it was me he was licking. "The only thing better would be if you were looking at me from your knees, with those pouty red lips wrapped around my cock."

My eyes momentarily shut as the image of his words is projected into my mind. Desire to do exactly what he is describing fills my body, and heat rises, like flames licking at my skin, while my needy core throbs to be filled. I reopen my eyes, and my gaze meets his heated one and roams over his sexy features before dropping to his chest, watching the deep inhales he's taking and lowering still to the tented fabric of his slacks. He's hard and thick in his pants, the shape of his cock pushing against the fabric. His own words and my response have him sitting there looking like a deviant warrior king off to collect his spoils.

A sharp exhale leaves my parted lips, and heat rises up my chest and neck. Jaxon Stratford is the definition of "*big dick energy,* " and luckily for me, he has the goods to back that shit up. Not so lucky for me. I can't seem to control the fiend.

"Hmm, not as unaffected as you'd like to make everyone believe, my devious little wife." He leans forward until his breath is mere inches from mine, and I can feel the heat coming off of his body and smell his fresh, minty breath skating across my skin. Desire races through my body, and my own breath sounds loud to my straining ears.

"You like the idea of having my cock so deep in your throat that you can't take a breath without me, don't you, *little wife?*" His long, warm fingers smooth over the skin of my cheek before reaching my jaw and tightening around it. An edge of pain makes its way across my skin as he pulls me towards him. The gap rapidly closing between us. "Oh, don't worry, Stella, I plan to have my cock deep inside all of your holes, and when I'm done, you will never forget who you belong to."

His tongue licks along the side of my jaw, warm and wet, causing goosebumps to break out across my body and a traitorous moan to leave my lips before I can stop it. My hands trail across the soft fabric of his dress pants, feeling the thick, strong muscles beneath. I grab a fist full of the material on his thigh in order to ground myself. His lips move down my neck, rotating between soft kisses, licks, and his teeth scraping along my heated flesh. I tilt my neck, giving him further access without a thought. He's creating a volcano of heated lava inside of me. One that begs to erupt and takes us both to the unrelenting void of hell and heaven combined. With Jaxon Stratford, there will never be just one pinnacle to reach.

"You belong to me, Stella. I escaped the fucking darkness and near death to return to you. There is a hole near my heart that has your fucking name on it. You will stop trying to manage and control me. I am not your enemy; I am your keeper." A deep groan leaves his lips as he bites down on the sensitive flesh of my ear lobe, causing my back to arch and a gasp to leave my parted lips. My pussy is spasming and weeping for him. His touch and words are an enticement that it does not want to resist. "This pretty cunt is mine, Stella."

My breath comes out wispy and faltering. My nipples are two hard pebbles in my bra, and my panties are soaked. *How can he do that to me with just his words and lips on my ear?* The rasp of his voice and the threat in his tone have me almost bending to his will. I want him with a desperation that I reserve for only one thing... power.

I crave power and control. The two items that will have me determining and managing my own future. Jaxon would have me giving up both to have a taste of him between my thighs. *Why can't we have both? Power and Jaxon?* My mind questions with a faltering breath.

I pull back until his lips are forced to part from my heated flesh, and I can look into his graphite gaze. "I belong to no one but myself, Jaxon. If you returned from death at my call, it must mean that you belong to me." I let my fingers skate up the fabric of his chest, reaching the open neckline of his shirt and slowly unbuttoning the first two buttons, then the next. I watch, transfixed, as his powerful throat struggles to swallow, and his breathing quickens as I unbutton another two buttons until his shirt is almost wholly opened and gaping before me, and all his beautiful golden skin and the ink along his ribs are exposed.

My fingers skim over his warm flesh, which pebbles with goosebumps at my touch. When I reach the pink puckered bullet wound in his chest, I slowly slide my finger over it—admiring the texture and the sacrifice this man made for me. That bullet went straight through but caused so much damage. *He almost died because of it, because of me.*

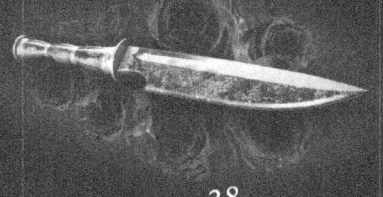

28

Stella

"Only a struggle twists sentimentality and lust together into love."
E. M. Forster

I LEAN FORWARD, MY lips gently touching the mark as his breath leaves him in a shuddering gasp, and I feel his body tighten. The tip of my tongue traces over the freshly soft, pink skin as his hands shift up my back. One of his fists makes it into the hair at my nape, and his fingers tighten around the strands, a small whimper leaving my lips at his harsh treatment.

I breathe in his scent and lean more of my body towards him until I'm half out of my seat, half-standing before him. My hand slides down his waist and over his firm and lean hip, following the groove between where his leg encounters his pelvis. My fingers meet and stroke over his hard cock, tenting the material of his pants and marking its presence and demand to be unleashed known. His cock twitches under my touch, and my breath falters.

I slowly wrap my fingers around his fabric-encased girth, a shudder running through him as a growly moan leaves his lips. "Unzip me, Stella. I want to feel those fingers wrapped around my skin." For a brief moment, I hesitate. My heart is beating rapidly in my chest, my senses all filled with nothing but Jaxon. My mind is at war with my desire for him. I should pull back from what is happening here. I should deny him and myself; nothing good can come from giving in to him other than a fleeting moment of pleasure. I refuse to be one of those simpering women that become dickmitized. I don't care how long and thick Jaxon's cock is; I'm not going to be controlled by it.

He almost died for you. My brain screams with frustration. The thought has me closing my eyes tight and once again kissing the soft spot on his chest. The one that will forever be a symbol of his heroic action. *My brave, unhinged husband.* There has to be a way that I can make it up to him and honor his sacrifice without losing my power to him. I can control myself; I just have to be firm with Jaxon. I have to keep my head focused and my heart out of our shared moments. This can just be about mutual gratification. I can pleasure him and myself without ceasing my control or power. *I can, can't I?*

I slowly unzip his pants, and warm flesh greets me. *Fuck me; this man did not come here, commando.* I trail my fingers along his length, tracing my finger over the wide, velvety crown that is wet with moisture. His cock jumps at my touch, and a gasp leaves his lips. My fingers wrap around his girth, and they aren't even enough to cover half the length of his cock. A moan escapes my lips as I realize how my body would have to stretch to encompass him, and the needy slut inside of me can't wait to feel the burn. I move my hand up and down for a few deep strokes; pulling back from his cock, I lean my face forward and spit on his cock, then retighten my grip on the upstroke as little animalistic grunts leave his lips.

"That's it, my little viper, tighter. Show me how you enjoy taking control of my cock."

My eyes leave his cock and make their way across Jaxon's face. I admire the blush across his high cheekbones, the way his lips are parted and slack, and his eyes are at half mast, filled with pleasure. His hips move forward into my grasp, forcing my strokes to be tighter and longer. His other hand reaches out and caresses my breast through the soft fabric of my shirt, which does nothing to disguise how hard my nipples are. The desire to watch him come undone before me fills me; it's a craving that I don't want to deny.

"I want to see all this creamy skin, Stella. I want to taste the perfection of your soft skin and leave my marks all over you so that when you look at yourself, you realize who owns you." His hand tightens on my breast and pulls at the fabric of my blouse, sending buttons flying everywhere with his rough handling. "That you are a Stratford, and the only man that will ever touch you is me."

Suddenly, his hand leaves my breast, and his fingers encircle my throat, tightening his grasp until my breath is trapped in my throat. I try to pull back from the hold, but he tightens it further in warning. His words are gritted through clenched teeth, and my grip on his cock tightens.

"There will be no other men, Stella. Not fucking Ajax or any other fool that tries to convince you to leave me." My face is going red, and I'm seeing white spots in front of my eyes. "I will slit your fucking throat if you are ever even slightly swayed. Then follow you into hell because even the devil can't have you. You're mine." I can't take my eyes off his enraged face, the menace and promise of violence and danger in his features. "Do you understand me, Stella?"

I release my hold on his thick, hard cock, and I wrap both my hands around his wrist and pull, hoping to dislodge his hold. I can feel the darkness calling me; my chest is so tight with the air trapped inside me. I slap at his grasp, but other than making a sharp sound, it does nothing to release his hold. I believe he might kill me for a moment, that he's lost control. I'm fumbling on the desk, trying desperately to grab onto anything I can use to break his hold. My fingers grasp the blade's hilt, tightening around its rough material. I quickly slide it up against his chest and point the sharp edge against his skin. I watch as he realizes that I have a blade to his heart. His grip releases until his fingers are just merely encircling my throat, stroking my delicate and bruised flesh as a raspy breath enters my lungs, and I swallow the saliva that had pooled in my mouth. *Jesus, fuck, he could have killed me.*

"You would stab the heart that barely survived the last attempt to save you?" His voice sounds bleak and weathered as his head lowers until he's staring at the blade in my tight fist. Sorrow fills me with his pain-filled words. I watch as my hand trembles, holding the blade, the tip against his skin, causing a bead of blood to rise along its surface. A few meager inches to the right, and I would be right over the healing bullet wound. I watch, entranced, as a drop of blood races down his golden skin and disappears into the fabric of his shirt, another bead of blood rising to replace it. "Have I not shed enough blood for you, Stella? Would you have more?"

His hand grabs the blade hilt still in my grasp, and he tightens his fingers over it, pushing the tip deeper into his skin. A sharp exhale leaves his lips, and a cry leaves mine as we both watch more of his lifeblood drip down his chest. His other hand releases my throat, and his fingers run through the trickles of blood now coating his abdomen. He slides them through the bright red mixture and raises them to my parted mouth, outlining my shocked lips before slipping his finger in between them.

"Taste what I'm willing to sacrifice for you, Stella, so you understand that there is nothing I won't do to have you, no length I won't go."

The rich taste of salty copper fills my mouth, and my tongue lashes at his finger, cleaning off all of his life-giving fluid. My eyes rise to his heavy, pewter ones, fringed with long, dark lashes. His eyes widen and gleam as my lips close over his flesh, and I suck deeply. My hold on the blade loosens until he pulls it away from his chest. My eyes meet the small cut on his chest, and the urge to lick him there, to claim him in such an animalistic way, fills me. I move my lips away from his finger and slide my tongue across his chest, licking up the small drops that remain on his golden skin. "Fuck, Stella. You will be my undoing."

His hand grabs onto mine, and he lifts it to his lips. His soft, warm lips make contact with the palm of my hand before his tongue slides across its surface, and a growl of satisfaction leaves his mouth. I look away from the perfect expanse of his chiseled chest and meet his eyes that sparkle with desire and the need to consume me. His tongue peeks out once again, and I notice that he has blood on his lips, blood from the palm of my hand. I must have sliced it as I grappled with the blade. He eagerly licks, groaning in satisfaction as if he is eating the finest of desserts, before he pulls back and stares at me. His handsome features are filled with hunger and desire. I no doubt am mirroring the same look back at him.

His hand strikes out and yanks the ripped shirt from my shoulders, causing it to slide down my arms and trapping me as he pulls on the fabric and forces my arms behind my back. His other hand grabs a fist full of my hair at the top of my head and pulls me forward until I'm bent at the waist, and my mouth is inches from his proud hard cock. He doesn't utter a command, just tightens his hold on my strands and pushes my head closer until the beads of precum coat my lips like some macabre lip gloss. I open my lips wide as the crown of his cock slips into my wet mouth. The taste and feel of him hitting my tongue has my knees almost buckling. His hold tightens on my arms, forcing me to remain where he wants me—controlling me, like he does indeed own me.

I trace my tongue over his slit and down the ridges of his thick head, sucking on the very tip until a moan leaves his lips. I let my tongue stroke over the large vein on the side of his thick dick, lashing it over and over. He allows me to have my way for a moment, learning his taste and the feel of all that hardness in my mouth before he starts a slow rhythm of thrusting into my mouth. The thick head hits the back of my throat, and I gag, saliva filling my mouth along with his heady taste. My eyes water as he picks up speed and force, hitting the back of my throat and going deeper with each stroke. Loud and vicious choking sounds fill the room, along with his soft growls. The combination of the sounds helping to edge me towards an orgasm of my own. *Fuck, if I could just get my fingers under my skirt and on my clit, it wouldn't take much to make me explode.* The noises he and I are making are a symphony of erotic passion and sweet music to my ears. "That's it, my little viper, milk me, suck me down hard."

I have never enjoyed giving head and gagging on cock like I'm right now. My few experiences with Ajax were never like this; they were never all-consuming and filled with molten heat. I never allowed anyone to manhandle me like Jaxon is doing and certainly never thought that I would enjoy and crave the rough and forceful way he is making me suck his cock. Jaxon's punishing grip on my hair is ripping out strands of my hair. The air is momentarily trapped in my throat every time he forces his cock deep into my throat. The feel of the tears sliding down the side of my face and saliva pooling on my chin. It's degrading, forceful, controlling, and sexy as fuck the way he's forcing me to take his cock, without questioning if I want him. I would never willingly put into words how much I want and need this, but that's the thing about Jaxon; he somehow knows.

"What a good *little slut* you are gagging on my cock; look at the mess you're making of yourself." He drags a finger along the side of my stretched lips and down my chin, running the digit through the spit that is trickling out of my too-full mouth. *"Mine!"*

He pushes my head down hard until my nose is flush against his pubic bone, forcing me to take as much of him as I can down my tight throat and holding me there so that I can't push back up. I struggle in his grasp, choking on his length, desperation for air filling me. A loud groan leaves his lips as his cock spasms deep in my throat, and warm salty cum fills my mouth. I try to swallow as much as I can around his thick cock, but there is no way I can swallow enough, and it slips out of my mouth and down the side of my face. "Swallow me down, my ice queen whore; every drop is yours."

When he finally stops shuddering, he pulls my mouth off of his cock with a pop, threads of spit and cum trailing between his hard dick and my swollen lips. *How the fuck is he still hard?* I barely get the question in my mind before I'm face down on the desk, and Jaxon is moving behind me, his grip still tight on my arms and his movement so quick that I don't even have time to register what is happening.

He grips the hem of my skirt, throwing it up and over my lower back, and his strong, rough hand pulls my panties down off my ass. I feel them pool at my ankles before he forces me to step out of them with his tight grip on my thigh. His knee slides in between my thighs, forcing them to part and my feet to widen my stance. His fingers caress softly over the inside of my thigh, rising higher and higher until he meets the soft wet skin of my pussy lips.

"This cunt is soaked, Stella. Is it craving my hard cock deep inside? Does it want me to claim this needy pussy?" His warm, labored breath pants near my ear, causing a shudder to go through me. His finger slips through my moisture and makes its way up to my puckered hole. "Maybe you want me to fuck this tight, little hole and stretch you wide, my little whore." He rubs his finger over and over across my tight hole as I clench my ass cheeks. His hold on my arms releases suddenly, but before I can lift my upper body off the desk, a harsh slap rings out across the space, and the flesh of my right ass cheeks feels like it's on fire.

"JAXON!" The shriek leaves my lips with shock.

"Did you know I wanted to murder you and my best friend, Stella? That I heard every fucking word." *Slap.* "That I knew you had been alone with him. Were you planning to betray me, little wife?" *Slap.* His finger pushes slightly into my puckered hole, a sharp pain tears through me, and a cry leaves my lips at the strange feeling of being filled back there. Jaxon slaps my other ass cheek hard, causing fire to be branded across my skin. "All your holes belong to me, Stella, and I plan to fill them with so much of my cum that you will never be empty." *Slap.* "You will never be rid of me, my dirty little slut."

Tears are sliding down my face and landing on the hard surface of my desk. The pain is euphoric, causing my breathing to pick up and electricity to race through my body. My clit is throbbing and begging to be touched. Jaxon slips the finger in my ass further inside of me and starts a slow rhythm of fucking my puckered hole with it. "Jaxon... oh my God." The words leave my lips in a moaned cry.

"Tell me who you belong to?" The ringing sound of another slap on my heated flesh is music to my ears. I have never been this turned on in my life. I can feel my moisture slipping down my pussy lips and coating my upper thighs and probably leaving a wet spot on the desk. I bite down hard on my bottom lip to try to quiet my cries.

"Tell me, Stella, who does this ass and cunt belong to?" He slides another thick finger into my ass, stretching me further. Another hit of pain races through me, yet as he plunges deeper and starts thrusting in and out of my tight hole, he has me seeing stars. My body tightens painfully, aching for the release that Jaxon is just keeping out of my reach.

I can feel bliss just within my reach. A part of me just wants to give in and let him use me like the wanton whore I am when he takes charge of my pleasure. The other part is feeling defiant and wanting to push him over the edge, so he, too, loses control. I have a feeling Jaxon Stratford, wholly unhinged and consumed by pleasure, will be my favorite version of him.

"Myself, Jaxon," I mumble through the pain of another slap.

29

Jaxon

"Women have to be extremely careful about choosing something that they consider an act of defiance that can really be used to further their enslavement." Alice Walker

"**Y**OU DEFIANT LITTLE ICE queen. I should fuck you in this tight hole, teach you what it truly means to be owned and used." I'm losing control of myself. Stella's warm flesh and scent are pushing me close to the edge of insanity and reason. Her puckered hole tightens against my fingers as I fuck her ass with them. The soft red flesh of her ass cheeks just begging me to sink my teeth into them. *Fuck, I want to mark her up, leave my teeth as a tattoo across her beautiful creamy skin.*

Her defiance, even now, while I have her spread face down across her office desk, amazes me and pushes me forward to take from her delectable little body all that I can. She won't relinquish control without a fight, even though she enjoys it when I take it by force from her. Her soaked cunt is proof of that. As are the moans of pleasure that are leaving her lips with each slap of my palm on her soft skin. *God, she's fucking perfect for me.*

Prickles of heat are racing across my skin as I push my fingers as deep as they will go inside of her, and a soft, mumbled cry leaves her lips. Controlling and dominating Stella is a longing I can't seem to deny myself. "I wish you could see my fingers thrusting deep inside this ass, Stella. How beautifully you clench them."

A groan leaves my throat as I spit down in between her ass cheeks, watching as it travels between her crack and inside her tight hole that I'm stretching. Fuck, I want to shove a third finger in there and make it gape for me, stretch her wide so that my thick cock can fit inside of her. I let spit leave my mouth again and watch as her hole swallows it as I slide another finger inside her ass. A desperate moan escapes her lips, and her neck bows, her forehead pressed against the top of the desk. Fuck I wish I had a collar to wrap around it so I could choke her out as I spank and fuck her holes. *We definitely need to get her a collar for the future.*

My cock is rock hard and begging to be included in the fun. Precum is dripping from the tip and sliding down her creamy thighs, coating them with the part of me that I desperately want to see leaking out of her. *Fuck, I want to cover her in my cum! Squirt all over her body and in every one of her holes.* The thought has me pushing the crown of my cock between her swollen pussy lips. I slide back and forth through her wetness, bumping her clit each time I stroke forward. Little moans leave her lips as she begs under her breath, my name a symphony on her lips. "Jaxon... Jaxon... oh my God... Jaxon."

My fingers continue to fuck her clenching hole, and I trail my other hand over her thigh, squeezing the soft skin before moving around her body and rubbing her hard nub. A sharp cry leaves her lips and fills me with deep satisfaction and hunger. *I need more of that fucking sound. I need to hear her scream my name.*

Stella cumming and deeply enthralled by the desire my body can create in her is my new favorite music. I wonder if she even realizes that she's saying the word *"Please"* repeatedly, like a prayer. One that is filled with desperation from the vortex of pleasure and emotions I'm creating in her. Her body arches and pushes back into the feel of my cock at her entrance, the tip barely breaching her tight hole each time I shift forward. I slide forward an inch, a groan leaving my lips as her pussy tightens around the head of my cock. "Please, Jaxon... please! I need you! Fill me up!"

Her moans and cries are my undoing. I wanted to be gentle with her the first time I fucked her. My good intentions go out the window when I feel her ass clench down hard on my fingers as more of my throbbing dick makes its way inside her wet channel. My forefinger and thumb pinch down on her little nub, and I propel the rest of my long length inside of her in one go. "Shit, you're so fucking warm and tight!" I hit the end of her and bottom out inside of her. My balls slap loudly against her perfectly plump pussy lips and cause my fingers to slip deeper into her puckered hole. A strangled cry leaves her lips, and her core clenches me so tightly that sweat breaks out all over my body. She tries to push back, to dislodge my hold on her and my cock's deep intrusion. "Too much! Fuck, Jaxon! Please! You're going to tear me in half! Fuck, get it out!"

Her cries of pain amuse me, and a chuckle leaves my lips as I fuck her in deep strokes, her body both welcoming me and trying to push me out. She's so wet I can feel her arousal dripping down my balls. "That's it, baby, baptize me in your fire, strangle my cock."

Her pussy is so hot and tight; my dick feels like it's in a tight vise. I can feel my cock moving inside her with my fingers in her puckered hole. The thin membrane between her pussy and ass allowing me to feel each stroke and non-stop spasms in her pussy. I pull my body back slightly so I can watch where our bodies are connected and how my cock slides inside of her, drenched in her wetness. She's creaming for me, her arousal coating my dick, and what a beautiful sight it is. A growl leaves my lips, and I bare my teeth. No one will ever take this away from me.

"Jaxon... holy... fuck!" She's panting hard, her body shaking underneath me. I drive into her with deep, hard strokes, making sure she feels the entire length of my cock with each thrust in her tight hole, hitting the end of her and knowing that she's mine. "Jaxon... fuck. I can feel you so deep... omg, too deep!" She moans.

I can feel her core tightening further, her pussy spasming and getting ready for the orgasm that is about to take her. My strokes become harsher and rougher until we're moving the heavy desk across the room with our motion. The sound is loud and jarring, combining Stella's screams and my moans. My cock is impaling her in deep strokes as she pushes back to meet my thrusts. I don't doubt that everyone outside her office can hear her moaning and crying out. The thought that we have an audience spurring me on to fuck her even harder. I want them to know I'm fucking her, that every part of her is mine. *This pussy is mine.*

I drape myself over her, my slick skin meeting hers, my lips connecting with the side of her face, and I lick up all the salty tears that are skating down her face. *God, she is the most beautiful woman I have ever seen when she cries.* My lips greet hers in an open mouth kiss that threatens to consume me and drag me under. I pinch her clit one more time, and she explodes, squirting all over my hand and cock. I swallow her cries into my mouth, her body clenching hard and dragging me into another orgasm with her. My cock throbs and spurts hot cum deep inside of her warm cunt. It feels like I have entered heaven at this moment, and I never want it to be over. I never want to leave this paradise.

I rest all my weight over her, crushing her into the table. My heart rate is through the roof, and I can't really catch my breath. *Fuck, I am starting to see prisms of light before my eyes.* Maybe fucking Stella this hard after almost dying wasn't the smartest thing I have ever done. *Totally fucking worth dying over.* My mind whispers contently back at me. I try to take calming breaths through my nose and exhale through my mouth. Fuck, if I die with my cock inside if her, I'll die happy.

My fingers are still knuckle deep inside Stella's tight ass, and my cock is experiencing the most delicious aftershock spasms inside her clamping pussy. She's breathing hard, too; her eyes are closed, and her body is completely flattened against the desk.

"Jaxon... please don't die inside me." Her voice is light and filled with humor. I raise my head slightly to stare down at her causing a wave of dizziness to hit me. *Fuck, that can't be good.* I have no desire to make this woman my widow, especially now when I have entered heaven between her thighs.

Once my vision isn't seeing two of Stella, and I'm sure I won't collapse back on top of her, I lift my upper body off of her and pull my fingers from her ass. A moan leaves her lips, and her pussy clamps down on my cock. I'm already semi-hard again, but I think if I go another round with her right now, she may get her wish and become a widow. *Death by orgasms*, what a way to go... my body cheers loudly.

I pull out of her cunt and move my body entirely off her, stepping back and falling into the chair behind me. Stella's pink cunt, is on display before me and glistens with her own arousal and my cum that is dripping out of her. *Fuck that's a sexy sight.* I roll the chair forward on its wheels and lean forward, using my fingers to spread my cum over her pussy lips and up to her puckered hole, slipping my cum inside of her there. She cries out, and her body shakes with the feeling of my fingers once again inside of her. *Fuck I need a taste of her.*

I slip the three fingers of my other hand inside her seizing core, and my lips latch on to her swollen clit, sucking it hard and then using my teeth to graze the overstimulated bundle of nerves.

"JAXON! FUCK!" Her cries are loud as she thrashes against my fingers and mouth. I suck harder and fuck her with my fingers, pushing her into another orgasm.

When she detonates, her arousal leaks out of her covering my face and dripping down my chin, and satisfaction races through me.

"Please... no more! I... can't! No... more!" She begs, and I finally relent, removing my digits from inside of her. I lean back in the chair, completely blissed out and feeling like a king who just plundered the kingdom. That right there is my kingdom, my paradise, and I mean to enjoy it every chance I get.

I watch with a grin breaking across my face as Stella tries to regain feeling in her legs, looking like Bambi trying to take her first steps. She falters hard against the desk, her body trembling, and it causes delicious shivers to skate across my heated flesh. She's boneless, ravished, and wholly undone, and I'm a proud peacock for having caused her condition.

She turns towards me, her eyes sparkling with mischief and satisfaction as she braces herself against the desk. Her skirt lowers so I can't see her beautiful cunt, but her breasts are still displayed through the flimsy blouse I ruined and her sheer bra. The desire to slip my semi-hard dick between the two creamy globes fills me, but just as I move to grab her, a sharp pain racks my chest. Fuck, what was that? Was that my heart? *Well, you did almost die a fucking month ago, you savage heathen. Then you rutted your wife like a goddamn animal—my* mind sneers.

"Jaxon, are you alright?" Stella's hands land on either side of my face, concern races across her stunning features, and fear is immediately evident in her arctic eyes. I know her being scared shouldn't fill me with fucking joy, but it does. What the hell is happening to me? How did this woman get so far under my skin?

"I'm fine, beautiful." I wrap my arms around her body and pull her towards me so my lips can meet hers in a tender kiss. When I break the kiss after a few moments, a pink blush is across her cheeks, and her lips are swollen and red. She pulls back, taking a few steps, sitting atop the desk, and staring back at me. Whatever she is going to say is one hundred percent about to piss me off. I can already tell she is reigning in her emotions and putting up her frosty walls.

I pull myself to my feet, happy that the dizziness has subsided, and I don't immediately fall on my ass. Before she can open her little viper mouth and take some of the glow off our amazing fucking sex, I kiss her lips and move away from her, tucking my cock back into my pants as I shift towards her office door.

"Where the fuck are you going, Jaxon?" She calls out with annoyance. A grin crosses my lips at her tone. I love it when Stella is angry and annoyed at me. I look forward to enraging her over and over for the rest of our lives together. Another sharp pain in my chest seizes me, and I almost falter in my steps toward her door. For however long that may be, I look forward to make-up sex with my little ice queen. *Better be a fucking long time, I've only just begun claiming and leaving my marks on her body, don't you quit now, motherfucker*, I admonish to my heart.

I look back just as I open the door and stare at the disheveled and satiated mess that is my wife. "I'm off to plunder the rest of my kingdom, little wife. Make sure you return home early tonight. I feel like enjoying more of my spoils with that pretty cunt of yours." I walk out the threshold of the door and turn back around. She's standing there with her hands on her hips, looking irate and like she wants to throw something at me. Maybe even the damn blade in my back. "Little viper, there will be no more separate rooms from this moment forward."

Then I walk away, my shirt still wide open and blood drying on my chest, passing the shocked face of her assistant and the smirk on the face of the armed guard, who both heard me loudly fucking and spanking my wife. I wink at her fucking assistant and lick my lips obnoxiously until a red flush appears on his clean-shaven cheeks. *That's right motherfucker; she belongs to me.* All in all, this has been a glorious fucking day.

Just one more stop before I can head home. I need to teach a traitor about touching my fucking prized possession.

30

Stella

"I have learned to hate all traitors, and there is no disease that I spit on more than treachery." Aeschylus

As I walk through the front door of my house, the house I share with my asshole husband that left me boneless this afternoon, anticipation is sizzling in my veins. The thought of seeing Jaxon after this afternoon's activities and his promise of more enjoyment has kept me company and distracted all afternoon. It didn't help that he left me filled with cum, pantiless and in utter disarray. I had to ask Tyson to grab me another shirt, as mine was utterly ruined.

The embarrassed look on his face, when he presented me with a new shirt, had my blood pressure rising. I don't want men looking at me with sly smirks or knowing that I was a brazen whore for Jaxon. *You were a brazen whore, you even let him fuck you with his fingers up your ass, and you enjoyed it. You cummed over and over like his very own porn star.* The snide bitch in my head replies.

Shit, the memory of the feeling of his fingers and that hard long cock inside of me has me clenching my thighs tightly. I should be embarrassed, never mind, I should be horrified with myself, but all I care about right now is getting more of that hard dick pounding that Jaxon teased me with. He has created a fiery need inside me, one I mean to satisfy with his long cock.

"Mrs. Pox?" I call out loudly. Usually, the staff is present the minute I pull into the driveway at night. Tonight seems to be an exception; where are they? Did Jaxon send them all off tonight so we could have the estate to ourselves? Maybe he plans to fuck me in every room of the house. A whimper leaves my lips at just the possibility. I should try to show some damn restraint. I saw the way he looked pained after he fucked me so hard across my desk.

The one I will never be able to sit at again without picturing myself getting pounded into. The one I had to have Tyson and the guard move back into place with complete mortification as it was almost across the room when Jaxon finished with me.

I need to rein in my desires and needs. Jaxon is just barely out of the woods from his injury and heart attacks. The doctor said no strenuous activity for two months, yet I let him rut into me like a lion marking his territory this afternoon, and I want more, so much more. Maybe he can lie back and let me take over all the hard work tonight? A smile crosses my face at the anticipation of the power and control that will give me over him. I'll ride him into the fucking ground and cum all over his face again. I can't wait to watch the heat rise in his dark gray depths as I take charge of our intimacy. Maybe he'll even let me tie him up?

"Fergus?" I call out but get no response. I climb the stairs to the master suite, needing to get out of these clothes and have a shower before anything more happens with Jaxon tonight. I enter the bedroom, slipping my heels from my feet, and come to a dead halt.

What greets me has shock racing across my face and my mouth hanging wide open. Ajax is gagged and tied to a wooden ladder-back chair next to my bed in my bedroom. His face is battered and bleeding. One of his eyes is partially swollen shut. His clothes are torn and bloody in various places, and he's struggling fiercely in his bindings.

If that wasn't enough of a horrifying sight, Jaxon is sitting across from him on the edge of my bed with a glass of red wine in one hand and a bloody knife in the other. *Jesus fucking Christ, he's lost his mind!*

"What the fuck is this, Jaxon?" I question and move further into the room. Fear is sliding up my back, and my brain is trying to comprehend what it's seeing. What the hell is happening here? Has he completely lost it now?

"This, my lovely viper, is called retribution." Jaxon snarls and takes a deep sip of wine, looking relaxed as if he doesn't have a man bleeding and tied to a chair next to him. "My best friend here tried to take something of mine. In fact, he tried to do more than that, didn't you, Ajax?"

As I move closer, I realize that Ajax's left hand is hanging limply and oddly in his lap, and all four of his fingers are broken and bent backward. *Holy shit!* I have to swallow back the cry and the feel of immediate nausea at their grotesque appearance.

"Release him, Jaxon. Have you lost your fucking mind?" I scream and move towards Ajax to try to release his bindings.

"I wouldn't touch him if I were you, Stella unless you want to see me break more of him before we have our fun. Every piece of your delicate flesh that comes into contact with his will have me carving his flesh right off of him."

His words have me stopping in my tracks and staring wide-eyed at a screaming Ajax. His cries are muffled by the thick gag in his mouth. Tears trickle down his battered face, and his brown eyes plead with me to help him. I don't know what to do here. Jaxon has obviously lost his mind. He's behaving unhinged and possessive again, and I genuinely fear for what else he will do to Ajax and what end result he's trying to achieve.

"This is sick, Jaxon; you're deranged. You can't hold him here like this. You can't punish him like this for trying to take me from you."

Jaxon stands and moves towards me, a graceful predator, the blade still grasped tightly in his hand. He discards the wine glass on the side table, where I notice another one is already poured, and the bottle is placed. Is he really enjoying a glass of wine while his best friend bleeds before him? I don't know what to make of this Jaxon before me. Should I be afraid that he's going to hurt me next in his quest for retribution? Have I married a psychopath, after all?

"You see, little ice queen, I can hold him here like this, and I can punish him. In fact, he has gotten off lightly so far. My blood is calling for further vengeance, and it will have its price. He tried to take something of mine not only with his words, not only by trying to convince and seduce you, Stella but with his reprehensible actions." He trails his warm fingers down my cheek, cupping my jaw and leaning forward, his breath skating across my lips. "He almost took your life with his callous actions, and that, Stella, is unforgivable. Your. Life. Belongs. To. Me. Alone."

My gaze is riveted on Jaxon's strong jaw and Roman nose, the way he parts his full lips, and the swirling anger in his dark slate eyes. His hand wraps around the back of my neck, and his fingers tighten, pulling me forward into his hard chest. His firm lips land on mine, forcing mine to part for him and give him entry to plunder my mouth. For a moment, I lose track of my very wits and kiss him back, small whimpers leaving my open mouth with how thoroughly he kisses me. My temperature is rising, and my nipples are puckering in my bra. Jaxon pulls back from the kiss and trails small open-mouthed kisses along my jaw and down my neck, shivers and goosebumps rising everywhere he lingers.

My eyes meet Ajax's tortured ones over Jaxon's shoulder, and I return to myself, pushing Jaxon away from me. He takes a step back, a smirk of glee on his face; then he turns to stare at Ajax. "Explain what the hell is going on here, Jaxon. If you've done all of this in a jealous rage, you have wasted your time."

"Oh, Stella." He sighs deeply and takes a step back away from me and closer to Ajax. Ajax whimpers and flinches in the chair the closer Jaxon moves towards him while still holding the blade in his hand. "You always think of me as the villain, don't you?" He slides the blade's edge down Ajax's cheek, and tears cascade down his face. "This time, though, I'm not the heinous villain you portray me as. I'm not a saint either, but I will be your avenging angel in this instance."

He yanks the gag down from Ajax's mouth until it sits just below his jaw and places the sharp blade across his Adam's apple. "You get one chance to confess to her what you did. If you try to stray from the whole truth, I will slit your fucking throat like a pig at the slaughterhouse and then fuck my wife in your blood."

Ajax stares up at Jaxon with resentment and rage across his damaged features. "You're a psycho; you don't deserve her." He mumbles, and I watch as a smile breaks across Jaxon's face. He brings the blade next to Ajax's ears and trails the tip into his flesh until blood wells up and tricks down Ajax's neck. A cry leaves Ajax's lips and has my shoulders tightening. "I warned you, didn't I? To stop being a fucking coward. Tell her the truth!" Jaxon roars.

Ajax turns his gaze away from Jaxon and meets mine. He has a look of abject fear and distress across his face. His eyes beg me for forgiveness, but for what? I'm not yet sure. Realization hits me and has my breath stuttering in my chest; he's not just scared of Jaxon and his unhinged behavior. It's what Jaxon is about to reveal to me that has him truly frightened.

I take a step forward toward the two men, both of whom are earning my suspicions at this point. I don't know what to think about what is happening here, but I have the sense that whatever is going to be revealed will devastate me. "What does he mean, Ajax?" My words are uttered softly, but there is ice present below their tone.

Sweat breaks out across Ajax's forehead, and he gulps loudly. A lone tear trickles down his cheek, sliding down his blood-smeared jaw and disappearing into his blotchy neck. Ajax licks his bloodied and busted lips and stares at me with fear and trepidation. "I... I... never." His voice stutters, and he tightens his lips closed into a straight line. Jaxon pushes the blade's tip back into his skin, and a whimper leaves his mouth.

"I... I never meant for you... to get hurt." Jaxon's fist connects with the side of Ajax's chest with a hard thud. A grimace and a groan make their way to Ajax's lips. "You were never supposed to get hurt..." He takes a deep gulp, and Jaxon punches him again, this time causing his air to wheeze out of his mouth, "not... more... than... a scratch."

"What are you talking about, Ajax?" Dread fills the pit of my stomach. He's looking at me with such despair that I feel it right in my own bones. I'm frozen to the spot, unable to move or walk away from the site before me. "Tell her, you fucking, dirty cunt." Jaxon grits between his teeth, the wrath flashing across his face has me taking a step back.

Ajax's eyes flash in a moment of anger and spite toward Jaxon's before returning to mine. "The gunman... he was never supposed to hurt you. He was just there to... scare you. To scare you to... leave with me."

My legs threaten to give out at the words tumbling from Ajax's lips. "What? You... you sent him to scare me? I don't understand. Why would you do that? You had someone shoot at me." Disbelief is making its way across my mind as I try desperately to make sense of Ajax's confession.

A look of shame crosses Ajax's face, and he can no longer meet my own horrified gaze. My eyes rise to my husband, whose eyes are two fiery pools of molten steel, and his jaw is locked in fury. I can feel the current of electricity and violence between us. He wants to hurt Ajax. No. He wants to do more than hurt him. He wants his pound of flesh and to destroy him.

"I just wanted you to leave him... Stella. You wouldn't listen... to reason. I thought if you realized how... how dangerous being his wife could be... you would leave him."

My hands are two clenched fists at my side. My nails dig deeply into the flesh of my palm as I shift forward until I'm no more than a foot or two away from the two men who both look like unhinged psychopaths before me. One holding a blade to the other. Who is more dangerous to me here? The one holding the blade or the one confessing to having someone shoot at me and strapped to a chair?

"You paid a man to shoot at me, Ajax? How could you? He could have killed me! He almost killed Jaxon!" My hand flies out and my knuckles meet with Ajax's nose in an awful crunch. An anguished cry leaves his swollen lips. "STELLA! Please! Please, I love you! I have always loved you. He... he was just supposed to graze you. Just to scare you. Jaxon wasn't even supposed to be home!" Ajax's blubbers, blood pouring from his nostril. "Jaxon seeing him and charging into the room surprised him, and his shot went wide."

"YOU ALMOST KILLED HIM!" I have never felt so completely filled with burning anger as I do now. My whole body is trembling, my breath leaving me in quick pants. I can't control myself when I slam my fist into Ajax's nose once again. It's not enough, though; it doesn't cause him enough pain. Not nearly as much as Jaxon suffered. He almost died because this fool tried to manipulate me and control the narrative. He almost killed his best friend.

"Stella... I... love... you."

"Give me the blade, Jaxon. I want to slice him open." I hold out my palm in my husband's direction, my hand vibrating with energy between us.

"No, beautiful wife, you will never have to dirty your hands. I will always be your vengeance." He moves the blade over the side of Ajax's head, cutting off chunks of his hair and nicking his scalp until blood trickles down the side of his face. He slides the blade down, slicing through the fleshy part of Ajax's ear and then across his cheek, leaving cuts in his wake.

Ajax's screams fill the room, echoing off the walls and causing my stomach to clench painfully. "Stella, please! Have mercy!" Ajax begs loudly as I watch my husband slice him open, one cut at a time, until his face, neck, and head are covered in so much blood that it's all you see. I should be appalled. I should be reining Jaxon in and stopping this madness, but I don't utter a single word in protest of his actions.

If anything, glee fills me at seeing Ajax's blood after knowing the horrors that Jaxon suffered because of his reckless actions. This deranged animal really thought that I would have run off with him after he had a trained assassin shoot at me. I would have been frightened enough to leave my empire behind and run off into the sunset with him. How fucking pitiful and weak he must have believed I was. He never valued me; he, too, saw me as just a possession to steal for his own.

"She will show you no mercy, you fucker. You could have seriously hurt her; you could have killed her. You would have rather risked her life so you could manipulate her than see her have a future with me. I will send you to the devil for almost taking my queen from me." A large cut opens on Ajax's shoulder blade, and blood slides down his chest. "She was always mine. She will always be mine." Ajax's screams are getting louder, and Jaxon looks like he's losing control of himself. The sound should be frightening to me. I shouldn't be standing here watching this. No normal person would just watch as a man is tediously tortured before them, but I can't seem to force the objection to cross my lips or my body to move to stop Jaxon's actions.

Maybe there was never anything normal about me. Satisfaction, pride, and lust rush through me, watching my husband carry out painful justice against someone who tried to hurt me, hurt us. My core clenches, and wetness trickles down my inner thigh, my nipples getting painfully hard underneath the shirt I'm wearing at every slash of the blade in Jaxon's hand. I am so aroused at his anger, at him taking justice into his own hands against the man who tried to take me from him. His nostrils flare like he's scenting me, like he knows I am aroused by his actions. At the blood of an enemy coating his hands. Make no mistake, Ajax is an enemy.

"Are you wet, Stella?" The question comes out raspy and filled with need as Jaxon halts the blade's motion over Ajax's heaving chest.

I want to dispute that I am, I shouldn't be turned on by the sight in front of me, but I can't. I bite down hard on my lower lip and nod, a deep animalistic growl leaving Jaxon's lips. *Fuck.*

31

Jaxon

"Give them pleasure. The same pleasure they have when they wake up from a nightmare." Alfred Hitchcock

"**U**NBUTTON YOUR BLOUSE, REMOVE it and your bra, and take off your skirt, Stella." My command comes out gruff to my own ears and filled with heat. My cock hardens at the sight of my wife turned on before me. She's enjoying the torture and retribution I'm seeking on Ajax's flesh. The color has risen up the smooth pale column of her neck and over the creamy soft skin of her cheeks. Her eyes are luminous and so large that they almost seem to glow with blue fire. She's breathing heavily, but I don't think it has anything to do with her act of violence or rage. She's turned the fuck on, and I need a taste, just like a parched man needs a drink in a desert.

Stella's eyes are two sapphires sparkling and never leaving mine. I watch with rapt attention as she unbuttons her silk blouse and then unlatches her bra, leaving her glorious round breasts loose and on display. Her dark pink nipples are hard, begging to be sucked and nibbled at in my mouth. She unzips the skirt, and it pools at her bare feet, leaving her completely naked before me. I had forgotten that I had taken her panties earlier, and now seeing her like this makes me so happy I did.

Ajax releases a harsh cry, his head moving back and forth on his neck, pitiful moans and tears escaping him. He keeps repeating the word "No" repeatedly, but it is ignored. "Do you see the perfection that is mine, Ajax? My wife, my queen, and my whore." I slam the hard metal end of the blade into the side of his head. "You tried to take that from me. You tried to steal what was mine, and now you will fucking suffer."

I step towards Stella, my hands still covered in Ajax's blood as I reach out and squeeze both of her round breasts, pulling on the hard nipples between two of my fingers on each hand and unleashing a cry of pleasure from her mouth. The blood leaves fingerprints on her skin against all that creamy pale flesh and has my cock standing at attention and weeping.

Fuck I should drench her in his blood and then my cum, fucking her over and over in every one of her tight holes. "Get on your knees, Stella, like my *good little slut*, and take my cock into your mouth." She hesitates for the briefest of moments, her eyes wide at my command, but my hand yanks on her lengthy hair, forcing her down on her knees.

Her breathing leaves her in ragged pants, and a pink flush crosses her heaving chest. She's tightening her thighs, rubbing them against each other in obvious need, seeking friction. A need I plan to fulfill shortly, but first, I need to make a point to our very captive guest. She lowers herself to her knees before me and unzips my pants, sliding them down my legs and removing my shoes, pants, and socks. Her small fingers slide back up my calves and thighs. Her soft lips follow the same path and leave trails of kisses in her wake that have the hairs on my body standing on end. A rumble leaves my chest when her small fingers encase my hard dick. "My good little whore." I murmur.

My head falls forward until my chin is on my upper chest, the feeling of her fingers so exquisite that it makes me tremble in my stance. I grasp a fistful of her hair, yanking on the strands until a small whimper escapes her lips. I wrap my other hand around her breast, squeezing the fleshy globe tightly before slapping it hard with the palm of my hand. A moan breathlessly leaves her lips, and her lungs expand and contract rapidly with her arousal, causing her breasts to sway before my eyes.

"Did you know that my wife likes to be used like a dirty slut? That she craves a little pain with her fucking? That degradation excites her and makes her pussy gush?" A chuckle leaves my lips as Stella's tongue licks my length. "I bet you were gentle with her as if she was some fine China doll and not made for fucking sin." I slap her other breast with my open palm; the sound is loud in the room, and a whimper leaves her lips as she continues to use her lips to nuzzle and kiss the veins on my hard cock. Her lips drag from my base to my tip and back down, where she licks my balls before sucking one into her mouth. *Fuck, that feels so good.*

I yank on her hair and pull her back, and she releases my testicle with a plop of her plump lips. I slide my bloody fingers across her lips, smearing Ajax's blood across her mouth and cheek. "Open, my little slut." I watch with amusement as she opens her mouth wide, and I spit into it, forcing her mouth to close with my fingers as she swallows. I drop the knife on the bed next to us and wrap my other hand tightly around her throat, ensuring that tomorrow, my pretty wife will be wearing a hand necklace in my exact size. Maybe just maybe, I'll reward her with a cum one to match.

Her breath leaves her in a sharp gasp that has my tip leaking drops of precum down my shaft. She opens her lips wide to beg, and I shove my hard cock to the back of her throat until my lower stomach is flush with her face. She struggles wildly on her knees, scratching me and trying to pull away, but my hold on her hair and neck prevents her from moving away from me. I fuck her mouth hard and with pent-up violence, all the while watching my best friend's devastated face with joy.

His world is crumbling around him now, realizing that he never really knew her this way. This sinful, passionate creature who likes to be taken charge of and used for pleasure. She was always mine, made for me, even if he had her first.

I release the hold on her throat and let air make its way back inside of her with a shuddering and pleasurable gasp. I yank her by the hair to stand up, my cock slipping from her wet mouth coated in strings of her saliva and my precum.

"I bet that pretty cunt of yours is drenched, isn't it, my pretty whore?" Her tongue slips out of her mouth and licks her bottom lip, her blues dilated and large. "Climb on Ajax's lap Stella and rub that soaked pussy on his dick. Let him see what a whore you are. What he missed out on with his sad dick and kind ways."

She stumbles as she rises but refuses my hold on her arm, tearing it from my grasp. Her eyes flash with rancor as they meet and narrow on mine. She looks like she's going to slap me hard for my demand that she ride Ajax's lap. Her defiance intrigues me; we both know she's immensely turned on and that she likes to submit to my brand of control and depravity. Have I misjudged her? She tilts her head, and I read her loud and clear. She will allow me to play my games for now, but if I push her, I'm likely to end up with a blade pressed up to my own neck.

Her gaze turns away from me and centers back on Ajax, and I watch as the look of pleasure races across her face. But it's not pleasure at the thought of being on the fucker's lap; it's the look she gets when she seizes control and power. She feels powerful right now. Her gorgeous face strips me bare of oxygen. She's so sexy and lush, her breasts tinged pink from my palms, swaying as she moves. She pauses as she shifts to straddle Ajax, and I see the look of not only hunger but also defiance and a giant *fuck you* to both of us cross her features. Her eyes never leave mine, even as she grinds on his lap, his hard pant-covered dick rubbing against her clit. For a moment, rage and jealousy fill me, and my actions backfire on me.

She is fucking mine; I don't want my cunt touching him. Every part of her is mine. I watch the pain across Ajax's face, the way his breath is leaving through his flaring nostrils, and how hard his jaw is clenching. He wants her; even seeing that she is my dirty little whore he still wants her.

"Tell Ajax whose dirty cunt that is Stella." She grinds again on his lap, her head falling to the side on her shoulder, her dark waves cascading down her back. A moan leaves her lips as she gasps, "Yours, your whore." Her full breasts bounce on her chest with each undulation of her waist on that traitor's cock.

I'm losing control, my cock leaking beads of precum, watching her get herself off on Ajax's restrained lap. I need to reclaim her, to rein in my rumbling chaos. The need to drive my cock into that sweet pussy and reconfirm that she is mine, strumming through my veins and causing an animalistic rush to pour through me.

"Get on the bed, Stella." She climbs up, moving slowly, her ass and swollen cunt on display before us and her creamy breasts bouncing. I grab a fistful of her loose, rich waves and pull her off Ajax's lap, roughly pushing her toward the end of the bed. "Lie on your back and spread your legs wide so Ajax can see that pretty, pink pussy that belongs to me."

She hesitates, her eyes meeting mine with fire, and I know she's close to refusing me. Stella will give me control in sex, but only up to a point. Power calls to her like a seductive mistress, and right now, I'm using all of mine to teach this piece of shit a lesson and to fuck my wife raw, so she never forgets who owns her. Electricity zaps down my spine at just the thought of being deep inside of her.

Will she deny me my right to own her? To show this fucker once and for all that she is mine in every way? If she's as intelligent as I know she is, she had better not. My control is precarious right now. My fury is seething through me, knowing I'm amongst a traitor and a thief. I bare my teeth at her like a wolf, and a growl rumbles from my chest.

Her eyes dart to Ajax briefly and then down to my erect cock. She bites down hard on her bottom lip as she leans back slowly and lies on the bed, opening her legs wide, and bending her knees. Her beautiful bare pussy glistens in the light with her arousal. Her pussy lips are still swollen from me fucking her earlier, and what a beautiful sight they are. It gives me so much pleasure to know I filled up her with my cum at her office, and I mean to do it again now.

I grab the blade off the bed and move towards her, a cry leaving Ajax's lips at the movement. *Does the fool really think that I would hurt her?* Never, she's mine in every way, and I have no intentions of damaging her, at least not permanently.

I slide the handle of the blade over the inside of her thighs and then across her swollen pussy lips, the metal sliding through her wet slit and getting coated in her juices. She lets out a little moan, and I slip the end of the handle into her tight hole, letting an inch and then another sink inside her as her body locks up tight. She thrashes her head on the bed, her hands fisting the linens beneath her. I push another two inches inside of her until I'm only holding an inch of the handle and the sharp blade in my hand. I slide it in and out of her cunt until the whole thing is coated in her juices. "Does that feel good, my dirty little queen?"

A moan rents the air simultaneously; a groan leaves Ajax behind me. "Please, Jaxon, stop this!" Ajax begs. A deranged smile crosses my lips at how he's suffering, watching how wet she is for me. How her cunt is dripping and soaking the bed below her, with how turned on she is. I fuck her for a few more strokes with the handle, the index finger of my other hand rubbing tight circles around her nub. Her tight pussy swallows the handle, and I have to be careful not to slice her with it in my eagerness to fuck her with it. I pull it out, and her cum soaks it. I move back over to Ajax, sliding the handle over his lips, coating his mouth with Stella's cum. Stella leans up on one elbow to watch me while she tugs on her own nipple, amusement on her beautiful face.

"Did she ever taste so delicious to you? Was she ever dripping for you like she is for me?" I can see by his expression and the way he is licking her taste off his lips that she wasn't. He didn't know how to make her wet like this.

Didn't know that the fierce, strong, and conservative Stella Stratford gets off on exhibitionism. That she leaves her fight for feminism at the door when she wants to get her pussy destroyed. That Stella enjoys the thrill of getting caught fucking by strangers, pain, and sexual control. She is perfect in every way for me, and I'm going to make sure she can never leave me. If she ever tries, I will slit her fucking throat.

I slip the blade handle into his mouth, and he sucks her taste off of it with a greedy groan. Stella watches from her raised elbows, her lips parted, and her thighs tightening in arousal at me feeding another man her cum. "That's as close to my wife's cunt as you're ever going to get again, motherfucker." I pull the handle from his mouth and move back to my wife.

She spreads her thighs wide for me, and I slip two fingers inside of her warm wet pussy, pumping a few strokes before pulling them back out and sliding her wetness over my thick cock. I slip three fingers back inside of her, fucking her hard and stretching her cunt wide, all the while making sure that Ajax can see her soaked pussy being used by me, stretching and making her gape for me.

Her breathing is getting ragged, and her hips are undulating and rising quicker and quicker. She's close to orgasming for me. My thumb rubs over her hard, little nub, applying a little pressure to create friction and circles on the little ball of tissue. I pull my soaked fingers back from her cunt and slip two inside her puckered hole without warning or prep, causing a cry of pain to leave her lips.

"You never got to feel how tight her puckered hole is, did you, Ajax? It's so warm and tight, like a vise. She clenches it so beautifully. Watch how my thick fingers stretch her." I taunt him as I fuck her ass with my fingers, preparing and stretching her for my cock. I'm determined that this fucker is going to watch me take all of her holes, so that he sees that she is entirely mine. *Tainted and filled by my cum.*

I grab the base of my cock and move it to her pussy hole, slipping just the tip inside of her and coating myself in her wetness. I plunge in hard in one go, bottoming out as a scream leaves her lips, and she claws at my shoulders and back with her nails. My fingers continue to stretch her asshole. My other hand lifts and urges her legs over my shoulders so I can pound into her warm cunt. "Fuck, her cunt is even tighter like this. My fingers can feel my cock moving inside of her."

"Jaxon, oh my God!" Stella cries out, her head thrashing on the bed and her hands fisting the linens.

"That's right, baby, I am your god. Pull on your nipples, and stroke that pretty clit for me, baby." She does what I ask, and I move my hand from her clit up to her neck, choking her out. I fuck her cunt in hard strokes that have her shifting up the bed with each thrust. "Are you going to come for me, my slut?" I groan at how tight she is, her pussy is clamping firmly even more around me, and her limbs are locking in place. I watch, amazed, as she comes hard, her breath trapped in her throat against my grip, her eyes rolling to the back of her head, and her legs tightening around my head. She cries out repeatedly, and the sound is music to my ears but devastation, no doubt, to the fucker behind us.

When she finally comes down from her high, I pull out of her pussy and flip her over onto her stomach, slapping her ass hard and pulling on her hair to arch her back for me and forcing her to her knees. I slip my face down between her folds, licking up her delicious cunt, over her clit, and slipping my tongue in her tight hole before pulling out and licking her puckered asshole and slipping my tongue inside. I fuck her for a few moments with just my tongue and then pull back, yanking on her hair until her neck arches for me and a pained moan leaves her lips. "Open your mouth Stella, nice and wide." I spit a wad of saliva, a mixture of her cum, and my cum from earlier, and the taste of her sweet pussy. "Swallow, my little whore."

I pull back, hawk up more spit, and let it slide between her two perfect ass cheeks and hit her puckered hole. My hard cock nudges at the puckered ring of nerves, and I slip the crown inside. Stella releases a cry of pain and then a moan, her head falling forward to the bed linens. I push forward until half my dick is trapped in her tight heat. "I can't, Jaxon; it hurts, please!" She thrashes. I push in another inch, and she tightens further around me. I slap her ass again and again until her body stops fighting me, and my palm is hot from her flesh.

"You will take all of me, Stella. This ass is mine." I push forward, sinking the last couple of inches inside of her until her ass cheeks are pressed firmly against my abdomen. I thrust slowly, not wanting to tear her, but wanting her tight ass to adjust to my size. When her cries turn into moans, I thrust harder, her ass gripping painfully around my thick cock. I know I'm not going to last long with how warm and tight she is. I need her to go again, though, before I fill her up with my cum. I reach around and slip three fingers inside her pussy until she's impossibly full and strum my thumb over and over on her throbbing clit.

"Jaxon! FUCK!" Her loud moan is everything I dream about.

A few more harsh strokes and her body locks tight again, dots of perspiration and goosebumps breaking out across her skin, and she screams into the mattress. I follow her quickly into oblivion, my cock throbbing and pumping her puckered hole full of my creamy, thick cum.

When I can finally catch my breath, and my chest doesn't feel like it will explode, I pull out of her holes. I stumble off the bed to stand next to my former best friend, wrapping my arm tightly around his neck as we watch rivulets of my thick cum drip out of her puckered hole, down her pussy, coating every part of her and dripping onto our bed. I bend my face next to my traitorous friend's, tears trickling down the side of his face.

"Do you see how beautiful she looks, filled with my cum? I'm going to fill all those holes daily, and eventually, I'll put a baby in her womb. While you, you will live with the regret of having lost everything. Your heart, the girl of your dreams, your best friend, and all of your family's money. I'll take everything from you like you tried to do to me." An evil smirk crosses my face at the look of horror across his face.

"When you have nothing left to lose, Ajax, remember I still have her; she is mine. Remember, you are watching the rise of an empire before you. My empire, with my fucking queen."

Stella sits up, wrapping the duvet around her and looking thoroughly fucked and ravaged but incredibly uncomfortable now that her passion has been assuaged. She stares at Ajax, and her emotions are in that mask that she hides behind. I want entry into that mind of hers. I want to know what she's thinking, how she's feeling. Everything about Stella Stratford interests me; I'll never get enough of her.

"Why the chicken and the spa? Why did you keep trying if you didn't mean to hurt me? That masseuse took a knife wound meant for me." She questions with a raised eyebrow.

Horror crosses Ajax's features at her words. "What the fuck are you talking about, Stella? I never sent anyone other than the idiot to the house who ended up shooting Jaxon!"

"You didn't make more than one attempt to scare her or go after her?" I question, fury rising once again inside of me. I grab his neck and tighten my grip until he is forced to look away from her and into my eyes. I see nothing but confusion, concern, and fear there. *Shit. He didn't send anyone else.*

"Fuck Stella, there's more than one person after you, and I don't think the other person is just trying to scare you!" I release my grip on Ajax and move back to the bed, pulling Stella sharply into my arms, and holding her tight in my grip as my heart thuds erratically in my chest. Fear races inside of all of my limbs now that I have once again come to the realization that someone is trying to hurt her.

Someone is trying to take what is fucking mine!

32

Stella

"True love is like ghosts, which everyone talks about and few have seen." Francois de La Rochefoucauld

I MUST HAVE PASSED out after my shower when Jaxon left with a broken, sniveling, and pitiful Ajax. I couldn't even look at him as Jaxon dragged him from the room by the hair, and he stumbled about. I heard his cry of pain on the stairs as Jaxon pushed him forward. He must have fallen the last few steps, landing in a disgraced heap at the bottom.

My stomach recoiled when I rushed out and witnessed how much pain he was in and how he was begging Jaxon for mercy. A mercy that Jaxon would not grant him. The look of complete satisfaction across my husband's face scared me deeply. Was there a possibility that Ajax wasn't ever making it home? Was Jaxon's rage enough to have him doing something that would cause irreversible damage?

I wanted to call out to him and ask him not to do something he would regret, but the words stayed trapped in my throat. The truth is I wanted to see the destruction he caused. I enjoyed his rage and possession. I craved it, deep inside of me. I wanted to know that he would burn the world down for trying to take what he thought was his.

It lit a fire within me and called to me like a seductive lover's embrace, wrapping around me tightly until I was warm and safe. I should be worried that I'm starting to think of myself as his, worried that I'm as insane as Jaxon is, that I, too, enjoy the suffering of others who have wronged me.

My mind is still reeling, trying to comprehend all that happened here tonight—all that I allowed to happen. Would Jaxon have stopped it all if I had asked him to?

Somehow, I know that he wouldn't have. His need for vengeance and domination was right before me and would not be denied.

I'm still finding it difficult to swallow the knowledge that Ajax hired someone to shoot at me. Regardless if his intent wasn't to actually kill me, only to scare me. Look at what ended up happening with his reckless behavior; Jaxon almost died of a gunshot wound to the chest. *That could have been me; he could have killed me.*

Anger once again surges like molten lava through my body; how could he have been so stupid? How did he think hurting me was ever going to get me back? Would I have left Jaxon if I felt I was in danger? All these questions circulate in my mind in a never-ending cycle.

Then, there are the two other matters to wrap my brain around. The first is that a second person is out there trying to actively harm me. Someone left the headless chicken on my desk, and someone tried to stab me at the spa a few weeks ago. *Am I dealing with multiple people, or is it just one more enemy trying to hurt me?* Enemies seem to be sprouting out of every corner, and my mother's warning echoes back in my mind. *"You are making waves when you should be making ripples."* Is she right? Is this all because I have taken power, or is it because I have married Jaxon? Could these be his enemies and not only my own? *Does it matter? Any enemy to Jaxon is an enemy to you*, the thought whispers across my mind.

The last matter brings heat to my face at the slightest image of the memory entering my mind. How wanton I was, allowing Jaxon to fuck me like that in front of Ajax. To enable him to dominate and control me. To show Ajax who I genuinely am behind the facade. Jaxon brings out feelings inside of me that I don't seem to have a way to control. His ruthlessness and power call to me like a siren's song. Some part of me wanted to hurt Ajax badly for the pain he inflicted on Jaxon and all the stress and worry I had to live through, not knowing if Jaxon was going to live. Still, I have never lost control and never behaved submissively before, and now it's like an addict's craving in my blood.

There is no point in trying to delude myself. I enjoyed the whole interaction a bit too much. For the first time in my life, I let go of the need to control the situation, the need for power. I allowed my inhibitions to run rampant and just savored the experience, the intoxication that Jaxon always seems to put me under. The pleasure that Jaxon produces with every touch, lick, and caress of my body. The way he takes control of me, never truly giving me an option in the matter. He used me for his pleasure, knowing that he could, and it caused electricity to race through me.

The knowledge that we had a captive audience just intensified the whole situation and made it sexier and more depraved. The pain we caused Ajax by forcing him to bear witness was incredibly arousing. Knowing that Ajax was watching Jaxon claim and control me over and over had my orgasms ripping out of me painfully.

I'm unsure if I should worry about how readily I succumbed to Jaxon's ministrations and commands. A part of me is horrified at my loss of complete control and the fact that he called me his *'dirty, little whore,'* the other part of me is clenching my thighs tightly at the memory of his voice and the look in his gaze as he said it. *Am I his dirty, little whore?* The thought doesn't offend me the way it should. If anything, the desire to hear him utter those words once again is a thrill in my blood.

Light shines through the open curtains that I forgot to draw in my exhaustion last night. A heavy arm is wrapped around me, and a warm, hard body is pressed tightly against me in bed. I should be shocked at the feeling of someone in bed with me, that Jaxon took that liberty without asking me first. *He did warn you after he fucked you raw on your desk*, my mind snickers.

I open my eyes and turn my head to see Jaxon's face up close and his jaw nestled into my shoulder, trying to hide from the daylight streaming across his gorgeous features. I try to dislodge his arm and move further away from him in the large bed, but he tightens his grip, pulling me more snugly against his hard body as a sleepy groan leaves his lips.

The silk nightgown I slipped into last night after showering is doing nothing to stop me from feeling every rugged ridge of Jaxon's body, including one that is currently poking me in my ass cheek. I study his features up close, starting with his thick, dark eyebrows and the long, dark, full lashes that rest like soft feathers against his skin. The light freckles spattered across his straight nose, high cheekbones, and delectable mouth, with his full pouty bottom lip and upper lip, parted in sleep. He has the beginning of a five o'clock shadow across his jaw, and for some reason, I don't comprehend. I find his disheveled state incredibly alluring and sexy. The desire to run my hand across his stubble is heady, and I have to force myself not to reach out and touch him.

"You keep staring at me so intently, *wife*. I might get worried you're not enjoying what you're seeing." His words are rumbled, still coated in sleep, and he opens both of his eyes to greet mine. The deep gray depth looks like two bright and shiny circles of silver in the daylight. He lets his lips rest against the skin of my shoulder in a soft kiss before dragging his lips up my collarbone and neck, leaving a trail of soft kisses before reaching for my lips. I melt into the embrace without any thought and have to force myself to swallow the moans of pleasure that are trying to escape me.

I pull back from him, horrified. "Jaxon, I haven't brushed my teeth yet!" My voice comes out shrill and filled with indignation. A chuckle leaves his lips, and he pulls me even tighter until every inch of my back is pressed against his warm skin. "I ate your ass last night, Stella. I think I won't be the slightest bit offended if you have morning breath."

He rolls me underneath his warm heavy body, and bears his weight down, crushing me into the mattress. His knee parts my legs so he can slip himself between my parted thighs, his morning wood making itself at home pushing against my rapidly dampening pussy. His lips drift over mine in a soft kiss, his tongue tracing my bottom lip before nibbling at it and then pushing against the seam of my closed lips, requesting entry.

I give in immediately, parting my lips, and his warm tongue meets mine, causing a groan to leave both our mouths. Warning bells are going off in my head that we are losing our precious control to this man. There will be no Stella Stratford left, just Jaxon's possession if we don't tread carefully. *Do we even know who we are anymore?* My mind questions with irritation.

Jaxon and I spend the next few moments kissing deeply like two teenagers who can't seem to get enough of each other. He sucks my tongue hard into his mouth, and a growl escapes his throat that sounds like a wolf about to devour his prey. Moans and whimpers are loud in the room, and the temperature rises inside of me with every swipe of his tongue.

An all-consuming feeling rushes through me to submit to him and let him take me any way he wants. To use and devour me because, in this heated moment, I am his. We rub against each other, warm flesh against warm flesh, causing my heart rate to increase. His hard cock pushes against the silk of my panties until they are soaked, and my core is begging for his hard dick. "Jaxon..." His name leaves my lips in a moan that has goosebumps breaking out across my skin.

Jaxon pulls back from me and sits back on his folded legs, pulling the linens with him until I'm lying here spread open in nothing but a flimsy chemise that covers next to nothing. He's got a pair of dark gray boxer briefs on and all that glorious golden inked skin exposed to my view. The Stratford crest prominent on his chest, the desire to trace it with my tongue, is almost overwhelming. The wound on his chest is the only imperfection visible on his gorgeous body, and yet, it fits perfectly with the man before me.

He is sexy, powerful, dangerous, and ruthless. All the attributes women dream of in naughty romance books that have your heart pumping in your chest. I brace myself on my elbow, letting my fingers run across all the hard muscles of his chest and abdomen. I know he started working with the personal trainer again last week to help rebuild some of the muscles he lost while in the coma and recovering, and it is definitely paying off.

I run my finger lightly over the pink wound before skating it down his chest across the black swirls of ink and the Stratford crest. I let my red nail graze over the defined six-pack definition in his stomach and follow his happy trail of dark hair into the band of his boxers. Leaning forward, I give into the need to taste his skin and let my tongue trace the outline of the Stratford crest before pulling back and grinning at him. Goosebumps rise across his skin in my wake, and his breathing increases, causing his chest to rise and fall more rapidly. *Fuck, he is so sexy, all mused from sleep and desperate for my touch.* A desperation that I, too, feel. I want him, and I won't pretend otherwise.

"Are you hungry for my cock, Stella?" He smirks with devilish intent at me. "Which of your pretty holes needs to be filled first, hmmm baby?"

His crude words and term of endearment have my core clenching painfully and my nipples perking and hardening. I never realized before, Jaxon, how sexy a filthy and vulgar mouth could be. He leans down, sucking my nipple through the silk fabric of my nightgown as my back arches into his touch. A whimper leaves my lips at how sore I am between my legs, but how much I crave his cock inside of me. He sucks my right nipple while rolling the other one between his fingers, then switches to the other one providing the same treatment.

"Are you sore, baby?" His words are whispered into the flesh of my breast, and the vibration against my skin makes my nipple throb. I nod, not even sure I can produce words right now with how glorious he is making me feel. "Good. I want you to always feel me inside of you, so you know who owns you."

His cock presses against my barely there panties and pushes against my throbbing clit. A groan leaves my lips as I run my fingers through his dark, thick hair, pulling on the strands and forcing his head down my body towards my core. "I need... you, Jaxon," my voice is breathy as I moan the words, trying to encourage him to suck on my clit.

"Is your needy cunt throbbing for me, baby? Does this juicy wet pussy need my tongue inside of her, eating her like a starving man?" He moves further back on the bed, until his body is sprawled between my legs, and his face is up against my mound. I watch as his tongue peeks out between his lips and runs up my folds through the silk and lace of my panties. A groan leaves his mouth as he tastes my arousal on the fabric. I'm so wet that the material at my crotch is completely and embarrassingly soaked. He drags it to the side with his finger, and his tongue licks me from my puckered hole to my clit and then back again. "What a pretty cunt." He moans into my skin.

"Jaxon..." I mewl. The sound filled with surprise and heat. Fuck, he makes my body scorch with warmth and excitement at how quickly he can get me so close to the edge with just his mouth. Everything about Jaxon Stratford is an enticement, his body, face, voice, and all the naughty words he lets loose from that filthy mouth. He releases a growl that sounds more beast than man and slips his tongue into my hot channel, fucking me over and over with it until I'm a writhing and soaked mess on the bed and yanking on his hair, trying to ride his face to my completion.

The fire builds within me, a searing burn across my limbs, and electricity races through my blood. He sucks hard down on my clit as he slips two thick fingers inside of me and strokes my front wall. All the sensations have my breathing coming in frazzled pants and prisms of lights bursting behind my eyes as my orgasm races through my body. My core tightens painfully over his thick fingers as he bites down lightly on my throbbing nub. I lose all control, coming all over his face in a gush of fluid, a loud cry leaving my lips with my stalled breath.

"Mmm, you taste like fuckin' heaven, Stella. I'll never get enough of this sweet pussy." He licks me through my aftershocks and then moves up my body, his face wet with my arousal and his lips glistening. His fingers pull my lips open wide as a drizzle of spit leaves his mouth and falls into mine. "See how delicious you are, my little ice queen." I taste my salty and musky flavor in the spit, watching Jaxon's reaction as I swallow and lick my lips.

"Mmm..." A moan leaves my parted lips, and I watch him slip his boxers off and part my legs wider.

"Are you too sore from my cock last night, Stella?" He holds his long, veiny, thick erection in his tight fist, stroking it over and over until drops of precum leak from the slit and drop on my pussy lips. Watching him touch himself is so erotic, the way his breathing picks up, and his abs clench tight with each stroke. "Yes," I answer in a whispered moan, biting down on the inside of my cheek, feeling embarrassed because I'm really sore, even slightly uncomfortable, but I'm also needy, and I'm trying to keep from begging him to take me hard. He slides his crown back and forth over my skin, coating himself and me in his precum.

"Good baby, I want this pretty cunt to hurt and feel its master." His fingers part my folds, and his cock fills me with a hard thrust. The sensation and soreness causes me to cry out as he starts a punishing rhythm of pounding into me hard, never giving me a chance to adjust to his length and girth. The burn and pinch of pain both feel euphoric and sting as he thrusts relentlessly inside of me. The sound of our skin slapping against each other is loud and echoes through the large room. The grunts leaving his lips, the mewling sounds leaving mine, and the sound of how wet I am, are obscene in the otherwise silent space.

I grasp tight to his shoulders, digging my nails in before dragging them down his back with purpose. Wanting to mark him up, so that he, too, has a memory of me all day. "Fuck, Stella, that hurts so good." My legs wrap tightly around his waist, and I meet each of his hard thrusts urging him to fuck me harder. Sweat is coating his brow and chest; I lean forward and lick up a drop that's making its way from his neck downwards. His breathing is rough, and his neck and cheeks are turning crimson with the exertion.

Once again, common fucking sense tries to enter my mind, and the thought that this is too much strenuous activity fills me. I should stop him; we should move slower. He's still recovering from three heart attacks. *Fuck, we are being so reckless.* I try to push him back and off of me, so we can slow down or stop, but his hand wraps around my throat. "I'm fine. Shut up and enjoy the ride, Stella." He thrusts hard into me, and his fingers tighten further. "Open your mouth, my pretty whore."

I open my mouth as wide as possible with his fingers still tightening on my throat. He pulls out suddenly from inside of my throbbing core and straddles my chest, his hard cock, the head dark red and throbbing in his hand. He strokes himself once, twice, and on the third stroke, ropes of cum leak out and fall into my open mouth, covering my lips, chin, and cheeks. He's making a fucking mess of me, covering me in his essence like some wolf marking his mate. Once he's done cumming he runs his thick cock through the mess on my face, coating himself in it before slipping it into my mouth.

"Suck baby, suck all of my cum off my cock. Be a good little whore and swallow every drop. Lick your master clean."

He releases his hold on my neck, and I lick every drop from his semi-rigid dick, my tongue rubbing down his shaft and over his balls, sucking and licking one and then the other and back up the side of his dick until I reach the crown. I lash my tongue over the slit, cleaning off any cum, and suck it vigorously between my lips. "Jesus, Stella, you're going to have me blowing my load again down that tight throat if you don't stop."

I pull back with a smirk on my face as he watches me, but notice the color on his face has risen, and sweat is beading on his forehead and trickling down the side of his face. His chest rises and falls rapidly, and his breath leaves him in ragged pants. *Fuck, now that I know how much pleasure he can give me, I don't want the fucker to die on me.* I pull him down next to me, and he wraps me in his arms, holding me tight against his chest. I can feel his heart thumping quickly against the palm of my hand.

"Jaxon... we need to slow down. You almost died a few weeks ago." I try for a soothing way to get my worries across.

"Stella, don't ask me not to fuck your cunt dirty and hard. It's all I think about. I'm not denying myself any of your holes." He releases a deep sigh and kisses my hair. "I don't want to talk about me almost dying. I want to talk about how you're still in danger from some unknown asshole and how we're going to protect you."

"I have the security, Jaxon; no one is getting close to me." I nestle further into his warm embrace, leaning my cheek over his heart and feeling the intense beating behind his golden skin. What would I do if something happened to him? Would it really matter in the grand scheme of things? In my quest for power, is Jaxon necessary or just a diversion? Do I have feelings, other than gratitude and guilt for him?

Yes, I'm incredibly attracted to him, but is that a place to grow a marriage from? All these questions are a cyclone of thoughts running problematically through my mind. I have no answers for any of them, and I try to avoid focusing on why that is.

I am not in love with him, right? He is just a man. An incredibly sexy man, with a fantastic body and an earth-shattering and orgasm-inducing dick. I don't have to like him or have feelings for him to take advantage of that, do I? Is it the guilt that he took a bullet meant for me? For some reason, that thought no longer convinces or validates my reactions to him.

"It's not enough, Stella. One slip and someone could get to you."

"Jaxon, I'm not going to hide out in our home, cowering from an assailant or whoever means me harm. I have two companies to run, two empires to build." The thought is not lost on me; that is precisely what I've been doing to him for weeks. Holding him hostage here in our home while he recovered.

"Speaking of those empires and those companies. We are building one empire, Stella. The Stratford empire, one we can leave to our future offspring." He presses his lips to my neck and sucks hard. "There is no, your company or my company. They are both ours, and I think it's time they became one, with you and I jointly at the head."

"You want to merge both companies and run them together?" Fear and excitement race through me as I pull back to stare at him. The look on his face is so intense and severe, but I see the sincerity there. He means it. He wants to merge the companies together and run them as one, together as Stratfords. I'm a Stratford now, no longer a Penticton. He is right; we would be unbeatable if we merged them. Laying waste to any and all of our enemies and anyone who seeks to challenge us.

"Stella, you have an awe-inspiring mind and a ruthless knack for business. Your father was an imbecile not to have seen what value you bring. I won't make that mistake. If I'm going to make the Stratford name a powerful empire that others cower in fear of, I need you. Not just for your name or a baby. I need your mind, your ideas, and the ruthlessness that lives inside of you.

"I don't want to be your husband in fucking name only Stella. This is not a power game between you and me. It's us against the world, baby. I want to be your husband in all aspects, the father of your children, the man you come to with your problems, and I want to be your business partner as an equal."

His words cause tears to race to my eyes, but I hold them back, refusing to appear weak before him. My heart feels like it's cracking open for him. All the resentment and rage that fills me daily at being thought of as less than starts to thaw at his words. He wants to be my equal, someone who sees value in me, not because of my appearance, who my father is, or for my womb.

Do I trust that he is being sincere? Do I let my guard down and meet him halfway? I notice he doesn't say that he's in love with me. Does that really matter? For a brief moment, pain sears through my chest at the thought that Jaxon will never love me. A longing fills me to hear those words leave his lips. Will he ever utter them to me? *Do I love him?* I desire him in a way that overwhelms me and makes me feel off balance, but do I love him?

This could all be a ploy to gain control. Maybe he is just saying all of this now because it's what he thinks I want to hear, and then he will take Penticton Industries from me. *He could have already done that; he didn't need to give us the board seat or the shares.* Yes, but I would have made his life a living hell if he didn't. *Did you see what he did to Ajax last night? Jaxon is not afraid to get his hands dirty.* The thought vibrates through my mind.

Jaxon has a reputation for being ruthless and manipulative in business. I know that he is involved with some unsavory characters as well. His underworld connections are well hidden from the general public, but not from my prying eyes. I know of some of the destruction he has caused to his enemies without the slightest indication of regret. Do I trust him, or do I guard my heart and mind? If I let him in, will he attempt to destroy me, turn me into some weak woman who follows where her husband leads?

I would rather fucking die than become one of these powerless women. I think I will play it safe for now, take the pleasure he is offering, and work as a partner to build our empire. As for my heart, I need to rein that bitch back. She's already softening towards him, and that is dangerous territory. I'll hold on to that piece of myself and see how this all plays out with my new *devoted* husband until I know his true intentions.

33

Stella

"It's so easy to be wicked without knowing it, isn't it?" Lucy Maud Montgomery

IT'S BEEN WEEKS SINCE the incident with Ajax in our bedroom, and I've been on the receiving end of daily and nightly pleasure from my union with Jaxon. His threats and promises that we would be sharing everything going forward from the afternoon when he had my ass up across my desk have come to fruition, and my needy pussy couldn't be happier with the arrangement. In fact, all my holes seem to be singing his unrelenting praises. *I'm becoming a thirsty bitch where he's concerned.*

Jaxon has awakened a libertine in me that I didn't realize existed. One that craves him at all hours and never seems to have enough of the pleasure he provides with his hard cock, mouth, and long fingers.

We have ventured out of the Stratford estate and had experiences I never considered myself capable of. Jaxon is insatiable, taking what he wants, whenever and wherever he wants it. Even if it be in compromising situations like in the parking lot of the theater we attended. Or finger fucking me at a charity gala under the linens while we sat at a table filled with fellow wealthy elites, and I had to swallow my moans, almost biting through my cheek to try to contain them.

There are no limits, it seems, to his depravity. Last Sunday, he fucked me raw in a curtained confessional while Sunday mass was happening a few feet away. The horrified looks on the parishioner's faces when we made our way out of the small, confined space had both of us giggling until we couldn't breathe. Needless to say, my mother sent me a scathing note the same day about showing some restraint and being a lady. Jaxon just crumbled it in his fist and fucked me on the floor next to it.

We just completed the merger of Penticton and Stratford Industries yesterday, to my father's horror and vivid objections. Stratford Industries is now one of the largest and wealthiest businesses in the world. I hope everyone's trembling at our feet. We're about to make history as we clear the board of our competitors. The feeling of so much power runs through my veins, putting me on cloud nine. I can't wait to watch them all cower with fear, especially those who have underestimated me.

My naughty and vengeful husband didn't sit idle while waiting for our merger to be complete. He decided Ajax Pickering hadn't received enough punishment for his actions. He took apart the Pickering family's holdings one section at a time, until nothing was left. Buying it up piece by piece and then selling it for pennies on the dollar to make a point. I almost feel sorry for Ajax, but when I do, I remember what holding a pillow to Jaxon's chest while he nearly bled to death felt like.

Things have been going so well between us that I'm wondering why I ever resisted him, to begin with. We talk like equals, discussing business and our future. He warms my bed every night, providing me with earth-shattering orgasms, and surprises me at the office by bending me over his desk and fucking me raw or hiding under mine and eating my cunt while others are in the room. The man has no shame and gets off both torturing me and pushing my limits. I'm discovering all these different factors about him and myself.

He is also obsessively protective and possessive of me. A fact that any man that has come within a two-foot radius has had to learn the hard way. The memory of the charity business luncheon we attended last week makes me grin. I had just stepped out of the private bathroom that Jaxon and I had a little quickie in, where he bent me over the vanity, fucked me hard and quick, and filled my pussy with cum when a male business acquaintance wrapped his fingers around my forearm in greeting.

My unstable and highly jealous husband just happened to come out of the bathroom door at that moment. The next thing I knew, the man was in a headlock and being slammed into a wall. The spectacle it caused was embarrassing and dramatic. The police were called, and the event coordinator looked on in horror. Luckily, the man refused to press charges despite the giant goose egg on his forehead.

We made the gossip section of every paper, and the warning was clear to any man who would think to approach me. My husband is unstable and territorial, so it's best to keep at a safe distance from my body. I could say I was enraged at his behavior, and despite raking him over the coals about making us tabloid fodder, I secretly enjoyed every minute of it. I'm the happiest I have ever been, a knowledge that should scare me but that I can't seem to dial back. Am I being reckless with my heart? *Only time will tell.*

"Mrs. Stratford... I apologize for disturbing you, but I think you should see this." Tyson walks into my office unannounced, looking like he's about to head to an electric chair. His face is pale, and sweat is beading on his forehead. He's holding a tabloid magazine in his tight grip in front of him.

I watch him approach with a sense of dread pooling in the pit of my stomach. It takes a lot to rattle Tyson, as Jaxon has come to discover. My assistant fears no one but me and puts himself in my husband's path of wrath more than any sensible human would. He hands me the magazine, and I watch him swallow harshly, his Adam's apple moving up and down with the movement. "I have already contacted our lawyers to get it stopped, but I don't know if we will be able to halt it completely before it's released. A contact I have there snuck this copy to me."

I stare down at the magazine cover in complete shock. My hand trembles as I place it on the desk in front of me, smoothing over the cover with my trembling fingers. On the surface of the gossip magazine is my husband dressed in a black tuxedo from last night's gala that he attended solo. Wrapped around his body with her hands in his hair and kissing his neck is none other than Kalista Cain in a daring silver gown that barely covers her sinful model body.

The urge to rip the cover apart fills me, and my hands clench, my sharp fingernails digging deeply into my flesh. The photographer caught them unawares. You can tell by their intimate posture and the way his eyes are at half-mast. The way his eyes are when he's turned on and enjoying himself. The gala signage is clearly visible behind them, so it can't be a photograph from the past. Instant rage and hurt fill me; the pain is so staggering that I have to brace myself on the edge of the desk.

They look enraptured with each other, both of them stunning in their finery, their sexual attraction and intimacy explosive. You can feel the heat coming off the page. Heat that I thought he reserved for me alone, but foolishly, I was mistaken. What a fucking imbecile I have been! I am the biggest fool walking around, with my emotions on display, just waiting for Jaxon to crush me. How easily I was convinced to let down my guard, to fall for him and his lies.

I raise my gaze to Tyson's, and I see a moment of pity there before he wipes it away and schools his features. "Where is my husband now?" I question through gritted teeth.

"I believe he is with the corporate lawyers tying up loose ends." Tyson's gaze never leaves mine, and I feel the strength and anger simmering from him to me. Is he the only man I can trust and count on? Is this young man who took a chance on being my assistant, my general, the only male who will never let me down and disappoint me? I stare back down at the image of the man that just this morning made me scream in ecstasy and now makes me want to cry in pain.

How could he do this to me? To us? Were Ajax and Kalista both right? Will he never be faithful to me? Will he keep going back to her? With this merger, he got what he wanted; his empire expanded to unprecedented lengths. Was fucking me and playing me a way to get what he wanted? Was I too naive and stupid to see that I was being manipulated? He used me; he used my attraction for him and my willingness to grow our empire to control me, to make me lax in my vigilance.

He went back to her, despite having me. Despite all the passion that we share. Does the bastard think he can have his cake and eat it too? I fucking warned him what I would do if he strayed if he tried to play with me. He obviously took my threats as ineffectual nonsense spewed by a weak woman. He's about to learn that nothing about me is weak. I will have my vengeance, my pound of flesh, and he will pay it in blood. He constantly reminds me that a Stratford always gets his revenge and pays his due. Did he forget that I was one now? That he himself forced me to become one? I will have my vengeance until the only thing left of him is my new name, and even then, I may bury that too.

"Ensure that this doesn't ever see the light of day. Buy the fucking magazine company if you have to." I stand there with the proof of my husband's treachery in my tightly clenched hand, moving from behind my desk and heading towards my office door, with fire racing up my spine and the need for retribution filling all my pores. War is calling my name, asking me to avenge the hurt that Jaxon has just caused with his deceit. I plan to answer it with all of the might I have before me. Jaxon thinks I have given him power over me; I can't wait to show him how fucking destructively wrong he is. He will regret the day he even breathed in my direction when I am done with him.

I will take what he seems to value more than me, more than the empire we were stupidly building together. I will bury that bitch in a shallow grave, where he can never find her, and then I'll take his legacy and ensure his name dies with him.

In my experience, only three types of fucking people ever really tell the truth: children with their innocence, the drunk with their incapacitated minds, and the angry through their fury. Jaxon and the world are about to learn my truth, that I am destructive and entirely without mercy when I'm angry and betrayed.

"Where are you going?" Tyson questions with trepidation, fear across his features.

I stop in my tracks, an evil grin crossing my face. "To start a war and teach my husband a painful lesson."

34

Jaxon

"Bitter people are not interested in what you say, but what you hide." Shannon L. Alder

W*HAT IN THE HOLY fucking hell!* My fucking car is on fire; flames are erupting from all of the shattered windows. I can't believe the sight before me in the parking lot of my corporate lawyer's office. Bystanders are standing around and gawking at the sight. I can hear the shrill noise of loud sirens heading in this direction. A loud groaning sound leaves the vehicle, and then I'm thrown back from the explosion that rocks the parking lot. My back hits the asphalt hard, and my breath leaves me in a loud whoosh!

Holy shit, did someone just blow up my car? Is someone trying to kill me? Fuck, where is Stella right now? Maybe it's the same person trying to hurt her. I need to get my ass up and to my wife to ensure she is safe. I sit myself up slowly, feeling shards of glass embedded in my skin just as the fire department races into the parking lot, and I watch them in horror as they hook up their hoses and try to control the blaze.

"Jaxon, are you alright?" My new assistant, Jake, helps me to my feet. The man is a grizzly bear and hefts me with such force that I bounce a bit when I regain my balance. I stare at him with dumbfounded shock. Is he stupid or something? How can I be alright? Someone just tried to blow me up!

"Where is Stella right now?" I demand, already moving away from the emergency service personnel and back towards the entrance of the building. I need to get into contact with her or that fuckhead assistant of hers, Tyson, to ensure she is safe. Panic is clawing at my throat, and I'm struggling to take a deep breath. Shit, she has to be alright! God, please let them have come for me and not for her. *I need her! I need her alive and well.* My heart races as my mind supplies vicious images of Stella hurt and bleeding. I clutch at my chest, air suffocating me and causing it to tighten painfully.

"She had scheduled meetings with the marketing team this afternoon outside of the office," Jake replies with abundant fear. He's finally coming to the same realization as I am, She may not be safe right now.

"Get me there now!" I bellow.

After the tensest and most frightening forty minutes of my life, and yes, this beats the time my former *best friend* had a shooter put a bullet through my fucking chest. I finally make it to the marketing company's offices and burst into their meeting room with my chest painfully heaving. I can't seem to get enough air into my lungs. I'm starting to feel light-headed and nauseous, and sweat is trickling down my back, causing my dress shirt to stick to me like a second skin. *She has to be okay, there is no world that I can live in without her now.*

"Sir! Sir, please wait! You can't go in there!" A secretary yells at me as I storm past her and slam open the door, completely disregarding her objections. As I walk into the room, my eye makes quick work of going over each of the inhabitants who are sitting there with shocked expressions on their faces. Where the hell is Stella? She's not here! "Where is my wife?" I demand with agitation and impatience.

"Your wife?" The bald man at the end of the conference table questions with fear across his features. He should be scared; I'm a moment away from destroying this whole fucking room!

"Yes, my wife, Stella Stratford. Five foot-nothing brunette with arresting blue eyes, Usually wearing a malicious and determined expression. My wife! Who is supposed to be in this meeting right now!"

A timid blonde with a pixie cut raises her hand, and I can see her trembling as she stands up. "Sir, she canceled the meeting earlier. She's not here." *Canceled the fucking meeting?* Where the hell is she now, then? I turn around to a red-faced and visibly winded Jake; my head is ready to explode. The fear that something could have happened to her is having an almost crippling effect on me and is triggering my need to get my arms around her.

"Get that brick of a cell phone out and find out where she is." I walk back out of the meeting room, allowing the door to slam behind me as I head to the vehicle I pilfered from one of my lawyers. The fucking thing is a station wagon with brown faux wood paneling, a monstrosity, but I couldn't be choosy. I needed a vehicle to get to Stella; this was the closest one without damage from the blast.

I hear Jake mumbling on the stupid phone behind me while desperately trying to keep up with me. The man needs to get more cardio; he's going to have a heart attack. The irony is not lost on me, having had three heart attacks myself this year, but I get lots of cardio daily between my wife's creamy thighs.

"They believe she is still at the office, sir." He heaves as he pulls the passenger side door open and tries to squeeze his six-foot-three, two-hundred-pound frame into the chariot from hell.

This fucking car is filled with children's toys and car seats, and the God-awful smell of grape juice is making my stomach turn. If this is what I have to look forward to, once I put a baby inside of Stella's womb, I may have to rethink the whole thing. I drive back to my office at the quickest speed this vehicle can manage, my fingers tightly wrapped around the steering wheel and my knuckles blanched.

Once I reach the office, I don't even bother to park the damn car, abandoning it while it's still running in front of the building and rushing inside. I pass security in the lobby, who gives me a strange, alarmed look, and then slip into the elevator up to my office. Once the doors open, I'm practically running down the hall towards mine and Stella's offices. People are moving out of my way as if I was on fire. Her cunt of an assistant isn't at his desk as I pass, and her door is shut. I slam it open in my eagerness to see her but am greeted with an empty room. *Where the fuck is she?* I have a sinking feeling starting in the pit of my stomach and an irrational fear that she is avoiding me, prickling at the back of my mind.

I rush from her office to mine just as Jake runs into the room. "Jaxon, you need to take this call! Miss. Cain is on the mobile phone, hysterical and screaming about her parents' house being on fire!"

What the fuck? Kalista's parents' house is on fire? Why the fuck is she calling me? I don't have time to deal with this shit; I have to find Stella. "Tell her to call the fire department. Why the fuck is she calling me?" I yell back, turning back into my darkened office.

"Sir, she's screaming that Stella had her parent's house set ablaze."

I rip the brick-shaped phone from Jake's hand, and even before I place it up against my ear, I can already hear Kalista screaming and crying. "Kalista, what the fuck is going on? Why are you saying Stella had your parent's house set ablaze?" I demand, losing my patience with this whole mess. Wretched sobs greet my ears, "She left a message Jaxon. She had it burnt into our fucking lawn." Another sob sounds loud against my ear. "The message says, 'I warned you'." My stomach feels like a ten-pound bowling ball just landed in it. What the ever-loving fuck is going on here? Why would Stella go after Kalista and set her house on fire? My wife's insane, but she doesn't tend to do things without provocation.

"Kalista, why would Stella go after you?" Fear slithers down my back. The image of Kalista yesterday at the gala trying to get me to kiss her, draping her body all over mine, and encouraging me to compromise myself slips into my mind. We were alone, though; no one was in that part of the lobby when it happened, were they? "What did you do, Kalista?" I question through gritted teeth, my jaw locked tight and my grip on the phone punishing. "What did you do, you stupid, fucking, reckless imbecile!"

"You are mine, Jaxon. I... I need you back." The need to wrap my hands around her skinny neck and strangle her at those words fills me. I am *NOT* fucking hers, not anymore! Stella is my *wife*. She is my fucking everything, and whatever this cunt has done, has triggered her. This idiot just baited a master predator and is crying about the fucking consequences. She's lucky she's still breathing. She won't be, though, when I get my hands around her fucking neck.

"WHAT THE FUCK DID YOU DO, KALISTA!" I yell into the phone, completely losing my control as I make my way to my desk. There's a pain in my chest spreading like wildfire, and fear is literally trying to strangle me. It can't be what I'm thinking; she wouldn't have been as reckless, wouldn't have had the guts to try something like that. My wife already destroyed her once. My wife who has zero chill and no fucking mercy. The one that is destructive in her fucking rage. Did this imbecile not already learn that firsthand?

"I had a photographer hidden and taking pictures of us... in the lobby." *FUCK!* Pictures that would have appeared like I was participating and enjoying myself with my ex-girlfriend, while my very jealous and possessive wife was not present. This idiot has damned both of us to hell! Ah fuck, if she set fire to Kalista's parent's house, then she's also the one that set fire to my fucking vehicle. She started with fire. Will the world burn at her feet once this is all said and done? Stella is unmanageable and relentless when consumed by rage.

My eye catches on a magazine pinned to the top of my desk by a very familiar blade. "Don't ever come near me again, Kalista. What we had is over. Whatever Stella does to you, I won't stop her, and in fact, if she doesn't kill you, I will." I end the call and pull the blade handle, releasing the magazine and falling into my seat. Right there in front of me is the means to crash my world down around me.

The photograph on the cover of the gossip rag is of Kalista wrapped around me seductively and kissing my neck, while my hand is braced against her hip and my eyes are at half-mast. I'm giving the appearance that I'm a very willing participant enjoying myself and about to fuck her.

The article title is a nail in my coffin, and with it, I know my little wife is about to serve me a world of pain.

35

Stella

"Anger kills logical thinking and logical thinking kills anger.... the choice is yours" Ketan r Shah

*F*OUR DAYS. IT'S BEEN four fucking miserable days since I saw that magazine cover, and I've spent all of that time scheming and planning. The war I've begun has consumed me day and night. *Am I hurt that Jaxon manipulated me with his tailored lies and played me for a fool?* I'm beyond crushed; the bitter taste of deceit coats every pore in my body and is a sharp barbed wire in my throat. He played me perfectly just as I let my guard down and thought he had genuine feelings for me. Worse yet, I realize that I have fallen in love with the fucker. The knowledge brings terror and a sense of helplessness to my soul instead of joy.

My chest feels like someone has taken an old, rusted, and jagged ice cream scoop and ripped out my heart, one horrendous piece at a time, while laughing as it shatters into splintered fragments of who I thought we were and what our relationship was turning into. We were nothing but a fucking tragedy, a tale of caution to those watching. *Oh, woe, the tale of the Stratfords who sought to build an empire yet ended up destroying themselves and each other.*

I should have never trusted him. I should have never let him inside my body or my heart. The mistake was mine; I bent too quickly. I gave too much of myself, and he took it all like the greedy and unsatisfied bastard that he is. The betrayal cuts so deep that it is a festering, oozing wound in my chest. One that has me sobbing behind closed doors but the picture of elegance and vengeance to all who are watching. I will not allow anyone to see my weakness, to know firsthand of my destruction at the hands of my callous husband. That would be the final straw that broke me, knowing that the world sees me as weak. Let them picture me as vengeful and spiteful instead;

it paints a prettier picture. *A woman with a heart made of ice; after all, I am their reigning ice queen.*

We weren't able to stop the publication in time, despite buying the company and firing all the executives. A wasted effort on my part trying to hide the actions of the slimy fucker that I married. A printed retraction was issued within hours, but the damage was done. Both to our image and to my bleeding heart.

The elite held its collective breath waiting for what I would do, and I didn't bother to disappoint them. Let them worry about my wrath being directed toward them. It will keep them all in line and under my merciless thumb.

Did I have Kalista's parents' house set on fire, *you bet your fucking ass I did*. I couldn't very well set fire to her condo building; the rest of the inhabitants would have perished with her.

Did I have someone blow up my husband's precious car? *Of course, I did; I made it rain fire in front of his eyes.* My only regret is the bastard wasn't sitting in it at the time.

Did I have a billboard placed in every prominent city, in every fucking state, and in all the major cities in Europe with Kalista's picture calling her a home wrecker? *You bet your tits I did. I'm a petty fucking bitch, after all, with billions of dollars at my disposal.* She wants to play games with me? Let's see how she likes it when she becomes one of the most hated women in America and abroad. There is nothing like a woman trying to fuck over another woman to get people's ire up.

Guilt doesn't eat at me for my actions. In fact, my heart begs for satisfaction, for me to cause both of them even more pain. To see Kalista and Jaxon both in ashes at my feet. I welcome the rage and the hate; it tempers the feeling of loss and betrayal. If I can just focus on hating Jaxon, then maybe I can plug this gaping bleeding hole in my heart.

Did I veto every single one of Jaxon's corporate decisions in the last four days, ensuring he can't get anything done in our joint business and looks like a fool? *You bet my fucking billion-dollar bank account I did.*

I even went as far as having half our combined bank account amount, a staggering four billion dollars, transferred to a Swiss bank and inaccessible to him. Did that cause him to throw a tantrum at the bank and look utterly unhinged? *It sure fucking did*. I just wish I could have been there to witness his palpable rage.

The only thing bringing me the slightest inclination of joy right now is knowing that I'm destroying Jaxon's world around him. My desire to see him on his knees before me is unmistakable and unforgiving.

As for Jaxon's hostile and threatening demands for Tyson to tell him where I am. They have fallen on deaf ears, much to my unfaithful, deceitful husband's frustrations. Tyson doesn't fear him; he knows who the scarier of the two of us is, and it isn't Jaxon. No threat will have him giving Jaxon my current whereabouts. My cheating husband is currently looking for a needle in a haystack. *Good fucking luck to him finding me without help.*

I haven't returned to our home since that first day, although I did let poor Mrs. Pox know what was happening. She was understandably upset to hear of Jaxon's repeated dalliance with Kalista and vowed to make him also pay for it at home. She's been serving him nothing but fried liver day and night, a food that he absolutely hates for the last four days. To my gleeful understanding, all his clothing met with an unfortunate bleach incident, and his shoes somehow ended up on the back lawn while the sprinklers were going. I had a good laugh at her attempt at vengeance on my behalf. I miss her and the staff dearly; it's incomprehensible how much she and they have come to mean to me. How the life I was building for myself and Jaxon has turned disgustingly upside down with his reckless actions.

I also haven't stepped foot in the office in the last four days, preferring instead to linger at the beautiful home in the Hamptons on the ocean that I purchased under a shell company. The one he knows nothing about. The house I meant to surprise him with so that we could eventually start a family, now it will do nothing but provide my refuge from our imploding marriage. A safe haven from the tumultuous storm I'm trapped in.

Some would say I'm off licking my wounds, a betrayed woman. They wouldn't be wrong, but what they fail to see is that I'm about to wage war and using the time wisely instead of steadily drinking myself into a coma over my husband's betrayal. I'm not going to lie, though; a few bottles have been consumed, and a few raged-filled tears shed.

"Tyson, make sure the lawyer sends those documents through to Jaxon today. I want the divorce papers served publicly, and my assets untangled from his immediately." I listen unamused to Tyson's repeated counsel for patience and to speak to Jaxon myself over the phone. I disregard all of Tyson's advice and hang up the phone, once again going back to laying my plans out.

I have no intention of divorcing Jaxon, although no one knows that but me. It's a scare tactic I'm playing at, one that will have my misguided husband's hair falling out in chunks. Jaxon wants nothing more than to build his precious empire and to have the Stratford kingdom rise in glory. What will happen to it once I threaten to take half of everything he owns? Will it crumble and go up in smoke like my trust in this marriage and his fidelity?

I almost want to kiss my father for his foresight in demanding that no prenup be drawn. It's almost like he already knew that Jaxon would betray me. Maybe he did; perhaps he was trying to protect me in his own way. Our empire is in the billions, and if I leave, I am taking half. He can try to fight it, but I'm the wounded party. A wound inflicted very publicly, and he would lose if we ended up in court. He's not a stupid man; he won't let it get that far. *Well, you didn't think he would cheat with that cunt again, either, but here you are.* The sinister bitch in my head cackles.

Will all of this chaos destroy whatever roads we had made together in our relationship? The bonds that I believed were strengthening us and causing me to fall in love with a lying, manipulative snake. The ones that allowed me to fool myself into believing that he genuinely cared for me. I'm more than willing to set a blazing gasoline-infused torch fire to them; *good fucking riddance.*

My poor, sensitive, and supportive mother has been calling and threatening to have her driver bring her straight to me. She is the only person other than Tyson who knows where I am. The chances of Jaxon getting any information from her is about as likely as the *Toronto Maple Leafs* ever winning the *Stanley Cup* again. She, too, had some threatening words for Jaxon once she saw the article. Her disappointment left her stupefied like everyone else, I imagine. She gave me a nonsensical comment about warning him about a blade to his throat, but I was in no condition to question her threat.

Shame fills me at my mother, seeing me once again smeared through the tabloids at Kalista's hands. The wretched bitch is going to pay until there is nothing left of her, but right now, I need to turn my attention to fucking up my husband's miserable life. Gone is the sympathy and guilt over him getting shot in my place. Right now, if I could, I would personally pull the trigger on him myself.

The knowledge that he went to another woman, with my scent still on his body, causes wrath to pour through me. The memory of that night, as we both prepared to go to separate events, plays out before my eyes again and again like a vicious cycle, determined to bring me to my vengeful and unforgiving knees.

I was completing my makeup, sitting in nothing but my undergarments, when he approached me, pants wide open, his cock already hard and precum slipping from the tip. "I need you to wear my cum inside of you, Stella, as a reminder of who you belong to, baby." He leaned forward and licked the side of my neck, causing a moan to leave my lips and my core to throb, soaking the crotch of my panties.

I took his cock between my red-painted lips, licking and sucking the crown before taking him to the back of my throat and gagging on his veiny length. He pounded into my throat mercilessly, his hands deep in my hair and pulling apart my updo that took me an hour to create. He pulled out of my mouth, yanked me up from the chair by my hair, and forced me to bend over my makeup vanity. All the items on the surface scattering and falling to the ground with jarring thuds.

"Fuck, Jaxon!" All the air left my lungs, with the bruising impact of my chest hitting the table.

His fingers dug into the fragile fabric of my panties, ripping them to shreds. His hard dick stroked my tight entrance before he slammed into me in one go, causing a cry of pain to leave my lips and forcing me to brace against the table or slam my face on it.

"This soaked cunt is mine, Stella. Cry for me, baby; I need to hear your screams." He was an intense animal, rutting into me and marking me everywhere he could with his hands and lips. His hand wrapped around my throat tightly as he came inside of my throbbing pussy. Then he got down on his knees behind me and sucked me to completion until he was as much covered in my cum and his as I was.

A deep groan left his lips as he licked me one final time and stood back up, his fingers pushing any escaping cum back inside of me. "Good girl, now I taste like your cunt, and you're filled with my cum. Make sure you don't clean that shit up, Stella. I want your thighs coated in my cum." He patted my ass and walked away like he didn't just wreck my pussy, to finish getting dressed.

I shake the memory away; it brings me nothing but shame and pain now. My hand slides over my neck and the lingering marks his mouth left on my fair skin. I imagined in my naivety that he didn't want to be without me at that event. That he felt he needed to mark his territory because he was possessive and falling in love with me.

Meanwhile, nothing could have been further from the truth. He was meeting his lover on the sly and just wanted to manipulate me. How many other times have they been together in the last four months of our marriage? *How many times has he made me feel special and desirable only to leave my side and head to hers?*

I pick up the vase filled with white lilies, the flowers symbolizing grief and death, much like my emotions for my husband, which is next to me, and throw it at the wall in a fury. The sound of the glass shattering is the same sound my heart is making over and over, and a welcome accompaniment to my grief—the destruction fueling my ever-present fury.

How could I have fallen in love with the fool? I am the biggest idiot walking around, an acknowledgment I can no longer deny. I have fallen in love with a man who used and deceived me. One who had no genuine intention of spending the rest of his life with only me by his side. A liar that led me to believe that we could build an empire and a life together. One that made me believe that I could crave something other than power. My folly was allowing him to become more important to me than my desire for greatness, world domination, and power. His transgressions have destroyed us even before we had a chance to begin.

Now all I care about is hurting him like he's hurt me. The wound that will not stop its incessant bleeding, demands retribution and satisfaction. I will hurt and destroy him until no memory of us is left.

He shattered my heart; I'm about to take his whole world. *This will be the end of both of us.*

36

Jaxon

"We should regret our mistakes and learn from them, but never carry them forward into the future with us." Lucy Maud Montgomery

MY OFFICE DOOR SLAMS open, causing the walls to vibrate around me. I look up from my computer, the one I had been staring at but not focusing on for the last hour, to greet a red-faced and angry Thomas Penticton. *This day just got fucking worse, if that's even possible.*

Is all of the world trying to test my patience and mental stability today? Do they not realize that I'm almost at the end of my rope and about to start burning shit down? Once I lose control, there will be no going back. I can feel myself free-falling towards the abyss, darkness, and my rage calling to me, begging to be let loose on the unsuspecting world and set it ablaze.

My lovely viper of a wife had me served with divorce papers very publicly at the country club this morning. *Why was I at the country club having breakfast instead of at my home, where I have staff ready to serve me and cater to my needs?* Let's see, oh, because my staff are a bunch of fucking traitors and are trying to drive me insane by serving me fried repulsive liver, nonstop. A food that I can't even stand the smell of. If that wasn't bad enough, I had to buy a whole new wardrobe since an unfortunate bleach attack happened in my closet three days ago. Let's not even talk about the fact that I'm down to one pair of shoes and sleep with one eye open.

My life is falling drastically apart, and it's all due to my scheming and vengeful wife. The one that won't even allow me to speak to her so that I could explain my side of the story. The one that every day she is gone is destroying me little by little. My heart and emotions are taking the constant battering of hits she's sending my way. I have become a cautionary tale to the married men around me, and she has become an inspiration to scorned women everywhere.

Literally! A random woman spit on me yesterday on the sidewalk outside of my office. She very eloquently let me know she was on Stella's side. Then there was the barista two days ago who spit in my coffee while I watched and passed it to me with a smile, telling me that I deserve everything Stella is serving me. When I venture out my door, the women in my office sneer at me with distaste, and even some of the men have started giving me pitying looks. I am *persona non grata*; pretty much everywhere I go now, thanks to Stella. I'm sure she's sitting back and enjoying my misery.

Now here is her fucking father to aggravate the rest of my already miserable day. What the fucker could want from me right now, other than to destroy what's left of my sanity, I don't know. *Maybe he wants to kick me while I'm already down?* Stella is close to bringing me to my knees, a place I reserve solely for eating her juicy cunt. The one I can't get to, because she is hiding from me in parts unknown.

"I will have words with you, Jaxon!" He bellows, coming further into the room and shoving the chairs before my desk aside, causing them to go flying. He leans down, both fists braced on my desk, and proceeds to bring his blotchy, red, angry face closer to mine. So close that I can see the large vein throbbing dangerously in his forehead, his nostrils flaring like a deranged bull, and I can smell his rank breath. *I wonder if that vein will explode like a geyser?*

"Thomas, to what do I owe the pleasure?" I try to smile, but it's hopeless. I can't even feel any joy in egging Stella's dad on. Stella has even taken that joy away from me. It doesn't have the same appeal if she's not here to witness it. *Fuck, I am really falling apart here.*

"You reckless idiot. You humiliated my daughter publicly with that blatant whore. The one you reassured me you were leaving in your past on your fucking wedding day!" His giant fist collides with everything on my desk, including my monitor, and sends it crashing to the floor. "You have managed to destroy everything in less than six months. How is that even possible, you maggot?" He slams his fist down again, making the solid wood table shake. "I was informed my daughter publicly served you divorce papers today at the fucking country club!"

I shift in my seat, watching his breathing increasingly ragged. My own leaving me in angry pants. Does he think that I, too, am not humiliated? Does he honestly believe that I would have done that to Stella? That I would have cheated on my possessive and spiteful wife? Of course, he does; what reason have I given him to think otherwise?

"I thought when you took that bullet meant for her, there was a real chance for this marriage to succeed. That you truly understood the precious, valuable piece I placed in your greedy hands. That you would honor my daughter, and together, the two of you would grow a legacy, ensuring mine and your father's bloodlines never ended."

I try to interject, but he slams his fist down again, and the remaining items shatter to the ground. "Shut up, Jaxon. I am fucking speaking! You had better get down on your miserable knees and beg my daughter to take you back. Crawl through broken fucking glass if you have to." He leans forward until his hot breath is inches from my face.

"If she doesn't, Jaxon, I will use all of the money and power I have left to ensure she takes everything you own. I will help my daughter destroy you, you miserable, traitorous piece of shit!" His fist flies out and slams into the side of my face, causing my office chair to slide back and crash into the windows behind me. My face is throbbing, and I'm a bit dazed. I watch him turn his back and walk towards my office door, his shoulders rising and falling with rage.

Shock and disbelief race through my body, not only because Thomas just hit me but also because he obviously cares deeply about Stella. I have never seen this side of him. He always made it seem like she was nothing but a prized piece to pass back and forth to get what he wanted. Has he come to realize the value of my beautiful wife? Could he want a healthy relationship rather than the strained and miserable one they share now?

"Thomas, I love her. I never fucking cheated. I was set up!" I rise quickly, approaching him and grabbing his arm, forcing him to halt his steps and turn back around to face me. I meet his furious gaze with mine and let him see the truth of my words.

"I love her; I'm in fucking love with her." I should be shocked at my own words and declaration of love for Stella after such a short, volatile time of being married to her, but I feel them deep in my soul. I am in love with her, and have been for a while now, if I'm being honest with myself. *She is my everything, and without her, I'm just fucking broken.*

He stares at me for a moment, still breathing heavily, and then shrugs off my hold. "Then you had better find her, Jaxon, before she destroys you both in her quest for vengeance. Stella can be hell-bent and determined when she sets herself on something, and right now, that's on destroying you."

He leaves my office without a look back, and my heart thuds painfully in my chest. I run both of my hands through my thick hair, yanking on the strands and trying to come up with a way to get to my wife. I need her to listen to me and give me a chance to explain my side of what occurred. *Do you think it will really matter? She doesn't love us; she hates us.* My mind whispers with vehemence. It has to; I can't live without her. *I refuse to live without her.*

I'm making my way through the underground parking lot toward my temporary vehicle when something slams into me from behind, knocking me off my feet and forcing me to my knees. Someone grabs me from behind, locking their forearm around my neck and cutting off my airway. I try to fight off the assailant, forcing myself to try to stand, only to have the back of my knee kicked out and be forced right back down. A cold metal object is pressed against my cheek, and I can see from the corner of my eye that it's a gun. My whole body stills instantly, letting the air leave me and my frame to go slack in the assailant's arms.

"Oh, Jaxon, how you disappoint me, after I had high hopes for you." The voice is feminine and sweet, coming from behind me as her footsteps echo off the parking lot concrete. She moves before me, and I watch as she tilts her head to one side to stare at me, disappointment and hurt across her features.

"Ra... chel." I try to gasp through the tight hold. *Fuck, fuck, fuck.*

"I warned you what I would do to you if you hurt my daughter Jaxon, and you have. You have hurt my daughter horribly. The one that sat next to you endlessly when you were in a coma. The young woman that has done everything to help you build your precious empire up, despite her horrid father selling her to you like a prized cow."

Rachel moves closer to me until I can see the flecks reflected in her blue eyes. Eyes similar to my wife's, yet strangely different. One's that are currently staring at me, filled with malice and rage. Unadulterated terror fills me as I stare into Rachel's eyes with the promise of retribution and pain. She did fucking warn me. *Please, God, don't let me die at my mother-in-law's hands.*

"Lo... ve her," I force out through a choked breath. The forearm of the brute behind me tightens against my throat until I start to see nothing but shadows as my vision dims.

A snort leaves Rachel's lips, and she motions for her rough minion to loosen his grip so that I can finally take in a stuttering breath. "You love her? Is that how you think love works, Jaxon? Do you think love includes cheating on my daughter with Kalista Cain?"

Her hand strikes forward, slapping my face and making my ears ring. *Fuck! She hit me in the same damn spot as her fucking husband earlier!* My face is going to be black and blue, that is if my cheekbone isn't already broken with Thomas' hit. Does everyone in the Penticton family mean to take a swing at me today? *Shut up and be grateful she hasn't shot you yet, idiot!*

"I was set... up, Rachel. I never cheated." I gasp, trying to shrug off the hold of the fucker behind me. The gun is now very firmly pressed against the side of my head; one wrong move and this fucker could blow my brains out. "I went out... to that... lobby... alone." I should be perturbed that Rachel Penticton has men doing her dirty work. *What the hell is she involved in?*

"So you told my husband earlier. Here's the thing though, Jaxon, I'm not so easily convinced, and my daughter will be even harder to persuade."

"I was set up... by Kalista in a way to get back at... Stella and to try get me back. I didn't cheat, she made it appear as if we were together, cornering me and trying to compromise me, but I pushed her away. I FUCKING PUSHED HER AWAY!"

I shout in rage. "The look on my face was for my wife. I was remembering earlier in the evening when I was with her. I needed to step out of the room... umm... because I was..."

Rachel's eyebrow rises at me in expectation, and fuck it if I don't feel spite at being forced to spit my truth in front of her. "I was fucking hard, Rachel. Hard because I was daydreaming about my wife's pussy. Is that what you want me to confess? FUCK!"

Everyone believes me capable of such villainy against my wife. The one I took a bullet for and almost died for. The one I dragged myself out of the darkness to be with. The same woman I am deeply and irrationally in love with, despite my unsuccessful attempts to stay away from her. "Kalista surprised me and forced that embrace. I pushed her away and told her to stay away from me. I never knew there was a photographer present. I didn't cheat, Rachel."

She stares at me with a cold blank look across her face, and I can't tell if she believes me. "How much do you truly love my daughter, Jaxon? Enough to give up everything for her? Think that through for a moment; your answer will determine whether your brains are splattered on this floor."

I swallow the lump in my throat and truly think over Rachel's question. How much do I love Stella? So much that I can no longer function without her. *No, that's not true; I don't want to function without her.* Life has no meaning without her by my side. She is mine, and I will not release my hold on her. Not even death could take me away from her. I would haunt her in the afterlife. There is no me any longer without her. I'm waiting for her very touch to bring me back to life, stuck in this gray nothingness that I'm calling living without her. What would I give up to have her back, to have her in my arms? *Everything.* I would give up everything that I have, will have, and am, to have her back. The thought should scare me, but it doesn't. It settles on me like a mantel of truth.

"Take it all, Rachel; without her, it means nothing to me now." I take a shuddering breath and then close my eyes, awaiting her order to shoot me and end my miserable existence.

"Good, Jaxon. Then you finally understand my daughter's worth. You will sign over everything to Stella, right here, right now. Your life will be forfeit if you don't.

Then I will tell you where you can find my willful daughter, and you can try to convince her yourself that you are worthy of her." My eyes open quickly, and the brute behind me releases his hold, shifting away from me but still holding the gun aimed at my head. My glare returns to Rachel and the folder she is pulling from her purse.

A chuckle leaves my lips at the vision before me. Stella's mother is a little gangster, strong-arming me at gunpoint to sign over all of my assets and wealth to her daughter—the daughter I love and would willingly have given everything to anyway. "You know you're incredibly frightening, Rachel. You look like this pristine little wealthy housewife, but really, you're a *mafioso*, aren't you?"

A devilish smirk crosses her pink-tinted lips. "Where do you think my daughter got her ruthlessness from Jaxon?" She hands me a pen and the folder and watches as I read through the document before me. It's a legally binding contract, one that gives my wife sole ownership of our newly merged enterprise and all of my financial assets other than my house. I'm about to go from being a billionaire to being just a semi-wealthy fucker with no legacy left to leave behind when I die. *How the mighty have fallen at the hands of vengeful women.*

"Did she ask for this?" I question, hoping that it's not my wife who is demanding this sacrifice. Let's be clear, I will pay this pound of flesh to get her back willingly. I just hope that it doesn't become a thorn of resentment between us.

"No, Jaxon, she didn't. She doesn't know I'm here. Stella will destroy you one chunk at a time, enjoying herself and breaking her own heart as she does. My stubborn daughter is as much in love with you as you seem to be with her. I am demanding this sacrifice so that I know your feelings for her are sincere and so I don't follow through on my promise to end your life."

I don't even bother reading the next document. I just sign my signature at the bottom of each page and hand the folder back to Rachel. She looks them over with satisfaction, a smile gracing her beautiful face, one that resembles an older version of my stunning ice queen wife. Is this what Stella will be like in forty years? *Naw, fucker, she is going to be so much more ruthless, you better pray long and hard she lets you live a long life at her side.* The thought brings me so much pleasure that I can't resist laughing out loud again.

Rachel places the documents back in her purse and hands me a piece of paper, an alluring smile reaching her blue eyes. "It seems my daughter bought a house in the Hamptons, Jaxon. You might want to wear a bulletproof vest when you try to convince her of your love. She is really quite irate with you right now." She turns and walks away from me, leaving me standing there like a complete and useless dumbass. *She bought a fucking house?*

I stare down at the piece of paper in my hand, with the scribbled address of a house I knew nothing about. This paper is worth my entire fortune, I have literally signed it over in order to have it. There is nothing I wouldn't have given up for this one small bit of hope.

Rachel says Stella is in love with me. *Can that be possible?* I fucking hope so. My pulse accelerates rapidly, causing my chest to tighten. I'm not sure if it's from fear, excitement, or a combination of both. Maybe after Stella is done bloodying me, she will listen to reason, and then hopefully, I can spend the rest of my days balls deep in all of her pretty holes.

I unlock my car and get inside, a smile broad across my face, making my throbbing cheek hurt. Even that pain and annoyance cannot simmer, the joy filling me. I now know where my wife is, and I'm going to get her fucking back.

Stella Stratford is mine, and it's time I made sure she understood that there is no me or her; there is just us.

37

Stella

"Looking back, I have this to regret, that too often when I loved, I did not say so." Ray Stannard Baker

I LIFT THE GLASS of red wine to my lips as I lean more fully against the island cabinets, leaning my elbow on the stone countertop. The gorgeous dark walnut and cream kitchen I planned to share with Jaxon and the family that we would have raised here, surrounds me, causing me further sadness. *It was all for nothing.*

I take a deep sip, the aroma and taste soothing yet not fulfilling me, as I slide my hand lovingly against the cold marble counter, cold like my supposed ice queen heart. I wish that the rich wine would make me forget all my problems, but nothing seems to be able to do that lately. My mind and heart are at war with each other. One bleeding through a series of sharp cuts and calling out for a man that has deceived and fragmented me. The other demands retribution and the infliction of pain on that same man.

A noise crawls its miserable way out of the depth of my chest as tears slide down my face. I sound like a wounded animal ready to die in captivity, knowing that there is no way to freedom. I'm so tired and conflicted with this struggle. Do I even want to continue in this petty war against Jaxon, or do I just want to have him back in any way that I can? *Is my pride worth all this pain?* What is that proverb? *"Pride goes before destruction, a haughty spirit before a fall."*

The sound of soft footsteps on the stone floors outside of the kitchen reaches my ears and has me turning back towards the entrance and wiping quickly at the tears across my face. *Damn it! Can't I even be weak in the solitude of my home?*

My eyes quickly scan the counters while I wipe away the moisture from my eyes that continuously falls like an unleashed tap, sprouting salty tears. Did Tyson forget something here? He left not even twenty minutes ago to return to Manhattan after delivering me the latest acquisition report and advising me of my father's impromptu visit to Jaxon at the office. One that apparently has caused all kinds of gossip to spread at the water cooler and will most likely make it to the tabloids by morning. A sob catches in my throat as I clear it. I don't want even Tyson to see how weak I have become. How this situation with Jaxon is almost unbearable to me.

I don't see anything here; as I turn back to face the kitchen entranceway, shock and surprise fill me. My eyes widen as my breath catches in my throat, and a chill of fear rushes down my body. I release the wine glass from my grip; it hits the Calcutta marble counter and then slams against the stone floor with a loud shattering sound. The sound of the glass breaking pulls me out of my frightened and frozen state and has me spurring into action.

There's a man dressed entirely in black with a ski mask over his face coming at me with a large knife in his hands. Pure terror races across me, and my mind scrambles for what to do. Grappling with the horrific sight before me, that's right out of a nightmare or a horror film. *How the hell did this fucker get inside? How did I not hear him until he appeared before me?* I dart across the island, putting it between the attacker and me. My body is trembling with a mixture of fear and anger. How dare this fucker sneak up on me to do me harm. I launch all of the items sitting on the counter, including the wine bottle, in his direction. My eyes dart all over the room, while also keeping him in my sight for a way to escape. Some things hit him; others never make contact. With nothing left to throw, I scramble backward and reach for the chef's knives on their block behind me.

"Who the fuck are you?" I demand, my grasp making contact with the largest knife and brandishing it in front of me, while moving slowly around the island and towards the open kitchen doorway. He takes a step back in the same direction, trying to prevent my escape. My mind is running quickly with options, searching for a way out of the room and to safety. Do I try to fight him? Will I be able to hold him off long enough to get out of the room?

Fuck, if I fight him, he might be able to corner me or bring me down, and then I will be at his mercy. I don't think he's here only to scare me. The way he's stalking me around the room tells me clearly that he's going to hurt me, even kill me.

I only have one chance to escape if I can make it through that doorway. Otherwise, I'm going to die here in my beautiful kitchen. I need to try to get to the front door and out of the house, or try to get up the stairs to the small closet-sized panic room I had installed and lock myself inside. My heart thuds loudly in my ears, and my hands feel wet with sweat. A feeling of revulsion and fear shudders through me. This man is here to kill me, and I'll be damned if I'm going down without a fight. Fuck him; I'm a Stratford; nobody's taking me down without me raining hell on them.

He doesn't answer me but tries to lunge across the island to slash at me, catching me in my bicep with the edge of his blade, just as I slash at him and catch the side of his face covered in the mask. The fabric gives way instantly and bares a glimpse of bloody skin below. "Fucking whore." He shouts at me, as he pulls back.

The sting of the cut on my arm is sharp and has my breath catching in my throat as I move out of his way, sliding around the other side of the island and making a run for it out of the room. Panic is threatening to suffocate me; I have to try to keep my fucking head, or this guy is going to kill me. I slide across the stone floor, almost losing my footing, and race towards the solid wood, white front door.

The nearest house is still a half of a mile down the road. I'll never make it with him chasing me. I don't think I can outrun him. *No, I refuse to die here at the mercy of this man. FIGHT STELLA!* My mind screams at me. I grab onto the large vase I have at my front door and launch it back at him, grabbing the table lamp on the console and doing the same thing. I scramble to open the door, the locks still in place. As I turn the deadlock and pull on the knob, I can hear his heavy breathing as he's coming towards me.

Finally, the door opens, and I try to dash out, but just as I do, he gets a gloved fist in my hair and pulls me roughly back, my body jarring and hitting his with a pained grunt, and I lose my grip on the knife, it goes skidding across the floor. A scream escapes my lips as I kick back, trying to hit him in the crotch and using my elbows to ram his face. My attempts to dislodge his precarious hold on me have him loosening his grip slightly. I take the opportunity to tear out of his grasp, ripping strands of my hair from my scalp as I run in the opposite direction towards the stairs. A grunt leaves his lips, and he tries once again to grab onto me and fails.

"Whatever they are paying you, I will triple it!" I scream as I lunge up the first step.

I make it up to the landing, pushing benches, art, and anything I can get my hands on at him as obstacles to prevent him from reaching me. If I can make it up to the main bedroom, I have a gun in there to defend myself. I can lock myself in the room and call for help. The panic room is in the other direction and further away, and I'm not sure I can make it in there without him tackling me.

He lets out a panic-inducing chuckle. "They want you dead cunt. I don't bargain with dead whores."

Who is this man? Is he still the same person that tried to hurt me before? Fear and dread skate up my spine. Tears rush down my face as I climb the stairs two at a time, stumbling in my attempt to escape from him and to safety. I let down my guard, thinking I was safe here with no security. That no one knew where I was, but I was wrong. Deadly wrong, and I'm about to pay the consequences if this man gets his hands on me.

"I'M COMING FOR YOU BITCH!" He shouts behind me.

I race down the hallway towards my room, pushing through the door and slamming it shut. I manage to just turn the lock as he slams into the frame, making the door vibrate loudly. It's a thick solid wood door, but it will only hold him off for so long. I scramble across the floor to my dresser and reach for the gun, taking the safety off and pointing it at the door with a shaking hand as I reach for the phone on the nightstand. He's slamming his immense body against the door repeatedly, trying to break it down. I can hear wood splintering; in moments, he will be inside. *Jesus! Fuck! What should I do?*

I press the numbers, nine-one-one, but there's no dial tone. The phone is dead in my tight, desperate grip. He cut the phone lines. Tears cascade down my cheeks, and my arm throbs from the knife wound, blood dripping down my side, soaking my shirt and abdomen and hitting the floor. My breath is coming in ragged pants, so quickly that I'm wheezing. I bite down hard on my bottom lip to try to contain the scream that wants to leave me. *I'm going to die.* This man is going to get in here and stab me to death.

He thuds against the door again, and I see it buckling inwards. One or two more shoves, and he will be inside the room. I should have headed straight for the panic room. I should have run in that direction instead of here; that door was made of reinforced fire-proof steel. I could have locked myself inside the small room and been safe. For how long, though? He cut the phone lines, and no one knows you're here but Tyson and your mother. *You would have eventually died inside, there. He wouldn't have left.*

No! Fight! This is not the end of us! My brain demands, filling me with strength and adrenaline. If we die, we die here, standing our ground, not as a coward hiding. I point the gun at the door, steadying it with both my hands, and wait for him to come through the broken door.

I don't have long to wait; with one more hard slam against the door, it splinters and allows him entry into the room. He moves quickly into the space, his arm raised with the large blade and coming at me menacingly. I don't hesitate, pulling the trigger once and then again. The bullets make an impact with his body, one in his shoulder and the other in his abdomen, causing him to stagger back. A cry of pain leaves his muffled lips, and he reaches down to place his hand over the wound in his stomach.

Blood is pouring from the wounds and making wet splotches against the dark material of the black shirt he is wearing. He looks down momentarily, stunned at the fact that I shot him, but then recovers and continues moving forward toward me with the knife. "You fucking bitch! You're going to die slowly for that!" He slashes once again in my direction, making contact with my side and forcing me to take a step backward, giving up ground. My hand is shaking and sweating, and I'm losing my grip on the gun. He moves to knock the gun from my hand, but I pull the trigger at the last minute, and the shot goes wide, grazing him as it embeds in the wall plaster.

"You're... going... to die... cunt!" He breathes heavily into the mask, his steps and movement slower. Blood is pouring quickly from his wounds, and he can't seem to catch his breath. *NOW STELLA!* My mind screams at me to shoot him again. I lift the gun again and press the trigger, watching as the bullet leaves the gun in a blur and embeds itself in his chest, forcing him to take a step back and then collapse on the ground.

I watch in petrified horror as he tries to get back up to his feet and come at me again. *END IT STELLA!* My mind screams over and over until it's the only sound I can hear. Turning my face away from the sight, I pull the trigger again and again until the gun clicks empty. My breaths are loud exhales coming from my mouth, as my blood rushes in my ears. Tears trail down my face like little rivers, and my body releases a shudder with all the adrenaline still running through me. My whole body is shaking, my teeth rattling in my mouth. I force myself to turn my gaze back to the attacker. He's lying there, a rattling noise leaving his body and his limbs jostling against the once-cream carpet.

My knees give out on me, and I fall to the plush ground, the sound muffled as I hit it hard. A deep red blood stain is soaking it and making its way towards my shaking limbs. A cry leaves my lips, and I drop the empty gun at my side. A horrific noise leaves him, and then the only sound in the room is my whimpers, harsh breathing, and cries.

Tears continue to slide down my face rapidly and soak the neckline of my shirt. A sharp pain catches my attention, and I glance down to see that blood has soaked my shirt in a sizable pattern. I lift the hem up to see a significant, deep slash across my abdomen, one that is streaming blood out in thick trickles. My vision blurs, and my head feels dizzy. I shake my head to try to clear my vision, and it helps for a brief moment.

I need to get out of here, I need to put pressure on the wound, or I'm going to bleed to death. I sluggishly rip the shirt off my body and push it as hard as I can against the wound. The minute I apply pressure, I feel the injury on my arm, which is slowly dripping blood down my bicep and creating a trickle down the other side of my abdomen. The pain makes me flinch and cry out. I try to get my feet under me to stand up, but my legs tremble and give in, refusing to hold my weight. *I'm going to die here.* I'm going to bleed to death, and no one is going to even know for days. The thoughts race through my mind on a loop.

I'm going to die here alone, without Jaxon. The only man I have ever loved. Now, all the games I have played, all the moves I made, and the petty ways I hurt him seem ridiculous and childish. I loved him, and then I left him, and now I will never even get the chance to tell him how much he means to me. How much I desired our life to work. That I wished to one day be the mother to his children. That all I wanted was for him to love me back and to build a life with me, and an empire we could rule together. All my dreams are crumbling before me, brought crashing down by a lie and a blade.

It's too late now. I won't survive, but maybe I can still tell him. Let him know that my final thoughts were about him. I release my hold on the shirt and slide my fingers through the thick blood coating my stomach and dripping down my waist and hips. I reach out to the carpet at my side and press my bloody fingerprints into the carpet. I drag my fingers through the thick fibers and back to coat them over again through my blood until words form before me like grotesque red smears. Once the final letter is spread across the carpet, I pull the shirt back hard against my wound and lay down in my own cooling blood, and wait for death to take me.

Maybe in my next life, I won't be so headstrong and willful, and I will get to tell him those words in person. *Jaxon, my love. I'll meet you in the next life.* My eyes flutter close, and darkness takes me into its heady embrace.

38

Jaxon

"With pride, there are many curses. With humility, there come many blessings." Ezra Taft Benson

I'M SPEEDING LIKE A fucking lunatic through the hills, a feeling of impatience and fear coating my whole body. The need to see Stella and wrap my arms around her is all I can think about; it's an urgency in my veins. "Jaxon, you need to slow down! We are going to crash in this tin can, and you'll never reach Stella!"

Jake holds on tight to the inside handle of the doorframe and braces for the next curve I take at over a hundred miles an hour. I've ignored his complaints for the last hour. I'm determined to make the trip that would usually take over two hours in just over one. My need to get to Stella is all-consuming and frightening. She has to hear me out; she has to forgive me. I will fucking tie her ass down until she listens to my side of what happened. *Are you ready to be bludgeoned when you attempt to tie her down?* My mind snickers.

"What are you even going to tell her once you get there?" Jake grits through his clenched teeth.

"I don't fucking know. I'll think of something when I get there!" I take the next curve and feel the back wheels come off the asphalt for a moment and then slam back down, making the car skid across the two-lane highway and causing me to bite my own tongue. The coppery taste of blood fills my mouth as a sniggling feeling of dread skates across my neck, causing the hairs to stand on end.

"You don't know? Boss, I think you should slow down a bit. Maybe even stop and get your thoughts together before you go storming in there and Mrs. Stratford hands you your ass, no offense meant."

I chuckle at his words; he's probably right. Stella will hand me my ass, one way or another, regardless of whether my words are practiced or spur of the moment. I wouldn't even put it past her to react with violence. She craves it as much as I do. I know it turns her on when I'm forceful with her, and I make her submit to me. Maybe I'll go in there and wrap my fist around her neck and force my cock into her tight pussy until she mellows out a bit and then agrees to listen to what I have to say.

The thought of doing just that, of Stella, fighting against me, and the sounds that Stella makes as she takes my cock to the hilt has my dick thickening in the constraint of my pants. I take the next bend wide, and a small little blue Mercedes sports car almost collides with my new Porsche. I slam on the brakes causing dirt and rocks to fly around us. The other idiot slams hard on his brakes, fishtailing, losing control of his vehicle, and slamming into the weed-infested embankment. *For fuck sake!* I shift the car into park and climb out to see if he's hurt. I can hear Jake complaining loudly behind me as he exits my vehicle that if I was going a little slower, none of this would have happened.

I reach the vehicle just as the driver's side door opens, and my wife's fucking asshole of an assistant pops out. "Are you fucking crazy, Jaxon! You almost killed me!" He shouts, his face red and his blue eyes wide with shock. He stumbles towards me, unsteady on his feet, and we turn to watch his car slide further down the embankment. "Ah, hell!" I shake my head with irritation; I guess he's lucky he wasn't still inside of it. Not going to say I wouldn't have liked it if the little prick disappeared, though.

I don't have time for this shit; I have to get to Stella. I turn to walk back to my car as two different voices shout after me. "Jaxon, where the fuck are you going?" "Jaxon, you can't leave me here like this, fucker!"

I turn back around with rage filling my veins. These two fuckers, are trying to stop me from reaching my goal. To get to my lovely viper of a wife. I won't fucking have it! I will leave them stranded on the side of the fucking road if I have to, but I'm getting to Stella. "Get in the fucking car and shut up, or I'm leaving both you fuckers behind."

They both race across the asphalt and into the passenger side door. Tyson squeezes his long-fit body into my back seat, and once again, I'm reminded that I don't trust the handsome fuck around my wife. After we reconcile, she needs to fire his ass and find an ugly-looking assistant, maybe one covered in moles with a droopy eye.

"Where are you going, Jaxon? She's going to be furious if you charge up there!" Tyson questions in that voice that annoys the fuck out of me. The one that suggests he knows my wife better than I do. *Fuck you, asshole!* I know every part of her intimately, and all my parts are about to be thoroughly reacquainted with hers.

"He's going to get his wife back. He hasn't quite figured out how he's going to do that or even what he's going to say, but he's determined to get her back." I hear the humor and sarcasm in Jake's voice as he replies to Tyson. I should fire his ass at the same time I have Stella fire, Tyson. We can share the ugly, mole-covered new assistant.

"You're not serious? Please tell me you actually have a plan on how you are going to get her to listen to you?" Tyson inquires with exacerbation. "Jaxon, she is beyond hurt. She's crushed by everything that happened, and she's angry. She's really, really angry."

"I didn't fucking cheat! I was set up by Kalista. She forced that compromising-looking situation and had a photographer hidden to take photos. I didn't touch her; I wasn't with her. I would never fuck around with another woman behind Stella's back, especially with Kalista Cain. Give me a little credit, assholes; I know my wife. She can be a vengeful demon when she wants to. Why would I put myself in that position where someone could catch me?"

A pang of regret fills me at my words, because they are lies or at least not complete truths. I did fuck around that very first night of our marriage, and with Kalista. I brought that cunt home on my wedding night. That shame and regret lives inside of me of how stupid I was. That was before, though, before I really knew Stella. Before I realized the precious gift, I had in my wife. In the past, before I came to the realization that I am deeply in love with her.

As for being led into the compromising situation, I should have realized what was happening. I should have seen the signs of vengeance in Kalista's face. While I didn't go out there with her, and I pushed her away, I still should have known better. I had a duty to have stayed away from her and refused to speak privately with her. I ought to have realized that she would do something to try to hurt Stella. I'm an idiot; I readily admit it. Some part of me never believed that Kalista would try anything against Stella. My wife is the boogeyman of the elite; who would be stupid enough to go against her? *Well, now I know who.*

I'm a fucking mindless imbecile, one who placed himself in this situation, not once but twice now, and caused my wife and the love of my life devastating pain. I don't even know if Stella should forgive me, even if I grovel on my knees, *which I fully intend to.* I have now given her everything; the only thing left I have to offer is my heart and my sincere apology. Part of me feels like that won't be enough, and I may lose her anyway. The other part of me refuses even to acknowledge the possibility of ever having to let her go. *Fuck that shit; she belongs to me. She's mine.*

"I have signed over all of Stratford Industries to her. I will give her anything that she wants, anything that she needs in order to punish me further, other than a divorce. I will spend the rest of my fucking days making it up to her!" I shout in the enclosed space, finally causing both these fuckers to shut their gapping traps.

"Boss, you really signed over the whole company to her?" Jake asks in a quiet voice.

A sigh leaves my stiff lips; my jaw is clenched so tight, I'm pretty sure I have cracked a molar. My hands tighten on the steering wheel, and I take my eyes momentarily off the road to meet his astonished brown ones. "You still don't understand. None of that matters if I lose her. She's my everything."

"Fuck! Okay, well, she's up at the new house, probably still crying into that bottle of wine she was drinking before I left. She's for sure going to throw something at you, and I wouldn't put it past her to call the cops and have you charged with trespassing. Hopefully, between the three of us, we can get her calmed down enough to hear you out. But whatever you're going to say, it better be good. I don't think she will give you more than one opportunity." Tyson sighs and leans between the two front seats, fierce determination reflecting back at me from the rearview mirror.

"Jesus, she's going to maim all three of us." Jake groans.

"It's a good thing she doesn't have security up there with her, she probably would have had one of them shoot Jaxon." Tyson spits out with humor. I almost take my hand off the steering wheel and backhand the fucker for enjoying the thought of someone shooting me.

I round the last quarter mile, pressing my foot down to the floor of the accelerator and causing both men to slam back in their seats. "It's the blue one, coming up! Slow down, Jaxon, before you miss it!" Tyson grabs onto the back of Jake's seat with a white-knuckled grip.

I spot the house and pull up the long, narrow driveway until I stop in front of a wide white porch surrounded by square white columns, dark blue cedar siding, large windows, and a massive white front door that is currently wide open into the rapidly fading evening light. *What the fuck? That doesn't look right.*

"What the hell? I made sure that was locked before I left." Tyson's words have me rushing out of the car and up the porch. Tyson and Jake on my heels. We enter the foyer to complete chaos, furniture, and pieces of pottery everywhere. A struggle clearly evident from the destruction. Terror races through my body, someone is here. Someone who is trying to hurt Stella, and clearly, she fought back. I race through the house, Jake taking the left and Tyson the right corridor, each of us moving with caution as we search. "Jaxon!" Tyson calls, and I follow the sound at a run entering the impressive large kitchen to see more destruction and blood across the Calcutta marble island. My stomach drops at the smears of red blood across its surface. Is it hers, is Stella injured somewhere?

I race out of the room and up the stairs, seeing more evidence of destruction, and struggle up here. I follow it down a wide hallway to where I assume the main suite must be located. The large wood door is barely hanging on its hinges and looks like a battering ram has been taken to it. There are no sounds coming from anywhere in the house other than Jake and Tyson's footsteps rapidly approaching behind me in the hall. I hesitate, reaching for the door, a sense of trepidation filling my bones. My stomach lurches and tightens painfully as my heart spasms in my chest. *Please be all right; please be all right.* It's a mantra going over and over in my mind. I push the door open, and the sight that greets me has me falling to my knees.

"No!" The anguished sound is ripped from my body and sounds like an animal roaring.

39

Jaxon

"Love grows. Lust wastes by Enjoyment, and the Reason is, that one springs from an Union of Souls, and the other from a Union of Sense." William Penn

TYSON PUSHES PAST ME as I fall to my knees and heads towards Stella, while Jake rushes to check on the masked assailant lying a few feet from her. I can't make my legs work, can't seem to force my body to stand up and obey me, so I crawl towards her. My heart feels like it's going to explode in my chest. *NO! No, this can't be.* I can't have lost her. I can't have come this close to having her, to having my whole world, only to lose her.

"No, no... please baby, no," I beg as I approach her, the knees of my pants soaking up some of the cooled blood drenching the carpet.

"This one's dead, shot multiple times!" Jake shouts from behind me.

"We need to get an ambulance!" Tyson screams and reaches for the discarded phone on the floor. My eyes focused on Stella's beautiful pale face. Her dark, feathery lashes make contact with the creamy skin of her cheekbones. Her lips are tinged a purple-blue, and blood is streaked across her skin. She looks like an angel, lying there so still. I reach my finger and stroke it across her chilled skin as tears stream down my face. I stare at my heaven and realize that I was too late. That someone *has* taken her from me.

"Jake, run back to Jaxon's car and use the car phone! Call a fucking ambulance!" Tyson yells and pushes me aside. Pulling the shirt that is soaked and up against her pale skin back. I look down in shock and realize that she's just wearing a bra, and every part of her abdomen, waist, and hips are drenched in her blood. Where the hell is all the blood coming from? "Fuck, she's bleeding out, and I'm not sure she's breathing!"

Tyson shoves me hard. "Get it together, Jaxon! Put pressure on her wounds to slow the bleeding while I start CPR."

My mind is slow to process his commands, and he shoves me hard once again, forcing my hands to hold the balled-up soaked fabric at her side. I watch in horror as he removes his own shirt and wraps it around her bleeding arm tightly.

I shake my head to clear the fog and watch as he starts compressions on my wife's chest, counting loudly before tilting her head, checking her airway, and then giving her mouth-to-mouth. I want to be enraged that he has his lips over hers. That he's shirtless, and her blood is streaked across his skin, but I am so scared right now. I just want her breathing; I just want him to tell me she is still alive. *Is she alive?* She has to be; there is no world that I can live in without her. The fates would not be that cruel, giving her to me and then taking her from me before we even had a chance.

My head tilts to the side, and I see blood streaks across the pale carpet next to her. At first, my mind can't make out what it's seeing. There's so much blood underneath her and on her. Then slowly, the shapes seem to form into words, and I realize it's a message. A message for me streaked in my wife's blood.

I

luv u

JS

The words cause both a thrill to enter my soul and terror to fill my heart. She knew she was dying and wrote those words in her own blood, with fear that she would never get to speak them to me in person. Sweat breaks out all over my body, and a furious roar leaves me sounding like a wounded wolf, one that has lost his mate.

NO! I refuse to lose her, not now, not fucking ever. She is mine, and I will follow her into hell & fight the devil for her. I can't fucking breathe; my chest feels like it's caving in on itself, and I can hear my blood rushing loudly in my ears. Saliva pools in my mouth, and I feel like I might just get sick. Every part of my body is trembling, snot, and tears sliding down my face. *I can't lose her, please; I can't lose her!*

I watch as Tyson repeats the process over and over again, time seeming to slow to a fucking crawl as I hold tightly to the wound on her side and do something I haven't done since I was a little boy and my mother was dying. *I pray.* I pray to a God I'm not sure I believe in and promise him anything that he wants if he lets her live. If he will, just give her back to me. *Please, I can't live without her.*

"The Ambulance is on its way, two minutes out. I left the door wide open and cleared what I could from the stairs." Jake rushes back into the room, but I can't look away from Stella and the compressions Tyson is performing on her chest. *Breathe, baby, please, just breath*e, I beg.

Loud voices fill the space, and a stranger tries to pull me away from Stella's side. I react by throwing my fist at him before Jake yanks me back and restrains me. "Let him do his job, Jaxon; he's trying to save her!" I watch as the paramedic takes over for Tyson, checking Stella's vitals. He removes the bloody shirt and tries to clean the wound before placing gauze on it and wrapping it painfully tight, lifting her upper body to wrap it securely around her. She's limp in his grasp, her head tilting on her neck like a rag doll. *Holy fuck, is she even breathing? Please, God, please let her be breathing!*

"She's breathing, but barely. We gotta go now." You! Are you the next of kin?" He directs his question to Tyson, and finally, my senses return to me.

"I'm her husband!" I shout and pull away from Jake's grasp. "Okay, let's go; you're going to put pressure on the wound while we get her on the stretcher and down the stairs. Do not stop, press hard, don't worry about hurting her; she's bleeding out." He doesn't wait to see if I comprehend his instructions, he and his partner move forward and lift Stella as if she weighs nothing and place her on the stretcher they brought with them. I race to her side, using the palm of my hand to put pressure on her wound, and we move out of the room and down the stairs in a complicated and quick maneuver that almost has me falling down the steps.

The police arrive just as we get to the foyer and try to talk to me, but I disregard them and go with the attendants into the ambulance. I can hear Tyson speaking with the police behind me but I couldn't tell you what his words consisted of. Everything right now is a buzzing sound in my brain. We get Stella into the ambulance, and I sit by her side. The paramedic moves back and forth with different machines and straps an oxygen mask on her. The vehicle pulls away and races down the road at a fast speed, sirens blaring.

She looks so small and delicate on the stretcher, her beautiful dark hair fanned out behind her and matted with blood. An angel with all of her creamy skin marred and stained with her life essence. I don't know what to do with my hands, the paramedic took over applying pressure to her wound. I grasp her cold fingers, threading them through mine, and hold tight, kissing the palm of her blood-tinged hand. "I love you, Stella. Please don't leave me." I whisper into her palm.

The ride to the hospital feels like I blinked, and we were pulling up in front of the emergency bay, doctors and nurses are already waiting on us. The ambulance doors open, and the paramedics work quickly to get her out, giving her care over to the doctor, who is impatiently waiting. He rambles off some words I am not even sure of, the only thing I catch is her pulse is low, and she's bleeding out.

The nurses grab onto the stretcher and rush her inside. The doctor in dark blue scrubs who was barking orders grabs onto my arm as I move to follow. "Are you the husband?" I nod my head, yes, my mouth unable to form words. "Does she have any allergies? Could she be pregnant?" He questions urgently.

"I... I don't know. We... are newlyweds." I stammer at the knowledge that I actually know very little about my wife, the thought horrifying me. *I don't know if Stella has any allergies, I never thought to fucking ask.* What kind of piece of shit husband doesn't know what his wife is allergic to? I drag my fist through my hair, pulling on my strands. *Could she be pregnant?* Fuck, I don't even know if she's even on birth control, and we have been fucking like rabbits!

The doctor doesn't bother waiting for me to come to my senses. He runs off after my wife and leaves me standing there like the useless turd I am in the emergency bay. *I can't breathe... I can't breathe!* My chest is too tight, and my vision is dimming; my breathing is becoming shallow and erratic. I stagger forward; I *need to get to Stella.* I take a step and then another and collapse forward onto my knees. I can't seem to get any air into my lungs; my chest feels so tight. A sharp pain is coming from my left side. I need to get to my little ice queen. I have to make sure she's alright.

"Shit! Get a gurney, this one's going into cardiac arrest!" A woman's voice yells around me. I don't know who she's talking about. Is she talking about me? *Am I having another fucking heart attack? Now?*

NO! I need to get to Stella. She's mine! I try to get back to my feet, but this time I fall forward and land on my face, my chin hitting the dirty concrete as my vision dips out until darkness consumes me. My last thought is of two beautiful arctic blue eyes and words written in blood. I love you, Stella Stratford, fucking fight for me, fight for us. *STELLA!*

40

Jaxon

"Time is too slow for those who wait, too swift for those who fear, too long for those who grieve, too short for those who rejoice, but for those who love, time is eternity." Henry Van Dyke

"**U**GH... FUCK!" MY MOUTH tastes like a donkey's ass and is dry like the Arabian deserts. *What the fuck did I eat?* My lashes flutter but feel stuck together, and my eyes are crusty and gritty. I rub my hand across my face and force them open. Bright overhead lights greet me and momentarily blind me.

"Jaxon, thank fuck, you scared the shit out of me, bud!" My assistant Jake's voice greets me. I narrow my vision and stare at him, standing in front of whatever the hell I'm lying on. *What am I lying on?* My eyes dart across the space, and annoyance fills me instantly, another damn hospital room. What a fucking surprise, *not!* I'm going to have to have words with this fucker about talking to me like I'm one of his drinking buddies and not his boss. Why am I once again lying in a hospital bed? This shit is getting ridiculous and starting to get old as fuck. *Maybe we are getting old motherfucker*; my mind snickers at me. Fuck that shit. I'm not even thirty yet!

My glare returns to Jake just as the memory of Stella lying in a pool of her own blood accosts me, and my body goes icy with panic. "Stella, where the fuck is Stella?" I shove the blankets back, push my legs quickly off the side of the bed, and try to stand up. Wiring across my chest and tubing in my arm pulls me back down, and I reach forward to rip it from my body while dizziness attacks me and my stomach cramps. "Hey, boss, slow down. You can't rip that off!" Jake tries to grip my hands and prevent me from removing the heart monitor currently attached to my skin.

"Stella, where is she?" Why is he not answering me? A scream crawls up the back of my throat and threatens to choke me. My shoulders curl forward, and I wrap my arms tightly around myself. My chest feels like it's caving in, bile races up the back of my throat, and I have to force myself to swallow to keep it from spewing out of my mouth. A wave of dizziness hits me at the same time. *Is she dead?* Is that why he won't answer me? No, she can't be! Stella is a fighter, she would have fought to stay alive. *She wouldn't have left me, not like that.*

"Hey, Jaxon, breathe, buddy! She's alright! She's alive!" His ruddy face is filled with concern, and sweat dots his massive forehead and upper lip. I reach forward and grasp onto the front of his shirt, pulling him closer to me in a tight grip. The material making a ripping sound at my harsh treatment. "She's alive?" I question in desperation, my mind refusing to hope while my heart thuds painfully in my chest.

"She lost a lot of blood, but she's alive, Jaxon." Jake pulls back, trying to dislodge my grip. "You had a mild heart attack when you got to the hospital with her. The doctor thinks it was all the stress of the situation. You're being monitored right now just in case you have another one, so you need to stay calm."

I had another heart attack? Like shit, how many can a man have before his heart gives out? Am I a cat with nine fucking lives at this point? Honestly, I hope that's the case. I have a feeling I'm going to need more than one life with the way shit is going with Stella. She's alive but lost a lot of blood. I need to get to her, to be by her side when she wakes. My little ice queen is fighting for her life, and mine will mean nothing if she doesn't survive.

"How long was I out?" Panic surges through me, and my stomach clenches tight at the thought that I have been unconscious for hours while she has been alone. What if someone tries to get to her here in the hospital? The thought has me pulling the intravenous from my hand with a sharp yank. Blood trickles down my hand and drips onto the white hospital linens as Jake stares on in horror at my actions.

I need to know who attacked my wife and why. My thoughts are a chaotic mess. "Do we know who the attacker was?" I fidget with the electrodes on my bare chest, and as I unhook one, the monitor lets out a shrill beep.

Fuck, that will have the nurses charging in here any second. I don't give a fuck what they have to say, my place is next to my wife. If I need to be monitored, they can do it from wherever she is right now. I refuse to be separated from her for a minute longer. The fear that something could still happen, somehow I could still lose her, runs through my mind and causes my body to lock up tight, and my heart to lurch. Terror stabs my heart, and more alarms go off around me. *Damn it! I need to stay calm. Apparently, I now have the heart of an eighty-year-old mother fucker.*

That's going to suck big time when I want to pound into Stella's perfect cunt. *Don't think about Stella's pink, juicy, tight pussy right now, asshole. We need to bring our heart rate down, not up, plus we don't want a boner when the nurses walk in here.* My mind screeches in irritation at my stupidity. That would be fucking humiliating, not to mention hard to explain without looking like a deranged psychopath. Yeah, my wife is in critical condition fighting for her life, and I'm standing here thinking about sliding my cock inside of her. *I roll my eyes at just the thought.*

"The police believe he was hired to attack her. There was a vehicle found a block away with her picture and a picture of Tyson's car in the glove compartment. They think that he followed Tyson and that's how he knew where she was and that she was alone once Tyson left to return to Manhattan."

"Who? Do we have any leads on who might have hired him?" Who the fuck would be brazen enough to hire someone to kill my wife? Who hates her enough to do that? Could it be Kalista? Would she have been able to organize something like this? She hates Stella for sure, especially after the incident with her parent's house burning to the ground and the billboards all over the place. She would still have the financial means to hire someone, but somehow even with all the malice between them, I can't see Kalista having the audacity to go after Stella that way. She wouldn't have had the ruthlessness nor the brain power to pull something like this off. No, it has to be someone else other than Kalista, but who?

Originally, I had thought that it might have been Thomas Penticton who was trying to hurt his own daughter. To get back at her for taking his board seat at Penticton Industries and forcing him into an early, unwanted retirement, but then that information about Ajax suspiciously fell into my lap and I didn't know what to think. *Did he give me that information?* He could have still been responsible for the other two threatening incidents, but after his display in my office where he clocked me, I'm less convinced that it was, in fact, him. He seemed to finally have realized the true value of his daughter. A little too late, because now she's fucking mine, and I have zero intentions of giving her back.

Who the fuck is out there trying to hurt my Stella? Now that this attacker has failed, will they stop, or will whoever they are, keep coming after her? How many new enemies are out there just waiting to plunge a dagger into her chest? I need to be more vigilant, no matter how irritated Stella gets with me. I need to keep her safe, and in order to do that, I need to be by her side. I rip the last of the monitor wires off and pull myself to my feet just as a nurse and a doctor rush inside the room.

"Mr. Stratford, you need to get right back in that bed, sir; you just had a mild heart attack three hours ago. You shouldn't be up and walking around yet." The doctor tries to corral me back into the hospital bed, but I'm not having it.

"Get the hell out of my way and tell me where my wife is!" My voice is icy with panic and fear. I take another step away from the bed and watch as Jake shakes his head at me in disbelief and, annoyance.

"Sir, your wife is in stable condition. She is being looked after, there is no need for you to rush in there." The doctor, who wants my fist down his fucking throat, utters and then takes a rushed step back when I direct my furious and malignant gaze in his direction. I*'ll fuck him up if he doesn't move.*

"No one is going to keep me from my wife, not you, not fucking death, mother-fucker. You had better just point the way before I wrap my hand around that thick fucking throat of yours."

I make a move in his direction, and he lets out the most undignified squeak and hides behind the nurse, who supplies him with a look of utter disbelief. *Fucking coward.* "Nurse... take Mr. Stratford... to see his wife." The doctor's voice comes out at an octave that would suggest the fucker's balls never dropped.

She moves away from the trembling coward and leads me out the door with Jake quickly at my heels. "Great job, boss, threatening violence in a place trying to keep you and Stella alive." Jake whisper-shouts from behind me.

I follow her down a long corridor, wearing nothing but the boxers I was wearing this morning and the shitty thin hospital gown that is wide open in the front instead of the back. No doubt to allow them to have all those electrodes attached to me, and that is way too fucking short on my six-foot-one frame. I keep my head held high as I pass gawkers on my way down the hall, giving everyone a menacing look that has them lowering their gaze. I can hear Jake trying not to laugh behind me, but I don't give the slightest fuck.

Nothing matters except getting to Stella. Not these people's opinions of me, not if my ass is hanging out, nothing. Nothing can touch me as long as she is still breathing. My impulse to protect her, to keep her safe, is so strong that it is becoming an obsession, and the only means I have for satisfying it is to get to my little viper.

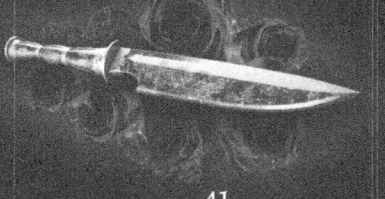

41

Stella

"A woman is like a teabag — you can't tell how strong she is until you put her in hot water." Eleanor Roosevelt.

M Y BODY IS SO sore that even the slightest movement brings pain and fire ricocheting through my limbs. My fingers are tightly imprisoned in someone else's hand and going numb. My eyes flutter open to the mirage of Jaxon slumped down in a chair opposite of where I am lying. His eyes shut in slumber, a grimace painted across his haggard and pale features. His arm is fully extended, and his long, graceful fingers are intertwined with mine.

How can this be? How can he be here with me? I look around in a panic at where I am, and the tell-tale beeps and distant noises confirm my suspicion that I'm in a hospital. A groan leaves my parted lips at the pulling sensation from my side. I cheated yet another attempt on my life. *I. Fucking. Survived.* Somehow, I survived bleeding to death on the floor of my room. *How did I? Who found me? Did Jaxon find me?*

"Ja... xon," I try uttering his name, but my voice comes out raspy and dry. He twitches in his sleep but doesn't wake. I pull on our intertwined fingers, and a groan leaves his lips before his eyes open at half-mast.

"Stella! Jesus, thank fuck you're awake!" He quickly leans forward in the chair, a moan of pain leaving his lips as he clutches his chest and focuses on me. He brings our intertwined hands to his pouty, full lips and kisses my knuckles. The sensation of his warm lips across my skin makes the hairs on my body stand on end, and warmth fills my limbs. He is so beautiful to look at, so stunning even when he is a disheveled mess.

"Tried... to... kill... me." I force the words out after clearing my parched throat. Jaxon reaches over to the bedside table for a cup and a pitcher, filling it with water and a straw and bringing it to my lips. I study him from below my lashes as he holds the cup steady. He looks exhausted, bedraggled, and pale. Dark shadows mar his handsome face, more than a few days' worth of facial hair graces his jaw, and he's got a massive bruise on the side of his cheekbone, just below his eye. One that makes me irrationally mad that someone has hit him, someone other than me, that is. He's wearing a hospital gown opened in the front, which is weird, and patches of his golden skin and hidden ink tempt me as he moves. He pulls back once I've had my fill, and his slate-gray eyes meet mine, filled with fear.

"I almost lost you, Stella. Someone tried once again to take you from me."

The memories of what happened flash through my mind. Running for my life while a masked intruder chased me through my new home, while he threatened me with a knife. Rushing upstairs to the main bedroom and locking myself inside with a gun, only to have the intruder break down the door in an attempt to reach me and end my life. Pressing the gun's trigger over and over, while bullets landed in his body, causing macabre red spots to appear. The sound that he made as he took his final breath, a noise that will forever haunt me. A cry leaves my lips, and tears cascade down my cheeks. *I killed someone; I murdered the man that was trying to kill me. I'm now a murderer.*

Jaxon moves to sit on the side of the bed, pulling both my hands into his and leaning down, his lips kissing each of my eyes and then my forehead. "You are safe now, baby. No one is going to hurt you."

"I killed him." The three words leave my lips, but I feel like acid is in my throat, corrosive and sharp, the knowledge devastating. I always knew I was ruthless and cold, but I never imagined I was capable of murder. Now I know that my soul is genuinely tarnished and that I'm the ice queen they named me. I want to regret my actions. I want to say that I would change what I did if given the opportunity, but the truth is I would pull the trigger again and again if that man came at me to hurt me. I'm an unredeemable sinner.

"You protected yourself, Stella. You saved yourself. You saved what's mine. Don't fucking ever regret that, baby." His words are fierce and filled with anger. He pulls back from me, and the look on his face has fear skating down my spine. He looks unhinged and wrathful, like he's just one moment away from setting the whole world ablaze. Is he angry that someone tried to kill me or that I had to save myself? Perhaps his alpha caveman tendencies are hurt, knowing I didn't need a white knight as my rescuer, that this ice queen saved her damn self. His lips open, but before words escape, the hospital door crashes open with a jarring noise.

"Get the fuck away from my daughter, you heathen!" My father's loud voice booms into the room as he makes his appearance in the doorway evident. His frame, large and intimidating, as is the scowl across his malignant face. A part of me, the little girl that always feared him, wants to cower back into the bed, but Jaxon tightens his hold on my hands, preventing any movement.

"Daddy?" I question in a small voice.

I can see my mother in the small space behind him, her worried expression is evident as she holds firm to his arm, preventing him from charging into the room and accosting Jaxon. Their difference in height and body size is almost comical. She is David restraining Goliath.

"Thomas, calm down!" My mother's stern voice rents the air.

"Don't tell me to calm down, woman! Someone almost killed my daughter, *AGAIN!*" He shrugs off her hold and charges into the room as Jaxon stands up, like a knight putting himself before me and danger. It gives me the chance to get a good look at him. He's in nothing but a pair of tight boxers and an open hospital gown, which does nothing to hide his body from anyone's view. He has electrode stickers across his chest that I didn't notice before.

What the hell happened to him? Was he attacked, too? Panic that he has once again been hurt fills me, and I move my body forward to reach for him, causing a sharp pain to sizzle up my side and a whimper of pain to leave my lips. Jaxon turns his head to stare back at me, his eyes locking onto my hand, holding tightly to my bandaged side. His nostrils flare, and his eyes widen, showing the whites of his eye, speaking to the anger and panic he's feeling. *Oh shit!*

"Thomas, I won't have you coming in here and upsetting Stella further! She needs rest. Whatever your feelings for me, I had nothing to do with this! We can take this outside like men!" Jaxon faces off with my father, his spine rigid and his hands tight at his side, the veins in his forearms protruding with restraint. Have his arms and veins always been that sexy? I shake my head to clear my mind, which is obviously in the gutter, and focus back on the two raging bulls before me. The ones my tiny mother has put herself in between to try to calm down.

"Upset her? You have got to be kidding me, boy! Ever since I gave you my daughter, the world has been turned upside down and set on fire. Someone has been actively trying to kill her the whole length of your marriage! You are a danger to her!" My father's face is beet red, and sweat is dotting his forehead. In all my years of being alive, I have never seen concern for me across his features. Most of the time, all I see is regret and disdain in his eyes. Right now, he looks like a terrified man. Is his fear genuinely for me or for the remainder of his legacy? After all, if I had died, the Penticton line would have died with me.

"Thomas, I am sure Jaxon had nothing to do with this." My mother places a firm hand on both of their chests and pushes them apart. I can see the determined look on her face. To my surprise, my father steps back and acquiesces to her demand to move away from Jaxon. His large body is tight with frustration, and he cracks his neck from side to side in a blatant intimidation effort. I'm watching two fucking wolves trying to outdo each other. God, give me strength to deal with the foolishness of men.

"In fact, I know it." She gives Jaxon a chilling stare, one that sends a shiver through his large body. *What the hell was that? Is Jaxon afraid of my mother?* The thought of Jaxon being afraid of my five-foot-nothing, hundred-pound, timid mother is laughable, but still very evident in his wary look. I'll need to get to the bottom of that sooner rather than later.

"Folks! I need you all to vacate this room immediately!" A gray-haired older nurse in light pink scrubs enters the room, arms crossed against her large chest, and gives each of us a determined glare. "Mr. Stratford, you just had a mild heart attack. You need to be in bed under observation." She turns her glare in my direction. "Mrs. Stratford, you were just stabbed and lost a lot of blood, ma'am. You need rest!" Her fierce, dark eyes turn towards my father, and I watch as she straightens her posture, preparing to do battle with a grizzly bear. She must be used to dealing with wealthy, obnoxious tyrants in the Hamptons. She doesn't even blink an eye. "You, sir, need to lower your voice and calm down! This is a hospital, not a boxing match. If you cannot keep your voice lowered and your tone respectful, I will have you removed."

My father stares at her in horror while my mother does her best to try to hide the satisfied smirk on her face. If I had the energy to give this woman a high-five for putting my father in his place, I would. My father is not used to women talking down to him, and right now, he looks like he swallowed something sour, and his anger is eating him alive from the inside out. I have no doubt, though, that if he replies back to her in rudeness, she will have his ass forcibly removed from this room. Whoever she is, she's my new fucking hero.

"We will all be leaving shortly, and they will behave respectfully, nurse." My mother nods at the queen of nurses, while raising an eyebrow in my father and Jaxon's directions. Her glare almost daring each of them to dispute her words.

With one last look at each of the testosterone-fueled idiots in the room and a wink at my mother, the warrior nurse steps back out of the room. My mother shifts away from Jaxon, and my father approaches me on the bed. Her fingers reach out to cradle my cheek, and tears glisten down her face. "Stella, my darling. How scared I was that I almost lost you." My hand cradles hers against my skin, and I feel her warmth and strength in the touch. Strength that I desperately need to get through this ordeal and process all that has happened to me.

"I'm alive, mother," I reassure her, the thought of the alternative, causing my breath to stutter in my chest.

"No thanks to this asshole here." My father seethes, glowering in Jaxon's direction. I can see Jaxon's chest rising and falling rapidly as he takes deep breaths to calm himself down at my father's accusations. They are two alpha male gorillas, moments away from beating on their chests. I roll my eyes at the amount of male toxicity in the room.

"Do we know anything, Jaxon? Who the assailant was? Why he was after my daughter?" My mother questions, her hand dropping from my face to reach for my hand and squeezing my fingers in support and reassurance. My mother's support strengthens my ability to speak my thoughts aloud.

"Ajax?" I question, although that doesn't feel right. Somehow, my gut knows Ajax wasn't involved in this, despite what Jaxon and I did to him, despite his attempt to scare me into leaving Jaxon. No, this attack was vicious, premeditated, and meant not to scare me, but to end my life. Ajax truly believes that he loves me, I don't think he would try to have me murdered. *What if it was the only way to keep you from Jaxon? Would he do it then?* The thought whispers through my mind, but I dismiss it.

"No, my darling, this wasn't Ajax." My mother replies with conviction.

"How do you know that, Rachel? He's tried to scare her once before. I'll fucking kill him with my bare hands." Jaxon drags his hands through his dark hair in frustration, leaving it standing in all different directions with his aggravation, and gives my father a side-eyed look that I'm not sure what to make of.

A snort leaves my mother, and her eyes twinkle with mischief. "Because I have had him... occupied, where he wouldn't have the ability to make another move against my daughter. Well, at least, since you maimed and punished him viciously for his last one."

"What?" My father's voice echoes in the silent space.

Mine and Jaxon's mouths hang wide open in shock at my mother's words. What does she mean she has had him occupied? How does she even know about Ajax's betrayal? My father has a look of miserable confusion across his face, like he's missing a large piece of the pie. *Me too, dad, me too.*

"It was you. You sent me that information, not Thomas." Jaxon stares at my mother in astonishment. I can see respect blooming in his eyes as he stares at her and maybe a tad more fear.

"Yes, Jaxon, I was the one that let that information drop into your lap. I wanted to see what you would do with it. If you would avenge my daughter, before I took matters into my own hands." She smirks in his direction. "As for Ajax being behind the current assassination attempt, it's highly unlikely. He's been a guest of a... friend of mine, for the last couple of weeks since Jaxon dropped him off beautifully broken on his doorstep. The man can barely speak and certainly wouldn't be able to make the arrangements needed from his current location. This was someone else."

"What have you done, Rachel?" My father questions with horror and fear. My mind wonders who her "friend" is. My mom is a wealthy socialite, who attends charity galas and spends time at the spa. What friends does she have that could keep a man under lock and key? I'm starting to see that my mother is a prism, one I took at face value, when I should have been looking at all her refractions.

My mother turns her cold, vengeful glare on my father, moving away from the bed and grabbing his fat chin in her pink-tipped fingers. "What you should have done, Thomas protected our daughter." She squeezes tight until a small gasp of pain leaves his lips and then releases her grasp, wiping her hand across her pant leg, as if the mere feel of his skin underneath her fingers disgusts her. For the first time in my life, I watch my father stare at my mother in abject fear. The woman that he often took his frustrations out on with his raised hands. She is no longer a cowering, whimpering mess, but a terrifying militant queen rising.

"If not Ajax, then who?" I question, my eyes darting a glance at each of the inhabitants of my room, confusion at what is happening with my parents adding to the muddled mess in my mind. The realization of why I am even in a Hampton's hospital rises, *Kalista*. The cunt, she's the reason I hid in the Hamptons like a vengeful deity.

Kalista and Jaxon, intimately embracing on the cover of that magazine, unaware that they had been caught. How he humiliated and deceived me, after all, we had been through together, how my last thought before I passed out from blood loss was how I loved him. I stupidly and weakly wrote that message to him in my own blood. Did he see it? Did he lay witness to my weakness, when I thought I was going to die?

A chorus of emotions makes their way through me all at once—*betrayal, loathing, sadness, and love.* Jaxon must see the direction of my thoughts; he braces himself as he lowers himself to his knees on the floor by the side of the bed. His features rapidly turn over with different emotions. I watch as his eyes widen, and he licks his bottom lip nervously. He takes my hand forcefully in his and smooths out my clawed fingers, the ones that want to scratch his and Kalista's eyes out.

"Stella, I swear to you… I swear I never cheated. She set me up, with a hidden camera and made it appear like… like we were together." His words race and stumble from his lips, his eyes never leaving mine. "She wanted to hurt you, to get back at you… and I was an idiot that walked right into a trap."

42

Jaxon

"Love is the wisdom of the fool and the folly of the wise." Samuel Johnson

"**I** WAS AN IDIOT that walked right into a trap." The words make bile rise up the back of my throat. I have never felt such shame at being a man, and not seeing what was happening right in front of me. The truth is I was weak; I should have known better than to let Kalista approach me. I didn't see the warning signs of being led into a trap. I should have been more observant and noticed what was happening around me instead of daydreaming about Stella's perfect cunt. I ought to have realized that she would want to hurt Stella. To get retribution for my wife's vicious smackdown, and the best way to do that was through me. *I was a blind, dumb fuck.*

My male ego, though, was flattered, like a fucking preening peacock. Even though I knew what I had with Kalista in the past was over, I could never compare it to the intensity of what I have with Stella. For a tiny moment, a split second in time, I was flattered that two sexy, beautiful women wanted me, that they would fight over me. Isn't that every man's grotesque fantasy? Never in my wildest dreams would I have thought my little ice queen would be so deep under my skin. That she would be a dagger in my heart that I could not live without, unless I wished to bleed to death from the gaping hole that she had carved.

I should have realized it the first time, when I placed myself between her and a bullet. But it took her leaving me, destroying my sanity, and ensuring that I couldn't function without her to realize the depth of my true emotions. Finding her bleeding to death on that bedroom floor, her blood written declaration next to her was the ass kicking that I needed to realize that without her, there is no point in living.

Had she died from her wounds, I would have found a way to follow her into the next life. She will never be rid of me now. Stella Stratford will call to me even in the ether; her soul is forever intertwined with mine. We are bound as one, and I will never release her from my hold, not in this life or any of the next ones. I will murder anyone who tries to get in my way of having her. *She. Is. Mine.*

"Stella…"I meet her intense blue gaze and have to swallow the lump in my throat. My eyes dart to my in-laws, and I watch as my mother-in-law raises her eyebrow at me with expectation. Thomas looks like he's getting ready to throttle me with my next words. I really fucking wish I didn't have an audience for this. This should be a moment just between Stella and me where I beg like the loser I am for her forgiveness. I can see, though, that no one is going to give me that option, so fuck it. I have to man up and tell her exactly how I feel.

"Stella, I swear to you… I… never cheated. I was done with Kalista after you and I started our relationship in earnest." Thomas lets out an unintelligible response behind me and grunts in pain from the swat Rachel gives him with her hand. *For fuck sake… this is not going well at all.* Like how the fuck do I confess to the beautiful woman in front of me that she is my everything?

"I… I care for you deeply, Stella. I would never have done that to you…" I stumble on my words, my tongue feeling thick, and the words I'm desperate to utter clog my throat.

"Oh, Jaxon, you fucking coward, spit it out already. Tell her the truth!" Rachel's harsh words have me staring back at her with rancor. I watch as confusion crosses Stella's beautiful features. She parts her lips to refute the words I have said so far. A deep painful breath leaves my chest, and with desperation, I spit it all out, "I'm fucking in love with you, Stella! I couldn't have cheated because there is no one but you for me. Not Kalista, not any other woman, just you." *Eloquent as ever, asshole,* my mind laughs at my expense.

My fucking knees are starting to hurt, and so is my pride, and I can feel heat up the back of my neck. I watch as my words wash over Stella, and the disbelief on her face is evident. She thinks my words are insincere, that they are platitudes of a man caught with his pants down. How do I make it crystal clear to my beautiful little viper that she is my everything?

A green file folder flies over my head and lands in Stella's lap, to my shock and her confusion. I watch as she grabs it, pulling her hand from my grip. I feel the loss of her touch, my hand craving hers back in its grasp automatically, with the desperation that my whole body feels to ensure that she is mine. "What is this?' Her voice comes out restrained and small, as if she thinks whatever is in that folder will hurt her. *It won't, baby; I love you.*

"Proof of his true feelings and intentions, daughter. He's not lying; he does love you—more than even I could have imagined. He has signed everything over to you solely, Stella. You control Stratford Industries and all its assets."

"YOU DID WHAT!" Thomas shouts behind me. I ignore his shock at Rachel's words and keep my eyes pinned on my wife as she opens the folder and reads the documents. Sweat combined with dread drips down my back. What if that's not enough to convince her? I have nothing left to give her but my very life. I will gladly hand it over to her if she asks for that, too. *What am I without her?* Nothing, I am nothing.

Thomas is swearing a litany of profanities behind me, but I could care less about his opinion of me. He deems me weak for signing over everything to Stella. What he fails to understand is none of it matters without her. *She is what I want. She is my everything.*

"Thomas, let's leave these two alone." From the corner of my eye, I watch as Rachel yanks on his arm and pulls him from the room. The door closes quietly behind them, and finally, I'm alone with my heart's greatest desire. My greatest possession, the one that has yet to utter a word. *Fuck.*

"Stella, I know... I have wronged you. That I'm a callous fucking idiot, but I swear to you. I love you, Stella, with all of my being, and with my dark and tainted heart. With everything I am, I swear I love you and will never let you go. You will never walk this earth alone without me. I will be your shadow and your sword for all of eternity." I pull her hand into mine, turning it over and kissing her warm palm.

"Jaxon... I don't understand... the picture?" Stella doesn't finish her words, and I can see the questions across her features. Maybe there is still a bit of doubt. Can I really blame her? If the tables were turned, would I readily believe without an explanation?

I drag my hand back through my hair, her palm still clutched in my other hand. I'm afraid to let her go, that somehow something else will try to take her from me. "I hated going to that gala without you, but I knew it was our responsibility to do our duty for Stratford Industries." I inhale a deep breath and push the rest of my words out, praying that Stella will give me a chance and listen to me.

"I couldn't focus, Stella. I was in that room, but you were all I could taste on my lips. Your pretty pussy was all that was on my mind. I couldn't keep my dick from going painfully and embarrassingly hard at the thoughts of you. So I... I excused myself to the empty lobby, trying to calm myself down. Kalista followed me, she... ah fuck! She caught me rubbing one out over my pants and took advantage of the situation, pressing herself against me and trying to kiss me. I moved my face away from her, and she got me in the neck." I pull Stella's hand tight to my lips, kissing her knuckles. My hand is clammy, holding her intertwined fingers, and sweat trickles down my back, making the hospital gown stick to my body. *Jesus fuck, this is embarrassing, but fuck it if I won't endure it for her. I would walk through broken glass and set myself on fire for her.*

"I pushed her away, Stella, so hard that she almost landed on her ass. I told her to stay away from me. That what we had was in the past, and all I wanted was you. That you were my future. I never knew a photographer was hiding and taking photos. I underestimated what lengths Kalista would go to to try to get me back and to hurt you." I meet her gaze, deep blue blazing into gray. I watch as she pulls her bottom lip between her teeth and bites down on it. The desire to pull it from her and suck it into my mouth almost overwhelms me. "I was naive and stupid even for not seeing the danger, but I swear, Stella, you are everything I want, all that I need."

I stand up and move my body next to her on the bed, pressing my forehead to hers, and she allows it. The look of trepidation is still warring in her eyes and I know I have to clear all doubts from her mind about my feelings for her. She needs to understand that this is real, this is everything. "I love you, Stella Stratford." The words leave my mouth, as I press my lips to her skin. When I pull back, I see the tears in her eyes, waiting to cascade down her beautiful face. The face that belongs to my future. "There is nothing I wouldn't give you; everything I am belongs to you. My wealth, my name, our empire, and my heart, without you, there is nothing worth living for. My miserable, weak heart would fail without you. It only beats for you, Stella."

A tear slides down her right cheek, followed by another, and a whimper leaves her pouty mouth. She reaches for my face tentatively. Her touch is a balm to my soul and thudding heart. "Take everything, Stella. It's yours, it's all yours." I kiss her hand and then lean my face closer until I'm just a hair's breadth from her lips.

"You are *mine*. You were always meant to be *mine*. You are my possession, my greatest desire, my heart, and my soul. I will never let you go, Stella, so please don't run from me. Don't run from us."

43

Stella

"When a woman is talking to you, listen to what she says with her eyes." Victor Hugo

T HE SHOCK OF HIS words and the documents before me make me feel light-headed. Jaxon loves me? He truly loves me and has signed over all of his legacy to me. How is this possible? Am I still in a dream state, or did I die, and this is all some fucked up place my brain has been transported to? One where I get everything I've ever wanted all at once, only to realize that I'm dead?

Could this be real? I feel the weight of all this information and his declaration of his feelings coming at me so suddenly. It makes me feel like I'm suffocating or drowning under its weight. While I had hoped that he had feelings for me as more than just a warm body to spend the night with, I never for a moment imagined the depth of his feelings, not even after he took that bullet for me.

Did I think that he enjoyed fucking me in any way he could and got off on controlling my pleasure? *Sure, fucking did.* Did I acknowledge and welcome the fact that he's a bit unhinged and insanely possessive where I'm concerned? *Yes*, but did I think that in any way meant he loved me? *Not for a second.*

Now, lying here in this hospital bed, hearing him declare his feelings and intentions for me and his denial of what happened with Kalista, I'm not sure what to think or feel. Can I trust that his feelings are genuine? *He just signed over his fortune to you!* My mind screeches with disbelief.

"Stella, my little viper, that mind of yours is working overtime, and smoke is pouring out of those pretty ears. Stop trying to overthink it." He leans forward, his warm lips brushing against mine. His taste lingers on my lips, and his scent invades my senses. He doesn't try to deepen the kiss, letting me decide how we are to proceed.

My eyes are wide open, blue staring into molten silver. *Is he what I want? Do I believe him? I want him more than I have ever wanted anything.*

Maybe I'm the biggest fool who has ever lived, but I believe him. I believe that he loves me in his own possessive and demanding way. He wouldn't betray me with Kalista once he realized he had a genuine affection for me. The sacrifice of his legacy and empire, the two things he has always desired above all else and is consumed with, proves that he wants me more than he wants the future he originally married me to create. Can we move forward together and create our joint destiny, one where I'm his world, and he is mine?

I press my lips firmly into his and open my mouth to allow his tongue to enter and rub against mine. The kiss begins soft and gentle, but with each stroke, Jaxon adds fuel to a fire that will not be held back. The kiss deepens, and we're ravenous for each other. Little whimpers leave my lips, and groans leave his as our tongues tangle, teeth clash, and our breath is passed back and forth between us. Right now, Jaxon is my air and strength, and at this moment, I cannot imagine a world where he is not mine and I am not his. *Please let all of this be true and real; I will not survive the heartache if it's not.*

Does all of this fix all our problems? *Not even a little bit.* Great, we love each other, but we still don't trust or respect each other. Although, we do hunger for each other as if we were two starving beasts. We're still two strangers tied together by fate, the will of wealthy men, and a massive fortune. Not to mention our most pressing issue. The one there is no way of avoiding or ignoring, someone out there is still trying to kill me. I pull back from this kiss, both my palms flat against his heaving chest.

"Jaxon... I believe you about Kalista, but this doesn't solve our problems. We started this marriage with coercion and untrue emotions... I can't help but think that we will never be happy..."

"STOP! Stop right there, Stella, don't utter another fucking word. If you are about to tell me we should not be together because of how we began our relationship, don't even bother my little ice queen. I'm not fucking having it." His lips peck mine once more, and he leans back to stare at me. "You need to understand a few things, Stella, so that we have no misunderstandings going forward from this moment on."

He groans as he shifts beside me on the small bed, making himself comfortable and causing a smirk to cross my face. He grabs both of my hands and puts them in his lap. I bite down on the whimper that struggles to leave my lips with the shift in my torso. I think this fucker has forgotten I was just stabbed in his overwhelming need to confess his love for me. He's adorable when he's behaving like a love-besotted sap, so I hold in the snappy words that want to leave my lips.

"You are mine, Stella Stratford, now and forever. I will allow nothing, and no one to take you away from me. No man or woman, no test of fate, no fucking deity in the sky. Hell, if the devil tries to take you, he and I are going to have a big fucking problem." He releases my hand, and his fingers stroke my cheek tenderly. "You are mine. Every part of you, from that pretty, dark head to those sexy arctic eyes, right down to that sexy, pink pussy and those delectable toes. No one, Stella, gets any part of you but me."

His declaration has my chest expanding, the breath I was holding exhales, and relief pumps through me. I needed to hear these words expressed from his demanding lips. To know that he feels as much for me, as I do for him. His words are a soothing balm to my soul and a lit match to my passion. My hand reaches out and grabs the back of his neck, pulling him closer.

"I will not share you, Jaxon, not with another woman, not with the fucking world, not even with your precious legacy. You are mine just as much as I am yours. If you ever hurt me again, ever make me suffer as you have, I will sink a blade into that heart of yours and meet you in hell." I crush my lips to his, and the raging fire travels once again between us until I cry out in pain from jolting my side.

He pulls back, his features filled with heat and amusement sparkling in the polished silver of his eyes. "As much as I want to fuck every one of your sweet holes right now, my little viper. It would probably kill both of us." A groan leaves his lips as he pulls away and retains the seat next to the bed, putting distance between us.

"I need to know about the intruder, Stella. Someone out there wants to hurt you. Someone knew to follow Tyson to get to you. You're not safe until we kill whoever is after you."

His words cause a shiver to race down my spine. He doesn't mention stopping them or apprehending them, he wants to kill them. *Can I kill another person? Can*

I let Jaxon be tainted with someone's death to protect me? I don't want to think about what happened. About how my actions led to a man riddled with bullet holes taking his last breath in my presence and me almost bleeding to death alone. There's no avoiding it, though; Jaxon is right. Someone out there will try again to hurt me. Possibly using him or even my parents to get to me. I need to figure out if this is just about me seizing power or about us. We have too many enemies hiding in the shadows, waiting to do us harm.

"He somehow got into the house without me sensing he was there or any of the alarms going off. I realized someone was there, when I heard footsteps on the stone floor and he was already making his way towards the kitchen. I thought at first that it was Tyson coming back for something he had forgotten. He tried to trap me in the kitchen and attack me with a blade, but I managed to escape and run for the front door. There, he once again tried to trap me, but I managed at the last second to thwart him off and run for the main bedroom and lock myself inside." I watch as anger races across his features, his eyes turning to hard flint and his jaw tensing with the grinding of his teeth. "I had a gun in there, and when... when he broke the door... I shot him."

"Did he give you any clue as to why he was there? Did he say anything to give us an idea of who hired him to hurt you?"

I rack my brain, going through each of the memories from the attack, scene by scene. It's like a vibrant movie reel in my mind. Did he say or do anything that would give an indication of who wants me dead? The memory of the stairs keeps coming back to me over and over, and with it, trepidation fills me. What was it he said to me as I tried to escape him? Did he mention a name? No... he never said any names, he just called me a cunt and a whore.

"Fuck! He said they! He said *"they"* want you dead, cunt." I stare at Jaxon with shock. The memory once again rolls through me until I'm certain that those were the words that he uttered. "Jaxon, do you understand what that means?"

"FUCK!" He shouts, stands up, and kicks the chair until it falls backward. "Yeah, Stella, it means, baby, there's more than one person after you, and we need to know who the fuck they are so I can kill all of them."

44

Jaxon

"Your biceps, six-pack abs, and daring attitude are of no use if you cannot protect and respect women!" Avijeet Das

*T*HREE WEEKS LATER...

I watch Stella from the doorway of her office, she's a vision of power and confidence. Her sexy slate gray suit, offset by the pop of red in her shirt, makes her skin look luminous. The desire to slip under her desk and tongue her pretty cunt, a vicious craving in my bloodstream, one I'm finding difficult to control, much like the woman herself. *Fuck, just one taste and I would gladly give her my soul.*

My beautiful, relentless wife refused to stay home to continue recuperating from almost bleeding to death and leaving me in this miserable world alone, despite my very best attempts at teasing her with my hard cock. I should feel dejected that she still insisted on coming to the office after all the effort I put in this morning. I can't stop the smirk from crossing my lips at the memory of her expression when I pulled out my cock and made her choke on it before she even had a sip of coffee. Fuck, my balls are already pulling tight into my body just with the thought of fucking that tight throat of hers again. Once a day is never enough with Stella; I need inside of one of her delicious, tempting holes all day long.

Stella is determined not to hide from whoever is trying to hurt her. I get it, I do. She's a little hellion who pushes through her fear and refuses to cower. She's the strongest, fiercest woman I know. The knowledge that someone wants to end her life causes me endless hours of panic and fear. The nightmares I relive every night of finding her lying in her own blood cause me to wake, shaking and gasping for breath. The only thing that calms me down after having one is pulling her tightly into my arms and feeling her breath skate across my skin. Holding her as tightly as I can so that I can reassure myself that she is still alive and here with me and that no one has taken her from me. How can I protect her if she won't stay behind the walls of our fortress? *Would you hide?* My mind questions.

FUCK! My grip tightens on the doorframe. No, I wouldn't hide. I would taunt whoever means me harm in hopes of baiting them and forcing them out from hiding so that I could kill them. It's the same thing my lovely ice queen seems to be doing. I look over at the new head of our security team, standing in full tactical gear like a sentry just outside of her office. The guy is one giant, scary motherfucker. A shiver runs down my spine at the thought of having to fight the fucker now tasked with my wife's life.

Clark Abbotts came highly recommended, but not from law enforcement like you would have expected. Oh no, Clark has an array of talents. Ones that those just outside of the bright lights of the law prefer. His skill set is not strictly legal in this country, but that's the appeal of having him work for us. I needed someone just as ruthless as I am to protect Stella at all costs. Someone who would not hesitate to do what was necessary by any means, legal or not, to keep her alive. A killer to protect my wife from other killers.

My underworld connections led me to the young man from Canada—a ruthless mercenary with an honor code. Within a day, he had overhauled all of our security measures. New ex-military guards were hired, ones that shoot first and ask questions later. The Stratford estate is now a state-of-the-art fortress. Every window and door is bulletproof. Weapons and panic buttons are hidden on every floor. Our gate now sports high voltage electricity, one that will kill a human that tries to climb it instantly and can be armed from inside our home. There's surveillance all around the perimeter of our estate, with someone constantly monitoring it. Fuck, even Fergus is now walking around with a gun strapped to him, much to Mrs. Pox's horror. *Fort Knox, who?* My estate is locked up tighter than a devoted catholic nun's knees.

We even temporarily moved Stella's parents into the estate to ensure they couldn't be used against us. Let me tell you how much fucking fun it has been trying to fuck my wife raw with all these people in my house and with my father-in-law giving me death stares every time we are in a room together.

The one time in the last two weeks I managed to make Stella scream from me eating her perfect juicy cunt under her home office desk, I ended up with a gun pressed to the back of my fucking head. Let me tell you how quickly my boner disappeared. *Poof, motherfucker.*

Yet, here we are at the fucking office, because Stella won't stay put! "Stella, are you almost done?" I walk into her office, and she looks up from whatever she is reading on the screen in front of her, a look of confusion marring her perfect features. God, I want to bite down on that plump lip and make her bleed for me. Unfortunately, we are supposed to be attending a charity dinner tonight to benefit the "*Widows of Fire Personnel.*" A function that Stella refuses to miss and one that I'm attending with a bowling ball of dread in my gut. *Fuck, she has to be okay. I can't lose her.*

This will be our first public appearance since that magazine cover came out, and she was stabbed. Not that anyone knows that happened. No, the home invasion and her killing her assailant was made to disappear with a lot of zeros from our bank account. We wanted to make sure that there was no mention anywhere of the attempt, let whoever hired that fucker wonder if he's still out there or if he's six feet underground.

"Just one more moment, Jaxon. I'm just going over this acquisition. Did you authorize this purchase two months ago of a bunch of construction sites in the south that had taken over an area of low-income housing?" Her eyebrows furrow, and she bites down on that lip I'm craving to suck. "The developers have gone bankrupt and lost millions of their investors' money. The sites have been overrun by gang violence and set ablaze. Why did we buy this?"

At first, I have no clue what she's even talking about. It doesn't sound like an investment that I would have made. Why would I have acquired construction sites in a low-income housing area? I rack my thoughts and move closer to her desk, making my way around and leaning over her to look at the document on her screen. Her glorious scent invades my senses, and I lean down to rub my lips against the warm column of her neck. I'm just about to suggest we skip the dinner and lock the door of her office, when the memory of my wedding reception niggles at the back of my mind.

A devious smile crosses my face as I remember fucking over those cretins weeks after my reception that were bragging about being able to steal low-income housing from the poor for pennies on the dollar and transition them to condos for the wealthy. Leaving all those poor people displaced and without suitable housing. I wanted to fuck up their plans and throw a wrench into their progress, so I called in a couple of favors from the local gangs and had the construction sites terrorized and set ablaze. I paid off local law enforcement to look the other way and the insurance adjusters to refuse payment. When their investor tucked tail and ran for the hills, I bought all the properties up for basically nothing. My plan was to transition that area back to affordable housing and even build a few schools and some daycares. Ones that would help the people of those areas prosper rather than continue to struggle daily while rich fucks like me prospered on their hardship.

Nothing brings me such joy as being able to fuck over and destroy other wealthy assholes. Do I make enemies that way? *Maybe*. Are they too chicken shit to do anything about it? *You bet*.

"I was playing a little game of chicken and bulldozer with a few of our wealthy friends. It's nothing to worry about, love. We are going to make an investment in the community and earn some goodwill and some tax incentives from the government. Even build a school that is dedicated to my father." I kiss her neck again, swirling my tongue over her soft skin and then sucking hard on her flesh to leave a mark. Fuck that has my dick hardening in my pants. I love to see Stella covered in my marks.

"Jaxon, this is not a small investment, we are talking about over two million dollars." She shoves me away from her. Her eyebrows raised closer to her hairline, and a grimace across her beautiful face. *Fucking great I have once again displeased my little ice queen*. Just with that look of annoyance across her features, I know there is zero chance I'm getting into her panties. *Damn it! My fucking cock is already hard!*

"It's chump change. Nothing to worry about. Now let's go and get this fucking night over with so I can go home and fuck your ass." I drag her up from her seat and kiss her soundly until her breath leaves her in harsh pants, and a pink color is streaking across her cheekbones. *Mine*.

I'm fucking angsty sitting here while my wife is steps away, shaking hands with different widows. All I want to do is get this night over and done with. Stella's supposed to be making some fucking speech in a few minutes and handing over a check for a million bucks to this charity. I wish she would hurry the fuck up. I don't know what it is, but a feeling of unease is skating up and down my spine. My eyes keep tracing over all the different people in the room. I don't see anything out of place, but my gut is telling me something is wrong.

I must not be the only one because Clark is no more than two feet away from Stella, looking menacingly at anyone who approaches her. His eyes are on constant patrol through the room, meeting the other security personnel across the space. They communicate soundlessly with each other, and each goes back to patrolling the room's inhabitants.

I shake hands with another acquaintance, but don't focus on any of the words he's blithering out of his mouth. My attention is solely on the dark-haired beauty I desperately want to wrap my arms around and take home. She looks up over her shoulder, feeling my eyes on her. Her blue eyes are bright and filled with mischief as they meet mine, a small smile graces her pretty lips. She doesn't look worried, Stella always projects strength even when she doesn't feel it. It's one of the qualities I most admire about my little ice queen.

The event organizer leads her away from the crowd of recipients, and to the side of the stage area; Clark follows right behind her, ever her faithful and lethal shadow. My eyes skip once again over the room, and I feel the hairs on the back of my neck standing on end. I begin searching for whoever is staring at me, giving off the malevolent energy I can feel in the room. My glare centers on three acquaintances off to the side, deep in conversation. They are sending me dirty, scathing looks. I gift all three of the fuckers with a snarky smirk. *Fuck those assholes.*

Fisher St. John, Jeffrey Cain, and River Stanton. The same fuckers from my wedding reception that were so smug and the very ones that Stella and I were discussing earlier about that investment I made. I stare them down, daring them to approach me and reprimand me for sweeping in and fucking up their investment. None of them will meet my glare, *fucking cowards.* Jeffrey Cain looks agitated and unkempt, a look of malice across his features as his eyes track Stella across the room. *What. The. Fuck.*

The look and anger radiating off of him has me paying closer attention to their little group. I nod at Clark in their direction when his eyes meet mine from across the room. Jeffrey Cain has every reason to hurt Stella. Kalista's father has suffered the brunt of my wife's temper, after all, she did set his house ablaze and destroyed his daughter's credibility and future. I want to feel sorry for the man, but even after all these years as his acquaintance, I never liked the fucker.

The organizer is now walking across the stage, and tapping on the microphone to get our attention and requesting for everyone to return to their tables. I sit my ass down, still feeling out of sorts, and watch as my gorgeous wife walks across the stage after her introduction in those sexy as fuck heels. The ones that will be up by my ears later on if I have anything to say about it. I don't see Clark, but I know he can't be far and will be positioned in the best way to protect Stella.

"Ladies and gentlemen, it's an honor to be here tonight and bring light to the Widows of Fire Personnel Fund. On behalf of myself, my husband, Jaxon, and Stratford Industries, I would like to present this check for one million dollars to the director of FPF..."

She doesn't get another word out before someone yells from the back of the room. The words *"die you fucking whore"* are shouted, and then it sounds like fireworks are erupting throughout the room. Except it's not fireworks, it's fucking bullets! Various people are shooting from different parts of the room. People are getting hit and falling to the ground, others are running in panic. Some have fallen to the ground screaming and are hiding under the tables.

It's pure fucking chaos! *Where the hell is Stella?* I push away from a man in front of me who took a bullet and stumbled into me. His heavy body knocked me into the table behind me and caused me to lose my balance. His blood gushes from his neck wound, spraying me. Screams are all I can hear, coming from every direction. I crouch down and start to move between the tables, making my way towards the stage and the last place I saw Stella standing. There are casualties everywhere, the shooters are still hailing bullets throughout the room. A large grunt greets my ears as the man hiding below the next table gets hit and stumbles backward. *Holy fuck! I have to get to Stella. Where is Stella?*

I spy a glimpse of gray and red and move toward where I think Stella is hiding off the side of the stage. I'm just a few feet away from her when the shooting suddenly stops, and a loud voice thunders through the room.

"Stratford, you had better come out if you want your little whore of a wife to live."

45

Stella

"Holding on to anger is like grasping a hot coal with the intent of throwing it at someone else; you are the one who gets burned."
Buddha

*O*H MY GOD! SOMEONE is spraying bullets across the room. My eyes land on the event coordinator, Sasha, lying prone on the floor a few feet away from where Clark has me crouched. Her eyes stare sightlessly up at the ceiling, blood streaming from the wound in her forehead that ended her life too short.

Who the hell is attacking us? My eyes try desperately to dart around Clark and search for Jaxon. I lost track of him when the shooting started, and fear slithers across my whole body. *He's going to be okay, he has to be.* My throat clogs with sobs, and tears slide down my cheeks unchecked. I need to get myself under control and be strong. I can't break down when I need to protect Jaxon and myself.

There seem to be multiple shooters throughout the room, gunning people down without reason. Is this some terrorist attack against the wealthy, or is this someone after Jaxon and me? My questions are answered with a loud shout from across the room, which has me trying to stumble to my feet in horror. *NO! Fuck, no!*

"Stratford, you had better come out if you want your little whore of a wife to live."

Clark grabs my wrist painfully and pulls me back down to the ground. "Mrs. Stratford, I need you to slowly start moving backward, crouch as low as you can." Clark's hushed words meet my ear. His dark suit jacket is wide open, and the array of weapons strapped to his body are displayed. He slips a dark gun into my hand and tightens my grip around it. "You press the trigger until it clicks empty if anyone other than me or Jaxon approaches you. Do you understand? Stella, do you understand?" He questions again as a humming begins in my ears.

My frightened eyes meet his, and I nod in understanding, my grip tightening on the weapon. I back away slowly, crouching so low that I might as well be a worm slithering on my stomach. Screams and sobs are still echoing off the walls in the confined space. My eyes meet a scared waitperson hiding under a table as I keep moving in the direction Clark is pushing me towards.

"JAXON, YOU FUCKER! COME OUT FROM HIDING!" A man's irate voice screams over the chaos. "Find the whore, he will come out of hiding to protect her."

"Stella, listen to me. When I signal, I want you to run towards the emergency exit at the back of the stage. Don't look back, and don't stop running, even when you're outside. You head to our designated area. Our team is outside; they will protect you with their lives."

"What about Jaxon?" My voice comes out in harsh gasps. The pain from my wound is a stitch in my side at the crouched position I'm in. My hand gripping the gun trembles, and I keep my finger away from the trigger for fear that I will accidentally shoot Clark or myself.

"Let me worry about getting to Jaxon. You do exactly what I tell you. They want you so they can hurt him." Clark's face is thunderous, his eyes so cold and frightening that it has me backing up a further step. Fuck I should have listened to him and Jaxon about not attending this event. I was so reckless, putting all of us in danger just because I refused to cower in my own fortress. How many people have died because of my decision? My eyes again shift over to Sasha's body, *I did that, I caused that to happen.*

"Now! Go!" Clark pushes me back and stands from his crouched position, with a gun in each hand, raining bullets across the room toward the assailants. I get up and run towards the emergency exit sign I can see in the distance. My legs feel like two wet noodles that want to cave in on me as I sprint toward the red words and beacon of hope. I don't look back, even though my heart begs me to look for Jaxon. Clark is right; they will use me to hurt him; I need to put myself out of their reach.

A grunt from behind has me turning and looking over my shoulder just as I hit the bar on the emergency door. The waitperson who was hiding had tried to escape after me and is down on his knees, clutching his abdomen as red blood soaks his white dress shirt. "Please help me!" He begs with frightened eyes.

I almost turn back around to help him, to try to drag him with me to safety, but another shot rings out, and he falls face down onto the ground. *Fuck, I got to run now!* I slam my arm into the door, and it opens with a shriek. I don't hesitate running out the door, my heels hitting the hard concrete of the side entrance. I keep moving, trying to use the shadows created by the overhang of the building and the darkness of the night to hide in.

I make it almost to the front of the building when another shot rings out in the night air. "You're going to die, you fucking whore!" Footsteps are rapidly approaching behind me. I duck down between two dumpsters, trying to control my ragged breathing, my hand tightening on the gun. "You can't escape whore; we have Jaxon, and we're going to put a bullet between his eyes while you watch."

I bite hard down on my lip until I can taste rich copper to stop the whimper trying to escape my throat. I have to trust that Clark got to Jaxon, that this fucker is lying, and trying to get me to come out of hiding. Crunching sounds greet my ears as he approaches my hiding spot. I quickly slip off my heels, knowing I will have one chance to run and I won't be able to do it with them on. A shot fires into the night air a few feet away from me and echoes off the wall of the building. "Come out, little Stratford whore, I plan to fuck that icy cunt of yours before I put a bullet into you!"

I don't recognize the voice of who is stalking me, but it doesn't matter who he is. I'm not going to allow him to hurt me. *What about if they actually have Jaxon?* My mind cries, and my chest tightens painfully. The best thing I can do for Jaxon is to make it to safety and get help. They want me, they want to hurt me, and maybe if I can get away, they won't kill him yet. A loud noise comes from behind us and startles the attacker; he turns and fires back into the darkness. I don't hesitate, jumping out from my hiding spot and firing the gun in his direction. I don't stop to see if my shot hits him. I run towards the alley's opening, lights, and the racing cars I can see beyond.

Another shot fires into the night air, and shards of brick rain down on my head from just above me. A scream leaves my lips, and I fall to my knees and look back.

He's quickly approaching in the shadows. I still can't see his face, but I can hear his ragged breathing. "Fucking cunt!" He grunts with pain.

The street light is mere feet away, I have to fucking get out of here. I jump back to my feet, point the gun at the shadow approaching me, and pull the trigger. The sound is so loud that my ears ring, and the blowback has me banging back into the brick wall before I stand up and run.

I make it out of the alleyway and into the light just as another shot rents the air, and I feel it impact with my shoulder. I stumble forward, slamming down to my knees once again, the gun going limp in my arm. Pain sears up my back and down my arm. *Fuck, he shot me.* I grab the gun in my left hand, stumbling with it, as adrenaline fills me, and I gain my feet and run for my life. Cars are whizzing by quickly on the road; people are running in different directions, trying to get away from the shots being fired. I make it further down, hiding behind a dark parked vehicle just as the shadow morphs into the body of a man.

River Stanton stands at the end of the alleyway holding a gun in one hand while his other hand clutches at his side. Momentary satisfaction fills me and spurs me on with the knowledge that I hit him with that shot. His eyes look over the parked vehicles as he searches for me. He's grunting in pain and shifting slowly forward, the look of crazed obsession and fury across his face.

Why is River Stanton after me? I've never done anything to him, to my knowledge. I don't even know the guy personally. I don't have time to analyze his reasoning behind wanting to kill me as he approaches my hiding spot. My shoulder is on fire. The pain making sweat slide down my back and bile to rise up my throat. I hold the gun awkwardly in my left hand, trying to get a firm grip on it. Another shot echoes in the air, and the windshield on the car behind me shatters, raining glass shards all over me. I'm going to die if I don't shoot him. He's going to kill me out here on Madison Avenue, and no one is going to stop him.

Flashes of my life with Jaxon rapidly cross my mind. His smile this morning as he tried to entice me to stay home with him. His words of love last night as he held me tightly in his arms as we fell to blissful sleep. His declaration of love in my hospital room back in the Hamptons. My mother's kind smile and warm embraces and my father's attempt at trying to have real discussions with me in the last couple of days flicker through my mind.

Fuck it! I refuse to die now! I refuse to cower before this man and let him take my life. If he wants to kill me, I will fight until the last breath leaves my lips, and I will take him on the journey to hell with me. *We can go meet the devil together.*

I stand from my crouched position, moving around the other side of the car and approaching him from behind. His deranged eyes are searching for me everywhere. I can see people running away from us, and others crouched down, trying not to get hit with bullets. Sirens are loud in the distance and approaching rapidly.

A shout from behind us, has him turning rapidly and gaining his attention. I don't hesitate, lifting my shaking arm, the gun grasped tightly in my fist. My eyes meet his for a moment, and then I pull the trigger, my finger squeezing as shots rain out across the space between us.

46

Jaxon

"Never interrupt your enemy when he is making a mistake."
Napoleon Bonaparte

"**J**AXON, YOU FUCKER! COME OUT FROM HIDING!" Jeffrey Cain's voice screams over the chaos. "Find the whore. He will come out of hiding to protect her."

From the corner of my eye, I see a brief flash of gray and red before it disappears further into the backstage area. A whoosh of panicked air leaves my lungs. I have to hope that Clark is managing to get Stella out of the building and away from these crazy assholes that want to kill us. It's all that matters right now. I don't care if I die, but if I do, I'm taking all of these fuckers with me. None of them will harm Stella if I have anything to do with it. *Stella, I love you. I will gladly die for you.*

My chest tightens painfully, and my breath stutters in my throat. *Naw, fuck that shit, not right now, useless, weak heart.* You don't get to act the fuck up right now. We have to protect the one thing we love the most. *We have to save Stella.*

My attention returns to Jeffrey Cain, Fisher St. John, and two other men I don't know as they open fire once again into the room. The hail of bullets is hitting walls and furniture, and people are running, scared for their lives. I slowly move from one table to the next, using the linens to cover my tracks as I approach Fisher St. John.

I have never been so happy that I let Clark talk me into carrying a gun strapped under my suit jacket. While I've never actually killed anyone with a gun before, my fury is racing through me, knowing that these lunatics mean to harm Stella and me. Nothing will stop me from ending their lives before they attempt to end ours. My grip on the gun tightens, and I release the safety, moving my finger into position.

Jeffrey Cain moves further into the room, shooting at people trying to run away from him and screaming incoherently. Fisher is holding his gun high in his hand like some criminal vigilante in a comic book movie. The look across his middle-aged face is unhinged, his eyes wide, the white pronounced, his face red and sweat sliding down his ridiculous comb-over. I never in a million years would have guessed that this guy would be involved in trying to harm Stella and me. He has always been soft-spoken, awkward, and restrained in his business dealings with me. I would never have thought that he would have the courage to be shooting at innocent people and trying to kill me. I guess losing millions of dollars can make even the most restrained person lose their mind. *Fuck.*

Just as Jeffrey moves towards the backstage area, shots ring out over and over, echoing off the walls and the ceiling and causing further panic amongst the trapped room's inhabitants. I take Fisher's moment of distraction, jump up, and land my shoulder into his abdomen, tackling him like a linebacker and taking him down hard as his finger presses the trigger of his gun. The shot goes wide, and the gun slips from his grasp and skates across the floor under a table. I rain blows down on his face with the butt of my gun over and over until I hear a crunching sound, and he stops trying to fight me. His grip on me goes slack before his eyes roll into the back of his head. Blood is pouring from his nose, mouth, and temple, and his face looks like ground hamburger meat. My lungs are filled with fire as I straddle his large body while trying to catch my breath.

A woman hiding beneath a chair cowers before me, her eyes wide with terror across her face. She watches with tears drenching her face and her hands covering her mouth to silence her sobs as I move off of Fisher's body and crawl toward his gun.

"Get the hell out of here, go! Move under the tables towards the exit." I pant at her. She trembles like a leaf but follows my instructions, crawling on her hands and knees under the table beside her.

I return my attention to Fisher lying in a bleeding mess on the floor next to me. He's still breathing but out cold. The desire to put a bullet in his brain fills me. This fucker came after my little viper and me with the intention of hurting us. I would be doing the world a favor by ending his miserable life. My hand clenches on the gun, my finger tightening on the trigger as another shot rings out across the room and grabs my attention.

Clark is fighting Jeffrey Cain on stage, and his fist rains blows to Jeffrey's head. Just when it looks like Jeffrey will go down, he fires a shot that hits Clark in the thigh, and his leg buckles, but not before landing a hard punch to Jeffrey's temple. The man goes down like a ton of bricks, hitting the stage floor with a loud thud. Clark drags his bleeding leg across the stage, raining another blow to Jeffrey's head. I watch, mesmerized, as his head rises and slams again into the floor, and the back of his skull cracks, blood gushing from the wound. *Holy fuck.*

"Jaxon, are you alright?" Clark bellows from the stage.

I move quickly in his direction, my eyes scanning the room for any further shooters. There are injured people all across the space, some begging for help while others try to crawl out of the room to safety. Just as I'm about to make my way to the stairs leading to the stage, the hard barrel of a gun is shoved into the back of my neck and has my body stopping cold. Ice-cold fear fills me, fuck did Fisher get up again? I showed the fucker mercy, and look where it has gotten me.

"You picked the wrong woman, Jaxon. Look at all the damage she has caused."

"Kalista…" The name leaves my lungs in a whoosh of air. My shoulders tighten painfully and rise towards my ears. I can hear my blood racing through my ears, replacing all the sounds of chaos surrounding us. *This fucking bitch, I should have strangled her.*

She taps the barrel against my neck again, pushing forward against my skin and causing sweat to break out across my back. Her other hand brushes the side of my neck, her nails trailing down my skin, causing the hairs on my body to stand on end and disgust to flow through me. I try to hold perfectly still in fear that she will accidentally press the trigger and shoot me. "You loved me first, Jaxon. I would have given you the world. I would have been the perfect wife to you, but you wanted that whore to grow your empire. Now look at you, you will die here with a bullet lodged in the back of your skull. A name forgotten except when they speak of tragedies. But don't worry, I'm going to make sure that bitch dies a painful death with you."

I try to turn around, but the barrel of the gun pushes into the nape of my neck more tightly. I'm still holding my weapon firmly in my grasp, but there is no way I can use it in my current position. Another shot echoes through the space from behind the curtain. Kalista's body jumps behind me at the sound, and her gun moves away from my skin. I take advantage of the moment and turn sideways, pushing my weapon into her breast as hard as I can. She quickly resets her hold on her own gun, pointing it back at my head.

"Drop your weapon Kalista, or I swear I will blow a fucking hole in your over-priced tits."

Tears slide down her pale, distraught face, her mascara is in dark clumps on her lashes and running in black rivers down her cheeks. Her hair hangs limply down the sides of her head and looks unwashed and disheveled. Her lips are bleeding and looking ragged and chewed. She looks like she's lost a ton of weight, her shirt hanging off of her, and bones visibly protruding across her collarbone. She's a fucking mess and looks deranged standing here holding a gun on me.

"How could you have done this to me, Jaxon? You let her ruin my whole life! She destroyed me! You walked away from me as if I was nothing?" Snot runs down her face and over her lips.

She looks utterly pitiful and a mere shadow of the woman I once cared about. The woman I once thought I might have loved but never understood the true meaning behind the emotion until Stella. Now I know with certainty that I have never loved another person like I love Stella. She consumes every part of me, her being intertwined with mine. Two hearts beating in separate bodies but one in every way possible. She is my heart and my home, and this bitch and her father are trying to take her away from me. To shatter with a bullet, my heart's desire, and my one reason for living.

"You did this to yourself, Kalista. You tried to fight a war with a wolf, when you are nothing but a fucking worm. She is a queen, and you're dirt under her feet." Anger rages through me to pull the trigger, to fire bullets into her body. "It was you that left the chicken and tried to have her stabbed, wasn't it?" A whimper leaves her lips at my harsh tone. I press the gun further into her large breast, and a look of pain crosses her features. How could I have been so deceived? I thought her incapable of orchestrating this, of going after Stella. I believed her to be too weak, but I guess she found the strength when she had nothing left to lose.

"I wanted you back... I wanted my life... back. She took everything from me!" A shuddering breath leaves her as more tears cascade down her face. "You are mine!"

A snort leaves my mouth, and my upper lip curls in disgust, my warm breath trailing over her haggard face. "You are a cunt, and were a plaything, Kalista. Something pretty to stick my cock in. You were never going to be my queen. You are nothing to me. She is my everything, my heart and my soul. I will never return to you, you never had me. It was always her."

Kalista's hand trembles, the gun still gripped tightly in her hand, and pointed at my head. I take a deep breath, prepared to die here in this moment with the knowledge that I love Stella. I caused all of this and put all of it into motion the minute I accepted the deal with her father. The minute I forced my little viper down the aisle, I began this tragedy that would be my bitter end.

All my hopes for expanding the Stratford empire and my original reasoning for doing all of this were worth nothing in the end. None of it is of the slightest importance or significance in light of my love for Stella. Loving her will be the greatest accomplishment of my life and the only thing of value that I leave behind in the world. My only solace is that I will take Kalista with me into hell. Hopefully, if there really is a God worthy of my prayers, he has seen fit to save my little ice queen and get her to safety. *I love you, Stella Stratford.*

"NO!" Rage crosses Kalista's face, and her finger tightens on the trigger. My eyes meet arctic blue eyes, filled with emotion, terror, and sorrow. My heart is ready to explode with fear and devastation. How could this be our end? The story had just begun for Stella and me. A fucked up fairy tale to end all tales.

I close my eyes, prepared to die here and now, the vision of Stella crossing my mind. How beautiful she is, even when she's irate with me. Fuck it, especially when she's breathing fire in my direction. I love her, I will always love her. I squeeze my finger, just as the sound of another shot rents the air around us.

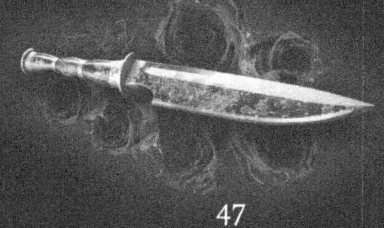

47

Stella

"In a world that wants women to whisper, I choose to yell."
Luvvie Ajayi

M Y ARM VIBRATES WITH the bullets leaving the gun. I pull the trigger until it clicks empty, and I watch as River falls backward to the ground, blood quickly soaking the dirty concrete around him. My ears ring loudly, and the sounds of bells in my head are so deafening that I feel like they will explode. I shake my head vigorously, trying desperately to clear my vision. I drop the gun to the ground, falling to my knees and trying desperately to catch my breath. My chest burns with the breaths that I was holding back. Tears fall down my cheeks, making my vision blurry again.

He's dead. He's lying mere feet away from me dead. I killed another person, another man trying to kill me. When will this all be over? Will they keep coming for me, trying to end my life? Will I ever be safe? *I'm a murderer... I am a murderer.* There will be no redemption for me now. My heart and soul were already stained with the first man's life that I took, and now another. *How many more stains before I am done?*

My sightless eyes focus on my surroundings, and the ringing in my ears settles down to a more bearable level. I can hear the shrieking of sirens around me, and flashing lights are visible out of the corner of my eye. There are men's voices loudly surrounding me, shouting orders. Ones I can't make out. Are they here to kill me too? I have nothing left to fight with. My hand moves to the empty gun on the ground next to me. My fingers don't seem to connect with it, missing its shape by mere inches as a searing cold sensation fills my body, and I force myself to swallow the scream that is desperate to escape my throat. *How many more will I have to kill, so that I can live?*

"Mrs. Stratford! Mrs. Stratford, ma'am. I need to get you to safety and medical assistance." My eyes meet dark green ones in a face I vaguely recognize as one of Clark's men. He's crouching down next to me and applying pressure on my shoulder. I didn't even feel him touching me until now. His face is laced with worry, his features stern as he stares at me.

"Stella, you are in shock and losing blood. We have to get you to the hospital!" He tries to lift me from the ground and get me to stand, but my legs refuse to hold me, and I crumble in his embrace. *Shock, yes, I must be in shock.* It's why I feel so cold, shivers taking over my body and making my teeth rattle.

"Jaxon..." His name leaves my lips, and dread fills me. *Where is Jaxon?* Is he still trapped inside with the rest of those madmen? My hand clutches the chest strap of the man in front of me tightly. "Where is Jaxon!" The words are ripped from my lips in a panicked scream.

"He's still inside. He hasn't made it out yet." He tries again to lift me, but this time fire fills me with renewed strength and I make it to my feet. Jaxon is still trapped inside with the men that want to kill him. I need to get to him. I can't let them hurt him. I turn in his grasp and push away from him, stumbling on my feet a few steps.

"Stella! Where are you going? You're hurt. We need to get you medical attention." He tries to grab onto me again, but I push backward, sliding in River's blood in my bare feet. *No! No one is fucking stopping me from getting to Jaxon.* There is no way I will allow them to take me away from here to get medical attention, while Jaxon is still trapped inside at the mercy of psychopaths.

My eyes catch on the glint of metal inches away from River's hand, his sightless and empty eyes greeting me as I bend down and grab his gun, lifting it in my left hand and gripping it tightly. I point the gun at the man moving slowly towards me. "NO! I'm going to get Jaxon, and if you try to stop me, I will blow your fucking brains out." I don't wait for his reply or to see if he will make a move. I turn and run back into the dark alley and the way I had escaped from.

"STELLA, WAIT!" I hear shouted behind me, but my blood is loud in my ears, and adrenaline is rushing through my body. I dash quickly across the alley and back towards the emergency exit door that is still partially ajar. Grabbing the door, I slip through it, my feet sliding across the floor, almost making me fall. *I have to get to*

Jaxon! The thought races over and over through my mind until it is a staccato beat along with the sound of my heart.

I move slowly through the backstage area, trying to get my ears to cooperate and stop ringing and my teeth to stop shattering. I don't hear the sound of shooting, just screams of fear and panic bouncing off the walls. I approach the curtained area just as Clark's man makes it to my back. He goes to grab onto me, but I point the gun at his head with a warning look. *He will not stop me.* If I have to shoot him, I fucking will. He raises his hands in a gesture of surrender, backing up a step. My eyes shift over the stage before me just as a shot rings out in the space and gets my attention. I move forward, and the guy slides in front of me with his gun drawn, ready to protect me. Over his large shoulder, I see Clark on the stage, his leg bleeding and drenching the ground around him as he slams his gun over and over into Kalista's father's face.

"Clark..." I don't even know if words are leaving my lips, but panic fills me. Clark is shot and bleeding. *Where the hell is Jaxon? Who is protecting Jaxon?* The guy in front of me motions for me to step further into the curtained area and move slowly and silently toward the side of the stage and the steps leading back into the main room area. "Clark's bleeding out. I have to get him out of here. You need to come with me so I can keep you safe." He whispers and grabs onto my right wrist, and shooting pain rises up my arm, over my shoulder, and across my back. A harsh, pained cry leaves my lips as I pull back from his grasp.

"For fuck sake. Stella, we have to get you to safety!" He tries once again to grab onto me, but I move away from him, quickly pointing the gun at his neck. "Get Clark out of here. I have to find Jaxon."

He seems he will try to force me to go with him towards Clark, but a shout catches his attention and mine. Clark is yelling Jaxon's name frantically. I peek out from around the curtain and spy my husband looking ragged a few feet from the stage.

A breath leaves my chest harshly at seeing him alive before me. It's replaced quickly with cold fury as I watch haggard Kalista slip up behind him, a gun in her grasp and pointed at the back of his neck. Jaxon stops cold in his forward movement, and panic is evident across his features even from the distance I'm standing in. I grip my gun tighter and move slowly forward, using the curtain to disguise my movements again, and slip down the first couple of steps, crouching low and making my way to the first table, ducking below it and using the tablecloth to hide myself. My shoulder aches with each movement, fire burning up and down my arm. I grit my teeth and keep moving forward. I need to get to Jaxon, nothing else matters.

I look back and watch as Clark's man stares at me with horror and frustration before moving stealthily toward an injured Clark. He takes off his belt, wraps it tightly around Clark's leg, and drags him back into the curtained area and out of view. My attention is drawn back to Kalista and Jaxon. He's egging her on, the ruthless idiot, as if he is trying to force her to shoot him. Their words echoing over the space clearly.

"You did this to yourself, Kalista. You tried to fight a war with a wolf, when you are nothing but a fucking worm. She is a queen, and you are dirt under her feet." OH. MY. FUCKING. GOD. This man is an idiot, baiting her with his words, causing her to get angrier at him and lose control. Does he have a death wish? Does the fucker want to make me a widow after all? I swear if we make it out of this, I'm going to dick-punch him for all this shit.

I slip under the table next to me, my body meeting the dead one of a man on his side. Shock races through me at the acknowledgment that I knew him; he was a friend of my parents and always so kind to me, and now he's needlessly dead under a table because of these assholes. *Motherfuckers!*

I'm going to end that fucking cunt once and for all. How dare she and her psycho father come in here and hurt all these people in an attempt to get to Jaxon and me! The recklessness and anguish of so many innocents suffering for her deranged perceived loss of my husband. *I'm sure your actions against her didn't fucking provoke her, huh?* My mind screams at me. Well, I'm as much to blame, I guess, but not for killing innocents. That is all on them. *Murderer...* my mind whispers back, and I shake my head trying once again to focus on Jaxon and Kalista's conversation.

"I wanted you back... I wanted my life... back. She took everything from me!" A harsh breath leaves Kalista's lips as I watch from my position underneath the table. Tears are ugly black rivers down her face, making her look grotesque. "You are mine."

I'm going to take your fucking life from you, bitch!

Her words make even more rage bubble up inside of me. How fucking dare she say that! Jaxon doesn't belong to her, he never has. He is and will always be mine. *Only fucking mine!* She has never understood that she would have never been enough for him. Not in this lifetime or the next. Jaxon has always needed a strong woman by his side. One that would challenge him and see that his legacy rises. She could have never offered him more than a warm cunt to satisfy his hunger. A hunger I stoke with the fire I create in him. Jaxon is an inferno, and I am his lighter fluid. He was put on this earth to be mine, and I am his. We are both made of the same thing, him and I. That eternal cloth that lets us push forward, be ruthless, and demand more than this world ever bargained for. He is my beginning, and I am his eternal end.

"You are a cunt, and were a plaything, Kalista. Something pretty to stick my cock in. You were never going to be my queen. You are nothing to me. She is my everything, my heart and my soul. I will never return to you, you never had me. It was always her."

OH. MY. FUCKING. GOD! This man and that mouth of his!

His words, while reckless, given a mad woman is holding a gun on him, fill me with the strength I need to move away from the table and stand slowly. I raise my hand, clenching River's gun tightly in my grasp, and point it at the back of her blonde head. Jaxon's eyes widen momentarily, catching mine, the look of desperation and fear on his features. Features that cause my heart to clench painfully, ones that I have grown to love with everything that I am.

In this moment, I see what our future could have been had fate been kinder. We could have grown an empire the likes of which hadn't been seen since the time of the *Roman Empire*. We could have had children, a little girl running around with Jaxon's mischievous smile and gray eyes, causing havoc on the male world around us. We could have grown old together, hand in hand, heading to the afterlife. In no world would I remain if the fates decided to take him. How could I when he is my heart and soul? *A body cannot live without either.* I love you, Jaxon Stratford, and always will.

48

Jaxon

"Love is composed of a single soul inhabiting two bodies."
Aristotle

S TELLA'S EYES MEET MINE from such a close distance, but it might as well be miles. I watch as fear flashes across her blood-streaked face. Her arctic blue eyes are panicked, blood is soaked across the front of her jacket, and she bites hard down on her lip. She trembles before raising her arm in the air between us, pointing a gun at the back of Kalista's head.

Kalista doesn't realize that my predator of a wife is behind her, about to end her life as she ends mine. Pride fills me, knowing that Stella is my ice queen who can defend herself against all comers. My wife never needed a prince on a white horse to save the day. *She is her own savior.*

I stare into the eyes that bring me so much pleasure and pain. The ones I would have never been prepared to live without, before I shut mine for what could be my final time. "MINE!" The battle cry rents the air with its fierceness. Two shots ring out loudly in the air, and I flinch, waiting for the bullet to penetrate my brain and cause me to take my last breath.

Seconds stretch before us, and then a body lands with its weight against mine, causing me to stumble backward before dropping down at my feet. My eyes fly open and meet two pools of blue mercury, a fire swirling from within them. *Holy shit!*

I watch as Stella drops the gun from her hand and sways before me. My gaze flies down to the body at my feet. Kalista is face down on the carpet, the weapon still in her tight embrace, but the back of her head is completely blown away, and brain matter is splattered everywhere and dripping down mine and Stella's faces. Kalista's abdomen has a large splash of red appearing and soaking the fabric of her shirt.

My panicked eyes look around for where the second shot came from, prepared to put my body in front of Stella's to protect her from any more shots being fired our way. My eyes meet the dark green eyes of Trig, one of Clark's men a mere two feet away. It's then that I realize he shot Kalista at the same time as Stella. *Jesus fucking Christ*, either one of them could have missed, and I would be meeting my father no doubt in hell to hear all about my failings.

I tear my gaze away from his and back to Stella, whose arm hangs limply at her side, her breathing rapid and her eyes dilated. "Mine!" She repeats over and over, her voice barely making it across the space between us. Her gaze stares down at Kalista, and her whole body shudders before me. I take a step forward, needing to wrap her in my arms and convince myself that she is real, that this is real. *That we are both alive.*

"Jaxon, she's bleeding from a gunshot wound. We need to get her to the medic right now!" Trig moves closer and approaches Stella. "Stella, it's over. I need you to give me the gun now." He approaches her as if she were a feral animal, and her eyes dart across his face before fear and confusion cross her features. Her body starts to shake, her teeth chattering loudly in the space between us. *Shit, she's going into shock.*

"Jaxon, I have to save Jaxon." Her voice comes out weak and breathy.

"I'm here, my little ice queen. You saved me. You saved me, Stella." I approach her, my hand sliding carefully to her face, my fingers caressing her soft cheek as her blue eyes meet mine, finally without the haze. Tears race down her face, and a sob wrenches from her chest.

"You are mine, Jaxon." It's the last words she utters before she sways, her legs giving out and her body trying to collapse before me. I reach for her at the same time as Trig does, and he catches her, lifting her lifeless body in his arms bridal style. Anger fills me at seeing her draped across another man's arms. The beast that lives inside of me wants to be let loose from his cage to reclaim what is his. *She is fucking mine!*

"Jaxon, we gotta move right now. She's been bleeding for too long." I shake the fury away from my mind and move with Trig towards the exit door just as the police force their way into the room with their guns drawn. "Police! Put your hands up in the air!" They shout, but Trig doesn't hesitate to continue moving forward, and I follow his lead. My only concern is the limp woman in his arms.

Emergency personnel rush through the room and approach us with a stretcher. Trig lays Stella down gently on the surface and begins cataloging her injuries quickly while they assess her. "In and out wound" and "Lost a lot of blood" make their way through the buzzing in my brain. I finally get a really good look at Stella. She's barefoot, and her feet and legs are covered in blood. Her suit jacket is blood-soaked and ripped, the fabric of the shoulder of her right arm barely present. Her face is so ashen and streaked in more blood. She has chunks of brain matter in her hair and dark streaks of mascara and dirt smeared down her face.

She has never looked more like an avenging angel, a violent queen, than she does now. My little viper, the one that just saved my life despite having a bullet wound and bleeding out. I move quickly with the EMTS as they move towards the doors of the building. Trig is moving with us and is still on high alert. My eyes never leave Stella's, but the memory of Clark being hurt enters my brain. "Clark, he was shot."

"Being taken care of now." His huge, frustrated sigh catches my attention and finally has my eyes moving away from my wife. "Jaxon, you should know, she was out of the building. She made it out. She killed River Stanton, then turned back for you. Refusing to allow me to get her medical attention and to safety." I can see the look of self-recrimination across his features. He's blaming himself for not forcing her away from here.

The awareness hits me like a brick to the chest that if he had managed to get her out of here, I would be the one lying dead on the floor of that room instead of Kalista. If my determined and stubborn wife hadn't come back to save me, Kalista would have murdered me in cold blood, and I would have never seen Stella again. My little viper truly did save me. I owe her my life, and I plan to make sure she holds it in the palm of her hands for all of the rest of our years together. *She truly is mine, and I am hers.*

I stare down at her features once again as they load her into the waiting ambulance, and I climb in beside her, holding tight to her hand and interlacing our fingers. I lean forward and let my lips brush tenderly against hers. "You are mine, Stella, and I will never let you go."

49

Stella

"Love doesn't make the world go 'round. Love is what makes the ride worthwhile." Franklin P. Jones

I WAKE WITH A groan and fire racing down my body, every part of me aches right now, this is becoming a common freaking theme in my life. "Fuck, that hurts!" The words tumble from my dry lips as I crack my eyes open. A chuckle greets my ears as my eyes open more fully and center on the man sitting beside me. "What did you expect when you behave like fucking '*Rambo,*' Stella?"

"Jaxon..." His name leaves my lips with relief. Relief that my idiot and reckless husband is still breathing despite tempting fate time and time again. I shift on the hard surface below me, and pain radiates down my back, forcing a gasp to leave my lips and a cold sweat to break across my neck. I swallow the sour bile that is just begging to leave my mouth. *Fuck, that hurts.*

"Easy, my little viper, you were shot in the shoulder a few hours ago; no sharp movements." Jaxon moves closer, pushing my sweaty hair back from my face and leaning forward to kiss my forehead tenderly, his hand grabbing and holding mine.

The memories of shooting River and then Kalista flash through my mind, causing me to grimace and cry out. *I killed two more people. I really am a murderer now, there is no disputing the truth.* He must see the turn of my thoughts, his other hand coming up to cradle my face gently.

"Stella, baby, look at me. Everything is going to be alright. We are safe, it's finally over." Jaxon's platinum gaze bleeds into mine intensely. His fierce words and tight grip on my hand have me leaning back into the mattress and staring at him with hope. *Over, it's over.*

Hope fills me that this might finally be over and we are safe. Safe from the villains of the world, *well, other than ourselves, I guess.* Hope that we won't have to keep fighting off people that want to hurt us. That I won't have to dirty my already filthy soul with more murder in order to stop anyone who comes for us. Hope is a dangerous thing for someone with dirtied hands and a stained soul.

"Clark?" The question leaves my lips with fear. He got me out of there and turned back for Jaxon, only to be shot himself by Jeffrey Cain. "Alive, in a room down the hall." A relief I didn't know I was craving fills my tired body at Jaxon's words.

"Jeffrey? Kalista?" Their names leave my lips and burn like acid across my tongue. Rage once again fills me with the knowledge that they were behind all of this. All those people were hurt and died because of their actions. Deeds of revenge against Jaxon and me. Conduct caused by our own actions in retaliation. I will have to forever live with the stain of all those deaths on my heart. *I caused that, me and Jaxon.*

"She's dead, Stella. She can never hurt us again." He stares at me with compassion in his gaze as I struggle to swallow the sour saliva pooling in my mouth. The memory of her head blowing open and her brain splattering across my face from the bullet I put in her skull at close range flashes before my eyes in vivid technicolor. A shudder races down my spine, the sensation of still feeling parts of her clinging to me, making me nauseous. "Jeffrey is alive, but in police custody. He confessed to it all."

"Why? Why did they do this to us?" My voice sounds pitiful to my own ears, a woman broken from the experience of bringing death to others. I need to comprehend how someone could cause all of this destruction and pain. I know that my actions were petty, burning down his house and robbing Kalista of her livelihood was indecent and harsh, but was that really a reason to kill all those people? What about River and Fisher? I never even did anything to provoke those two. What reason would they have had to join in Jeffrey and Kalista's cause to harm me? None of this makes sense.

Jaxon releases a deep, nervous sigh, pulling his hand from my grip and dragging both his hands down his face. Remorse and shame are written across his features. "What did you do, Jaxon?" My voice is a strangled scream, my heart pounding like a loud drum in my chest as I await his words.

"Ah, fuck!" He shakes his head and meets my gaze, blue meeting silver in a harsh embrace. "I'm going to tell you, Stella... but first... first, I need you to understand how much I love you. I need you to promise you won't run from me." His gaze is so intense that the fear in the room is palpable and clawing at my throat; warning bells are sounding in my head. *No, no, no, what did he do?*

I swear to God, if this man tells me he slept with another woman, I'm going to rise from this bed and end his fucking life. There is a limit to how much I can take right now before I completely lose my sanity. Any more betrayal, and I'm just going to give into my primal urges for darkness and allow it to turn my heart completely pitch black. I need his answers, like I need my next breath for why this all happened.

I swallow the bile rising in the back of my throat and grind my back teeth. "I won't run." I don't bother uttering any other words. If the next words out of his mouth involve his dick, he's a dead man, and it won't matter how much I love him. He must see it in my cold gaze. He sighs and grabs a fist full of his hair, pulling on it tightly.

"Remember the deal we were looking at right before we went to the charity gala? The low-income housing acquisition?"

I nod my head but am utterly confused about where he's going with this. "Stella, I stole that out and under from River, Fisher, and Jeffrey. They lost millions of their own money and investors' money." He tugs harder at his dark hair, his eyes wild with fear and remorse. "I had the local gangs terrorize the sites and set fires to the developments. I made sure that they couldn't collect on the insurance." I watch as he clenches his fists and forces them into his lap.

"What I didn't know was that Fisher and River had sunk all of their fortunes into it... hell, Stella, all of it is now gone. Jeffrey didn't invest as much, but coupled with everything you did to Kalista and the savage way you burned his house to the ground, well, he wanted just as much revenge as the other two, maybe more. Kalista has always been very close with him."

His words penetrate my thoughts, and finally, the situation starts to make real sense in my muddled mind. My thoughts race, and my stomach clenches tightly when I realize what we have done. He destroyed their lives as much as I did. He was the catalyst, and I was the goddamn spark. Together, we were an inferno, burning their world down to the ground. Unfortunately, we took innocents down with us in our need for control. I close my eyes, tears sliding down my cheeks at the realization that we together are a destructive force.

"Stella, please say something. I love you, Stella." For a moment, I wallow in the thoughts and knowledge of how much pain we have caused not only to ourselves but to others. "No baby, none of that shit." He grabs me around my waist and pulls me forcefully into his lap, a gasp of pain leaving my lips as it jars my shoulder. *Fucking brute!*

"You don't get to do that, my little viper. You don't get to wallow in self-pity. There is no such fucking thing for a Stratford. You are my queen, and queens do not fucking bend, they do not break Stella."

"Jaxon…"

"NO, STELLA!" You are mine. *MINE!* Do you fucking hear me? I own you as much as you own me. I will not watch you break over some pieces of shit that did not have our strength." His hold on me tightens painfully; his eyes are rabid and filled with fury. "You will not bow or break, and do you know why, Stella?"

I meet his intense gaze, fire starting to burn inside me at his anger. "Why?" The word sounds so small leaving my lips as I drink in his features. Jaxon's eyes beam brightly at me, molten silver threatening to drown me in their depths as his hand drags up the front of my chest. His fingers ghosting over my collarbone before meeting the front of my neck. They circle the delicate organ, and my breath stalls in my chest as his fingers tighten. Not enough to stop my breath, but enough that I read the warning loud and clear. He is in control right now, and he wants me to let him have his way, to let him exert control over me and my body. Tingles erupt all over my body, and my toes curl under the blankets.

"You, my little viper, will be the reason the Stratford empire survives and flourishes. You will give birth to the next generation of Stratfords that will burn this world down around their feet if it does not bow. Your strength will be our shield, your mind, the reason we prosper, your desire and will, our weapons. You are my mother fucking queen, Stella. I will worship at your feet for all of my living days and even into the afterlife. You are mine." His fingers tighten as he pushes me back on the bed and falls to his knees between my parted legs.

"Let me worship at your throne, Stella, so you know how much you mean to me." He doesn't wait for me to give consent, his other hand ripping the loose hospital gown up around my waist. I'm entirely bare underneath, and his words have started a raging cyclone inside of me causing my core to heat and weep for him. He skates his thick finger down the middle of my slit, and I bite down on my tongue, the taste of copper filling my mouth. A groan leaves my lips, even though I'm fighting to silence it. A quick glance behind him shows me the door to my hospital room isn't even shut completely. *Fuck, anyone could walk in at any moment and find us.* Excitement coils in my stomach at being caught with Jaxon's face shoved up against my pussy.

"You're soaked, my little viper." He slips his finger inside my tight hole and rotates it before pulling out and pushing a second one inside of me. A whimper leaves my lips at the sensation, and my core tightens around the thick, long digits. The heat of pain in my shoulder makes me grimace, but it's not enough to have me stopping Jaxon's actions. I need him to claim me, to make me feel how much he wants me after everything that has happened. To know that my dark soul and tainted hands don't repulse him, but instead make him want me more. My actions call to the sickness and darkness in his soul as much as they do to mine. We are twin fark flames, destructive and uncontrollable.

His gaze meets mine, and a devious smirk crosses those sinful lips, the ones I crave to taste. "Does my *little slut* get wet at the thought that any minute someone could walk in here and see me finger fucking her perfect cunt?" He pulls his fingers out of my needy pussy and spreads my moisture across my throbbing pussy lips before rubbing wet circles on my hard bundle of nerves. *Fuck, fuck, fuck.*

He leans forward, his tongue swiping at my clit and causing my hands to clench in his hair. A feral growl leaves his lips as he sucks down hard on my nub and grazes it with his teeth, forcing a scream to want to leave my lips that I have to swallow down. His wet tongue slides down my pussy lips until it finds my tight hole, and he slips inside with a groan. Both his hands grab onto my flesh, his fingers harsh and demanding as he spreads my inner thighs wide so he can press into my core. His stubble rubs against my over-sensitized flesh and adds another level of intensity. My hips undulate below him, pushing my pussy further into his face and coating it with my juices.

"Fuck Stella, I want to drown in this pussy." His nose skims along my pussy lips as he coats it in my scent. "Fucking perfect cunt, so pink and pretty."

The groan that leaves his lips has heat rising in my core and the hairs on my body standing on end. Shivers rack my body as he slips his fingers back inside of me while pressing his thumb over my puckered hole. He pulls back, his mouth slick with my wetness, and spits on my pussy, the sound forcing a moan to leave my lips. The spit slides down between my pussy lips and into the crack of my ass, where his waiting thumb rubs it across my tight hole.

"I need to fuck all your holes, to have you creaming and filled with cum spilling from inside of you." His thumb pushes inside of my tight hole, and his mouth and fingers return to my pussy. The feeling of fullness causes my breath to stall, goosebumps break across my body as his fingers curl, and reach up, meeting that spot inside me that has me seeing stars. The orgasm tightens all of my limbs, the pain in my shoulder long forgotten as I rub my nipples and pull on them, the hospital gown confining them and rubbing against their sensitive and tight flesh.

My breathing picks up, I'm so close, so very close. "Jaxon... fuck... close." The moan leaves my lips just as all of my body lights with a fire from within, tightening until I can't breathe and then gushing as I cum all over his face. *Jesus fuck.*

He continues to lick me through my orgasm and the aftershocks, his fingers and thumb still moving in slow strokes inside both of my tight holes. "Look at how pretty you squirt, baby." He pulls his fingers out of my pussy and his thumb from my puckered hole before replacing it with his tongue, thrusting inside of the tight ring of muscle. My head is thrashing on the linens as I feel the sparks grow inside of me once again. He pulls back and stands, leaning over me, his face in line with mine. His winter storm, gray eyes, heavy-lidded and fringed with dark lashes, meet mine, and I can see that he's losing the battle for control of himself. "Open your mouth, my little whore; taste how delicious you are." He spits into my mouth, my saltiness and musky taste filling my senses.

"Do you want me to fuck this tight pussy, Stella? Do you crave my big cock filling all your holes?" He leans forward, rubbing his nose down my cheek, along my jaw, and down my neck. "Tell me whose queen you are?" Breathless moans escape my lips as my body flails below him. Fuck as much as I want control, nothing ever feels as good or as sweet as submission to Jaxon. He is the oxygen I breathe, and I am the blood that makes his heartbeat. One depends solely on the other. *He is mine, and I am his.*

"Yours." My voice is husky as it leaves my lips, and I watch as he pulls back from me, satisfaction in his eyes and a sinister smirk across his lips. I watch, transfixed, as he unbuttons his pants, slowly pulls down his zipper, and releases his hard cock. The crown is deep red and engorged with drops of precum slipping from his slit. He rubs his thumb across the slit capturing a creamy drop and rubbing it across my parted lips. He wraps his arms around my waist, lifting me up, cradling my overheated body against his, and switches places so that I am now draped across his body. My core connects with his hard cock as he thrusts upwards, his tip meeting my needy clit. His chest rises and falls in an erratic rhythm that meets mine. Both our breaths sounding harsh in the otherwise silent room.

His hands grip my hips, and he moves me forward, my legs straddling either side of his body. Bolts of pleasure rack my body and skate down my spine as I drag my throbbing clit along the length of his hard cock. "Slide that pretty pussy over my hard dick and ride me, my *dirty, little whore.*" The pull of his command and the enthralled look across his face has me lifting and then sliding down his dick slowly, filling my hot, tight hole, one inch at a time. When he's finally balls deep inside of me, we both release breathless pants. My shoulder aches, but the bite of pain seems to add to my euphoric state. *More, I need more.*

"Show me you belong to me, Stella, that you're mine." I start slowly, building up momentum between us and making sure my clit rubs against the skin of his pelvis. His hand slides up my back and around my body, until he squeezes the globe of my breast in his large hand. The pink tinge across his high stubbled cheekbones and the redness of his lips make me bite down hard on my own with how gorgeous he is. He is the sexiest man in the world to me, and I will never not be turned on by the way he looks. He lifts his head and stares down to where we are connected, a groan leaving his lips.

"Look at how pretty your cunt stretches around me." His hand darts out and slaps the lips of my pussy as I pick up the pace and ride him hard.

I falter in my motion, my body sagging slightly with my thundering breaths leaving my chest, and he takes over, thrusting between my thighs and driving into me in deep, long strokes that have me biting down hard on the inside of my cheek. Jaxon takes complete control over my languid body, his fingers tightening on the flesh of my hip with a hint of pain. He makes sure to hit the end of me and ensures that I feel every inch of his long cock as he thrusts in and out of my tight hole. The sensation makes my toes curl and heat swirl through my body. I'm so close, so very close, and ready to go over that precipice with him.

"No matter how many times I fill this sweet cunt, it will never be enough, Stella." My pussy starts clenching tightly around him at his words. "That's it, baby, keep gripping my dick with that perfect pussy. Milk the cum from me, be my *good girl*, my perfect *slutty queen*." His words are my undoing as he picks up speed, pounding into me while his grip on my hip ensures I feel every single hard thrust. His other hand leaves my breast and makes its way to the column of my throat, his fingers wrapping around it as he pulls me forward toward him. His full lips meet mine in an earth-shattering kiss, one that has me seeing stars before me. "If you ever think of leaving me, I'll kill you, Stella. I can't live without you."

He deepens the angle of our connection, and it hits my 'g' spot hard, causing me to moan loudly and tighten down hard on him as my body gives over to the sweet, intense orgasm that erupts across it. He follows me down into euphoria, a moan leaving his lips as his teeth bite down hard along the skin of my neck.

He holds my body flush against his, our hearts thumping against our chests as we try to catch our breaths and come down from that exquisite release. "I love you, Stella Stratford. This heart only beats for you, and it is determined never to let you go. You are mine forever."

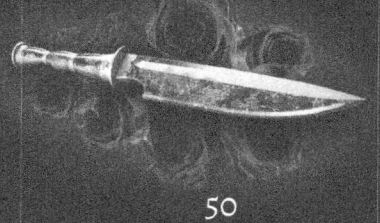

50

Epilogue Stella

"If you're going to live, leave a legacy. Make a mark on the world that can't be erased." Maya Angelou

*T*WO YEARS LATER...

I try to hold back the smirk that wants to grace my face as I make my way barefoot and in my silk nightgown down to the den. I know Jaxon is currently sitting in there drinking his scotch and sulking like an overgrown child. My parents left an hour ago from having dinner with us, and of course, my father couldn't hold back asking Jaxon when he was going to man up and place a baby in my womb. *As if that was his only purpose in life, my how the tables have turned.*

I watched as the love of my life restrained himself from throwing a dinner knife across the table at my overbearing father in response. My mother and I tried and failed to hide our laughter from the two male idiots in the room. I swear the male toxicity whenever they are near each other is nauseating, but also hilarious.

His response was mumbled under his breath, but I still heard it. "Not for the lack of fucking trying." *Poor suffering baby.*

While Jaxon has tried to make peace with my father. Even going as far as involving him in our merged company and asking for his opinion on different business ventures. My father is harder to placate. His stubbornness knows no bounds, and he just can't seem to forgive Jaxon for Kalista and Jeffrey Cain, and their attempts to kill me. His relationship with me changed dramatically in the months after the whole ordeal. Gone was the man who wished for a son and only saw his daughter as a chess piece to move across the board. It took killing both River Stanton and Kalista Cain and taking his company away from him for him to finally see me, the real me—the one who is ruthless and will do everything she can to protect what's hers.

His new understanding and appreciation hasn't swept all of our past under the rug. I still feel resentment at the memories of every time he raised his hand in anger at my mother and me. The only thing that makes me feel even the slightest retribution is the way my mother has taken charge of their lives. She stopped cowering to my father the same day I killed Kalista. The gun she later pulled on him when he raised his voice at her, helped to show him that she was not weak and afraid of him. Not to mention the realization of who my mother's *"friends"* are, but that's a story for another time. Let's just say my mom is a badass all on her own.

While I was cleared of all charges, the stain of the deaths could not be so easily wiped from my hands or the minds of the public and the elite that surround us. If they were hesitant and fearful of me before I murdered two of their own, now they are downright terrified of even breathing the same air as I do. My father's pride swelled with the knowledge of my ruthlessness. Finally, realizing he had everything he ever wanted right there in front of him, in his daughter.

Jaxon the fucker started calling me the *"killer ice queen"* whenever we were amongst company to remind them how truly horrifying I am. The name has stuck and now carries with it a weight of warning to those who would risk going against us. Nothing and no one will stop me from protecting myself or my family. I'm a Stratford, the top of the food chain, and we do not forgive easily.

The Stratford empire has grown under mine and Jaxon's combined ministrations over the last two years, becoming even more powerful than it was. In the next ten years, we will have expanded worldwide, acquiring companies and assets in every country on the globe. No small feat for two people who were forced into an arranged marriage and had near-death experiences in the first six months of wedded bliss.

Our love, too, has grown, not only from the passion that we still feel but also from our mutual respect for each other. Jaxon has become my best friend, and I am his. We enjoy every minute we are together and look eagerly towards our future. Well, that is when he's not moping around in a pissy ass mood or acting like a deranged possessive nut. His usual M.O. lately.

We discussed having children after I left the hospital from my shoulder wound, both of us agreeing that it wasn't the right time. We were greedy and selfish in our need for each other and not ready to share that with someone else. We also wanted the opportunity to grow our empire before we brought another Stratford into the world. Jaxon left the decision up to me for when we decided to start our family. *"It's your body, Stella, and as much as I want to see this tight little body stretch with my child inside of it, it has to be your decision."*

Instead of focusing on kids, we focused on pleasure. We are experimenting with what brings us the most intense gratification, where our limits are, and how to bring each other to our knees. Jaxon and I practice hedonism in our own way. We both came to realize quite early on that I enjoy a bit of exhibition, voyeurism, and degradation with my sex, and Jaxon enjoys controlling all of my pleasure and depriving me of my sanity and air. While we don't actively go out and fuck in public. We have gotten caught in a few compromising situations that have needed greasing of other's hands in order to be made to disappear from the tabloids. After one too many incidents, we started attending private establishments catering to our particular type of kinks and offering exclusivity and, of course, discretion.

"Still sulking, Jaxon?" I approach him as he sits back in his oversized leather wing chair in front of a blazing fire. *He looks good enough to eat, even if he's being petulant.*

"Your father's a fucking dick, Stella. He'll be lucky if I don't lose my shit one of these days, and he ends up swallowing that malicious tongue of his." I watch as he takes a deep sip of amber liquid, his tongue sliding across his full lower lip to lick up a drop that slipped from the cup. *Fuck, I want to be that drop.*

Desire pools in my core at how handsome he still is. I can never seem to keep my hands off of him. His gaze finally lifts from the fire and meets mine in a slow perusal, starting at my bare feet and legs. To the black nightgown that barely covers my pussy, over the mesh fabric that is tight across my chest, and up my neck sporting his hand necklace from last night, to my face. I watch as he slouches further down in his chair, his eyes heating into twin peaks of silver, as he watches my chest rise and fall with my quickened breath.

I had elaborate plans to take him to our house in the Hamptons this weekend, shackle him to our bed, and have my wicked way with him, but now I'm thinking I might have to move up that timeline. My poor baby's ego is bruised, and his feelings are hurt. A snort leaves my lips at the very thought. *That ego is the size of New York State.*

I know he has been feeling restless for the last few months, although he tries to hide it. Jaxon's desire for a child has increased, I watch him as he stares longingly at our friends' children. Of course, my father constantly at his throat about our lack of spawn has started playing havoc with his mind, too. It's one of the reasons I didn't tell him that I took myself off birth control three months ago. I didn't want to add any pressure to our already busy lives and figured if it happened, then it was meant to, and if it didn't, then maybe we needed to look into alternatives.

"Stella, have you come down to let me eat that perfect pussy for my dessert?" He quirks his sinful lips in my direction.

I quickly neutralize my face as I move closer to him in the room, stopping a few feet away from his sexy frame. "Only if you want me to suffocate you with it."

"Don't threaten me with a good time, Stella." He smirks, the light from the fire causing his gray eyes to glow and a look of smugness to cross his features. I take another step closer, and his scent of spicy citrus and musk fills my senses and has me trying to swallow a moan. *He's fucking delicious.*

He stands from the chair, his glass in his hand, and moves toward me like a graceful panther stalking its prey. His fingers trail down my shoulder, sliding over the mark left from the healed bullet wound before causing the strap of the nightgown to slip down and expose my breast. He repeats the action with the other side until the nightgown is pooled along my chest and barely hanging on. With a quick movement, he slices through the straps with the blade, I didn't even notice was his tight grip. The one he always has hidden on him in case someone tries to hurt us. The silk slips down my body and pools at my feet as he repockets the blade. I almost pout, seeing it disappear from sight. I have become very fond of that particular blade making its way across my body.

"Fucking sinful." He moves around me until I feel his thickness pressing against my ass, and his hand reaches around my body to palm my heavy breast and tug on my hard erect nipple. The sensation of him pulling and rolling the sensitive tip between his thick fingers has bolts of pleasure singing down my spine. His warm breath meets the side of my neck, and his lips drag a blazing path to my ear lobe, where he sucks deeply before finding his way back down my neck and leaving marks along the way.

It's one of his kinks, marking as many places on my body as he can and claiming me as his. *As if anyone would be insane enough to try to take me from him.*

His hand fists my loose hair, and he pulls tightly, pushing me forward. "Bend and touch your toes, Stella. I want to see my favorite holes gaping for me." I bend my spine forward, my dark waves cascading down before me as I reach for my red-painted toes, and my core contracts, feeling empty without his thick cock inside of it.

"Fuck." He growls the word, sounding animalistic as it drops from his lips. Jaxon's hand skates down my spine, leaving shivers and goosebumps in his wake. His hand grabs one of my ass cheeks tightly as he squeezes it firmly in his grasp, before releasing it and doing the same to the other side. I watch between my parted legs as he lowers himself to his knees, his lips trailing down my spine. He tips up the glass of scotch, and I release a whimper as the cool liquid slithers down my lower back and in between my ass cheeks, and his tongue follows its path, licking it up from my skin. *Fuck!*

"Grasp your pretty cheeks, baby, and spread them wide for me like the *dirty slut* you are. I want to lick that pretty cunt and eat that sinful ass."

I slide my hands slowly up my legs to the back of my thighs and grasp onto my cheeks, pulling them apart as a growl leaves his lips before I feel his breath hot against my center. He licks me from my puckered hole down my weeping slit and to my bundle of nerves just waiting to be teased. His thumb grazes against my tight hole before slipping inside, and I can't contain the moan that leaves my lips. "Jaxon... Jaxon, oh...my... God."

"Forget about calling for him, baby. I'm all the God you need." His tongue slips inside of my pussy at the same time, and his thumb strokes and moves inside of my ass, making my cheeks clench, and my legs tremble. *Jesus, that feels so good.* The combination of his dirty words and that masterful tongue will be my undoing if I am not careful.

As much as I want to cum, I also want to play, and teasing Jaxon is one of my favorite things to do. He fucks me with his tongue as he pours the rest of the scotch down my crack and licks me until I'm panting and breathing heavily. The glass drops to the area rug next to us just before a loud crack sounds in the air, and my right ass cheek feels scorching hot. A moan rips from me at the feel of my skin throbbing. *Fuck, fuck, fuck.*

"Do these holes need to be filled by my hard dick, Stella? Do you crave a pounding baby?" A second slap follows quickly to the same cheek, all while he never stops fucking me with his thumb and moves his tongue in and out of my holes. The sensation of being filled in both holes and the pain and heat of the slaps are almost too much for me, and my orgasm starts racing up my spine. I hear him chuckle as he watches my body tense before him, aware of my body's cues.

"Oh no, my little viper. You don't get to cum yet."

He pulls back from me, and I almost stumble forward, straightening my body and turning around to stare at him still on his knees before me. His pupils are dilated, his mouth and chin wet from my arousal, and a lock of unruly hair messily across his forehead. He is sex personified, a sinful dream, and he's all mine.

"Give me your belt, Jaxon." His eyebrow rises, and a smirk graces his face as I watch riveted as he removes his belt from his pants, unbuttoning and pulling down the zipper, and freeing his giant, veiny cock. His hand tightens around his length as he strokes himself from root to tip, his thumb gracing over the drop of precum already present. The sight causes my legs to tighten closed and my mouth to water.

I take the folded belt from his hand, sliding it across his forearm, up his bicep, to his shoulders still encased in fine linen, and down his back. "Strip Jaxon." A shudder runs through him, and his eyes spark as he does precisely what I have demanded. When he returns to his knees before me, completely bare, I move closer, putting my abdomen and breasts in front of his mouth, my nipple dragging across his full bottom lip.

"Suck." His lips wrap around my hard nipple, and he sucks deep as my hand slips into the thickness of his hair, fisting his locks and holding him to me. I pull back, and he releases my nipple with a pop before giving the second one the same treatment. His eyes remain locked on mine, staring up at me from his thick lashes. There's no mistaking the heat in them, he's enjoying me bossing him around. *I'm enjoying it too.*

I can feel the stirrings of my orgasm racing towards me, the electrical current along my skin causing all of my hair to rise on my arms. I pull back and move behind him, pulling one arm and then the other behind his back before using the leather belt to tightly wrap his wrists and forearms. "Are you craving control, my little viper? You want to dominate me tonight?" I can hear the laughter in his words, and I roll my eyes at his attempt to bait me. We both know if anyone likes to be controlled and dominated during sex, it's me.

Tonight is different, though. I want to not only take my pleasure from Jaxon but also to own him entirely in a way that only I can. As I move my fingers away from his confined wrists, my charm bracelets make a little sound, capturing my attention and making a smile grace my lips. The various charms catch the light from the fire. One of a gun, another a diamond heart, a skull, a little diamond house, and the letter "J" move together. My gift from Jaxon for our first Christmas to celebrate our survival and our marriage. I adore it and never take it off, much to his pleasure. To him, it might as well be a handcuff or a declaration of ownership, one that I'm increasingly happy to let him have.

My long nails trail across his back and up his shoulders, leaving marks as I go until my fingers wrap around his neck and tighten slightly. "You talk too much, Jaxon. I have better uses for that mouth."

I pick up the silk nightgown from the floor and wrap it tightly around his eyes, removing his sight. His breathing has picked up. His chest rises and falls heavily, showing me exactly how much he's enjoying this little reversal in our roles. The large tattoo of my name across the left side of his chest that surrounds the bullet wound that almost killed him catches my eye, and I lean down, running my tongue across his flesh. Further proof that his heart is mine and only beats for me. If the bracelet is his ownership, the tattoo is mine.

I move away from him towards the desk, opening a drawer and pulling out what I hid earlier. I make my way back to Jaxon. My fingers rake through his hair and yank on the strands. I force him to crawl on his knees before me until I'm sitting spread open on the sofa behind me. Like a queen before her paramour, a devious smirk crosses my lips at just the thought of Jaxon being my sex slave. *Maybe we can role-play that sometime.*

A pained grunt leaves his lips as his cock bounces before me, dripping precum along its length. "Stella, release me. I want to see that pretty pussy that belongs to me." I ignore his demand and pull his face harshly into the cunt that he craves, forcing his lips and nose to be flush against my soaked skin. His lips open, and his tongue licks my wet folds before meeting my hard nub and rolling it with his tongue. *Jesus, fuck, that tongue of his will be my undoing.*

I watch him for a moment. A man starved before me at a feast. He sucks and licks every part of me, sliding his tongue between my pussy lips, dipping in and out of my hole, and returning to my puckered hole to suck and lick. Harsh groans are leaving his lips, his chest rising and falling, a pink streak flushing across his skin. "Fuck Stella, this pussy tastes delicious. I can never get enough, baby."

I slide my fingers down my stomach, holding on to the item I retrieved from the desk, shifting it over my throbbing clit and my soaked pussy lips before nesting it between them and pulling Jaxon's head away from me. Excitement races down my spine at what I'm about to do. He cries out as I release my hold on his hair and pull the nightgown off his eyes and away from him. His heated gaze meets mine, hunger clearly evident as he licks his lips. I tilt my head to the side, a smile gracing my lips, and wait for him to see the gift that I brought him.

His eyes skate over my face, down the column of my neck, and over my breasts. They continue down their path, leaving heat behind in his wake. His gaze trails down my stomach and over my soft hips. The minute he sees it, his whole body stiffens, and his eyes rapidly seek mine. My lips quirk, trying hard to contain my smile. His jaw tenses, and he bites down on his lower lip, his eyes glass over with unshed tears, looking vulnerable and adorable. He bends forward, his lips gracing my stomach before kissing it with such sweetness that it has my heart aching. "Stella fuck... I... is it real? You're not playing with me right now?"

"No, Jaxon, I'm not playing with you." He yanks on his tied wrists, his muscles bunching below his golden skin, but the leather doesn't release him. "Baby, please let me touch you."

"I thought you wanted dessert, Jaxon? My cunt is not going to lick itself." A giggle leaves my lips at his irate glare before he leans forward and slips his tongue back inside of me. Fucking me with it and rubbing his stubble across my folds. I move the item from between my swollen pussy lips and up my stomach, Jaxon's eyes never losing sight of it. I skate my fingers across my nub, rubbing circles, and with the friction of Jaxon's facial hair and his tongue fucking me ruthlessly, I come hard across his face in no time. My wetness drips down his chin as he licks every drop off his lips. He pulls on the restraints again with frustration. He turns around and gives me his arms to release him from the captivity of the belt. For a moment, I do nothing, ignoring his request while I lie here in my blissed-out state.

"Stella, release me. Fuck! My cock wants inside of *his* pretty cunt." A giggle escapes me at the desperation in his voice and features. I finally release the buckle, and he pulls his arms free. The moment he does, he grabs the item as if it were the rarest diamond. He holds it close to his face, reading the symbol clearly marked before turning back to me.

"We're having a baby! Holy fuck, Stella! We are having a fucking baby!" His cry of joy makes my heart jump along with him. I've been keeping this secret from him for three weeks, not wanting to disappoint him if it didn't last more than a few weeks. I was going to make a massive production out of telling him, but somehow, right now, in this room, with him on his knees before me, it feels perfect.

His hand trembles as it clutches the side of my face tenderly. "Baby, I love you! This is the best gift you could ever give me. I'm going to love this little girl just as much as I love you, and I promise you right here, right now, I will protect her with my life."

That right there is why I love this man more than I love air, more than I love power. He wants a daughter rather than a son. To Jaxon, a woman is never second best, she is his equal. He will raise a daughter to rule the world around us. She will be powerful and fearless, our daughter, if that is what we're blessed with.

The rise of the Stratford empire has begun, and it's time for the *reign of the queen*.

Trust me, keep going; you don't want to miss the next part.

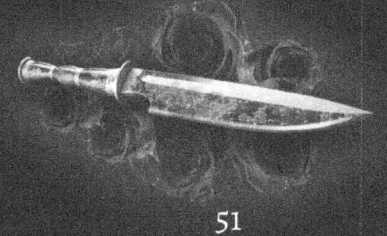

51

Bonus Epilogue Stella

*"Because I am a woman, I must make unusual efforts to succeed. If I fail, no one will say, "She doesn't have what it takes." They will say, "Women don't have what it takes."
Clare Boothe Luce*

36 years later...

T HE SUN SHINES BRIGHTLY as I walk into the room, the glorious rays warm on my skin. Today has been a fantastic day all around. The acquisition we just made will ensure further prosperity for the Stratford empire. One that has grown to a fifty-billion-dollar empire under mine and Jaxon's control. We are untouchable, and the world fears us, as it should.

Jaxon looked perkier at breakfast this morning, a welcome change from his pale pallor of late. I have to try to convince him to see the doctor again. Maybe I could give him something he wants in exchange for going? Perhaps a weekend away, just the two of us, where no one can reach us. It's been a while since we have indulged in each other freely. Memories of when we were first married and couldn't keep our hands off of each other warm my heart and keep me going, despite the fear in the back of my mind that something is wrong with him. *I can't lose him, I refuse to be parted from him.*

My husband is still the only temptation that I freely indulge in. His body, mind, and soul are a balm to my spirit at the end of each day. A smirk crosses my lips when I think of how we started, and where we are now, and the incredible life we have lived together. The fact that we are still together after all these years and our very rocky, contemptuous beginning amazes me daily. Who would have thought that Stella Penticton would fall madly and deeply in love with a demanding, possessive playboy like Jaxon Stratford? One that forced her into marriage, kicking and screaming. Certainly not me, if you had asked me thirty-six years ago. I would have told you to get your head examined.

Silence immediately greets me as I walk into my family room, and two little, dark heads turn toward me. Two pairs of blue eyes meet my appraisal. One pair is so much like mine that it's like looking in the mirror; the other is ocean blue and filled with trepidation. I stop before them, my face a mask hiding my emotions and thoughts from those watching. My *ice queen* persona is firmly in place. I catch Jaxon smirking at me from the sofa. I would love to wipe that smile off his devious face, but right now is not the time. He knows I am unhappy about this situation, and the only saving grace in this whole mess is standing before me in a pair of yellow overalls.

My gaze meets the little girl to the right. She's holding on tightly to Isabella's hand, but her gaze is fierce when it meets mine. *Hmmm, do we have a little fighter here?* She's hiding behind her thick, wavy dark hair. Her face is a tad pale, and she still has her baby-round cheeks. She resembles a little cherub, if that cherub had a fierce will. *I can work with that anger I see just below the surface.* Ensure that she channels it correctly.

I tear my gaze away from her to Isabella. My dark-haired princess, who resembles a little porcelain doll. Her skin is so pale, it's luminous. Her red lips lift in a semi-smile, knowing that despite whatever mood I might be in, she brings me such happiness. This one is deceptive, looking like nothing but sunshine and joy, but below the surface is an iron will that she has no doubt inherited from the women in my family. My poor little Isabella, who has already suffered at the hands of fate, but shows me every day that she is strong and will not be brought to her knees. She turns and whispers to the other little girl, and they giggle together before staring down at the ground.

Yes, these two will be thick as thieves in no time. The thought brings me immense pleasure, knowing that they'll be able to depend on each other for the battles yet to come. I stare at the heads of the two young women that will inherit my empire. The girls I will turn into fierce queens that will take on a male-dominated world and burn it to ash if anyone tries to harm them. I will raise and shape them to know they are powerful beings. That being a woman is a blessing, not a curse, and that they are mine no matter where they go in life. My granddaughters, my kin. *Stratfords.* Ones that fear nothing and bow to no one. *Queens.*

"Who is this?" I question, trying to keep the affection out of my voice. She meets my gaze with a little fear, but then I watch as she raises her head and pulls back her shoulders. She may be frightened, but she refuses to let me see it. She refuses to cower before me. *Good.* She will need that spirit in the future. Our enemies are many and would drag her down to hell if she allows them. *I am here to ensure they will never get the chance.*

My gaze travels over to my son, standing awkwardly to the side with his new bride. He knows very well that he's on my shit list. He ran off and married a waitress without even discussing it with his father and me. On top of it, with a waitress that already has a child. The woman, my new daughter-in-law, won't meet my gaze, making irritation slide up my spine, and my hands clench at my side. I can see what attracted my son to her. She's beautiful, her body slim and well proportioned, and her long dark hair an enticing feature. Unfortunately for us, she is weak and not a true Stratford. I can already see it in her demeanor. She will always cower to me or anyone else with strength. So, unlike the little version of her standing before me, the daughter obviously has not inherited her strength from her mother.

That won't do, though. We are Stratfords, we fear no one. I'll have to keep an eye on her. I'm not convinced that this is a perfect love match, as my son claims. Although she readily signed the prenup and adoption papers that Jared presented her with before getting married at some backward little southern town's city hall. Imagine that, a Stratford, getting married before a justice of the peace with only county clerks as witnesses. I have no doubt my dearly departed mother is rolling in her grave right now. I was livid when I discovered what he had done, but the deed is now done, and we have to move forward, even if it is with care. Before me stands the new Mrs. Jared Stratford. She may bear my son's name, but she will not lead my legacy. *No, these two little girls will.*

I have had investigators digging into Catherine's past. She has lived a hard life, one of sacrifice and pain. She was left all alone to raise that child without any assistance, while the father served time for horrific crimes. Ones that I cannot even envision her and her daughter surviving, but here she is, alive and married to my son. From the sounds of the reports, she is a hard worker, doing all she could to keep a roof over both of their heads. Now that they are both Stratfords, they will never want for anything ever again. I will make sure of it, just like I will assure that the child grows up from here on under my tutelage to guarantee she survives the perils in her new world.

I meet my handsome son's eyes, those identical to his father's, and love fills me. For a moment, my resolve weakens to be dissatisfied with his behavior and actions. He, too, has been dealt a harsh hand by fate. Losing his first wife within three years of marriage and leaving him a widower and a single father. I understand his need to find someone to share his life with and bring him happiness. If Catherine is that woman, then so be it. I will attempt to be civil to her and welcome her into the Stratford fold. The one thing his spontaneous actions have brought me that I welcome readily is another granddaughter.

My inability to give Jaxon more than one child has always plagued my heart, and then to have my own child only have one as well has always brought me heartache. I always wanted a house full of Stratford children, ones we could leave this vast empire to. If I'm being honest with myself, I always wanted a daughter and lots of granddaughters. Women, I could shape and teach how to navigate this world and the empire I have helped build.

It looks like some divine being up there was listening, as before me are two little women who will rule long after I'm gone, ensuring that the Stratford name continues for years to come and that the Stratford strength will be felt for eons.

"Amelia... Ham... Amelia Hamilton." The little voice responds, at first low and unsure but then stronger.

"Wrong." I return my gaze to her and meet her beautiful eyes, which remind me of the Caribbean Ocean. I hope they are deceptively beautiful, just like that ocean, and behind their stunning beauty hides peril. She will need to be strong to rule my empire. I watch as anger momentarily crosses her features, her nose flaring and her jaw tensing. *Hmm, we will need to work on that.* She will need to learn how to hide her emotions from those who would seek to manipulate her.

"What do you mean? That's my name!"

"No, it is not. That person no longer exists. Amelia Hamilton has disappeared, never to be heard from again. Do you understand me, young lady? Your name is Mia Stratford. You are a Stratford now." I bend down until my face is inches from hers, meeting her fierce eyes filled with fear and distrust. I sense confusion in her little mind, fighting against the knowledge that my son has adopted her, and that her name has been changed to prevent predators from searching her out and causing her harm.

"From this moment forward, you are Mia Stratford, a Manhattan princess, and my heir. With that comes responsibilities, Mia." I gently reach out a tentative hand to her jaw, taking it in my grasp. "Let me make it clear to you, child. You are not of my blood, but you will be of my heart. I am your grandmother, and you are a Stratford." I meet her wide eyes.

I know she was bullied back in that shitty backward town that she came from. I heard all about what those wealthy sons of tyrants put this child through. I'm determined to build her strength so she can one day avenge herself on her enemies. I will ensure she has all the power she could ever need to destroy their worlds down to the last stone. A Stratford never forgets and always demands her pound of flesh.

"You are a Stratford now, and no one will ever hurt you again. You have my promise."

The end.

You can learn more about the Stratford Princesses in the first book of Casbury Prep, *Reign of the Queen.*

STRATFORD

Long may a Stratford reign.

xoxo

Acknowledgments

L OVELIES!
    Let me start by saying how Im incredibly grateful and honored that you read my books!

Reign of the Queen was a labor of love for me. *Fall of a King* was a way to help me purge some of my internal demons. *Rise of a Kingdom took* chunks of my sanity with it. Stella would not release me from her vicious hold, without her story being told. In typical Stella fashion, it had to be told now, before I could move on to *Corrupted Kingdom*.

To the readers - thank you from the bottom of my heart and soul for reading my books. I am humbled and honored by each kind word, post, and video. They keep me going! Know that without you, there are no books! Thanks for giving this Canadian indie author a chance!

To my mother and mother-in-law, who will never read this book. Thank you for being the inspiration behind Stella. Two women that refuse to bow and refuse to take shit from anyone. You are both vicious little queens, and I love you.

To my ride-or-die, I'm so sorry I lost chunks of my mind writing this book. Thank you for putting up with me and bringing me copious amounts of chocolate! I love ya, *Pooh*! You are my rock, shield, and sword.

To my daughter, Katie. I know how difficult the last couple of weeks have been. Thank you for being a mountain of hope and inspiration. I could not do this without you. Thank you for reading another one of your mom's dark, depraved romances and not disowning me. Your input always makes me a better writer, mom, and human. I love you, *little momma*!

To my handsome son, who ignored me throughout this whole book while leaving candy out for my consumption. Thank you!

To my four-legged demon spawn, who suffered with less pets and walks while mom wrote this story and sobbed. I'm sorry, and I'll make it up to you with treatos! *I love you*, handsome fur demon.

Anna, Lillie, Katelin, and Tawny - thank you for reading this book during editing. You, ladies, have kept me sane, prevented me from DNFing this whole book, and rooted for me! You are amazing women, and I

Mia Fury & Darcy Bennett, you two are amazing women. Thank you for inspired and helping me with this book. I could not have done this without you!

My lovely members of the *Queen's Lair* on F.B. - You make me smile & keep me sane every day, and I am honored to have met you! Thank you for putting up with my cray-cray and still coming back daily!

To my arc team! I love you! Thank you for putting up with me and watching me stumble like a newborn calf at this. I promise I will be more organized going forward (at least, I hope!). Thank you for sharing my books and supporting me!

To the group of *Bookish Girls* and Issa, who keep giving my books a chance, making me smile, and sharing my worlds with other readers, I can never thank you enough. You have my gratitude & heart forever.

Thank you, to the other amazing book community authors, PA, and readers who have been very supportive, inclusive, and patient with me.

Thank you, Cady Verdiramo, for making this gorgeous non-discrete cover!

Thank you, H.E. from B&R edits, for helping to polish my words, and reducing down my vivid profanity!

I have so many new worlds and books to be published. I hope you all stick with me and continue on this amazing journey. I love ya, lovelies!

A.L. Maruga, xoxo

Resources

I RECOGNIZE CERTAIN THEMES within this book that could have been triggering. Please see the available resources below. Together, *we are stronger than our demons*.

If you or someone you know needs help for **assault crisis**, please view the following resources.

isurvive.org **USA & CANADA**

endingviolencecanada.org **Canada**

safehelpline.org **Universal**

myawayout.org **Universal**

If you or someone you know needs help with **mental health crisis**, please see the links below

wellnesstogethercanada **Canada**

mentalhealth.gov **USA**

988lifeline.org **USA**

checkpointorg.com/global **Universal**

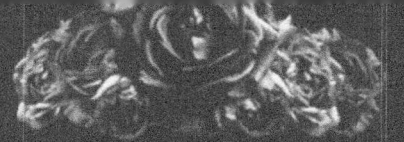

Come stalk me!

B E SURE TO SUBSCRIBE to her newsletter: https://www.authoralmaruga.com/

This will keep you updated on her craziness, book releases and giveaways!

Come join the naughty fun in her author's Facebook group!

A.L Maruga's Naughty Queen's Lair: https://www.facebook.com/groups/httpslinktr.eeauthoralmaruga

Stalk her on:

Instagram: https://www.instagram.com/authoralmaruga/

TikTok: https://www.tiktok.com/@almarugaauthor?lang=en or check out her LinkTree: https://linktr.ee/authoralmaruga

About Author

A .L. Maruga grew up in the big city of Toronto, in Ontario, Canada, reading romance novels and watching *Buffy the Vampire Slayer*. She now lives in a tiny suburb outside of one of Ontario's largest metropolises, with her two spawn, fur demon, and soulmate.

Her love of all things romance and paranormal has stayed with her over the years, and now she devours books at an alarming rate! Why she seems to always fall in love with the villains of the stories is anyone's wonder.

When she's not immersed in her writing, A.L. can be found indulging in her love for coffee, chocolate, and gardening. Her small town in Southwestern Ontario is her playground, where she can be seen with her loyal writing assistant, a four-legged fur-demon, or tending to her gardens. Her downtime is spent with her two grown children and her soulmate, a testament to her balanced and fulfilling life.

She writes about demanding, possessive, morally gray, and ruthless dark alpha-aholes and the strong women who bring them to their knees in her spicy dark romances.

Also By

R *EIGN OF THE QUEEN*, A.L Maruga's debut, dark enemies to lovers, why choose/RH, bully romance. Available in Kindle Unlimited, paperback, and coming soon in hardback!

Get your copy today! **https://books2read.com/Reignofthequeen**

The Fall of a King **is the second book in the Casbury Prep series. It is available in Kindle Unlimited, paperback, and hardback soon**!

Get your copy today! https://books2read.com/Fall-of-a-King

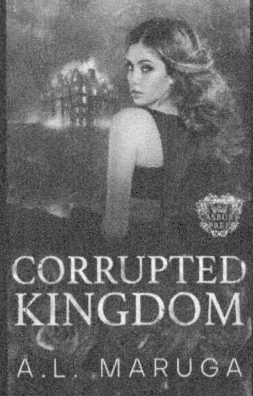

Corrupted Kingdom is the 3rd book in the Casbury Prep world; get your cop y today! https://books2read.com/Corruptedkingdom

The Queen's Serpent is the first book in the spinoff series from Casbury Prep and is the story of Stella and Jaxon's other granddaughter, Isabella. Get your cop y today! https://books2read.com/thequeensserpent

Made in the USA
Las Vegas, NV
13 September 2024

95192305R20213